BY CAROLINE KEPNES

You First

For You and Only You

You Love Me

Providence

Hidden Bodies

You

YOU FIRST

YOU FIRST

A JOE GOLDBERG PREQUEL

CAROLINE KEPNES

RANDOM HOUSE
NEW YORK

Random House
An imprint and division of Penguin Random House LLC
1745 Broadway, New York, NY 10019
randomhousebooks.com
penguinrandomhouse.com

Hardcover ISBN 978-0-399-59146-4
Ebook ISBN 978-0-399-59147-1

Printed in the United States of America

1st Printing

First Edition

Book Team: Production editor: Michelle Daniel • Managing editor: Rebecca Berlant • Production manager: Sandra Sjursen • Copy editor: Sara Robb • Proofreaders: Jill Falzoi, Catherine Mallette, Tracy Roe

Book design by Susan Turner

The authorized representative in the EU for product safety and compliance is Penguin Random House Ireland, Morrison Chambers, 32 Nassau Street, Dublin D02 YH68, Ireland. https://eu-contact.penguin.ie

For my mom, who taught me something new about the human spirit every day of her life and lives on in my heart for the rest of mine.

I love you, Mom. This one is like everything I write. It is for you.

YOU FIRST

1

There's the blonde to my left, a shy reader with tortoiseshell glasses who took her eyes off the page when I got onto the subway. The floor shook. I stumbled. I could've sat beside her, but I didn't. I'm six seats away, and we're the only two people on the train, in the universe that is a crowded New York subway car. The tension is there, here. She isn't reading, not anymore, and I can imagine a life with the blonde. Missionary mornings on a comfy sofa we found on the street, a frisky orange cat we adopt one lazy Sunday in Union Square after a long brunch because we do things like that. We adopt cats and sofas.

But then my Portnoy twitches. Jay-Z and Vince Neil see them too. *Girls, girls, girls.*

Another one calls, silently. A suited minx with short hair and dark red lips and she's right across from me. She doesn't adopt cats, and she would never just lie there and take it. She *is* the cat. Older. Wiser. Dirtier. Not a shy bone in her lithe, horny body, and did she *giggle* when I adjusted my pants? Yes. She giggled. She fakes a yawn and strokes her neck, and she won't look at me again. It's on *me* to make the next move. Do I do it? Maybe that's what I need. A martini of a woman who would hit me straight up, force me to get my GED, go to night school and *make* something of myself.

"Achoo!"

That's a wild sneeze and that's door number three and this girl is different. Not so nervous. Not so domineering. She's standing, unlike my exes—sorry, ladies, it was fun while it lasted—and she's holding her *Atonement* in that way where she wants me to know she walked into a bookstore and bought her *Atonement.* I *work* in a bookstore, so already you know we'd have something to talk about. Her coat is too big and too red, and she seems annoyed that she has to break away from *Atonement* to blow her nose and yeah.

That's it. That's my girl.

She's not a missionary mouse, and she won't push me to "make something of myself." She's cotton panties to the core, but then she crumples up her dirty Kleenex and gasps—I know that book, I know that part—and I can't do it. I can't be with someone who's just like me.

It's not time for me to atone. I'm seventeen years old. I've barely even lived.

This one down the way . . . This one fucking *lives.* 2:12 P.M. and she's visibly, clearly drunk. Wobbly legs in a skirt she put on last night. Chomping on a ham and cheese croissant in that way where you just know she'd devour my Portnoy.

She looks at me. She waves. What the fucking *fuck,* and I put my eyes on my tote bag. Do I get up? Talk to her? What would I say?

Doesn't matter. Not anymore. She licks her fingers that were just on the pole, and she scrunches up the tinfoil and tosses it on the floor like we're not all in this together, like litter isn't fucking *illegal.* Ham and cheese my ass, and it's true what Mr. Mooney says.

Girls really do have a sixth sense buried in that extra hole between their legs.

She could feel me losing interest. That's why she bends over and picks up the tinfoil.

Too little, too late, and I spy a *prescription* in her purse. She pinches her eyes. The pain. I can't go there. You can't make a sad girl happy, and I'm way too young to die trying.

"Seventy-second and Columbus!"

This is it. My last chance to make something happen. I freeze up. I do this all day every day. I talk myself into things and out of them and what the fuck is wrong with me? I don't know these girls and they don't know me, and it's all coming to an end. The train slows, a direct *fuck you* to my speeding, stupid heart.

I rise. Eight eyeballs and four holes to choose from. *Pick, Joe, pick.*

But it's predictable. I'm predictable. I don't make eye contact. I just walk up the fucking stairs into the street and—

"Wake up, asshole!"

I hold up a hand and wave at the justified old cabbie. "Sorry!"

I'm no good at being a New Yorker lately. I'm just not the same since 9/11, but then again, who is?

My appointment isn't until three, so I walk into an internet café and pick a computer in the back. It feels weird, choosing this place over the bookshop, shoving my ATM card into the slot like a junkie who needs a fix as I wait for the machine to rob me blind. This should be free, it really should, and I do what I do all day, all night.

I go on fucking Craigslist.

"Heya, buddy."

Craig doesn't say hi back. I don't even know if he's a real person with a last name. But God fucking bless him either way. The world used to be this black hole. You see a girl, you feel something, you chicken out and you know you'll never see her again. But now we have this magical place called Missed Connections. I've fallen in love in my head seventeen times today and there's a chance that one of the sweet seventeen can't get me out of *her* head. The page is loading and . . .

Nope.

I should be used to it by now, the rejection, but Emily Dickinson said it best. "Hope is the thing with feathers." It's still early. Maybe one of them will realize that she deserves to be loved by the cute guy with the bookstore bag because we *all* deserve to be loved.

Well, not *all* of us. Certainly not Angus Fucking Kaplan.

Of course he lives in a penthouse on the Upper West Side. The kind of place protected by soulless, scowling stone fucking gargoyles. Angus is a gargoyle. A crackhead who gets a pass in this world because he can afford a high-end crack den. A book buyer who burns the books in his fireplace. Everything about this is wrong, but it's like Mr. Mooney says. *That's capitalism, Joseph.* I am delivering Angus a signed first edition of *Goodbye, Columbus.* I could do something to save this book's life. Throw Angus in the fireplace. Punch his lights out.

But it's the same way with the girls on the subway. It's all in my motherfucking head, fantasies on my Moleskine as more foreskin goes untouched. *Use it or lose it.* I am losing it. I don't do stuff. I just *think* about doing stuff. And the whole point of being here is that you gotta live. Do something. Be something. Fuck someone. Pick a life and live it or you die in your head.

I press his buzzer.

"Yes?"

"Hey, Angus. It's Joe."

"Who?"

"Joe from the bookstore."

"I don't know a Joe."

EVERYONE KNOWS A JOE. "Angus, I got your Philip Roth."

He laughs. I hear it now. The flick of a Bic. I can almost smell the fumes. Real actual *crack.* He coughs and he belches, and he sighs. "Come on up, Jimbo."

Gargoyles are nipping at my legs, and I don't like the way I look in the lobby mirror. My head is too big for my body, or my body is too small for my head. I'm in the elevator, trying not to cry, and I can't go on like this. Malleable. Alone. Collecting typewriters and living in a four-by-ten room with cardboard walls. Yep, I got screwed. These NYU kids Chad and Hauser put out an ad for a cheap room "in the village." They seemed nice enough on the phone, so I said yes, sight unseen. Turns out that by "village," they meant Stuyvesant *Town,* a concrete mini-city in the far east. I don't have a window and I sleep in a "converted pod" that Dumb and Dumber rigged with cardboard and duct tape. I went from one Stuy to another. No privacy. A cloak of shame that I can't fucking shake. My jeans feel good at home but here I am tugging at them. Nothing fits, not really. I haven't touched a girl in centuries. I jerk off in the shower, on the sofa that isn't mine, in the basement of the bookshop. Dumb and Dumber made an innocent mistake, but maybe I am Dumbest. I threw my fate in Craig's hands, sight unfucking seen. Who does that?

"Jimbo!"

"It's Joe."

Even for Angus, this is bad. He's in a red-and-blue silk robe, and the belt doesn't belong. It's black. There's a wad of chewing gum stuck to the chest hair by his left nipple, and I shouldn't see his nipple. This can't be the only nipple I see every week.

He laughs. "Oh, don't worry about my eye, Jerry. Just a blood vessel. Come on in."

I didn't even notice his eye, because I try not to go there. The darkness of this penthouse. The long walk down the hall, a trail of septic breadcrumbs, cracked fucking crack pipes and vomit, and is that piss? That is piss. A chew toy for a dog—Angus doesn't have a dog—and I want to run. Flee. Live.

He rocks back and forth on his hairy-toed feet. "Hear that?"

"Peter Frampton, right?"

"Oh yes, Jake. That's my boy."

And then we're moving again, down the hall and past the foyer—more crack pipes and a bag of blow—and Angus pulls a Heineken out of his pocket and tosses it. I catch it, but this is new. This is not how we do this. "Thanks, Angus."

"Drink it."

"It's already open."

"Oh, relax, Jimbo, I'm clean. You're not gonna get cooties."

I do not sip the Heinie, and he grabs his fucking pipe. "So, you're never gonna believe this, Jack."

People who sell you on their stories before they tell you their stories are allergic to the truth. I clutch my Heinie. "What's up? And, Angus, I can't stay that long today."

He rolls a joint and rolls his eyes and jacks up the volume on the sound system and I tune it out. Him *and* Peter Frampton. I've been delivering books to this crackhead heir for eleven months. He lives up here with his butter-soft sectional in his sunken living room, sitting around putting out cigarettes on his own fucking carpet. He has the view everybody wants—Central Park is his living, breathing painting—but I've never seen it from up here because he never opens his blackout curtains. Everywhere I look there are books. Rare books. Special books. Signed books. All of them molested and abused by Angus and his crackhead friends. Bloodied and torn. Caked with leftover cocaine.

Angus is on the move. Stomping and smoking and ranting. The fireplace is on. The sunken living room is sinking, and I'm going down with it. Drowning from the contact high.

"All right," he says. "Gimme that goddamn . . . Are you Jewish? Never mind."

I should be used to it by now. Angus Kaplan is a rich man. Rich people do and say whatever they want. The last time I was here he told me that his *slutty mother* had a fling with Philip Roth, that Roth is his biological fucking father. Yeah fucking right and so help me God if I wind up like him, lying to myself and anyone paid to listen about where I come from. Chills, but the thing with feathers is strong. I always want Angus to change. Grow. Do the right thing.

Alas, no, and I pull Philip Roth out of my tote bag. RIP *Goodbye, Columbus.* "Do you have a check for me, Angus?"

He opens his robe, and I cover my eyes—*Don't look into the light,*

Carol Anne—but then I hear something snap. Spandex on skin and yep, the man is in a thong. The check was in that thong and it's in my hands and can you catch herpes from pube DNA?

"Drink up, Jerry." He spits at *Columbus,* and I can't be such a pushover. *Think, Joe, think.*

"You know, Angus, if you really wanted to stick it to Philip Roth, you could hold on to the book, make a shit ton off it when he dies."

He spits on the floor instead of the Roth, and did I do it? Did I save my literary hero? "Wow," he says. "You Jews really do stick together, don'tcha?"

Mr. Mooney is right. *A little bit of hope can do a whole lot of damage.*

And then he's talking, and there's no way out. He tells me his quote-unquote sob story again, how once upon a time he was a promising young author so good that he dropped out of the MFA program at Columbia because why bother? He was a genius. He was writing a novel, of course. *A good one, Jerry. Faulkner via the bastard son of Roth.* His working title was *The Twenty-Seventh Town,* but then a guy by the name of Jonathan Franzen came along with *his* debut novel.

The Twenty-Seventh City.

It sounds like a lie, so it might be the truth—life makes no sense, ever—but it's all coming together. If you don't live your life, if you give up or freeze up, well, you wind up like this sad fucker. Flat on your back, wiping your ass with Philip Roth.

I do what I always do. I tell him to chin up. "You know, it's not too late, Angus. You could finish your book. Find another title."

He grunts. "Leave it alone, boychick."

I leave it alone. And he rewards me by flicking the book into the fireplace like it's one of his fucking cigarettes, and he's up again. Up and at 'em.

"You don't get it, Jerry. A man steals your title, your thunder, and your youth. . . . You can't *find another title.* It's over. See, it's all connected. I lost my book. I lost my girl." Here we go again. "A man doesn't just get over a thing like Kelly Demon." Her real last name is Damon, and she isn't a thing. She's a woman. "She was it. A dead ringer for Carolyn Bessette. I knew her too . . . Carolyn. See, she settled for John-John when I broke it off. . . . We all knew one another at Brown." Sure, Angus, sure. "You can't rewrite a first novel, and you can't replace a girl like Kelly. She quit modeling to go to law school, Jimbo. It's like that."

"Wow," I say, as if this made-up story is new to me. Amazing, the way life fucks with you. Angus is a bitter crackhead but I feel like the outcast, the freak. There are no Bessette-esque willowy demons in my midst, no great thing I started but never finished. He paws at his CD player and *Frampton Comes Alive* and Angus tears off his robe.

"Did I ever tell you about the time I killed my mother?"

Yes. "No shit?"

"Oh yeah," he says. "She was in the hospital. Low sodium. I gave her a glass of water. Ten seconds later . . ."

He collapses onto the butter-soft sectional and cries like a little kid, like the boy who accidentally killed his mommy. This is where it's impossible to really fully hate people. There's a person in there, somewhere, and I'm glad I didn't throw him in the fireplace.

"Buddy," I begin. "Don't give up. It's what I tell myself, y'know? 'Hope is the thing with feathers.' "

He rubs his cheeks. Those famous gates of hell that burn incessantly aren't in Turkmenistan. They are here in his skin, his pores. "Jimmy," he says. "That thing you just said . . ."

"It's Emily Dickinson."

He rolls onto his backside. "Bullshit," he says. "It was me."

Outside, I breathe like my life depends on it. Out crack, in smog.

"Excuse me."

It's a girl, a pretty one.

My Portnoy comes alive. The thing with feathers is back, but I might be a little high on crack. I blink. I think. *Just be a fucking person, you idiot.*

"Me?"

She laughs. Brown hair. Brown eyes. Dimples? "Do you have a light?"

It's always weird when they do this, when they talk to me like I'm a real person, and this is the whole problem.

I like it better on the subway when you can't talk to the *girls, girls, girls,* when they can't talk to you.

I study her face. Yes. She has dimples. "I could buy you one at the newsstand."

The thing with feathers is dead. You don't do that, idiot. You don't offer to buy a girl a lighter, and she pulls out all at once.

"See you."

See you.

As in *fuck you.*

Four hours later and I'm still thinking about her. The girl with no lighter.

Mr. Mooney is in his office, and we're slow. Dead. He says I can close early and go home, but I don't want to go home.

I want life. Love. *Something.*

That's where Craig is such a good guy. He gets it. Sometimes you want to see if anyone out there is looking for you, and sometimes you want to be the captain of the ship. I sign into my account, and I use the same subject for every Missed Connection.

You . . . are still on my mind.

And then I get into it, really fucking into it.

You were on 72nd and Columbus. You asked me for a light, and you were gorgeous. Brunette Carolyn Bessette. I offered to buy you a lighter, and you laughed. There was something about you, and I messed up. If you want to know why I was a little off, there's a story there. A good one full of colorful characters. . . . Wanna get a coffee? I'll bring a lighter this time.

The second Craig informs me that my letter is online, in the world, I feel like a whole new real fucking person. I did something. I tried. I'm not deluded. I know what I am. I'm no better than Angus, hunched over this chunk of wires like a junkie in a sinking living room, like my mother at a blackjack table in AC.

Mr. Mooney clears his throat. I didn't even realize he was here. He sneers. "The radon in that thing will burn your brain out, Joseph."

No, it won't. "I'm almost done."

He tells me to get home safe, but I can't go home now—I don't own a computer—and he says what he always says.

"Beware, Joseph. Those machines are designed to make us fat and weak."

He's not wrong, but I'm not a total junkie. I can walk away, so I do walk away. I mop the floor and I put stickers on the signed Lucinda Rosenfelds and it's been a few minutes—okay, it's been nine minutes—so I hustle back to home base and check my Hotmail.

Nothing.

Night falls early in the winter. I do push-ups the way this kid in my ninth-grade algebra class said you should before you have sex, and I check my Hotmail.

Nothing.

The push-ups revved up my appetite and I forgot to eat, and I want a slice of pizza but there's no computer in the pizza joint, so fuck it. What's the harm? I check my Hotmail.

Nothing.

I go downstairs and open the door to the cage. For months, I thought Mr. Mooney was talking out of his ass, spouting off on how books need to breathe. It's New York; no one can breathe. But then some Bob the Builders showed up with plexiglass walls. They built a giant box where the smog and the *radon* can't fuck with the classics. The boss man was a little weird when I asked if I could stash my typewriters in here.

He smirked. "You're wasting your time, Joseph. You can't save the world."

But maybe you can, because he caved. It's my happy place, I come down here and fuck around with my rescues. They should be home with me, but there's no room for props in a cardboard fucking box. Same way there's no room for a girl.

I pet the first one I ever found, the green machine from Bushwick. "One day you're getting out of here, Hector."

If I were a girl, I'd be into a guy like me, and I turn red—that's a douchebag of a thought—but a few minutes with Emily Dickinson makes me feel like a good guy, like actual fucking boyfriend material. The girl who wanted the lighter kinda looked like Emily Dickinson, and I run upstairs and check my email.

Nothing.

Midnight somehow and I'm still up. Still hungry. I have to work tomorrow. I have to exist. I should get off the floor and go downstairs and catch a few z's on the cot. It's right there in the cage. Not a great bed, but something. I stand. Dizzy. It's almost one now and I can't go downstairs. This is the witching hour. Girls do things after midnight they wouldn't do in the day, so it's very possible the girl wrote back to me. I check my email.

Nothing.

I pop a Peter Frampton CD in the boom box. Is that weird? Am I weird? I do this sometimes. I mimic people. I told that girl she looked like Carolyn Bessette because Angus said *his* girl looked like Carolyn Bessette. Something is wrong with me, but something is wrong with anyone awake at 3:12 A.M. I check my Hotmail again, and then again, and then again, and then night becomes day. Mr. Mooney barges in and glares at me, disgusted as the sun.

"There's a fresh shirt in the back, Joseph."

"Yeah, I got sucked into that new King."

He knows I'm lying. He knows everything. Mr. Mooney is married. It's not like he's so in love, but he has something, someone. He says I'm not the same since we got this computer.

And he's right.

I turn off the computer. Fuck it. All of it.

I put on the fresh shirt. A new black Hanes T-shirt that's only here because I do this a lot lately. I stay in the shop, by the computer, by the list. It's fucking insane. That girl on the street is like those girls on the subway. I don't know her.

So why am I bashing my head into the mirror? Why am I making fists? Why can't I just say fuck it and let things go? Why do I wanna sleep in a prison?

It's true. Back in September, Mr. Mooney locked me in the cage to punish me for letting a girl walk out of here with a signed *Catcher in the Rye*. I liked it in the cage. I slept great. Better than I had in years. When I told him how good it felt, he hung his head.

That's because your mother didn't love you. Rest in peace, Joseph.

The way he said that . . . I didn't know if I was gonna get out of there alive.

Maybe I didn't. Maybe I'm dead.

I splash cold water on my face. *Stop it, Joe, stop it.*

The shop opens, and it's a good thing. I'm alive. Busy. I'm not dead, and the hope of something between me and some girl who asked me for a lighter won't be the death of me either. I'm gonna change my ways. No more Missed Connections. I'm done. I delete my pathetic post, and it feels good. The computer is bad for me, the way Craig never lets up. The real world is a breeze. Shit closes and you can't get what you want. But Craigslist is always there, it's the mother

I never had prodding at me, checking to see if I'm hungry, if I have a fever. Mooney is right. Sometimes it is that fucking simple. Mama didn't love me, and the *girls, girls, girls* all know it, because girls have a third eye, an extra hole. They *can't* love me, because they know I can't love them.

Poor Angus will never get clean. He can carry the rocks in his pocket—there is no escape for a crackhead—but I have a shot at a good life.

The computer is my drug, and it's not a mobile phone or a lighter or a crack pipe.

I can't fit one in my pocket.

I can kick it—*Yes I can*—and I kill it on the floor. I am clean and sober, *pushing* Lucinda Rosenfeld on a woman going through a divorce. Time for my lunch break and it feels good to be out in the world. I duck into a proper old-school coffee shop, the kinda place that won't fold and turn into an *internet café.* I open my Bukowski, but the guy in the chair next to me grunts. "Unbelievable, right? Get a room, lady."

He's irate because a woman is nursing her baby. In a better society, it would be legal for me to kick him in the nuts. In this shitty world, best I can do is ignore him. It's oddly soothing to me, the mother in agony with the baby that won't latch on. The poor woman is spent, apologizing to everyone as if she did something wrong. The jerk next to me storms out—I bet his mother didn't love him either—and I stay where I am. It's a game, like baseball or hockey, and finally, the guy scores! He latches onto that breast, and his mother sighs in relief.

I look down at my Bukowski. The old me would have crushed it, but I can't do it. I can't open my mouth, or my soul. I can't latch onto words on paper, especially when I spy a single, lonely computer in the back of this old-school café. It's calling my name, and that's okay. You're not supposed to quit anything cold fucking turkey. I'm allowed. I'm not "addicted." If I was a real addict, I wouldn't stop to tell the new mom that her kid's a keeper.

She needed that, and she looks up at me, into me. God, I love women, I really do. "Thanks," she says. "Thanks for not being a jerk. I mean, what am I supposed to do?"

I make my way to the back—computers are like porn, they hide them—and I sit at the desk. It felt good to lift that lady's spirits. We all need someone to tell us that we're not the worst person in the coffee shop. All babies starve without milk. Not just me.

I know what to expect from my Hotmail by now. . . . Coldmail. That's what I get. And that's okay. Life is long. I'll do better. I'll check Missed Connections one more time, and then I'll take a few days off. Learn to read again. Make a woman who's not a new mom smile.

But then I find my milk.

You: NYC Bookstore Babe, touchable brown hair, brown eyes, twinkling

The milk hits like heroin, like crack fumes. This is a first, the kind of high you spend the rest of your life chasing. Kafka shit where I metamorphosize all at once. My jeans fit! My head fits! I touch the mouse but I can't push it. What if I jumped the gun? What if you went into some other fucking bookstore and want some other fucking guy with touchable brown hair? I want to be your NYC Bookstore Babe. I *have* to be your NYC Bookstore Babe. I *am* your NYC Bookstore Babe, assuming this note is for me . . .

Is it?

It's a little scary. I am all in. I want you even though I don't know who you are. Even though you might not want me. But that's love, isn't it? Unconditional and pure. Simple as the black font on the white background of a Missed Fucking Connection. It's not just me anymore. Now there's someone else. You. You're not in my head. You're not *girls, girls, girls*. You exist. You walk into bookstores and you turn to Craig for help, but you might be after some other guy in *Brooklyn* or some shit. I could bail on you. Unplug the computer and throw it out the window, but no. I can't do that to you. Us. You have hope in you. Passion. You wrote a message, and you put it in the bottle and I am not some boy on the beach who happened to find the bottle in the tide. I am the prince who was built to open your bottle and drink every last drop.

2

It's crazy, the way life goes. I kinda wanna get out the phone book and see if Miss Frascatore is still alive. She was my guidance counselor in second grade. She was like one of those happy adults on *Sesame Fucking Street.* This one time, my mom sent me to school with a black eye. My teacher Mrs. Prince—big breasts, the kind that scream *over-the-shoulder boulder holder*—sent me to Miss Frascatore. A tiny person in a sweater with fucking *candy canes* and lights, the kind of thing a kid wears. Anyway, I was sent to her a lot back in the day. She always acted happy to see me. Sitting on the floor, smiling at me like I was some go-lucky kid with a belly full of homemade apple pie.

"Wanna know a secret, Joe? A really *good* secret . . ."

I gave her nothing. Most adults hate that shit. They want the kid from the Life cereal commercial. But Miss Frascatore took off her big glasses and clamped her hands over her eyes, and she smiled like she was watching a movie in her head, something funny, something like *Porky's.*

"Try it," she said. "See, Joey, there's a dirty little secret that most grown-ups don't want to tell you. Trusting someone feels good. I am choosing to set you free, to believe that you won't hurt me, and again . . . it's fun, Joe. It makes you feel good to be—"

I slammed the door on the way out. I was a fucked-up little dude, and she was the original *Little Red Corvette.* Too much, too fast. I wasn't a monster. I felt bad. The next day, I asked my teacher if I could go see her, and my teacher said no.

"Miss Frascatore is at another school now."

I never saw her again, and she's on my mind because of you.

You! You really *were* writing to me, thinking of me and the best part is my part.

I remember you too, Bookstore Babe.

You came into the shop on an icy rainy Tuesday in the dregs of post-9/11 December. You reminded me of Miss Frascatore the day we met. You with your little bright blue cape. Combat boots and a messenger bag that was almost bigger than you. Plaid tights that revealed something about your insecurity, like your legs weren't enough. This smile that screamed *inexperienced guidance counselor.* I watched you rummage through your too-big bag in EARTH SCIENCES. You were more of a large child than an adult, playing dress-up.

"Can I help you, miss?"

"Do people really buy this stuff?"

I was good with you. Cool with just a touch of cold. "This is New York," I said. "Yesterday, a woman came in here and bought three books about Beanie Babies."

You looked away as you smiled. Swayed. That ridiculous cape like a hula skirt hanging on your torso. Girls are silly. Clothes are silly. "I'm not gonna lie," you said. "I'm not here to buy a book."

"Oh, no?"

You were closer now, and when did that happen?

"Look," you said. "I know the drill. Restroom is for customers only. Yada, yada, yada. But you seem cool. You know how it is. I'm a hardworking assistant in the middle of my day, and if I don't finish my stuff, I'm gonna get fired and wind up living in my parents' basement back in Beverly Hills, and I know . . ."

I looked at you the way anyone would. *Beverly Fucking Hills.*

"No," you said. "Beverly Hills, *Michigan.* I'm not, like, I mean, I'm not a princess. I can't actually afford this Miu Miu cape, okay? I got it at work. Shit. My quarter-life crisis isn't even here yet and already I'm a nervous babbling wreck."

"You're not babbling. You're talking."

You undid a brassy button on that stupid fucking cape. "Okay," you went on. "All I mean is I know I can't just waltz in here and use the loo, but at the same time . . ."

"You want to waltz in here and use the loo."

"Need," you said. "I *need* to waltz in here and use the loo."

That was it. The first spark. The click. I offered to show you the way to the *loo,* and you laughed a little. "Oh God," you said. "I'm really getting my British on today. I might have a little too much Dido on my mixtape."

I didn't know who that is and I didn't ask you who that is. I knew enough to be quiet.

"Anyway," you said. "I'm a total Anglophile. I adore all things British."

"Me too," I said. It wasn't a lie or some intentional fucking deception. It was instinct. It felt right to agree with you, same way it felt right to let you break the rules. And then it was on. You told me you just rewatched *Sliding Doors,* and I told you I love it too. You asked what I would be doing with my life if *I* missed the train.

"Well," I said. "I think I'd be right here, honestly. I think I'd be me."

You said that was either *really deep or really shallow,* and I liked the way it felt, being on the move with you. I was at my best. Casually picking up some Clancy and reshelving it while you looked around the shop. You said it reminded you of the one from *You've Got Mail.* I pictured you naked. I imagined your body on top of mine. It felt different with you. Clear. I was nervous because I was gonna do the thing I never fucking do. I was gonna ask for your number. We made it to the back of the shop, and I opened the bathroom door. It was on the tip of my tongue. *Maybe we could grab a coffee or something.*

But then Mooney barged in. "This is not a paying customer."

You were tied to the railroad tracks, and I was there with pliers. "Actually, Mr. Mooney, this young lady was in earlier today. She bought a book."

I saw your lips turn up a little. *This young lady.* You liked that.

Mooney didn't budge. "What book?"

I was fast. Good. "*Portnoy's Complaint.*"

The lie played—Mooney let you into the can—but the shop got busy. You slipped out the door with a shy wave, like you'd lost your nerve in the bathroom. But who am I to judge? I fucked up too. I didn't leave the register and run into the rain.

Later that night, I tried to write a Missed Connection. Usually, it comes naturally to me, but I couldn't do it with you. I couldn't clap my hands over my eyes and trust the world. I couldn't reduce what we had and pack it up into a little post.

You couldn't either, not at first.

I pushed you out of my mind, and I'm sure you tried to forget about me too.

But this is where I love *girls, girls, girls, girls, girls I do adore.* You cling. You don't let go. You don't give up.

And as it turns out, we are lucky to be alive and young in late December of 2001. Yes, the world is fucked. Yes, we might all die at any moment. But there's one thing we do have going for us. . . .

The internet.

I pull up the World's Best Missed Connection Ever Written, and I do what a good reader does. I read it again.

MISSED CONNECTION: NYC Bookstore Babe, touchable brown hair, brown eyes, twinkling

This is a long shot because it's all probably in my head. And this is so not me. It's my first time here and all of it . . . Craigslist . . . Missed Connections . . . I am not that girl, okay? And yes, this is embarrassing, maybe even pathetic, but maybe also (gulp) romantic? I know. People who say they never do something or tell you it's the first time for them are usually lying, but I swear I'm telling the truth.

A couple of weeks ago, I walked into a random bookstore because it was raining, and I had to pee. Your boss barked at me that it's for paying customers only. I was in a mood so I kinda bit the old man's head off about how we're all supposed to be nice to one another right now because hello . . . Who DOESN'T have PTSD from 9/11? My voice was shaking, and he just kinda set me off, and I thought I was gonna burst into tears, but then you ran up to him—so sweet, the way you touched his shoulder—and you told him that I was *a paying customer.*

Him: "Are you telling the truth?"

You: "Swear to God."

Him: "What did she buy?"

You: "INSERT NAME OF THE BOOK IN YOUR REPLY SO I KNOW IT'S YOU."

Anyway. You saved me. Total hero move. A whiter, sweeter lie there could not be.

And yes . . . You were cute. Felt like you thought I was cute, but again, I totally get that you might be a good guy who does good things, and if you see this and you DO remember me and you were NOT into me . . . I wish you nothing but the best, and I promise I won't come back to your place of work and hunt you down. You totally have the right to see this, cringe, and move on.

If, on the other hand, it WAS personal . . . if you do remember me, if you think about me, if you think about me a lot, if you don't think it's creepy and weird and pathetic and gross of me to put this out there and you wanna see that new John Cusack movie with me, this is what you do.

Write back to this post with the name of the book and the name of the shop.

I know your name. I saw your name tag. The question is, do you wanna know mine?

I want to write back to you, but I have to be smart about this. I have to put myself in your shoes. After all, you're the reason we get a second chance. You're the one who put yourself out there for *me.*

And I know it wasn't easy. You probably had a few sips of something strong. You typed. You tweaked. You hemmed and you hawed and paced around your little apartment—it has to be little; they're all fucking little—and the liquid courage wasn't cutting it, so you called a friend. She thought you were nuts.

Nobody actually does Missed Connections. I mean, what if he's crazy?

But that's not you. You're not cynical. You're a dreamer, a romantic, a doer.

So, fuck yes, you cut open your chest and you shared your deepest, newest, most embarrassing dream with the world. Lucky for you and for me, I too am a hopeless fucking romantic. Sure, you got some of the dialogue wrong, but that's girls. You make everything bigger in the rearview mirror. You threw out a line. You let *hope* win, and one day, we'll frame this beautiful letter and hang it in our *very, very, very fine house.* We won't have two cats. We'll have a dog. And it won't be a house, technically. We'll live on the Upper West Side and—

Gently, Joseph.

You don't want to marry me, not yet. But you do want me.

I am *NYC Bookstore Babe.* I deserve this. How many times have I heeded the call of Miss Frascatore, closed my eyes, and trusted that some girl out there would read my letter, that I would read the letter from some girl? This is my first win, and I gotta relax. I can't come on too strong. And I earned a win. I should have seen it coming. At some point, someone had to walk into this shop and see me. If your life is one clusterfuck after another, if the first seventeen years are too *bad* to be true, it makes sense that you get a shot of too good to be true in the form of a comely caped crusader.

Gently, Joseph.

I scan the shop to make sure Mr. Mooney is still in his office—yep—and I put the pedal to the metal, my fingers on the keypad.

> Portnoy's Complaint. *Mooney Books. The Angelika has a* Serendipity *screening at 11:45 tomorrow. If that works for you, I'll be out front. No name tag, though.* ☺

My fingers hem and haw, they hover. You were in this moment. You freaked out. Hesitated. Worried that I might think you're nuts. It feels good to be in your shoes, wondering if I have the guts to go through with it, to answer your shot in the dark. And then I bite the bullet.

Click.

3

Time is bullshit.

I can't tell if it's been ten minutes or ten years since I wrote back to you and did I fuck it up? Did I stutter? Was I lame? Is tomorrow too soon? I chose tomorrow because it's that dead week that doesn't exist, the blur between Christmas and New Year's. But did I seem too eager? Lonely? There is no going back, and my stomach is on a warpath to take me down. Why did I add that smiley face? Did I sound like a telegram? You penned thoughtful, grammatically on-point sentences, and I sent you an order?! You'd think someone who reads so many fucking books would know how to write a simple email. A smiley face. Did I really do that? I did. You said you're pathetic, but that's not true. You're bold. You started this. *I'm* the pathetic one, and I should've played it cool. Held off on a response and waited to see if you were brave enough to come back to the shop. I don't know your name. I don't know anything about you, but I bet some evil friend of yours is telling you to ignore me. I can hear the evil friend, see her.

Um, do you realize that this guy only saw the Missed Connection because he goes *on Missed Connections? Think about that. How sad is that? I mean, it's kind of pathetic if you think about it, and beyond that . . . a smiley face?*

"Yoo-hoo. Is it possible to get some service?"

Great. Just what I need right now. A *customer.* "Sorry for the wait, sir."

He drops his Clive Cussler on the counter. I tell him it's a good one. He grunts. "In my day, we had our feet on the ground and our eyes on the world, but you kids . . . Mark my words. Those computers will be the death of you."

I laugh like the loser I am, the idiot who makes a smiley face. "Have a good one."

"Impossible," he mutters. "The good ones are all behind us."

The second the door closes, I check my Hotmail, but it's cold. Ice-cold.

My Portnoy is twitching. I look at the door. Why didn't you just come back? Sure, you put yourself out there, but you got to hold on to your fucking dignity. You got to be *anonymous.* Me? I blew my wad. I came too fast. I lost my privacy and my dignity. You pursued me in the most beautiful, gutsy way and I made a joke of it. A smiley face. A *smiley* face.

"Joe!"

"Coming!"

Oh, that's right. It's another problem about us, as if there is an us. Mr. Mooney is all I have, and he hated you—you didn't buy a book and you left the light on in the bathroom—and how does this work? How do we fall in love if the two of you hate each other?

I knock on the office door, and he says it's open, and I brace for impact. It will never *not* kill me. The hypocrisy. The man loves books. The man smokes cigars . . . in a *bookstore.* He smirks.

"What's that face, Joseph?"

"Nothing."

"What did we learn about lying, Joseph?"

"Sorry," I say. "Just a bad salad."

He nods and sighs. He *hates* salad. It was a good lie. I'm learning. Let him grumble about the evils of *carnivores eating leaves.* But not for too long. The more he whines about salad culture being the downfall of civilization, the more I want to meet you. I get it now. If I don't at least *try* to have a girlfriend, I'm gonna end up like Mooney, watching the security footage, *wanting* to be robbed, because I like to be angry more than I like to be sad.

I hold my stomach again and wince. He rolls his eyes. "Don't be a pansy, Joseph."

"Sorry."

Pansy and this is the opposite of a pep talk. I bet you don't like me, not anymore, and I want to unsend my pathetic message and take hot pokers to the eyes of the fucking *smiley* face—WHAT IS WRONG WITH ME—and I blew it, didn't I? Mr. Mooney is right about a lot. Maybe I am a pansy.

"Anyway," he says. "I reviewed our stock as well as our sales."

"Okay."

"You lied to me again."

I did. "I didn't."

"That's number three and it's not even six P.M."

I hang my head. It's been about four months since I fucked up and let a girl walk out of here with a rare, signed *Catcher in the Rye.* He put me in the cage. I swore I learned my lesson. Don't lie. Don't be naïve. Don't let women get away with murder.

"Joseph," he says. "We have six *Complaint*s in this shop. Which means we did not sell one in the month of December, which is no surprise, as people have no taste, particularly young women in *capes* and combat boots."

It's dark kismet. Bad magic. WHY DIDN'T I BUY A FUCKING *COMPLAINT*?

"Right," I say. "But she seemed nice, and sometimes . . ."

"Joseph."

He's picking up his keys, the keys to the basement, to the cage. I don't want to go in there, not on his terms. I want to fucking *live.*

"You're right," I say. "She was a cunt."

We're not even together and already I betrayed you. You wouldn't like me if you saw me right now. And maybe on some level you didn't come back because you did see me, even though you wanted to project all this good stuff on me. Maybe you're having second thoughts. You're probably at work—you seemed older in a way where you probably have a checkbook and a 401(k)—and I bet you read my email and realized that I'm not a hero. I'm just a dumb kid. A runaway *pansy* who sleeps in an extra-long twin bed in a cardboard fucking box of a fake bedroom. You can't call it a *room.* There is no window, and if you think about it, it's just another cage because of Dumb and Dumber on the sofa watching their big fat TV. I am cute, but not cute enough. I come too fast, and I wrote too fast—I should've made you wait and yearn—and Mr. Mooney snaps his fingers.

"Wake up."

"Sorry."

All at once, my flaws come barreling at me. I apologize too much. I read too much. I think too much. I do a *lot* of things too much. I am not "Too Much" by Dave Matthews, which is only annoying to some. I am annoying to all. Nobody loves me. Not my parents, not Mr. Mooney, not the one girl from the one time. Not even Dumb and Dumber. They don't invite me to watch football with them, and why should they? I live in a room that isn't even a room. No closet. No lock on my "door." Just a body in a makeshift box to help them cover the fucking rent.

"Don't be sorry, Joseph. Be smart."

"Okay."

"What happened with you and this girl? And I want the truth, Joseph."

"She batted her eyes at me because she wanted to use the toilet."

"Yes."

"She didn't smile at me because she liked me. She was using me."

"Yes."

I wish I had a computer in my pocket—did you write back?—and I wish he would stop with this shit, and if you did write back—did you?—and you're sitting there waiting for a response, you're probably getting antsy, having second thoughts, thinking it might be wiser to put it all behind you and pee somewhere else next time you're in a fix.

"Say it, Joseph. Finish it."

"She was using me because she knew she could use me."

"And why is that, Joseph?"

"Because I let women walk all over me."

"And why is that?"

"Because my mom walked all over me."

He lights a damp stogie. "Remember, Joseph. The best books are hard to read. They strain your eyes, your mind. They challenge you, boy. You've a lot more reading to do before you so much as dare to make your way into the hole of some cunt in a cape."

I barely make it out the door before I fold like a whiny little toddler who couldn't even get my own *mother* to like me. I cried too much when I was a baby, and Mooney is right. I'm weak. I get excited when any girl looks at me. I practically come in my fucking pants. I'm a bad seed. Desperate. I can't believe I didn't take my time with you. I wish I'd taken out a Moleskine notepad and a fountain pen, tried to match you, meet you, be you. There's no way I'll ever see you again and maybe it's okay. That's the thing about losing hope. Accepting defeat. I feel nothing as I tap the computer, as it comes back to life. And then I open Hotmail and . . .

It's you. As if you felt me jumping ship.

Hi. It's me, Vail. See you at the movies, Joe. ☺

4

I got here first—I am the man—and I look like a boyfriend, like *Romeo in black jeans.* I shaved. I ate a banana. I practiced my small talk in the mirror, and I walked all the way here from Stuy Town. There is a whole world out there. Zillions and billions of people and you are not *girls, girls, girls.* You are just one girl. I'm not risking my life, but my legs won't stop shaking. It's good. I'm good. I bought the tickets. They're a little moist—I am sweating—but first dates are a mind fuck, and I bet you're sweating too, wondering if I'll show up, if I'll still want you when I see you. I need to breathe. Be cool. Don't say *moist.* But it's one of those topics I made for us to discuss, the way it's always the coldhearted snakes in this world who are so fucking good at being relaxed. *Cool.*

The other topics are on the Moleskine notepad in my back pocket, but I don't need to check it. They're all upstairs, in my head:

- Our favorite Philip Roth books
- Our favorite books from childhood

- My advance copy of *The Lovely Bones* that I might lend to you
- Pizza
- The horror that is the Virgin Megastore in Times Fucking Square

I'm ready for you, Vail. My feet are planted on the concrete on the corner of Houston and Mercer, right in front of the main steps to the theater. But then a woman smirks at me and fuck. Am I *too* ready? Yes. There's this stink about me. Desperation, as if every passerby can tell I jerked off in the shower, the way I went from pulling at my Portnoy to clutching these fucking tickets. *Fix it, Joe, fix it.* I step aside to lean against the wall like James Fucking Dean, like I'm *cool.* It's just a date. You're just a girl. But my neck is stiff, and the wall is too hard and then . . .

You are here. Bare legs under a black miniskirt. No tights. Same messenger bag. Your hair is stick straight. Ironed and glossy.

"Hello, Joe."

"Hi, Vail."

You throw your arms around me, and I'm a soldier back from the war. You smell like a girl, like powders and peaches, and you have strong arms. Muscles that you use to hold on to me. And then you pull away, as if you think you came on a little strong. You size me up, and do you see good things? Bad things? Did you expect *me* to have a messenger bag? Should I have worn my brown sweater instead of the black one?

"So," you say. "Are you as nervous as I am?"

"Oh yeah. Just now I tried to lean against the wall to seem cool."

"And how'd that work out for you?"

"It didn't."

You laugh—you like me—and you pull your hair over one shoulder. You really are nervous, and that means I matter. "Aw, I get it," you say. "But come on. You guys have it easy. You throw on jeans and a T-shirt and you're good to go."

It's *December,* and I am wearing a sweater. "True."

"You have no clue. . . . Women, us, *me,* I went *nuts* this morning. My place is a mess 'cause I still haven't unpacked since I got home from Christmas. . . . Did you go home for Christmas . . . or Hanukkah?"

I laugh like I have a family, like I had a holiday. "I'm from Bed-Stuy, so there's no suitcase involved."

"Cool," you say. "Okay, my point, though . . . This morning, I changed my clothes ten times. I mean, jeans are okay if I'm feeling them, if they flatter me, but as a girl, every day you have a different body, so you can't plan these things in advance. And the whole time I'm melting down and worrying if a skirt in the day is too much and my slutty roommate is rolling her eyes and mocking me and oh my God this is so *not* what I planned on saying to you when I got here."

You are bursting with fruit flavors, with words. That's what you are, a pack of gum. Fruit Stripe that I used to count as lunch, and I like you, Vail. I like you. Your mouth that moves so fast and your exposed, weak knees. I get it, the nerves. I changed sweaters four times before I left my cardboard box, but there are some things girls can say that boys just fucking can't. "Well, you look lovely, Vail."

Lovely was the wrong word. I can feel you clock it and stow it in your giant busy-girl bag. "Thank you, Joe. And fuck me and my blabbing."

You said *fuck me,* and I stash that in *my* invisible bag. It's early, but it's clear. We're clicking. Open and yet shy all at once, as if we're surprised by ourselves, by our chemistry. I touch your elbow. "See, this is why people go to the movies," I say. "Because we have to keep our traps shut once we're inside."

You blow a little strand of hair out of your mouth. You say that's a *good point*—you think I'm smart—and I never knew that I had that opinion about the classic movie date until now, until you. You shift gears. "Speaking of movies, did you ever see *Annie Hall*?"

Your voice is high. The alchemy is getting to you too. I laugh and say yes. "I mean, I'm a fucking New Yorker."

"Mm-hmm."

You say this like it's a code, and it's my first real date. I do what feels natural. I do you. "Mm-hmm."

"Okay," you say. Yet another lick of the lips, and are you blushing? "Do you know that part where they . . ." You shake your little head, hair blown out for me, combed for me. "Never mind. . . . I can't."

"Sure you can, Vail. It's okay."

It feels good to say your name, to imagine it coming out of my mouth every day. Big bad thought, too much, too soon. *Down, Portnoy. Chill.* Your cell phone rings. It's work, you have to take it, and it's fancy, *Motorola.* You are sweet and sorry, talking by the fire hydrant, looking at me, promising *one more minute.* I am the good guy, patient. I like the way you check in with me. You're kind. You care. I could get used to this. I *am* fucking used to it, and you're back.

"Okay, hi."

"Hi."

And then we are quiet. I read about this kinda stuff, about "love." Time slows down, the planet dies, and we're the last two left on the sidewalk, in the world. I hear the opening lines of that song from *Shag,* that movie at that birthday party, in the dark, in Kelly Fuentes's basement, the first time a girl touched my Portnoy. *Touch me. . . . Love the way you touch me.* You sneeze, and the music dies, which is good. It's too soon. I can't jump off the bridge into you just fucking yet. You're a girl, you have a tissue. You dab your nose. A button that's a little too large for your face, probably the reason why you draw black circles around your eyes. You don't know that you're perfect as you are, but soon enough, I will show you.

"Okay," you say. "So, *Annie Hall.*"

"*Annie Hall.*"

"You know that scene when they're on their way into the diner and he says they should kiss before they eat so they can digest their food?"

I really am *Romeo in black jeans* and I'm a *cool cat . . . tapping on the toe with a new hat.* Collected. "I think I remember it. . . ."

Your eyes come at me, two little Polaroid cameras, and fuck yes, Vail. Capture me, expose me. I want this, you. You bite your lip in a deliberate, slow-motion music video kind of way. It's happening right here, right now, on Houston and Fucking Mercer. I take your hand, or you take mine—the blur is real—and you give me your lips. It's a fit, a good match, and your fingers work my hand, and your body melts below my other hand. This is my life turning around in real time. My eyes are closed but already *we are the world* and undoubtedly others are watching, vowing to get what *we* have. I deserve a girl like you. An *X* who marks the spot, quivering when I find the small of your back, and is that your tongue? It is. I put my message in a bottle, my tongue in your mouth, two lovestruck whales humping in a deep blue sea.

You pull back and squeeze my hand before you drop it. "Well, hello, Mr. Tongue."

The CD skips. Scratched. *Well, hello, Mr. Tongue.* You recede like a fucking tide and wait. What just happened? You started it. You brought your tongue into it, and I was only bringing mine to be polite. You fidget with your skirt and your messenger bag. . . . Did I imagine it? Did I just give you unwanted fucking tongue? Did I kill the whales?

You snatch the tickets and slap my chest with them. "So! Where do you live?"

Is this a test? "In the city."

You don't ask for specifics, and I don't offer. I can't. My tongue is MIA. "C'mon," you say. "I *live* for the coming attractions."

I follow you up the stairs, and it's wrong, all wrong. Fuck you, Mr. Tongue. Fuck you, Woody Allen. You grab onto the door with the same eager beaver gusto you had when you grabbed onto the tickets, and you screech, "After you, sir."

I'm the man. I'm supposed to ask the questions, to get the door.

Inside, you are casual and clucking, turning every tiny, quotidian transaction with every employee into an inter-fucking-action. Can't even hand off the tickets to the usher without complimenting his vest. Mr. Tongue killed it, he did, and I have to fix things. Man up.

I point to the concession stand. "Popcorn?"

"Mmm . . ." It hangs there, incomplete, and c'mon, Vail. Give me the fucking *hmmm*. "Nah, I'm good."

You don't want our hands to meet in a bowl of salty butter anymore. Assuming you did earlier. Did you? You dig into that giant bag and flash a box of peanut M&M's. "The snacks are always such a rip-off."

"True," I say, but not true. It's a date, Vail. I *want* to be ripped off for you. You won't let me feed you a fucking snack at the movies and is it true that girls turn on a dime after the first kiss? *Hello, Mr. Tongue.*

You grab the door for me and that's *my* job. No. No! "After you, kid."

Kid. Is that good? Bad? I DON'T FUCKING KNOW, and you want to sit in row ten, so we sit in row ten, and you want to be smack-dab in the middle, so we are smack-dab in the middle. You dump your messenger bag in an empty chair. You're the captain and I'm the guy with the big, sloppy tongue and it doesn't feel like a date, the way you talk about the plots, the bullshit actors, the *sets.* The movie doesn't matter. *We* matter.

You open your box of peanut M&M's. I don't hold out my hand.

"Oh," you say. "Are you allergic?"

Are you allergic to my tongue? "Nah," I say. "I'm just not a peanut guy."

As in YOU BROKE MY NUT SACK. But then you fiddle with the box like you don't hate Mr. Tongue, like you wish you brought the good M&M's. "I didn't know," you murmur. "Sorry."

Fuck it. I offer my hand, the palm. "Maybe I should give them another shot."

You pour cheapo, chemical-drenched nuts into my left hand—

I wish I were on the right, I'm a righty—but you're smiling again. Girlish. Maybe you *would* give Mr. Tongue another shot. "So," you say. "My boss knows the director of this movie."

There is no part of that sentence that interests me or distracts me from your legs, but I know the drill. Guys with bad tongues have to play the game. "Oh yeah? That's cool."

"Well, yeah. I'm in the industry. . . . In TV."

Ugh. "Cool."

"Oh, I'm not like . . . I'm not in it *in* it. It's not my 'dream' or anything. My friend had an uncle who knew someone who knew someone, and I'm just assisting this director dude."

Oh, great. A friend with connections and an older man with a shiny big job and a dozen or so years more practice with his Mr. Fucking Tongue. "That's cool."

"Anyway," you say. "It's not glamorous or anything. Mostly I run errands for his wife."

I like you for that, for knowing that I needed a little boost. "Cool."

"But the thing is . . . yeah. So, I work for *Sex and the City*. . . ."

You say this like it's a coup, like you edit Philip Roth. I don't watch that show, but I know the gist. Is that what comes next? You sit with *the girls* and tell them about Mr. Fucking Tongue over pink, stupid drinks? "Cool."

"And before you ask, I mean, no, I can't tell you what happens with Carrie and Aidan."

I say the only word I have left. "Cool."

You tuck the box of M&M's into your giant messenger bag. "Okay then. Message received. . . . I know I sound pathetic."

"You're not pathetic."

"Oh, come on. I'm a big girl. I hate the sound of my voice when I get nervous and start bragging about my job and you're just like, 'Cool,' as in *not* cool."

I touch your hand and smile. "It's all right. It's . . ."

If there's any chance for me and Mr. Tongue, you'll finish the sentence for me and then you do it, Vail. You look me in the eye and say the magic nervous word. "Cool."

I want to kiss your hand the same way I kissed your mouth, but no. Not yet. I tell you I'm even worse, self-conscious and nervous, obsessing over every word, every move. "Even the book."

"The book?"

"Why did I say you bought *Portnoy's Complaint*? Why didn't I go with *Goodbye, Columbus,* or *American Pastoral*? Why did I pick the perviest one in the bunch?"

It's time for you to assure me that there is no such thing as bad Philip Roth, but instead you just stare at me. "Huh?"

"The book I told Mooney that you bought . . . *Portnoy's Complaint.*" You furrow your brow, and I say it again. "*Portnoy's Complaint.* . . . The book I said you bought so you could get in the *loo.*"

You laugh now, as if you already forgot the origin of our love story, as if Mr. Tongue really did kill the potential. "Ah," you say. "I guess I didn't know it's a real book."

"It's Philip Roth."

"Who's Philip Roth?"

Blasphemy and your Polaroids flash in the bad way.

"Was it made into a movie?"

I choke on the end-of-the-world air in this dank, daytime dark slimy abyss of a fucking theater. "It's the kind of novel that you just have to read."

You shiver. You say it's cold in here and I didn't wear a coat so I can't offer you a coat and are you a Philistine? Is that the best you can do? Whine about the cold as if every fucking theater isn't an icebox? *Who's Philip Roth?* You fidget with your box of M&M's. This is bad. Maybe. I stare at you. "Sorry," you say. "I'm not like . . . Books aren't my thing."

This is all wrong. You seem like a reader, what with your messenger bag and your Woody Allen role-play and your writing, your beautiful, bold writing. "Oh. Okay. Cool."

Cool and you shrug again, candy girl, TV girl. "So, Phil Roth. . . . Did any of his other books get made into movies?"

"Philip," I say and FUCK YOU, MR. TONGUE.

You didn't like that—don't correct girls, ever—and the lights are dimming. The coming fucking attractions. My leg is shaking, and there are guns on the screen, blood. You elbow me and whisper. "How good does this look? That production design is whoa."

Maybe Mr. Tongue was right, the way he tried to poke your eyeballs out from inside of your mouth. "It looks good. And Philip Roth . . . he's . . . the man is a god."

"Mmm. Speaking of gods, do you know Mira Nair? Such a visionary. Her films, all film . . . It's everything to me. Everything. It sounds cheesy, but I love cinema . . . *movies* . . . I'm a visual person and oh my God, did I just say that out loud? I'm gross, I know."

You're not gross but my tongue is too big for my mouth—I freeze up—and you pick up your messenger bag and set it on your lap. A literal fucking cockblock. This is bad. Tense. You pout. "So, I guess you're a book snob?"

You are sassy and love is war. We are sparring. You judged Mr. Tongue and you don't know Philip Roth. I can do this, I can talk. "Oh, I wouldn't say that. I'm just a book *person*."

"Ah, well, just so you know . . . I've done that whole pretend-to-be-into-books-to-seem-deep thing or whatever. I mean, I like movies. I *only* went into that bookstore to pee."

"Okay."

"Truth is I actually . . . I kind of *hate* bookstores."

"You what?"

"Oh, come on. You know the way people act in bookstores, around books, all pretentious and performative like they're superior or whatever. *Monsoon Wedding*—the Mira Nair movie—it feels deeper than a lot of books. I mean, if it's a choice between a museum and a bookstore and a movie, I am *always* going to the movies. Always."

You cross your arms, and it's confusing. You took a dig at *me*. But in the dark theater, where it's almost just us, it's hard to let go of the thing with feathers. Hope. You are pretty and you smell pretty, and I want you to love books. Me. Bookstores. "It's okay, Vail. Seriously."

"The last guy I dated would drag me into bookstores and drone on about . . . No. I'm sorry."

I never dated anyone, which is probably why no girl ever told me what to do with Mr. Tongue. I don't ask for more details about your ex, and I don't launch into a defense of books.

You squirm. I squirm. We have nothing in common right now except the screen in front of us. It crackles. Another preview begins and it's bad, the way your Polaroids go crazy, as if the screen is a fucking *Poltergeist* and you're that little blond girl. Consumed. Enthralled. Possessed. You called them coming attractions, but that's bullshit. Those are *advertisements.* They don't make previews for *books.* My leg is shaking. Worse than Mr. Tongue, and you plunk your giant bag back in the chair. Was that your way of telling me to stop fucking shaking?

I clamp my hand on my leg. I thought I'd be holding on to you by now, your thigh.

And then you whisper in my ear. "He's *amazing*, right?"

I don't know who he is. "Yep."

I can't give up on you. Not yet. You showed up in a skirt. Maybe you're not a Philistine. Maybe you just haven't found the right book, the one that alters your soul and makes you want more. *Who's Philip Roth?* I glance at you, but you're still in it. Entranced by propaganda. I may as well be invisible. *The last guy I dated* . . . You're a woman, and my most recent relationship started at an eighth-grade fucking *basement* party. *Well, hello, Mr. Tongue.* The darkness falls to a deeper level—*Serendipity* is upon us—and you clap your little hands and curl up into yourself, all your *lovely bones.* It's almost like you came here to see a movie more than you came here to see me. If I made a run for it, you'd probably stick with *Cusack.*

The comedown is hard, a boner crusher. I was excited for you, for us. I thought of you in the shower this morning. I thought by this point we'd be knee-deep in conversation about Philip Roth, tempted to ditch the stupid movie so we could keep talking. I was a fool, naked with my Portnoy in my hand. But we are what we are. You can't read, and I can't kiss. This is not the ride of life, the beginning of my first love. It's just the predictable prefab setup of a schlocky fucking *rom-com.* Boy meets girl. Boy plays it cool because boy knows better than to kiss her on the street. Fuck that boy.

Fuck you, Cusack. Fuck. You.

5

Bless you, Cusack. Bless fucking you.

I probably want you more than I should in the middle of a first date, but you want me too.

Fifteen minutes into the Best Movie Ever, Kate Beckinsale pulls a copy of *Love in the Time of Cholera* out of her bag.

You look at me, and I look at you. Sparks. *Serendipity-do-do-zippity-yay.*

I go in for a whisper. "Score one for books." You knock your leg into mine. Zoinks! Beckinsale won't give Cusack her number even though they have chemistry, but she will scribble it in her *Cholera* and sell it to a used bookstore. My man Cusack is aghast, exasperated. He just wants her fucking number. But she believes in fate. She says that if they are meant to be together he will find her *Cholera* and call her.

It is the right movie at the right fucking time and you put your hand on my leg and whisper in *my* ear. "Okay, Bookstore Babe. Let's see where this goes."

My Portnoy chimes in the dark. That touch. Your breath. Every part of my body yearning to lean into you. You, who spends the rest of our time in the dark finding any excuse to bring your lips to my ear. I will buy a new Moleskine notepad so I can remember all your sweet somethings . . .

You kind of remind me of John Cusack.
He and Jeremy Piven are best friends in real life.
Molly Shannon is excellent casting.
This movie is like a master class in location scouting.
The lighting people killed it. And at a night shoot, that's impressive.
John has good range, right? He's so not Aidan, you know?

No, I don't know, Vail. I don't give a fuck about any of these people. Except the part where you said Cusack looks like me. And that's gonna be at the top of my Moleskine:

#1 I LOOK LIKE A MOVIE STAR, A GOOD ONE

The movie ends. I rise and you pull at my sleeve. You are one of those people who sit through the credits. Or maybe you just want to sit by *me.* And then we're up. The haze of exiting the dark of the theater and entering the light. You are all but skipping down Houston. Revved up. *Sprung.* Pontificating like a little overzealous professor. "It was brilliant of them to cast real talent like Jeremy Piven and Molly Shannon but not force them into a relationship at the end. There was a narrative confidence that stands out, you know?"

I smile at you. Can I kiss you again? Is that normal? "Mm-hmm."

You elbow me, shy. A little self-conscious. "'Mmm' what, mister?"

My eyes are the Polaroids now. "Vail," I say. "You lied to me."

You blink. Puzzled and doe-eyed, channeling Kate Beckinsale.

"Vail, you *are* a reader. Just now . . . I saw a movie. Cool movie, sure, but you . . . You read that movie the way I read books."

You look down at your little hands. "A lot of guys get annoyed with my commentary in the theater . . ."

"Yeah," I say. "But I'm not some dick in your sitcom."

You smack me. Again, with your inability to keep your hands off me. The thrill. The lust. The snow just starting to fall. "Watch out, Cusack. *Sex and the City* is not a sitcom."

"Point taken, Miss Beckinsale."

You like that. You like me. You murmur. "Come here, Cusack."

This time, Mr. Tongue plays it cool. This time, you don't say anything after we kiss. You just nuzzle me, nose to nose. "It's snowing."

"I know."

That's another entry for the Moleskine:

#2 REDEMPTION FOR MR. TONGUE

I am about to insist on taking you to the kind of late lunch that turns into dinner when your phone rings—your bossy boss—and you can't eat with me. Duty calls. I watch you cross the street. If you turn around, you like me and want more, and if you don't turn around . . .

#3 YOU LOOK OVER YOUR SHOULDER AND YOU WANT ME TO WANT YOU

You shake your ass and laugh, and *that's* when you become my girlfriend. I call your home phone the second you go underground and leave a voicemail. I want to be in your house, waiting for you like a bouquet of fucking flowers and it's scary, the waiting. Did I go too far? Was I supposed to fuck with your head? But then you call! You love my flowers and I am smart enough to send you to voicemail. And then I listen to it, your second lovely love letter.

Well, hello to you too, Cusack. So I have a crazy week, but maybe we can grab drinks? Just not frozen hot chocolate. I mean, we don't want to move too fast, you know?

I pop into the nearest stationery slash pepper spray store and drop a few bucks on a shiny new Moleskine and the kind of pen you don't ever lose. I jot down the first three wins and then it's the fourth one, best one yet.

#4 YOU WANT TO MOVE FAST

If you didn't, you wouldn't say shit like that. Slow and steady wins the race and all that bullshit. Life is different now. Work's not a drag. I'm preparing to be your man. I say things like "My girlfriend loves Lucinda Rosenfeld" and "My girlfriend's really into the new Ursula Le Guin."

I read. I know *girls, girls, girls.* I know that if you wanted to move slowly, you wouldn't say yes when I call you and ask to hang out two days after *Serendipity.*

"A little soon but . . . oh, fuck it. Do you know that bar we passed near the Angelika?"

I know they card. I know I am underage. "I was thinking maybe we get coffee . . ."

"Ah," you say. "I like it, Cusack. Coffee it is. Also you don't have to say it, but I was just on antibiotics for a throat thing last month and ugh it's *awful* when you can't drink."

I'm not on antibiotics—ha!—and I need handsome sleep to look my best but I can't sleep. But it's okay. I'm young. It's the longest shift and it's dead in the shop and Mooney catches me at the door.

"What's the rush?"

You. "I, um, I have to bring a book to this guy . . ."

He slaps me on the back. "As long as you get your dick sucked, boy."

I don't think that's in the cards—it seems like a third-date kind of thing—but I'm feeling good and looking good as I saunter into the romantic-as-fuck coffee shop in the West Fucking Village. You're already there and we do that quick hug hello thing. I pay for the coffees and after a couple minutes of nervous weather chat, your Polaroids widen. "Can I ask you something?"

"You never have to ask if you can ask me something."

"How old are you?"

Fuck. "How old are *you*?"

You squint. "Mmm . . . I asked you first."

"True," I say and I have to get a fucking fake ID. "But it's kinda like books."

"Oh boy. I guess I did sign up for this with NYC Bookstore Babe. . . ."

"The page count doesn't matter, Vail. It's the style, the pacing. A Dan Brown book . . . You fly through it at ninety miles an hour. But you get your hands on some Joyce, same number of pages, and it's a whole different thing. You take your time. You go slow."

For a second there, our second date is scary, the way you don't mount me. But then you burst out laughing in the good way, with me, not at me. "Well played, Cusack."

I wipe my forehead, and we are in it now, trading stories about our lives. You talk about your time at *U of M* and the angst over doing the undoable . . . moving to Manhattan. You share a *tiny two-bedroom* with *crazy, slutty* Cynthia in . . . *New York*. You leave it at that, vague, but *I Know What You Did Last Week*. It's a good thing when a girl keeps a secret. Like Mooney says, *The best strippers take it off one piece at a time*. You don't know what you want to do with your life. Sometimes you want to be *in the industry*, but sometimes you think it's ridiculous. You love dinner mints—there's a sea of them in the bottom of your messenger bag—and your parents *blah blah blah*, because I don't fucking care.

We're moving fast and my mind is a happy broken record. *I like you, Vail, I like you*. You notice I'm not drinking my coffee and leap up to go get more cream. You pour and tell me to say when. You stroke the back of my head as I take that first, second sip. And then you rub your hands on your thighs. Jeans this time. Blue and tight. *I like you, Vail. I like you*. You sit. "So where were you on September 11?"

I cough. I hate it; I hate that I have to lie to you. "You first."

You scratch your little nose. "Well, it's more about where you were before, right?"

I was locked in a basement, and it's almost like you relate. "Totally."

"See," you say. "I think of 9/11, and I go back to September 6. I was at the VMAs dancing my ass off to Britney Spears . . . Everything about it, the boa and the *song*. It felt like life was about to become this nonstop dance party, you know? 'I'm a Slave 4 U' is just . . ."

"I prefer 'Nothing Compares 2 U.' "

SHUT THE FUCK UP, GOLDBERG, but you smile like you care, like you know that I know that that was a lot. "Anyway, you know how it is, Joe. You're living your life. A few days later, I'm pissed at Cynthia for bringing a random home from Passerby and the next morning . . ."

"Everything changes."

"Yes, Joe! The three of us sat there staring at the TV. It felt like no one's ever gonna dance again, and I hated myself for thinking about dancing when people were. . . . Kinda the loneliest day ever." Your smile is a baby and a mother all at once. "So, where were you, Joe?"

I was hoping you'd forget about me, and I don't want to lie to you about something like 9/11, but what choice do I have? "I was in the bookshop."

"Yeesh, you guys open *that* early?"

I won't go there in my head. I was locked in the cage, in the basement. The only person in the whole fucking city who didn't know about the big bad day. "Well, we weren't open for business, but I was supposed to sign for some packages and do deliveries and . . ."

You pull lint off your cape; no girl is perfect. "And that never happened."

We go silent and I get scared. Is my secret gonna ruin us? But then you say you didn't mean to go there, that you're not that girl who talks about it nonstop or dwells.

And then you don your cape and I guess that's it. Off we go, outside, and was it good? *Do you like me, Vail? Do you like me?*

You rock back and forth. "So here I go again. Speaking of another big day . . ."

"New Year's Eve."

"Joe, honestly, I despise it. And I actually still can't drink right now, so if it's okay . . . can we skip it?"

"Absolutely."

"I mean, I would say that we could hang out and watch movies or whatever, but I don't want to do that to you. Every year I get really blue and I just . . ."

"Vail," I say. "You don't owe me an explanation. And I fucking *hate* New Year's Eve. It's amateur night."

"Totally."

"Can I kiss you?"

You come a little closer. "Totally."

The second-date kiss goodbye is better than our first-date kiss hello, and it's the next milestone in my Moleskine.

#5 MR. TONGUE DIDN'T FUCKING CHOKE

The second date was so good that we meet for coffee on New Year's Eve, before the shitheads take over the city. You are late and frazzled, and you do most of the talking. You are blue, as promised. Preoccupied with the enemies in your life. Slutty Cynthia. *I might have to put a padlock on my door because of the rando creeps in our house. I have to move out, I do.* Bossy Barry is no good either. *If I do become a director, I will never sexually harass the girl who gets my wife's dry cleaning, and in 2002, so help me, I will quit.* It's only the third date and already I am the shoulder for you to cry on. It's not third-date sex, but it is third-date progress.

"What about you, Cusack? Do you have any resolutions?"

"Not a one," I say, because I am looking at my resolution, you.

"But if this goes on . . . us . . . I mean, I'll kick your ass about yours whenever you need reminding."

Your Polaroids flash. Your cheeks turn red. "I probably shouldn't say this."

"But you will."

"It's just . . . With a lot of guys, you get the feeling they're just letting you talk so they can talk. But you . . . you listen. I mean, you really, like . . . you listen."

"I try."

"Are you on AOL IM?"

I don't know what that is and you don't make me say it out loud. You write down your *screen name* on a napkin. "I'm gonna be busy at work, so get on your computer and find me, yeah?"

We kiss on the sidewalk and race back to our respective homes to hide from all the idiots and a new year dawns in every fucking way! I get a *little* worried when you don't take my Happy New Year call at midnight, but the fear is short-lived. You hit me back in the morning. You had a full house. *Fucking Cynthia, Joe . . . I really need to move.* Yes, *life after* Serendipity *is good.* Rebirth-level good. I am a new man. "My" computer? Even that's different! It's a magical portal that lets us talk with our hands on AOL Instant Messenger, *AOL IM* for short. Best fucking thing in the world. You are *VailInTheCity* and I am *NYCBookstoreBabe,* and we can't keep our virtual hands off each other. I'm at work, daydreaming about your panties—Are they silk? Is that only in Skinemax?—and then a little ding, and there you are, reading my mind, pining for me in a little white box.

You: *Sup Bookstore babe*

Me: *Well, hello, Miss Gunderson.*

That's your name. Vail Gunderson. You are twenty-four.

You: *22nd and fuck it . . . Never mind.*

Me: *What about it?*

You: *That's where I live. I was a little evasive the other day but now . . .* ☺

LOOK AT THAT SMILEY FACE and oh, you like me. Why else

would you pop up and tell me every little thing? Old stories, like the time you had your appendix out sophomore year of college. New stories about your roommate who stole sheets from Loehmann's. You worry the cops are gonna barge in to arrest her, but you also know you're silly. If there was a book about you, I would read it. And I know you feel the same, because we're planning our fourth date, and it *won't* be in the fucking computer.

Soon, there will be sex. You don't say it. I don't say it. But it's in the ether. In the white box we share when we can't be in the same room.

You: *How's tricks? Did you watch Sex last night?!*

Me: *Ha. I am halfway through* The Lovely Bones. *It's unreal. How goes it with you?*

It's a lie. I can't read, can't focus. But I did read the first three pages, and you don't read at all, sooo . . .

You: *Cool* ☺

Me: *Cool* ☺

And then you disappear, because that's how it works. Your boss, Barry, is demanding, so when he shows up, you shut down. And it's good. I need the downtime to be happy and prepare for greatness. I buy Trojans. I score a shiny fake ID off a kid I knew back in middle school. Same name because why would I want to be anyone but Joe Fucking Goldberg? I like having two IDs in my wallet, and I've never been this good at being me, galloping like a well-hung stallion to the register, where a patron awaits. She's chipper, excited about her Dan Fucking Brown, and I am chipper. Work is no longer the center of my world; it's just a place for me to practice being me, being yours.

I smile at the woman. I do not picture her naked. "After you finish, come back, because you'll want to know more about NASA."

"Ooh, thank you for the tip, but honestly . . . I'll probably just want another page-turner."

We laugh, and this is what you don't get about bookstores, what I'm going to tell you when we meet at La Bonbonniere tomorrow. We have fun in here, we do, and I check AOL IM. You're still busy, so I grab the tape, the knife. I'm trying not to think about you too much, trying not to analyze every tiny thing and replay every second of every date. But it's hard not to think about you as I slice open the boxes, as I smell fresh books and wait for tomorrow to arrive . . . which it does.

Fourth date. Day date. La Bonbonniere. A West Village joint where a tabby cat jumps on your lap, and you order the jelly omelet just because it's there. My cell phone rings. You.

"Ugh," you say. "I hate to do this, but I can't make it."

"Are you okay?"

"You are so sweet to ask, and yeah, I'm fine, but Cynthia 'accidentally' gave some guy her keys, so we had to get the locks changed, which was a whole nightmare, and now Barry is making me go to Syosset to pick up his wife and . . . Do you hate me?"

I tell you the truth. "I could never hate you. Just let me know if I can help."

"You really are the sweetest, Cusack."

I puff up at my table for two. "You too, Sitcom."

"And Joe, next time we meet up, we are going to fucking Serendipity, okay?"

You follow through. The very next day you hunt me down on IM; *Are you free tomorrow, Bookstore Babe?* Fuck yes, I am free and tomorrow. Tomorrow we go to Serendipity for frozen hot chocolate and steaming hot sex. Tomorrow, we are going to fucking *fuck*. Forty-one minutes later, my screen lights up. You really can't get enough of me, can you?

You: *You still there?*

Me: *Always.*

You: *It's cheesy, but I left you a little present at that coffee shop in alphabet city lol*

Me: *The Beanery, right?*

You: *Yep, just a little something . . . that you might want to wear tomorrow night* ☺

I pull my Moleskine notepad out of my back pocket. Black leather. Cool. It might be cheesy to write down every little thing but what guy *wouldn't* want every little life-altering, dick-hardening moment on the record?

#6 YOU BOUGHT ME A FUCKING PRESENT AND WE HAVEN'T EVEN FUCKED

"Excuse me, son. Do you have a restroom?"

Oh, right. Real life. The here and now. A poor woman with a walker and two French cookbooks. I relieve her of the heavyweights. I am gallant, helping her to the back of the shop, standing guard as she unloads in a way that makes me wish we had another bathroom. Normally, this kinda thing would set me off, but I live in a new world now. I live in a world with you.

After my shift I make a beeline for the Avenue B Beanery and the bald guy sees me coming. He remembers me. I am memorable.

He grabs a black bag off the counter. "I think this is for you, guy."

I take the bag. Never got a present from a girl before. "Thanks, dude."

He gives me another bag with a free muffin. "No prob," he says, nodding at my gift bag. "The things we do to get some, right?"

I laugh like it was so fucking hard to make a pit stop for a *present*. "Thanks again."

He nods. "Eat up, son."

Love is like that Janet Jackson video from the '80s where New York is a fun place and the whole city dances for you, with you, even the bald barista! I wait till I get home to my cardboard box to open my present. I still can't believe it, Vail. You saw something and thought of me. You put your money where your mouth is, and there is tissue paper. Black. I never did this before, never pulled out the thin party paper to discover . . .

A hot pink Ralph Lauren shirt. Giant fucking *polo* player on the chest. It's not me, but you're psychic, so of *course* my phone is ringing . . . you.

I answer with a lie: "I love it."

"Do you? I felt silly and I don't want to scare you off. It's not like I spent money on it. Our costume designer had an extra and . . ."

"Vail, seriously. I love it."

"Good," you say. "And more good news. Cynthia is staying at her quote-unquote boyfriend's tomorrow night, some guy she met at Don Hill's."

Oh. Big O. Orgasm! "Oh?"

"So after Serendipity, I mean, I do have the place to myself, as long as you don't think I'm coming on a little way too slightly strong . . ."

Impossible. You are my girl. Nervous. Hopeful. Feathers all fluffy and shiny. The next day is the longest day of my life but eventually it's time for me to go into the restroom and change into my pink fucking shirt for lucky number seven. . . .

#7 SEX SEX SEX SEX SEX

It's D-Day as in Dick Day. Sex day. I'd be whistling if I could whistle. *Serendipity-do-dah-unzippity-my pants . . . My oh my what a wonderful—*

"Joseph!"

"Coming!"

Buzzkill, but I jog to the back of the shop—Mooney needs to hear my feet pound the ground—and I guess it was inevitable. Predictable as a fucking rom-com. Love always has an enemy, a form of cynical, toxic *Cholera.* And in our case, that would be Mr. Mooney, the Fox Books to your Shop Around the Corner.

He sneers at me. "Wipe that grin off your face."

"Sorry."

"Has this girl even sucked you off?"

I don't answer that—you're a lady—and he stabs at his papers with his long, pale fingers. You haven't kissed my Portnoy. You made it clear that you don't approve of Cynthia and the way she moves fast, a nonstop *parade of sketch pads from Passerby and Don Hill's.* It's your way of telling me that you're a good girl. And good girls only do bad things for nice boys like me who are willing to wait.

"Stand by," says Mr. Mooney. "And stop fidgeting with your wiener."

I adjust my Portnoy, but he's excited about tonight, and who can blame him? Frozen hot chocolate. Sex. "Sorry."

"All right, Joseph. These invoices need to be filed."

I reach for the invoices, but he pulls them back. Dick move, but I feel for the guy.

His old lady (his phrase, not mine) hasn't laid a hand on him "since *American Psycho* was in galleys." It's easy to put up with his shit, to be the bigger fucking person.

"So, what's up with the invoices?"

" 'What's up'? Are you twelve?"

"Sorry," I say, relieved that you hate bookstores, that I don't live in a world where there's a danger of you popping in and hearing Mooney lash out at me, or even worse, overhearing me refer to you as my girlfriend before we even do it. "What can I do for you?"

"For starters, I asked you a question. Did she suck you off?"

"Tonight, I'm staying at her place."

He grunts, and the poor guy really should leave his wife. "Moving on," he says. "How much is Ralph Lauren paying you to advertise his wares?"

"It was free. Vail got it from the wardrobe department at her job."

"Real men don't wear hot pink billboards."

He throws a raggedy old flannel at me, but I can't do this. It's your shirt. It's my sex shirt. "Well, I'm just about to go, so . . ."

"You're in my shop, Joseph. And I'm taking that blouse home to burn it in the fireplace."

No. You gave me this shirt. You want to see it on your bedroom floor, but then something bizarre happens. Butterflies swarm inside of me and number eight is motherfucking great . . .

#8 YOU LIKE ME FOR ME AND CLOTHES DON'T MATTER

No stupid shirt can come between us. I strip like a convict and don his old, ugly flannel and head to the subway.

To you.

6

Dream nights are *supposed* to come the hard way, after a few nightmares. So of course, I get all the way uptown only to get a frantic phone call from you. Barry needs you downtown just in case, so you are stuck there waiting for the green light.

"And believe me, Joe, I know how ridiculous I sound. 'On call' like I'm a doctor or something. Anyway, I got antsy after I got ready at work so I'm doing time at the Beanery. I was thinking you could wait with me if you don't mind coming . . . Do you want to come?"

Fuck yes, I do! The train can't move fast enough but a thousand minutes later I'm downtown, flying up the stairs in my stupid smellier-by-the-second shirt. I feel good. We're on track. I love the way you take your work seriously but walk it back a second later. *Like I'm a doctor or something.* I love that I'm not scared to show up for sex night in this oversize ugly flannel that reeks of stale cigars.

And when I walk into the Beanery, I almost collapse. You didn't just get ready for me, you went all out for me. Hot pink bra straps under a see-through shirt. A skintight skirt. Eyelashes that will come off when I fuck you, when I move your mountain.

Down, Portnoy. Not just yet. I roll up to the counter. "Hello, Sitcom. I like your skirt."

You startle. "Wow, um, thank you. I guess I got a little carried away."

The barista laughs. The guy who gave me the free muffin. "I guess grunge is back."

You ignore his dumb jab, and you pat my chest. "Now, this is *not* a Ralph Lauren."

I kiss you on the top of the head. A little bold, but fuck it. You're mine. The barista goes back to wiping the counters, and I tell you about Mooney, about the shirt.

You put your hand on my leg. "Joe, seriously. It's fine. I get it."

You really *are* the coolest girl in the world and the barista grabs his messenger bag. Same as yours, I think, and maybe I should have brought mine. "I'll walk out with you guys," he says. "And it's Dick, by the way."

I shake his stupid hand. "Joe."

You ask *Dick* what he's up to tonight. He looks around like he's waiting for someone. The poor guy does that a lot. I feel lucky. He's alone, and I am not. I have you.

"Well," he says. "I was supposed to pitch this financier about my movie."

You light up like he doesn't make our coffee. "So cool, D!"

He shrugs. You are kind, the type of girl who lets the generic insecure barista talk like he's the man, like he's Harvey Fucking Weinstein. You're as caring as Miss Frascatore and I know you see what I see. Overdone muscles and insecurity. The too-tight T-shirt. Imagine being Richard and choosing to be Dick. You are too nice for your own good, and he's never gonna shut up, so I sling an arm around your shoulder.

"Well, dude, good luck with everything, but we gotta hit the road."

"All good," he says. "I'm jonesing for some *mattar peetar,* so I'm gonna hit up this rad Indian place a few blocks away. You kids have fun."

You grab my hand. You squeeze. "Actually," you say, "I too am kinda *dying* for some good matar paneer. What do you say, Joe?"

No no no. We are sitting on the floor of *Malai Galli.* Our asses are on old green pillows. The floor is as hard as the food is spicy. I don't get it, Vail. Dick is on our date and he's at it again, going off on his *solo trip* to Costa Rica. He despises New York beaches because he prefers *soft sand,* and you say you are the same. I don't know shit about *sand* and the only reason I don't haul off and punch him is that he keeps looking at me like he feels bad, like he knows he's not supposed to fucking be here, like he knows we're not supposed to be talking about some movie he'll never make.

"Sorry," he says. "I get started on my feature and I can't stop. Gonna dedicate it to my brother. Use the earnings to make a doc about him."

He kisses his dog tags and you tell him he doesn't have to apologize and you're right. None of this is his fault. Dick is not the bad guy. His brother died in Kuwait—that's how he got the dog tags—and you don't read so you don't know *The Body* by Stephen King, but you might've seen the movie *Stand by Me.* If we're ever alone again, I will tell you that Dick is like a beefy gym rat version of Gordie Lachance minus the brains.

"Ooh," you say. "I am *living* for this pakora."

You don't sound like you. You're different tonight. Preening and polite. What happened, Vail? What did I do? You showered for me. You got dressed up for me. Your blouse is a gauzy plastic bag, and your bra straps are hot pink. I have a feeling that your friend in the makeup department did your eyes. The black lines are blurrier, smokier, and you look hot, ready to lure my Portnoy into your Beckinsale, but what the fucking fuck? WHY ARE WE HERE?! We had plans and the table is too low and too little and Dick's T-shirt is too much. We get it, *kid.* You have muscles. Tattoos. You surf. He does things, and they show up on his body. Me, I read things. I've never been more aware of it in my life. There's a difference, there is.

I don't want to make the other kind of list in my Moleskine. It's too soon. But it's flashing in my mind. Neon-black fucking Sharpie.

#1 WHY ARE WE IN INDIA WITH DICK?

Dick, who went north in Costa Rica because you *have* to go north, and he's like *Zoolander* via Rick Fucking Moody.

"Of course," you say, as if you've been to Costa Rica. And maybe you have been to Costa Rica. Maybe you don't like me anymore. Maybe it's the flannel. Maybe you like Dick.

"What about you, Joe? Do you surf?"

Before I can answer, you do. "Ah, Joe's a bookworm. The idea of you on a surfboard, Cusack . . ." And then you rub my chest—good—but then you coo like I'm a baby—bad. "Joe's a softy, an indoor cat, you know?"

I meow—what else do I do—and play it off like it's a joke, but men are dogs, not cats. Dick rips a piece of naan in half.

"You guys want?"

You take the naan. I take the naan. I chew slowly while you dunk it in a bowl of I CANNOT PRONOUNCE IT AND I AM TIRED OF BEING CORRECTED. The two of you are doing it again. If you're not discussing tropical paradises, then it's back to the fucking *food.*

I am my father's son. *Food is meant to keep you alive, not give you a life.*

I feel ignorant and soft—*The idea of you on a surfboard, Cusack*—and my mouth is burning and I know I am failing you, the way you nudge me and widen your eyes. "Are you okay?"

"Fine, just a long day."

You rub my arm, and is that soft too? "I'm sorry, Joe. If you're tired . . ."

I look at you and so does Dick. What do you want? What the fuck do you want? I pick up my Diet Coke, extra ice, because no, I didn't copy Dick and order a *beer and a shot of Jim Henson* or whatever the fuck you call it. Things are bad enough without the possibility of the waiter calling me a fake.

"So, what about you, Joe?"

It's Dick, and it would be so much easier if he *was* a fucking dick. But he keeps including me.

"Sorry," I say, because that's all I say at this table, all I am, the sorry, sourpuss fuck. "I missed it."

"It's cool, buddy. I was just asking if you have a favorite sushi place."

"Oh, I don't really eat sushi."

You gasp. "Not even salmon? I mean, *never.*"

"I don't like it."

"But did you ever try it, Joe?"

No. Ick. "Of course I tried it."

Dick knocks back another Jim Henson and laughs. "Chicks and sushi. Such a thing."

You press and push and why, Vail, why? "I mean, Joe, have you had a California roll? Because even if you think you don't like sushi, I just . . . You are so missing out."

And you are *so* hurting my feelings with this uncalled-for assault on my taste buds.

I look at you, but my eyes aren't Polaroids. They're glossy and burned out because of the fire raging in my intestines. "Have you ever had On-Cor Veal Parmigiana?"

Dick wants a high five, so I meet his hand. "Now that's what I'm talking about," he says. "That shit is the shit."

It could be so nice. We could talk about our favorite frozen foods so that I can participate, but it's weird. It's like you don't *want* me to participate. You cut off Dick—oh God, you do—and you start talking about your show again. You never do this when we're alone, but it's too soon to say never; I only did just meet you. You're rambling about an episode where the one named Carrie goes out with a guy who hates sushi and cracks bad jokes and she concludes that he's only good for one thing.

"Sex," you say, and if that was a jump, you did not stick the landing. You're not good at it, Vail. You're not good at summarizing that fucking *sitcom.* You sip your water. "I know," you say. "*Enough* about Carrie Bradshaw. I get it, boys."

Dick laughs. I laugh. The waiter brings more I CANNOT PRONOUNCE IT AND I AM TIRED OF BEING CORRECTED. You and Dick have tasted everything. You've lived. Am I dead? Was I ever even alive? Love is the thing that makes you alive. The stories you tell that make me feel special now make me feel like a nonperson, a half person. Your parents took you to sushi when you were twelve, and Dick worked at a seafood joint with his family at their place *by the lake.* My heart races, and not because of you. It's me, Vail. I don't have stories, not like that. The spices don't agree with me, but other people are fine. Everyone in here is noshing on their naan, their *Malai Galli,* so it's not the food. It's me. I'm not *NYC Bookstore Babe.*

I'm NYC loner teen runaway who lives in a cardboard box.

"Joe," you say. Not *Cusack.* Not *babe.* Not *honey.* "Are you okay?"

Dick looks around at nothing, just a nice guy trying to give us a second. I don't want pity, Vail. I want love. I force a smile onto my puffy, sweaty face. "I'm great."

I lied to you, and you know it, and the bad list in the Moleskine of my mind is growing longer, longer than the *good* list. It's too early for a night like this. Glitches where the CD skips and the page that explains the big twist is missing. You bite your lip and nod at the *Malai Galli.* And then Dick gets a call on his cell phone. Motorola flip phone just like yours. And it was some girl he knows, some waitress, so of course you're talking about food again, Zagat bullshit, *spice.*

I lived on cold pizza for three days in the cage. A cage in a basement that I still sleep in when the cardboard walls are too thin and *I'm a loser, baby, so why don't you kill me?*

My body turns on me. You make a face. "Whoa."

I farted at the table. *I'm a loser, baby, so why don't I kill me?* "Sorry."

My bowels are like me. Inexperienced and failing. I can't blame money. This is New York Fucking City and there is good cheap food everywhere. But who wants to try new things alone? It's me. Always just me. I lay my napkin on the table. The two of you are comparing your parents and their tech skills. I don't belong here with you and I never will. I can't keep up with you, Vail. I can't catch up with you. My intestines are too stringy, too weak. I tasted the matar paneer. I tried the masala dosa, and when you insisted, I took a nice big heap of that Hyderabadi biryani.

And now I'm not just the young dud in the oversize old-man flannel. My insides turn over—I'm gonna shit my fucking pants, I really am—and Dick raises another tiny glass of Jim Henson and why isn't *he* about to puke? "The shitter's downstairs, killer."

You grab at your bag. "I might have a TUMS."

I can't risk responding to either fucking one of you. I walk fast, bumping into the waiter and the curtains. I am that guy no one wants to be, that guy no woman wants to be with. I am not *NYC Bookstore Babe.* I'm a soft scrawny soft sad sack who gets the runs in public. Ugly and unworldly. Weak with no *pitches* or future prospects or exciting fucking stories, a letdown of a fuck-up who's never been to the airport, let alone been on a plane.

I hear your voice when I hit the stairs. "Feel better, Cusack!"

And I know: It's the last thing you'll ever say to me.

7

It's another dreary Dylan day in the shop. "You're Gonna Make Me Lonesome When You Go" on repeat. *Lonesome,* Vail. Worse than lonely. Lonely I can do. Lonely is *fuck everyone I just wanna chill with my typewriters.* Lonesome is a first for me. It's about you. I don't want to be alone, checking my lousy non-folding Nokia for the ninth time in ten minutes. The phone, the computer, the Dylan, they're all just torture devices. Empty crack pipes that provide active constant fucking confirmation that *you* aren't lonesome without me.

I snap the rubber band on my wrist. This "psychologist" in a self-help book said it helps to control your mind. The pain of the rubber band makes you stop being a whiny baby. Such a crock of shit, Vail, not that you care. When I left India without saying goodbye, I knew you wouldn't call. You proved me right. You didn't. It's so January in the shop, in my heart. I am living on bananas and coffee in blue-and-white Greek cups and I'm down on myself. Aware of all the people who are good at being who they are, deciding what they want and hatching a plan to get it. Where did I go wrong with you? How? When?

"Boo-hoo, Joseph."

It's Mr. Mooney. He caught me slouching again. "Sorry."

"They're all one cunt, Joseph."

I hate the c-word. My dad used it too much, and I hate that I still want you. I barely know you, I know, but it's how dealers get people hooked. They give you a taste. You're the closest I ever came to a girlfriend, and you're gone. Mooney tells me there's a customer and it's that woman from another century, a few days ago, the one who left with Lucinda Rosenfeld.

"Hey," she says. "I ate this book up. You *have* to thank your girlfriend for the rec."

Impossible. I don't have a girlfriend. Never did. "Sure thing."

I ring her up—more Lucinda—and then Mooney is in my face again. An adult in Charlie Brown. I can't hear him. I can only see my Moleskine, the way it mocks me on the counter.

"Are you listening, Joseph?" He groans. "Walk with me."

I follow him to the back, to his ashtray of an office. It's more bad news. Angus Kaplan is on the hunt again. He bought six signed copies of *The Corrections.* Mooney shakes his head. "That bastard Philistine. . . . *He's* the enemy of America, Joseph. Not those religious fanatics. Men like Angus, blue bloods with money who buy books the way their fathers buy stocks . . ."

I can't do it, Vail. I can't handle another lecture about the downfall of civili-fucking-zation from Mooney. I tell him he should start a blog, and he scowls.

"Stop it, Joseph."

"Sorry. I just mean, what's the point? Angus is an asshole, but we wouldn't be in business without that asshole."

"Joseph, don't lecture me."

"Just saying . . . At least he plays the game. At least he *bought* the books."

Unlike you and that pink shirt. You didn't put money into me. Were you always going to disappear? I pick up my cell phone, and Mooney coughs. I put the phone down.

"Don't be impatient with me, Joseph. Don't be smart."

I'm not smart. I'm stupid. If I were smart, I would know how to digest Indian food. "Sorry."

"The man is a crackhead. But because of his money, money he did not properly earn, we don't refer to that louse as a *crackhead.* We refer to him as an *eccentric.*"

Mooney slaps a Post-it on the counter. There are digits on the blue Post-it, six of them, and the idea of drowning in that sinking living room makes me miss you even more.

"What's this?"

"The door code," he says. "Franzen's *publicist* will deliver the books this afternoon. And you'll deliver them this evening. You're in luck. The Upper West Side eccentric is off in the Hamptons or some such. You'll enter the premises and leave the books. In you go, and then out."

Never got to do the in-and-out with you, and I nod. "Got it."

"Chin up, Joseph. Life is a dead end. So a cunt does you wrong. The sourness in you, that is your fault, boy. Remember the danger of hope, Joseph. Remember to kill it before it . . ."

Kills you. I'm back on the floor, behind the register. Sinking chair, sinking spirit. And it doesn't make any sense. It was a few cups of coffee, a few dates. I shouldn't miss you, not like this. I open some Bukowski and think about the girls before you, the subway beauties, and the one who did or did not have dimples, but none of it helps. I love no one and no one loves me.

I snap the rubber band on my wrist. Again I try to read and again I can't do it. I'm like *you* now. I go back to the computer and I open AOL Instant Messenger. You're online, but you're not talking to me. I should close my account, but I don't know how.

I snap the rubber band. Nothing.

I carry new Kings to FICTION, to HORROR and that's the thing about some guys. Stephen King. Dick the Barista. You put them anywhere, in any section, and people gravitate to them.

The door opens. The bell chimes. I do not shout hello. I have no voice left in me, no cheer. No reason to be alive. You made me lonesome, and the loneliness is worse, the way I can't even say you left me, because I'm the one who left you and Dick in India.

The customer moves slowly, and I wish we never met. Craig and his list . . . The man is a sick fuck who's trying to drive us all crazy, and why did you have to do it, Vail? Why did you claim that you missed me, that you wanted to connect?

I snap the rubber band. Nothing.

The customer settles in. KIDS section or the FINANCE section. Two things I'll never have: kids and money. I bet you'll have them both by the time you're thirty.

I snap the rubber band. A red mark on my wrist. Something.

I make my way to the front of the shop because this is what I am, all I am. I am a bookseller. I roll up my sleeves and walk through the dusty stacks and I think of Dick and his *parasailing* and you and your exes and the sushi and I reach for the rubber band but then no.

As in yes. "Vail. Hi."

"Hello, stranger."

You're smiling at me like we were never in India. You clutch a kids' book with both arms. Your arms cover the title, your heart. "So! How're you feeling, Cusack?"

Like death. I thought you were gone. Done with me. *Buh-bye.* "Fine. Good."

"Yeah," you say. "Well, I'm . . . I kind of don't believe that, Joe."

Dylan ends and begins again, and I don't know what to do with you, how to be, what to say.

"Joe, come on. Look at me. You got diarrhea, okay? It's not the worst thing in the world. It happens to everyone."

"I didn't get diarrhea."

You bite your lip and smile, and then you do a *ta-da* kind of reveal. You thrust the book forward, in my face.

Everyone Poops.

I laugh. You laugh.

You lay the *Poops* on the counter with tentative, nervous hands. It's a gift for your cousin, and you're breathless the way you were at the Angelika, before we had history, if that's what you call it. And I know. I know it wasn't easy for you to come here, but you did.

"Vail, I . . . I wanna say something."

"Me too, Joe, but you first."

"I'm sorry. I guess . . . I just assumed you were done with me because . . ." No one ever loved me. No one ever came back. "I mean, I thought you wanted me to go."

"Cusack, come on. I'm here. Would I be here if I didn't want to see you?"

It's tempting, Vail. I want to jump back into the ocean that is you, but you bailed on Serendipity. You brought a Dick on our date. I pick up *Everyone Poops,* and you grab my arm to stop me. "My turn now. Remember?"

"Sorry."

"Don't do that. Don't apologize when I'm the one who messed up. For you . . . there's no shame in being human. Ever. And that food . . . it was a lot. Especially if you're not used to it."

WE WERE SUPPOSED TO BE BATHING IN FROZEN HOT CHOCOLATE. "Yeah."

"You don't have to be embarrassed."

YOU BROUGHT A DICK ON OUR DATE. "I know. I'm not."

"Ah," you say. "There it is."

My eyes are black holes. How do you know what's in me? "There's what?"

"Well, you're obviously mad at me, Joe. That's why you left. The thing with Dick . . ."

Dick.

"Okay."

"But don't you get it? I'm a little . . . I was mad at you."

"Me?"

"Joe, come on. I screwed up and overreacted and then you screwed up and overreacted, and that's what I mean. . . . Everyone poops. Literally. You walked into the coffeehouse with that flannel, and I felt like you were sending me a sign, like you weren't into me. . . ."

"I told you what happened."

"Sure, but I mean it when I say it. I'm a visual person. I read into things. I'm sitting there done up like a wannabe Carrie Bradshaw."

"You looked beautiful."

"The point is I make this big, pathetic attempt to look sexy and . . ."

"And you are sexy."

Your pupils widen, maybe, and is it really that easy to make a girl happy? "Look," you say. "I know it was weird, the way I'm like, 'Yeah, barista, come join our party.' "

Incorrect. We joined *his* party. "Yeah, kinda weird."

"But now is now, right?"

"Now is now."

"And that's me. . . . I got nervous and insecure when you wore that flannel. And when I feel rejected, I can be a little . . . I mean, you have to know I don't like that guy like that. That whole me-me-me gym rat with a dream thing is just plain *not* my jam."

"Well, it's not *not* nice to hear you say that."

We're getting there, and you smile. "Good," you say. "Because all that was . . . I got nervous. Just like you. Just like everybody in this city, in this world. I mean, that's everyone. And in this case . . . I was terrible, and I'm sorry. I suck."

Not according to Mooney, and I like you like this, scared and caring, picking at the dinner mint stuck on your credit card. I take the card. I run it, and Bob Dylan starts moaning again. The air is shifting. Lightening.

You grin. "Wait," you say. "Are you . . . Is this on repeat right now?"

I could tell you the CD player is broken. But there's no need. Everyone poops, and I'm actually *not* a loser, baby. I'm the guy standing here with you. "It sure fucking is, Sitcom."

You run your fingers through your hair. "So, when do you get off?"

GET OFF. *Let a woman be a woman and a man be a man.*

This is it. *Serendipity redux*. Fuck everything else. "In about five minutes."

You lick your lips. "Well, Cynthia's on a bender."

"You don't say."

"And that means my place is all mine. And . . . it's silly, but it's Sunday, and we're back tonight, the show, and I kinda like the idea of starting a new season with you."

I want a new life with you and I am in, but then a call from the back, from the darkness that wants to keep me in my place, the one that doesn't feel like mine, not anymore now that you're here again. A voice I can't ignore.

"Joseph!"

8

The whole time I was in Mooney's office defending you and your *scatological children's book* and promising to deal with Angus, I was only half there. Mostly I was watching the little TV, the security camera footage. The Dylan was still on, faint, and there you were checking your makeup in a little mirror, nervously facing the possibility of a *lonesome* night without me.

I needed that, Vail. A sneak peek at you in your own torture chamber. And we did it!

I got out of work, as promised, and we're on the street. Arms linked. Heading north to Serendipity, to frozen hot chocolate . . . sex. I feel calmer. No more manic Moleskining in my journal like a reporter. We know each other a little better now, and it feels different. Like I was right to be so down because now I am so up.

"And that's another thing," you say, still grinding about *my* bossy boss. "Even the way he says your name. *Joseph.* Such an asshole, and I'm so glad you got outta there."

I don't like it when you call him an asshole, but I like your hot pink bra straps. The ones from the night we didn't make it to Serendipity. You came here to start over. Same outfit, less makeup. "Best part is, Vail . . . I'm not Joseph. On my birth certificate, it's plain old Joe."

You swing my hand and smile. "My middle name is Colorado because I was conceived—"

"In Vail, Colorado."

The sense of getting closer as you effusively lament your behavior in India. You're at your worst with *that barista* because he reminds you of your parents, who are always going on about some fucking trip. I quote my favorite line about traveling to San Francisco from *A Heartbreaking Work of Staggering Genius* and you hold my hand so hard it might break.

"I might have to read that, Joe."

"Oh no you will not. And there's no shame, Vail. Everyone poops."

You squeeze my hand even harder. "You know, Joe, the way you put out the fire with your boss, how you're so fast on your feet . . ." Your voice trails off, and I know where you're going, where you want us to be, and you're right. I *will* be a really good husband, and you *will* want to pull on my hair while I fuck you.

And then you blurt, "You'd be a really good assistant. You totally have what it takes."

I know you mean that as a compliment, but that's what *you* do. Not me. *Gently, Joseph,* and I force a fake smile. "Thanks."

Silence. Tension. *Seren-DO-ME-IN-HOT-CHOCOLATE-AND-CALL-IT-A-LIFE.*

"So how long have you worked in that bookstore? It's so depressing. The angry guy, the hours—I don't know how you do it."

"A few years."

"And how did you meet the old man?"

Can't tell you that, Vail. Can't tell you that I was twelve years old when my parents got back together for the millionth time and took off for AC. On day four with no money and no food, I left the house. I wandered into Mooney Books, and the "old man" gave me a cold slice of pepperoni and *The Catcher in the Rye.*

"I dunno. Just kinda happened."

You shrink a bit, and I'm losing you because girls are curious. That sixth sense, that extra hole, and why oh why can't we just fucking love people? Why do you want to know all my secrets? Why can't love mean that you don't give a fucking fuck about my past?

"Joe . . . Never mind."

A puddle in the sidewalk and we break apart, and is that what's happening to us? "Vail, come on. What's up?"

"Well, it's just . . . I want to know you, you know?"

And I want to fuck you and no one ever really knows anyone and I nod. "Me too."

"You say that, and I'm sure you mean it, but sometimes it feels like . . . Okay, like at the Indian place. I know that was shitty on my part. I'm a terrible person."

We settled this and I don't know why girls go backward when life goes forward. Push fucking *push.* "You were just nervous, Sitcom. We're past that."

You nod because you need me, because you're scared of losing *me.* "The thing is . . . The whole time we were sitting there . . . I know you felt sick and all, but I'm telling stories and barista dude is telling stories and . . . I want your stories, Joe. I do."

It's a test. Life is always a test, and you're doing it. You're testing me. Twirling your red scarf like a witch with a scepter. It's like that other guidance counselor I had in middle school, the one with a tight perm who said my mother had two days to get me new sneakers. If I don't open up to you about *something* right now, I'm going to lose you. But it's not fair. All the stories I have are bad and sad. No family dinners. No crazy plane rides to places like *Turks and Caicos.*

You take my hand. "Are you okay?"

I'm sweating and you know it. You feel my sticky palms. "Of course."

"Phew," you say. "No pressure, Cusack."

You hold my hand. Tight. And then your phone rings. You groan. *Cynthia.*

You take the call, and I wipe my hands on my pants.

"Slow down. . . . Well, why didn't you just leave? Well, I told you. The answering machine is broken. . . . Did he leave a voicemail on your cell? . . . Cynthia, I did *not* erase the messages. . . . You do *not* have a yeast infection. . . . It's okay. . . . It's fine. . . . I would but . . . Okay. Okay, just eat something. . . . Yes, Häagen-Dazs is a good thing, vanilla. . . . Yes, babe, it's good that it wasn't Rocky Road or mocha chip. . . . You just need to shower. . . . Yes, okay. . . . Okay, bye, honey."

You hang up. You sigh. "Sorry."

"Do I wanna know?"

"Ha," you say. "Well, if I have to know, you do too. She just woke up with some guy and she was glued to the sheets. I guess she blacked out with a quart of ice cream, and they were getting weird with it and . . . I think I am not in the mood for frozen hot chocolate."

It's all I've wanted to do since the day you kissed me, but sure. It's okay for Cynthia to have nothing but bad, sad stories, and yet it's not okay for me. None of this is okay. "Okay."

You nudge me. "Don't worry, Cusack. We'll get there. We will. But if you're *not* okay and you really wanna go . . ."

I'm not doing a good job with my face. You see the letdown. I put on a happy face. "Sitcom, I mean it. It's fine."

You lick those lips, the ones that came for me on Houston and Mercer. "So obviously, my place is out of the question, but your place . . . Whaddya say, Cusack? Do you guys have HBO?" You say that like it's my place, like Dumb and Dumber are my buddies, and nope. Plus, they're home tonight. They found new astrology sluts at a frat party. I can't let you see my cardboard box with the mattress I pulled off the street. It's one thing to get the runs in public, but to be *living in a box . . . in a cardboard box*. It's the story of my life. I don't have a place. Never did. But oh to be with you on a sofa, your boots off, your head on my lap.

"Yep, we can do that."

You are happy now. You can't *wait* to see where I live, but you *can't* see where I live. I need to buy time. I point at a diner.

"Oh," you say. "I'm good with snacks at your place. Or later tonight after . . . you know, we can order Benny's Burritos or something."

That's code for I WANT YOUR PORTNOY TO FUCK ME SIDEWAYS, and this should be a *good* thing, a great thing. You want *Sex* and sex.

"So which way do we go? You said you're downtown, right?"

I've never seen you like this. Openly pawing at me with those big eyes. I am the attraction, and you want me to come, but where are we supposed to go? The subway is two blocks away, but I can't take you home because I don't have one, not a real one.

"God," you say. "I am so that girl, you know? I can't wait to see pictures of you, baby pictures and school pictures and all that. Yee!"

I can't show you those things because I don't *have* those things, and I thought I was in the clear. In all the books, the girl wants the guy to go to *her* place. But you . . . You want my sofa, my bed, my Portnoy, my past. You squeeze my hand. "You okay, Cusack?"

That question again, and I make like a man who knows where he lives. "Yeah," I say. "I'm just wondering if we should take a cab or the subway."

"God, I love it up here. It's like being in a Woody Allen movie, and I keep thinking Nora Ephron is gonna pop up around every corner." You lean your head on my shoulder. "But, Joe, seriously, I'm not a princess. I'm good with the subway. I just want to get to your place in time for the opening credits, you know?"

No, I don't know, and why don't I have a friend? A buddy who would let me use his place. Cusack has his Piven, and you need a buddy when you're in a jam. The temperature is dropping. The clock is ticking. The traffic sign turns white. WALK. As if I know where the fuck we're going. As if I have a home, an apartment, a bathroom without a *Dumb and Fucking Dumber* poster taped to the wall.

Fix it, Joe. Fix it.

STOP IT, JOE. BREATHE.

All men lie for love. We improvise. Cusack and his sidekick didn't give up on getting the girl. They went to Bloomingdale's, and they went to *The New York Fucking Times,* because when you want the girl, when you need the girl, you do what has to be done.

I take you past the subway, not down its steps, and am I doing this? I am doing this. We turn south down Amsterdam.

It's a risk, but that jumpy spring in my step is a sign. I'm manning up, putting love first and going that extra uphill, possibly prison-bound mile for the one I want. Guys like me have to work with what we have. And I may not have a nice home, but I do have the *code* to a good home. And you are damn well worth the nerves and the paranoia that are the price of fucking admission.

I squeeze a little, just to make sure. "Sorry if I'm a little sweaty."

"Oh, Joe," you say, and you swing my arm. Frisky. "Just wait till we get to your place."

9

Ten blocks later and we're there.

You gasp. "Wow. I just . . . I can't believe you live in a place like this. The *gargoyles* . . ."

I'm full of shit. I can't do this. This is a crime. *Breaking and entering.* And I can't do this to *you.* But you loosen your coat and I see those hot pink satin straps and I do what any guy with a Portnoy and a passcode would do. Fuck the gargoyles. I open the door. "You first, madame."

You're in the lobby. You're a criminal and you don't even know it and you look over your shoulder. Skin. Bare. Smooth. "Joe, come on. The show starts in like two seconds."

It's another first for the Moleskine, Vail. Our first elevator make-out session. You look at me like I am the man, and so I am the man. I grin. "Well, hello, Miss Tongue."

You smack my ass. "So how do you afford this?"

The best lies are born in the truth, and a good man is fast on his feet. "I don't afford it. My Uncle Andy is a trader, and he's overseas a lot. It's kinda like . . . I'm house-sitting."

"Ah," you say. And you're a little disappointed that the big money isn't mine, but your gloom fades fast, and why shouldn't it? I'm young. I'm not supposed to be a fat cat, just a cool cat. Trustworthy. Solid. You kiss me again, and wait. What happens when we get there? Do I throw you against the wall and pull your clothes off? Do I play it cool? Do I push the red button and trap us in here for a *Fatal Attraction* fuck-fest?

Ding. No such luck.

You do your best to whistle, but then you sniff and frown. "Do you smell that?"

It's crack, Vail. Angus is a crackhead. "The painters were here all week."

You wiggle your way out of your coat, and I catch it as it falls—*Rico . . . suave*—and you swan down the hallway, avoiding a near miss with a stack of signed Raymond Carvers.

"This is like being in your store."

I like the sound of that. *My store.*

"Ooh," you say, stroking a *Manhattan* poster. "This is my favorite Woody Allen. . . ."

You're lecturing me about *Manhattan,* and this is a good thing. I need you to be distracted because holy shit. I have to make this crack house a home. He left the CD player on—*Frampton Comes Alive*—and I'm grabbing pipes and bags of *rock* and this pipe is hot—and *wait.*

Is Uncle Andy Angus here?

No. I shove the hot pipe in a pizza box, and you sink into the sofa in the sinking living room, and I am hard. Rock hard. Can we do it, Vail? Can we do it right now?

"Questions," you say. You pick up a lipstick-stained wineglass and you point at a pair of panties. FUCK YOU, ANGUS.

I stammer about a party. You laugh. "Relax. I'm not jealous. Where's the remote?"

ANGUS TOOK IT APART WHEN HE WAS HIGH ON METH.

"Shit," I say. "I have HBO at my crash pad, but my uncle isn't big into TV."

This might be the end, but nope. You want sex with me more than *Sex* and you untie your bootlaces. "It's all good. I mean, it's just a show. One day we'll sit down and start with season one, episode one. Anyway! Where are your DVDs? Got any rom-coms, my dear?"

We can't watch a movie, because I can't turn on the TV, and I tell you it's broken and that's NOT FUCKING FAIR. *Watching a movie* is code for "fucking our brains out." I failed you, and I can feel it in your bones. You don't trust me, the sinking living room, the *bras* on the floor. You pick up a bong, a glass fucking bong. "Wait . . . You smoke weed?"

That's for CRACK, not weed, and I grab it. "No, I mean, not really. It's not mine."

DUMB, JOE, DUMB. No one ever falls for that line, whether it's about *Penthouse* or crack pipes. Seconds ago, you were mine, and now you're folding your arms. I toss an old greasy *Times* on top of another errant fucking pipe, and you look at the walls, at the books. "So I guess the book obsession runs in the family."

If only you knew what he does to these books. "Ha. Yeah, I guess . . ."

"So, you have this all to yourself and you don't even have to pay him anything?"

A little tone in your voice and, right. No one wants a freeloader. Also I don't want you to worry I think you're digging for gold. "Oh, hell no. I pay rent. Angus is a serious guy."

"Wait . . . I thought it was *Andy*?"

FUCK YOU, ANGUS, and why do you want to know about things that don't matter? I tell you that *Andy* is a nickname, and I keep on cleaning. Empty baggies. Tinfoil. Spoons. *Filth.* Soon the place is in order, and you reward me for my labor. You slip off your boots. Butter and leather. Lace and skin. Tights . . . not sure how to get those off but not gonna get ahead of myself. You are at ease. This is progress. Did

I pass the test? Do I jump your *lovely bones*? You cross your legs like you just read my mind, like the answer is *Not just yet, Cusack.*

"Second things second, Joe. I have another question, but first . . . Not that I don't like Peter Frampton, but does it have to be on repeat?"

YES, VAIL. I DON'T KNOW HOW TO WORK THE CD PLAYER. I play the romantic, the *cool cat,* and tell you that repeat is my thing, same way I had Dylan on a loop in the bookstore and Jesus Fucking Christ. Are me and Angus the same fucking crackhead?

"Ah," you say. "Well, that is very *NYC Bookstore Babe* of you."

Is that a good thing? A bad thing? It might be a bad thing, and it's a fucking CD player. How hard can it be? I see things I missed. Left-over coke on the jewel cases, on the CD player, and I hit Play. Am I high now? Does coke get in your fingers the way smoke gets in your eyes? I push a button. Nothing happens, and the song begins again.

You tell me to relax. "I can do the repeat thing, especially with this song. Used to great effect in *Reality Bites*. . . . You've seen it, right?"

Fuck, no. "Only about five times."

I trip on my own feet, on another fucking crack pipe. You laugh. "Okay, I'm curious."

It's the Spanish Inquisition and I'm never going to Spain unless I pass this fucking test. "Shoot."

"Well, actually . . . First, can I have a glass of red?"

No, you can't, Vail. I don't know how to operate a fucking cork-screw. "Of course."

I walk to the cabinet of reds and whites, and I pick up a bottle. This is a new crime. This is *theft*. I pick up a corkscrew and *I'm* screwed. If you learn I can't pop the cork on a fucking wine bottle, you're not gonna let me pop your cherry. Stupid. No cherry for me—you're not a virgin—and the guy who popped yours probably knew how to open a bottle of wine.

"Joe?"

"Sorry. I, um . . . I think I left the lights on out on the terrace."

You motion for me to give you the bottle—phew—and I open the door to the terrace. Another first, not for our Moleskine, just for me. Finally, I see it, the city from here.

You join me with two glasses of red. I am loved, fed. "Wow, Cusack. What a terrible view."

I take the wine. "I know. Don't worry. I won't make you come out here."

You lick your lips. You liked that. "Okay, baby, I am ready for my tour."

I am *baby*—that's a first for the Moleskine—and I lead you back inside, into the kitchen—a pigsty that makes you laugh and groan, *men*—and now it's off to the den where it's books, more books, and movie posters, more posters. You gush about *Magnolia* and you're a little *too* fond of Paul Thomas Anderson, so I tell you the bedroom is a mess.

You slap me and smile. "I didn't *ask* to see the bedroom, baby."

Oh, you're good—and we make our way back home, to the sinking living room. Butter and leather. Lace and skin. You touch your neck and look at me like I'm James Fucking Bond. Bondage. Are you into that? I hope not.

You sit. I sit. Do I touch you? Kiss you?

You offer me more wine, and I can't do it, Vail. My Portnoy is nervous. Twitching. You set your glass on the table and stretch and now your feet are on my lap. Little feet. Trapped in plaid stockings. Stripes thick as the bars on a cage, and did you wear those tights on purpose? Are your legs off-limits?

"Okay," you say. "I don't mean it in a bad way, Joe. . . . I'm a little surprised."

That I didn't tear your clothes off? "About what?"

Your toes curl in the bad way. "Baby, I know it's not 'your' place. And I mean, it's nice to have rich relatives . . ."

I don't really have an Uncle Warbucks and your toes are stiff. Bent. "Yeah. Totally."

"What I mean is . . . well . . . You had a *party.*"

Angus had a party. I hate parties. "It was just one night, just a bunch of dudes."

You tilt your head at a wineglass, at a *lipstick* stain, and I make up a girl who showed up uninvited and you tell me to stop. "It's okay, babe. I'm not like that. You're allowed to let loose."

I love you. "Thank you."

"It's more just . . . I mean, it's a shocker, Cusack. Like I get it. We barely know each other . . . blah, blah, blah, but also . . . you never talk about partying."

You bring your knees to your chest and hold them with your arms, and there are two cages now, the stripes on your tights, the arms on your legs. "It's not a criticism, Joe."

THEN WHY ARE YOU HOLDING YOUR LEGS HOSTAGE?

"I know, baby."

You flinch like I'm not supposed to call you that, and you shake your little head. "It's just . . . It's not what I expected."

Think, Joe, think. "My buddy Jeremy was moving away, so it was a guys' night, a going-away thing . . ."

"Who's Jeremy?"

Piven. It's Jeremy Fucking Piven. "Jeremy Perry. He's the best."

"Did you meet in high school or college?"

I dropped out of the former, never even contemplated the latter. "Mooney's. He's a writer, or he wants to be. He came into the shop a lot."

You let go of your legs, and that's progress. That's the Piven effect, because girls are like that. You want guys to have friends. You smile. "So where did he move?"

Your feet return to my lap, and we are on the road to Serendipity. "San Francisco."

"Ah," you say, and you like it, this idea of me, you're buying it. "So why did he move?"

I tickle the top of your foot. "Well, he dropped out of school. . . ." I pause for reaction, but you don't react. "He's seriously like the smartest guy I know, and he was blogging, and now . . . now he got a job at a real paper."

"You'll have to show me his blog."

Not possible—it doesn't exist—and I thank my lucky stars that a computer can't fit in your pocket. You wiggle your toes—you want me—and I hold them in my hands—I want you—and you let out a little moan. I passed the test. I do have a place. My place isn't this place. My place isn't my place. My place just might be with you. You sip your wine. You feel it too. You touch your hair—you're teaching me how to touch you—and you gulp. I like you like this. Nervous. Opening slowly, *petal by petal,* and then taking a deep breath as you plunge into the deep end, the place you go because I went there first.

"So, my best friend, Anjanette . . . she also dropped out of school."

"Cool."

"And like you said, well, she's not the smartest person I know. . . ." That's me. "But she's the happiest person I know."

I rub circles on the pads of your little feet. You smile. Do you want me to kiss them?

"Joe, random question, but did you ever see *Coyote Ugly*?"

Fuck it. I can't lie anymore. "Nope."

"First of all, we're watching it, *stat.*"

Oh, you want me. You just planned our next date.

"Deal."

"Second, okay. It's so good, Joe. It's about these Jersey girls, right? And they were so us. One is a dreamer, and the other is . . . practical. The dreamer wants to be a songwriter, so she moves to New York, and by the end of the movie, she makes it."

"And the best friend?"

You have sadness in you, and that's why you wear those plaid tights, that awful cape. "Well, she's just happy to have her little home.

And it's like . . . it's enough for her to have this small little life, you know? She's not like *trying* to be things. She just is, you know?"

I hold your feet. You know that I know. You trust me.

"So, I fly home a few months back. Anj and I go see *Coyote Ugly*, and after the movie, we're like . . . *weird*. We can't decide where to eat and it's odd. Best friends, but we're like aliens. We go to Chili's and it's . . . I mean, it's not like Carric and the girls, you know?"

No, I don't know, but at the same time I do. "Weird."

"Yes. Weird is it. We get our grub, and we talk about the movie, and she's like, 'Gundylocks, slow your roll.' "

"Huh?"

"Oh, it's a nickname, only back home." The way you look down hurts, like this whole other part of you is inaccessible, tucked into your family's cookie-cutter hearth, steaming in a kettle I can't touch. "Anyway," you go on. "She says she's worried about me living in the city."

"Why?"

You're pouring more wine, and I will kill Angus Kaplan—I won't kill him—but I would if it meant we could live in the sinking living room, if I knew we could talk like this every night.

"Well, Joe, come on. She was right. She said I'm not like the girl in the movie. I don't have a dream. A purpose. A passion. And it hurt, you know? 'Cause Anj . . . she has her purpose, she's settled . . . and . . . She didn't want to hear about my 'crazy' life, and I didn't want to hear about her curtains. It's not a tragedy, but . . . Do you know those books . . . *Amelia Bedelia*?"

I know all the books and I remember the first date, the list I made for conversation starters. We are doing it before we do it and show me another guy who could say what I say right now. "Amelia Bedelia does everything wrong."

You laugh like you could love me—the sinking living room is rising—and I can't squeeze your little feet hard enough. I want to put them in my mouth, tights and all. And then your laughter fades. I let go of your feet. I love you. I love you! I love that you're rubbing your eyes and drinking your wine and showing me your sad side. Your Miss Lonely loneliness. You loved your best friend, and you lost her.

I never had one, Vail. But I get it.

"You know why I love going to the movies, Joe? Because you go into the dark with someone. You leave your lives and you go into this world together, and sometimes, in the dark, you see what you don't want, and that's the risk, right? If we'd seen anything besides *Coyote Ugly* that day, we might still be friends. It's like you too. . . ."

I pet your feet. Serendipitous little feet. "Yes, Sitcom."

You pull at your skirt. "Actually, baby, can we not do that anymore? Sitcom . . . Cusack . . . I know I don't look like Kate Beckinsale—"

"You're prettier."

You laugh, and it's good—I am sick of those stupid nicknames—and your petals are wilting, dropping like sweet flies. Your lips come together, and you lick them, and I swear I can feel your tight, scared heart starting to pound. "See," you say. "When you and *I* went to the movies . . . I forgot about how the power can be a good thing. We were so awkward at the start, and by the end of act one, it was like, oh, I like this guy. He's good."

This is the reason lovebirds need a nest. A sofa. Quiet. You're relaxed in a way that you can't be in a coffee shop or a bookstore. You forgot about how nice it is to just sit around listening to music, and the petals are opening quickly now, one after another, after another. You bite your lips, but there is something going on inside of you. Something scary, something sad. *I don't have a dream. A purpose. A passion.* You close your eyes. I squeeze your feet. You open your eyes.

"It's like this, Vail. Of course you don't have a dream. You're working your ass off. You can't sleep because you're on call for this douchebag who doesn't respect you."

"I know."

"Don't sweat dreams, Vail. Most people are lying when they tell you about their dreams, and the thing is, and seriously . . . You dream when you're in deep sleep. You're not dreaming right now but . . .

Since we met I'm, I'm dreaming a little bit more. And maybe telling you that will, you know . . . You deserve to dream too."

No more footsies and no more nicknames. You mount me. Legs and arms. Lace and skin. You do have a passion—your hands clinging to my hair, tugging—and you do have purpose—Miss Tongue wants Mr. Tongue—and you do have a dream.

You purr. "Come to Mama, baby. Come."

You are *Mama,* and Portnoy comes alive. Your hands are on the move, all ten thousand of your perfect milk bone fingers. Happy Portnoy. Hungry Portnoy.

"So much hair, baby . . . so thick."

Me? Is that good? Bad? Fuck it. On we go. Miss Tongue broadsides Mr. Tongue in the deep blue sea, and I'm learning the way of you. Slow and then fast. Fast and then slow. You're the elder, and it feels good, the way you steer my hands. *Oh, baby. Oh, Joe.* You grab my biceps and run a hand down my chest—I need a better sweater—and I could live like this, with you, read you all day, all night. That first day in the theater. *I'm a visual person.* Me too, and my eyes are open. I see you, Vail. I see you.

I pull your shirt over your head, and it's allowed. I know it because you pull my sweater off and run your hands over my chest, and then you . . . Wait. Did you just giggle?

The CD doesn't skip, but it does. "What's so funny?"

"Nothing, baby. I just love how you are. Soft and . . . soft and snuggly."

SOFT IS THE OPPOSITE OF HARD.

"Oh."

"Aw, no. See, it's a good thing, baby. It means you're not a narcissist gym rat. . . ."

Soft is for girls, and Portnoy isn't *soft.* Is he?

You grab onto my hair. Another giggle. Is there laughing in sex? Is there crying in baseball? "Baby," you say, "just promise me you won't get a haircut or go crazy at the gym. You're so pure, the Frampton on repeat and the 'let's just listen to music' . . . it's all so seventies."

I ask if that's a good thing, and you tell me to learn how to take a compliment. I kiss you—no more talking, no more words—and your hand finds my Portnoy, and he wants out of the pants. I reach for your waistband. You whisper in my ear. "Mmm . . . You first, baby."

You put a hand on my zipper. Zipper down. *Watership Down.* Portnoy up. Hard. You say it again. "Come to Mama."

Gently, Joseph. I can't rush this. You're a romantic. The anti-Cynthia. Sex matters to you. Love. We never saw Cusack and Beckinsale do the nasty in *Serendipity,* and Tom Hanks doesn't stick it to Meg Ryan in *You've Got Mail,* not even in the end, in the park, and then you go still. Still as a fucking stop sign.

I'm unzipped. I'm in your hands. I look at you. "What's wrong?"

"Nothing. I just . . . I've just never seen one like this, I mean, not in person. . . ."

WHAT IS WRONG WITH MY DICK?

"Sorry," you say. "It's exciting. . . . I can't believe this."

WHAT IS WRONG WITH MY PORTNOY?

"Oh."

"It's just . . . it's so rare to see one in the States. I mean . . . you're uncut."

I'm not un-anything. I'm *natural.* "Yeah."

"You don't see that a lot . . . not that I see a lot. And we did an episode about this."

Great. You made fun of my dick on national fucking television for girls. "Oh."

"Was your mom . . . Is she a hippie or something?"

You study me like a book, like suddenly you read *dicks.* I bet Tom Hanks is cut. I bet *his* mother was all over that shit and I don't want Alma Goldberg in my head, but she's there, lurking. I can't introduce you. I won't introduce you. It's my *dick* and the Mister Softee truck is ringing the bell, gunning for my Portnoy. You think you want my stories, but you wouldn't want my stories if you knew my stories are all laced with salmonella and I'm losing it. Us. You.

But then my chin is in your hand. "Baby," you say. "Relax. Tell me what you want."

Anything. Everything.

And then we're back. I want what you want. Portnoy wants to run, *yawp,* and jump out of his foreskin and slide into your Moleskine. *Down, boy.* But now your hands are faster and *wait* . . . Do you want it to end now . . . like this? I haven't touched your Beckinsale, and you order me to come, *come for Mama, baby.* No. That's not how it works. Not in the pornos or the poems. There are rules about this. *Mama don't take my Kodachrome* until I give you *your* greens of summer, and no cookies for me without cookies for you. I throw you onto your back. You squeal. You like it. I grab onto the waist of your tights. You wince. "Um, I sort of have my period."

A crackhead won't notice a little blood, and neither will I. "I don't care."

"That *too* is very seventies, baby, but . . . Wait."

Uh-oh. Is it my dick? Me? You sit up. "Did you, like . . . Did you invite friends over?"

You pull your shirt over your head, and you reach for a boot, and I hear it now. The elevator. I tell you I'm sorry, and you laugh. "It's fine, Cusack. All good. Totally!"

But I'm not laughing and I'm not Cusack. We got past that, I am *baby,* I am *Joe,* and you're regressing and the elevator is rising. Our love nest is collapsing, the living room isn't sinking, it's in free fall like my fucking Portnoy. Our first date flashes in my mind, the way they say your life does right before you die. Houston and Mercer. Philip Roth and Mr. Tongue. And now it's over. He's coming, not me, not you. Him. Angus Fucking Kaplan.

I rub my forehead, and you kick me like we're buddies, like I'm some random guy you hooked up with. You say it will be nice to meet my friend—HE'S NOT MY FRIEND—and you pull lipstick out of your bag and rub it on your mouth like I might just be the way you meet some *other* guy, some better guy with HBO and a common American cock.

The elevator groans, and I just fucking say it. "We should have gone to Serendipity."

10

Thirty seconds later, we're walking the plank on this sinking fucking ship because he's here. Angus. Slimy green robe. Velour. Same green as those pillows in India. Cigarette holes in the sleeves, and I am silent. Dead. He isn't holding a Heinie, and he isn't holding a crack pipe.

He's holding a fucking *gun*. You put your hands up and I put my hands up and my Moleskine heart is pounding—this is the worst kind of first—and you extend a hand like he doesn't have a gun, like this is fucking normal and you *smile* at the gun-toting crackhead.

"You must be Uncle Andy, right? I'm Joe's friend Vail." *Friend.* "And I gotta say . . . I am kind of in love with your robe."

He looks at you and he looks at me, and he takes the two steps down into our sinking ship. Your scarf is right there, and I'm begging that fucker, please. Don't touch that fuzzy red scarf. Don't kill us. Don't wreck us.

He spits. "The hell do you think you're doing, Jimmy?"

You get it now—this ain't my Uncle Andy—and that's why you

put your hands back up. You're scared again. I want to tell you it's not loaded, but last summer, he got mad about something Oprah said and shot a hole in the wall. It very well might be loaded, and you are never going to forgive me for this, for any of it.

"Angus," I say. "I can explain."

He leers at you and laughs. "Did you get me a present?"

You are *not* a present and I howl at him—*Drop the fucking weapon*—but you rest a hand on my arm—*Gently, Joseph*—and you look at me like I'm a child. "Let me, Joe," you whisper.

I can't say no to you. I am useless. I'm the reason you're in this mess, and you are so good at the world. You negotiate like a pro, like that lady on *SVU.* You ask Angus if you can sit down, and when he says no, you say that's okay, that we will do whatever he wants.

"You're the boss, babe. Truly."

He waves the pistol at you, at the sofa. "Sit, Ubu, sit."

You sit, and he calls you a *good dog.* I'm still standing here like the teenage loser that I am, and you're a genius, a regular Miss Frascatore. You stay calm, asking questions about his day, about his night. His answers make no sense. *I didn't have a day. . . . I don't do night.* You know to let it go, to let him lead, and so he leads. He says I don't belong here. He says I'm a *book bitch* and sometimes he calls me Jimmy and other times it's Jerome or fucking *Jimbo* and all the while I stand here with my hands up because he never told *me* to Sit, Ubu, sit.

"Hey, Angus," you coo. "Do you want some chocolate, hon?"

Hon and he falls under your spell, and drops the gun (junkies do like their sweets) and you dig into that messenger bag and peel the foil off the mints, the Andes. Uncle Andy. *Andy.*

I catch my breath. I try not to puke. Useless juvenile delinquent. Liar. Felon?

Angus eats his chocolate, and blubbers and mutters that we don't understand, and you sit by him, not me.

"How's that taste, hon?" You put a hand on his knee. I want your hand on *my* knee and he says it's good and you give him another and

I've never been smaller in my whole fucking life. Angus eats your chocolate, the chocolate meant for me, and you pat his knee (don't touch him, you're killing me) and he shakes his greasy head.

"You do not play Peter Frampton after dark."

"Amen," you say, and how do you know how to work him? I come here every week, and I still freeze up when he pisses me off. Not you. You met him at gunpoint, but you're bonding with him over some record store I never even heard of and how? Do you like him more than me? Are you over me already? I would be over me. I wrecked it. I lied to you. Did I kill it?

You slap your thighs (no), and I was gonna do that, Vail. I was gonna slap your thighs. *Love them. Touch them. Squeeze them.* Angus says you can go meet your friend and you put on your boots. The end is nigh, the dream is over, and I've never felt quite so young and dumb.

I catch your eye. *I'm sorry.*

You wink at me, and I don't know what that means. What's a wink? Is there hope?

"All right," he says. "I'm bored."

He's on his feet and we're on the move, following him down the hall to the elevator and maybe there's a chance. A way out of this for us because we are getting out now and that means we lived. I owe you my life, and I squeeze your hand and thank you. You chuckle and roll your eyes like it was nothing, and the earth splits open. An abyss that is the difference between us. You are older than I am, Vail. In this moment you know it. I know it. You've been places. You've seen shit. But you're still with me, walking by my side as Angus swerves off and kicks at Raymond Carver. I've read about this kinda stuff. Trauma bonds. We've been through something together, our own little September 11, and okay, you saved my ass. In an ideal world, I would've saved yours, but maybe that makes me seem like a feminist or something.

My fun, fucked-up not-an-uncle hits the elevator button and the door opens fast. *Schwing.* I wave you in and you're in the clear, and I'm on my way to join you and stay up all night talking about our crazy families and fucking our brains out the way we wanted to, but nope.

Angus slings his arm around my back. "Boys' night. Someone needs a spanking."

You wave goodbye to him, and he flips you the bird and I'm stuck. Invisible. Owned. And it hurts. The light agrees with you in the elevator (all light agrees with you), and the worst is when you take one last look at me and see it all. My impotence. My youth. You adjust your messenger bag like a doctor who made a house call, like a mother leaving her terrible sons alone to trash the house.

And then the doors close and Angus lets out a fart from the southernmost bowels of the gates of fucking hell.

"All right," he says. "Daddy needs a Heinie."

11

Angus's Heinie . . . *is crowding my icebox,* and I wonder if I'll ever see Mooney again, or my dad, the real one who doesn't know where I live. I am lost. You are lost. Out in the night alone. You thought you'd be watching your sitcom with your hot new boyfriend, but I fucked up, royally, and Angus digs a couple of Heinies out of the TV stand. He opens one of the bottles with his teeth and spits the cap on the floor. I won't give up on us. You're gone to God knows where and the thing with feathers is dying, but it ain't dead yet. There is hope.

You winked.

I hold on to my Nokia, the actual lifeboat, my only connection to you. "I should probably check on Vail."

"Why? She's a big girl. . . . Actually, no, she's pretty short."

THE WORD IS PETITE, YOU FUCKWAD, and he pours cocaine on the jewel case and sighs. "Did I ever tell you about my ex? Kelly Damon. Demon. Now *she* was something. . . . Dead ringer for Carolyn Bessette."

No time for this shit. It's my turn to save *you.* But Angus is getting higher by the second, replacing the Frampton CD with *Purple Rain.* He kicks at invisible Kelly Demons and I could make a run for it, but I can't do that because of his fucking gun. I need to keep my job at Mooney's. I need to get my own fucking apartment, my own fucking butter and leather.

On this goes for what feels like hours, Angus retelling his self-aggrandizing fake fucking tragedy while I sit in a wingback chair pretending to sip my Heinie that isn't even open. I have to call you. I need to know you're safe and I need to hear your voice before you tell Cynthia about this fiasco or some nightcrawler sinks his teeth into your skin and tears off your tights. Mine.

"Jacob," he snaps.

What choice do I have? I answer. "What's up, Angus?"

He tosses a first edition of *Beloved* into the fireplace. That's Toni Fucking Morrison and could I steal the gun and kill him? No. I can't even kill the mice that sneak into the fucking shop. I squirm. I suck. Will I ever feel your lips again?

"Angus, I gotta take a leak."

Normally, he says to piss in the fireplace, and usually, I'm okay to hold it. I don't want to catch a disease off the toilet, the hand towels, the air. But he's in outer space, trying to bite his toenails. I rise out of the chair while he thrashes like a fish that just turned into a human, and I'm down the hall. I close the bathroom door and I call you and it rings.

Is it over? Are we dead?

Then . . . "Joe?"

There is noise in the background. Life. *Men.* "Vail, thank God. Are you okay?"

You laugh and you've had a drink, maybe two. "I'm great. I met up with Cynthia at Jake's Dilemma and I ran into a friend. . . ."

Is that friend a guy? Does he have a dick? You drop your phone and thank a guy for picking it up and my Portnoy didn't like that, and you groan. "Fuck."

"Vail, are you okay? I'm getting out of here any second. . . ."

"Babe! I'm so dumb."

"You are not."

"No, I mean . . . I left my scarf. It's red . . . I think. Or maybe I didn't wear it? Omigod, I'm so fucked up. . . . I can't do shots. *Or* cosmos . . ." A man calls out to you. *Gundylocks!* From the sound of it, you tell him to *shhh.* And then you come back to me. "Anyway, grab it if you see it!"

The end.

Hearing your voice did wonders for me, even though you were drunk. I see the positives now. I didn't steal anything, and you're not physically hurt. You're self-medicating; that's natural. And you didn't send me to voicemail. You still want me. You got out. You used your feminine wiles. I don't have those—I don't think guys have wiles—but I have other stuff. I splash cold water on my face and slap my cheeks the way you slap a new baby's ass.

I *will* get your scarf and there *will* be frozen hot chocolate. And sex.

I return to the living room, and there he is, fucking floating in our leather and our butter as he picks at a Band-Aid on his nipple.

I ditch my *Heinie* on the coffee table and scan the room for your scarf. "So, Angus, my man, I'm gonna head out."

He laughs and picks at another Band-Aid on his belly. "She's not even hot, Joe."

Now he knows my name, and I grunt. "Angus, buddy, I'm sorry, but I really gotta split."

"Aw, the boy said he's sorry."

I don't want to die in here—the smoke, the farts—and Angus picks up his pipe. "You don't get it," he sneers. "You're not the victim, Jamie. *I'm* the victim."

Oh, for fuck's sake, and I bob my *'70s* head. "You're right. And I'm sorry."

He trades his gun for a lighter and *poof.* More smoke. I don't know how he does it, how he stays the fuck alive. Worse still, the idea of you at Jake's without me. Who was calling you *Gundylocks*?

Angus peels off the Band-Aid on his nipple. He chews on it. "I have cameras, Joe. All buildings like this . . . you might not know this, but they have *cameras*."

That's a threat, and could I do it? Could I pick up the gun and shoot him? Cut him up in pieces and toss him in the fireplace? If you could see me, if you knew what I was thinking, would you still want me to rescue your scarf?

"See," he says. "I bet you've never been to therapy."

It's more expensive than Spain and Costa Rica. "Not yet."

"Well, my mother made me go to sailing camp, Jerry. Can you imagine that? A kid like me . . . a certified genius learning to tie knots like some . . ." He shakes his fat head, and I can't kill him. If I blew his brains out, his mother who hates him would come back to life like a zombie in pearls just to preserve the family image. She would find his killer and hire someone to write some ridiculous obituary about how much her precious, sensitive son loved to sail. "It's the doves. Do you hear them, Jack?"

I hear them. I pray for them.

"I'm just like my mother," he says. "And I'm just like my father too. . . . Did I ever tell you what *he* said about my first novel. . . ."

It's not a novel if you don't finish writing it, and time is passing. You are out there, in the wild, and Angus moves in a circle, from his mother to Kelly Demon, back to his mother. The doves aren't helping, the way they peter out and then return, unknowingly egging him on. He swats at them, at his mother, at his father, at all his Kelly Demons, but he won't be alone. I can't lose you because of him. I have to kill the doves. Distract him. He lights a Marlboro Red that he found in the butter and the leather, and he wants something from me, but I don't have wiles or drugs or money and then it hits me. . . . *Franzen.* Sometimes you lie so much that you forget you're lying. I always tell Angus what Mooney *wants* me to tell him, that we don't have a galley of *The Twenty-Seventh City*. But we *do*. And it's the white whale, the one he sees as the reason he never finished his own fucking opus.

I cut him off in the middle of some sob story about his dad's Porsches. "Hey, did I tell you we got a galley of *The Twenty-Seventh City*?"

He drops his cigarette on the shag carpet and plants his bare foot on the butt. Sizzling skin. No pain, yet no gain, literally. "A *galley*? Are you sure, Jerry?"

I got him, Vail, *hook, line, and sinker*. You would be proud of me, *Mama,* and he's rolling a joint (it's not crack, yay!) and I'm kicking the gun under the coffee table. Safe.

"See," I begin. "Truth is, I was telling my girlfriend how that galley is the reason we don't have *your* novel. . . ." Feed the ego, stuff it. "She worships your ex, Carolyn Bessette, and she wanted to see your place. . . ."

"And drink my wine. . . ."

I laugh like the Cusack to his Piven and let that one slide. Eyes on the prize. "Ain't that the way? Anyway, like I said, we're buddies, yeah?"

"Course," he says. He offers me a warm new Heinie. A can this time. "Buddies."

I take the Heinie and pop it. I tell him the good news again, so it doesn't fall through the crack pipe. "I wanted you to be the first to know, buddy. Before Mooney lists it. We have a signed galley of *The Twenty-Seventh City*. And unlike Mooney . . . Angus, come on. How many times have we hung out in here? I'll sell you the book. You know me. You know I don't give a fuck what you do with the books."

The weird thing is, it's true, Vail. I really *don't* care about the galley. You come first—that happened fast—and what's a thought compared to a feeling? What's a galley compared to a girl? I barely know you, but already I give a little bit less of a fuck about the world. Already I know that I would and will do anything for you.

Angus rubs his belly. "I like a fire."

I'd like to set *him* on fire, and I smile. "So, let's do it. Let me sell you the white whale."

"Impossible. Mooney would never sell me that galley."

"Fuck Mooney. We do this on our own. Just you and me and the big white whale."

"Correction," he says. "'You and *I* and the big white whale.'"

I guess I'm no different from all the girls who don't like to be corrected, and I nod.

"Well, this is aces, Jimbo. Actual aces."

Only assholes say *aces,* and I sip from my can of warm Dutch urine. I wish I'd brought a toothbrush, but I didn't. "Aces," I say. "And you know the drill. Cash or check. Twenty-four hundred bucks."

He takes a deep pull on that joint and rubs his stomach and why is there a Band-Aid on his belly button? He pulls a scarf out of the sofa. Red. Yours. He ties it around his neck in this way where you know he will never love or be loved.

"So," he says. "How you gonna do it?"

I'll rip that scarf out of his cold dead hands. "Don't worry about Mooney. I got him."

"No," he says. "How are you gonna get the money?"

He must be high. *Dazed and Confused.* "I'm not the one buying it . . ." I remind him.

But he's not laughing, Vail. He's staring at me, smelling your scarf and licking your scarf. "Wait," he says. "You think *I'm* going to pay for the galley?"

HE LIVES IN A HAND-ME-DOWN PENTHOUSE AND I LIVE IN A CARDBOARD BOX.

"Angus, I make ten bucks an hour."

"You broke into my house."

"Only to impress a girl. I mean, you get that. You know how it is."

"You opened a 1949 Château d'Yquem."

"We can grab you a bottle."

"It's a ten-*thousand*-dollar bottle of wine, Jimmy. And it's my favorite."

CRACKHEADS CAN'T BE WINE SNOBS. "I'm sorry, Angus. If I knew anything about wine, I never would've opened that bottle, and if I had that kind of dough, I'd get you the galley and the wine, but it really is that simple. I don't even have a checking account."

"It's not about money, Jimmy," SAYS THE RICH FAT PIG as he pulls the Band-Aid off his belly button and chews on it. But I'm no better. Why didn't I just offer you a Heinie? "You know what my sober companion would say about you. . . ."

HIS SOBER COMPANION IS A FIGMENT OF HIS FUCKING IMAGINATION.

"Angus, I don't have twenty-four hundred dollars."

"So put it on a credit card."

"I don't have a credit card."

"Well, that's for the best, Jake. Don't get a card, and if you do, go with Amex. Or Discover. But pay it off every month. Your dad will chip in because all dads know about interest rates. . . . A kid like you, Jake . . ."

MY PARENTS ARE NOT THOSE PARENTS.

"Good tip, Angus. Thanks. Cool."

The living room is sinking, fast. I didn't think it through. Angus is on his feet. He's roaming around looking for an orange, so he doesn't get scurvy (help me), and he settles for a crack pipe and sighs.

"This is it, Jimmy. The moment it all changes for me. After I burn *The Twenty-Seventh City*, I'm going back to rehab. . . ." BULL FUCKING SHIT. "And not that dump in New Mexico. I'm doing it right. Going to Promises. . . . You know what they say." I don't like the way he pauses, the way he becomes my own private Joker. "You don't go forward until you hold yourself accountable, Jackie. . . ."

He tosses his pipe to fuck with the CD player and again, the doves are crying.

"So true," I say.

As he dumps coke on Prince: "In rehab, you learn about manning up. . . ." He does a big fat line and shakes his head, and I swear moths are in the air now. Tiny ones. "You broke into my house, and you say you're sorry, but those are just words."

"Angus, I can't . . . I can't pay for the book."

He grins and says that's not his problem and I am not *the only living boy in New York City.* I AM THE STUPIDEST FUCKING BOY IN NEW YORK CITY. NO ONE IS CHEAPER THAN THE RICH. *Breathe, Joe, breathe.* He does another line and the doves are crying, and I don't have it, Vail. I don't have that kind of money. I want off this ship. *Now.* I snap my fingers the way people do when they get the big idea, the big idea that came from *you.* "How about this, my man? What if I work it off? The twenty-four hundred bucks. I can be your assistant."

He stares at me like he isn't scratching at *another* Band-Aid dangling from the pubes sprouting out of his filthy boxers. "I don't need an assistant. I'm going to rehab."

NO, HE FUCKING ISN'T and he's still wearing your scarf, and he says he has *business* to deal with—no, he fucking doesn't—and the hallway is longer than it was when we got here and I tell him I have no money. No savings. I tell him about the box again. *I'm living in a box . . . I'm living in a cardboard box.*

He eyes my shoes. "Converse?"

I nod, and he huffs like Converse is Hugo Boss. "Think of it as your first Maine summer."

Oh, fuck you, Angus. Fuck you. "My what?"

"Your first Maine summer, Jimmy. Mom and Dad left me in the Maine house alone when I was fifteen or fourteen. All the help was gone. I had to do it all—make my breakfast, flush the jobbies . . . This is how the boy becomes the man. Seriously, Jack. Have fun with it."

With that, he calls the elevator and pushes me inside.

"Oh, Jimbo," he says. "If you don't survive your first Maine summer, if I don't get that Franzen before I go to rehab in two weeks, if you forget to cover the pool when it rains and it floods the patio . . . Ever been to juvie? Ever seen a pool overflow into the game room?"

He tosses your scarf at me as the walls close in.

Outside, I puke warm Dutch piss as the gargoyles scowl from above. 4:46 A.M. I dial your number. Voicemail. I call your landline. Answering machine. Serves me right. I can't go to you. I don't know where you live, but the walk helps. I did what you wanted. You asked me to rescue your scarf, and I came through. I bring it to my nose. I remember your hands on me. You want me. You still do. This scarf is not special. It's from the *Gap*. You hid it because girls do that. You leave a little something behind so you have a reason to come back.

Girls are like crackheads. You don't let go.

I'm no different—I think it's why I don't have a posse—and I am Gollum in the good way. I tell it to the world, the homeless guy talking to a trash can, the drunk girl crying with her friend. I shout the way you can in New York at five A.M.

"I love you, Vail Colorado Gunderson!"

Stone cold red hot truth right there. My life is a wreck. An eccentric monster just gave me two weeks to earn more than I make in a month. I could lose my job and the clock is ticking and my nose is running in the predawn freeze, but here I am with the biggest shit-eating grin of my life. It's the Jimi Hendrix of it. Growing louder by the hour, by the second. I don't fucking *panic* over mundane real world stuff, not anymore. Worries are smaller because of you, *my waterfall.* I'm actually happy that you opened the 1949 Château d'Yquem and I'm happy that you unzipped my fly. Hell, I'm even happy that you had your period. I want to go to war for you, *Gundylocks.* I kiss your red scarf. I'm ready.

12

I was wired. I couldn't show up at your place with your scarf because "22nd and Fuck It" is not in the phone book, so I went to one of those all-night diners. I'm a changed man, but I'm also me, so of course I sat there brainstorming get-rich-quick scams. After six cups of coffee, I made a beeline for the bathroom. That's when I manned the fuck *up*. I tossed my phone in the toilet.

It wasn't an accident, Vail. Sometimes a guy needs a fresh start. I don't have to worry about *Angus*. He's a crackhead! Empty threats from a junkie are kinda like kids from broken homes and Nokia cell phones. They all fall through the cracks. I'm flush and I don't owe him a dime, so I went and dropped a few hundred bucks on a Motorola just like yours. I haven't called you yet—I bet you're sleeping it off—and no judgment from me. Angus could drive *anyone* to cosmos. But it's 1:31 P.M. and I can't wait another second.

Neither can you, apparently. You pick up on the first ring. "Joe. Joe! Are you alive?"

You sound like a wife on a widow's walk who fears her fisherman is never coming back. I cling to your scarf. "I'm just glad you're okay. You had me a little worried there. . . ." *Drunkylocks.*

"Oh, I'm fine."

You drank your weight in cosmos and you were slurring in public. Of *course* you're a wee bit defensive. I am yours, undeterred. "What a night, right? We're lucky to be alive."

"Aw, come on. That was nothing."

WE ALMOST DIED. "Oh, okay. . . ."

"I mean, me and Cynthia have been in some *crazy fucking* places. Last summer, we met these guys and . . ." That's my punishment for ditching you. You want me to picture you with other men. "Anyway," you say. "Your uncle isn't scary. Just sad. Wait . . . Is he your uncle?"

It's a fresh start, and I don't want you to worry about my gene pool, so I tell you the truth, mostly. "No, he's a customer slash crack-head. He gave me the code, I hang there when he's out of town, but you saw how he is."

"Ah, well, I still can't judge the guy. Addiction is a tough thing, you know?"

I am Gollum. I am sniffing your fucking scarf. "I know."

"Did you ever see our episode about the guy who's in AA and gets addicted to Carrie?"

"No."

"Huh."

The silence is the bad kind, so I fill it up fast. "Anyway, the thing is I really am sorry. I was just . . . The truth is I live in a shithole with these idiots who get high and quote *Dumb and Dumber.* I didn't know how to tell you about my situation; they're pigs and I hate it but. . . . I'm sorry."

There's a silence. I can't read it; I'm too scared to fill it. Are you still there? Did you hang up?

"Okay, Joe. I get it. We're all self-conscious."

"Thank you."

"Wait. The thing is . . . It's like your uncle."

"Customer."

I did it again, I corrected you, and you sigh. "Once again, my dear . . . everyone poops. . . . This is New York. *Friends* or my show . . . People like us don't live in places like that. I mean, first of all, Carrie and the girls are in their *thirties.* We're in our twenties, you know?"

I don't tell you I'm seventeen. I don't want you to feel like a cradle robber. "Mm-hmm."

"So, you know how it is, then. We all live in a shithole. There is literally no shame in it, in stumbling along the way as you figure it all out, what you're gonna do, who you're gonna be. And second of all . . . I'm flattered. You wanted to impress me. You meant well. I know you care. . . . But, Joe, I wasn't expecting a penthouse."

I'm seventeen and I live in a box and life moves *forward* so that's what I do. I push us ahead. "I know, but anyway, can I make it up to you? Take you to Serendipity sometime this week?"

You tell me this is *a week from hell* and you have to deal with Barry and you promise to call a little later.

But you don't call *a little later* and you don't call at night.

In the morning, I don't have a voicemail from you, and it's a *lot* later. I try you first thing, and five rings later, I reach you in the bad way. Your motherfucking voicemail: "You went to Vail and all you got was this lousy voicemail."

I chuckle to seem calm, cool. So not Gollum. "Yeah, Vail, it's me. Just wanted to make sure you got my new number. Also, I really like Vail. I can't wait to go again. . . ."

So much for the coolness, and I blame that bastard Angus but then, when I'm dug in with Mooney, you call me and get my voicemail, so now *you* are the Gollum, the seeker.

"Howdy, partner! I'd call this phone tag, but I hate that phrase. I mean, this kind of communication has its merits or *You've Got Mail* wouldn't be such a good movie. Byeee!"

You called me your *partner,* and it feels good. Right. On we go like this for another day, and then another day, trading voicemails, ships passing in the night, a couple of put-upon "twentysomethings" trying their damnedest to keep the love alive. I want to see you and you want to see me, but your week from hell is getting worse every day.

Barry is riding you hard, I get it.

Cynthia is having an STD scare and she needs you, I get it.

You have to see the dentist *and* your cousin from California, I get it.

And I mean it, Vail. I do get it, and that's because of you. Constantly assuring me that this is your hell week, that you do *want* to see me, and I don't mind the distance. We're bonding with our voices. Trading details about our lives. Old-school love letters via matching Motorolas. I've told you about my plan to ask Dumb and Dumber to move the cardboard box, give me an extra couple of feet, and you've told me about this potential new job in fundraising for the arts. *We've Got Mail,* yes. But my Portnoy is antsy, and I am too. I want the back-and-forth. The ping-pong. And your period is over by now, right?

I miss you. Your red scarf is losing its scent, I am losing my mind and finally it happens—you are calling—and I want it so bad that I let it ring so I don't sound so fucking desperate. I picture you, crossing your fingers, hoping to hear my voice, and then I give you what you want. Me: "Vail!"

"Joe!"

"How goes it?"

"You first, Joe. Did Dumb and Dumber let you move the wall?"

"Nope."

"Fuck."

You know things now. You know about the astrology sluts who make me uncomfortable, and you know I don't belong with Dumb and Dumber. You're investing in me, in my journey. Gollum isn't nuts. He's just a guy who knows what he wants. So here I go again.

"Hey, what are you up to later?"

"I have to meet Cynthia in midtown."

"Right."

"I mean, I wish I could see you. I do. . . . Next week will be better."

I feel your scarf in my back pocket. Still there. "Don't even worry about it."

"Are you sure? Because I really do feel bad. It's just one of those weeks. . . ."

"I know, I know."

We hang up, and you said it—this is *one of those weeks*—so on the way home from Mooney's, I stop by the video store to pick up *You've Got Mail.*

The snarky shithead behind the counter grunts at me. "Chick flick," he says.

"Yeah," I say. "My girlfriend's coming over."

The lie felt good. At home, I drag the TV stand into my cardboard box. Dumb and Dumber are out with their astrology sluts. I have your scarf on my lap, and I turn out the lights and I feel you, Vail. It's like you're here in the dark with me, watching Tom Hanks and Meg Ryan talk pencil sharpeners and New York City. I picture you out with Cynthia, talking about me, thinking about me, picturing us as them, *You've Got Voicemail.*

After I finish the movie, I jack off. I do not rub my hands on your scarf.

And then I call you and get your voicemail. The words I know by heart: "You went to Vail and all you got was this lousy voicemail. *Beeeeep.*"

I do it, Vail. I do my best Tom Fucking Hanks. "So, I'm pretty sure you already know this, but Meg Ryan . . ." I count to three. I make you wait. "Well, she kinda looks like you. You're like that, you know? You bounce when you walk and . . ." I laugh a little so you can blush and feel like the princess that you are, my princess, my ring, *mine.* "The thing is, though . . ." I want book club with you, I want *connection* with you. "Tom Hanks is the man, always, but am I on crack? Because he's also kind of . . . I mean, you know he's the worst, right? He's Joe

Fucking Fox. He's Fox Books and he's putting the good gal out of business and he's lying about who he is and I would never . . ." People in cardboard boxes shouldn't throw stones. *Gently, Joseph.* "Anyway, I saw in the *Voice* that *Hannah and Her Sisters* is playing at the Forum this week. And it's only this week. So if you can, tell Barry I said to fuck off. Tell Cynthia I said to have some water. Let's go see *Hannah* on the big screen, yeah? See you on AOL IM tomorrow."

The night is like the others (it never fucking ends!), and the morning is no better. You didn't leave me a late-night treat, but you might call while I'm in the shower, so I put my Motorola in a plastic bag and leave it on the sink. You don't call. And it's fine. I didn't go too far with my voicemail, right? I have to be patient like Tom Hanks. I get dressed. I walk to work. I think Tom Hanks kind of thoughts—*I love New York in late January, when pink hearts pop up in all the windows*—and I make it to Mooney's. I turn on the lights in my *Shop Around the Corner* and I make small talk with Mooney—you still haven't called—and I log on to IM—you're not there, not yet—and I don't "obsess" over you. I do the Tom Hanks thing. I charm customers. I help a divorced dad pick out the right book for his sad thumb-sucking offspring, but then . . . wait.

Am I the Meg Fucking Ryan? The wide-eyed duped bookseller in the dark?

I laugh like you're here to tell me I'm being silly, and see how you do that? You make me feel better even when you're not around. Life is so different with you in it, Vail. I am never really alone because I get to talk to you in my head. And I'm on. I'm being the man I know you want me to be in case you walk into the shop and surprise me. Nothing gets me down, not even the bitter woman who tries to return a battered *Good in Bed.* No one would do that in Meg Ryan's fucking shop and okay. By 3:02 P.M. the wait for you to pop out of the blue has *me* turning blue. Tom Hanks was the captain of his ship. He was in charge, testing his potential bride, helping her soften and grow. Where are you? I get so *blue* that I leave my cell phone on the counter when I hit the head—I am *Dumbest*—but then I go back up front, and the light is blinking.

One new voicemail.

"Joe," you squeal. "Omigod so first, FYI, Barry made me kill my IM. He doesn't want me doing that when I'm working. And oh God . . . Cynthia got hit by a bike messenger. Pause for reaction. . . ." I smile at you. Do you feel it? I hope so. "I was in the ER with her, and it was a whole thing, and you know how it is . . . domino effect where much as I would love to go see *Hannah* with you, I can't do that because I lost the whole night to Cyn—" You sigh. You long for me. You *Meg* for me. "I swear, I am seriously questioning my life choices right now and kind of think being an indentured servant isn't the best job for me. Anyway! Drumroll . . ."

This is it—we're gonna make a plan, you need to see me, you want to see me—but then Mooney snaps his hairy-knuckled fingers at me. "Put that thing *down*, Joseph."

I put the thing down. "Sorry."

He launches into a tirade about a sales rep, but who cares?! Nothing matters except you and your drumroll, and I get it now. *Serendipity. You've Got Mail.* It's the same shit. Two sweet, good people belong together but life pulls them apart and the longer they go without seeing each other the more they *want* to see each other. Mooney snaps his fingers at me.

"Give it."

"Give it?"

"That cellular device, Joseph. You're not being present."

I love the old guy, I do, but I will knock his jagged fucking teeth into the back of his fucking throat. "Okay, sorry. I'll put it in my messenger bag."

"Don't say *messenger* bag, Joseph. Give me the device."

Gollum had teeth. Gollum would tear this old man's hair out before he gave up the ring. But Gollum didn't work in a bookstore. I give Mooney my phone, and he sneers at it.

"What's this envelope?"

"It's voicemail."

"Voicemail," he says. "A paradox and a lie, as all true mail is on paper, written with intention, with *ink*. How might I dispose of this *voicemail*?"

YOU WILL NOT DISPOSE OF MY VOICEMAIL. "I wish I knew."

He glares at me like he did the day the Salinger got stolen, and I feel like a fucking kid again. I am a boy and a bitch and he orders me to destroy your love letter and I don't have a high school diploma. I don't have a résumé. All I have is Mooney, so I do it, Vail. I kill your drumroll.

"Good," he says. "Now leave that thing in your *pocketbook* and tend to the new stock."

Unboxing pop culture nonfiction paperbacks is the hardest thing I ever had to do and what did you say to me? What came after the drumroll? What did I miss? I tear into a box. Cardboard, like my bedroom, and I stop in my tracks. Lo and behold . . . it's a plot twist in a fucking *rom-com*. Five advance copies of *Sex and the City: Kiss and Tell*. A work of nonfiction by a woman named Amy Sohn. Of all the books in all the gin joints . . .

My shift is never ending but then it does and I love calling you on a crowded sidewalk in front of other women, strangers who steal a glance at me and wonder who you are, why I love you and not them. You pick up on the second ring—you want me—and here we go.

"Joe!"

"Vail!"

The opening nervous laughter that's become our little tradition and you really can become a couple over the phone.

"So, how's it going?"

"You first, Joe. Did you get my voicemail?"

The drumroll. The deleted voicemail. "Mmm, we'll get to that. First, though, I have a surprise for you."

You give me an *mm-hmm,* and I am turning it around. I am Tom Hanks with the daisies, *the friendliest flower.* "We had a little visitor in the shop today."

"Oh, you did, did you?"

"Mm-hmm."

"And?"

"And what are you up to tonight?"

"Ugh, honestly . . . I ate some bad sushi. I'm sorry. But you know . . ."

"Everyone poops."

"Exactly." Not the news I wanted, but Meg Ryan catches a cold. Women get sick. "Anyway, Joe, what's the surprise?"

"Well, it wouldn't be a surprise if I told you."

"I am hunkered down in the bathroom with a bottle of Pepto."

"Do you know Amy Sohn?"

"No," you say. "Why?"

The perfect amount of jealousy, and it's good that you can't see me smile. "She's a writer with a new book about my favorite sitcom I've never seen. . . ."

"Ha."

"Anyway, she came into the shop today. . . ." It's not a *lie.* It's a little white one. Innocent. "She gave us galleys of her new book about your show."

"No way."

"I might have asked her to sign one for you."

"Oh, Joe. You're too sweet."

I stop at a green light. You're home sick. Sick like Meg Ryan in her robe attached to Kleenex. "You live in Murray Hill, right?"

"Sort of," you say. And you cough. "Sorry, I feel gross."

Gently, Joseph. "Well, I gotta make a delivery in the area. I could drop it off. . . ."

The silence is warm and fuzzy. You want me. You want me bad. "Hmm . . ."

Do it, Vail. Invite me over. "You live on Twenty-second and . . ."

"I feel like hell. And I look like it too."

I tell you that's okay but then you get call-waiting—it's Barry—and an icy rain starts to fall and it's okay. *I will survive.* This just isn't it. It isn't the night we come back together.

"Look," you say. "This is totally just a twenty-four-hour bug, and tomorrow night . . . How about some long-awaited frozen hot chocolate, my dear?"

My Portnoy wakes up, and *my dear* means I will be yours again soon. As in *baby.* I clear my throat. *Gently, Joseph.* "That could work. How is sevenish?"

"Seven is heaven."

Nothing can get me down on the happy walk home. Not even a call from Angus. I send him to voicemail and I listen to his whining—*I want a progress report, Jimbo*—and I guess his brain isn't as cracked out as I'd hoped, but who cares?! He can fucking wait. The "real world" doesn't matter. I'm about to sip your frozen hot chocolate and I let love obliterate me the way it does in all the songs. I can't eat. Can't sleep. *There's no doubt. . . . I'm in deep.* At 3:15 A.M. I pick up my Motorola. I leave my cardboard box and step over the astrology slut who didn't get "lucky," the one passed out on the fucking floor because her friends are banging Dumb and Dumber. It smells like weed and *Heinies* and Drakkar Astroslutfucking Noir.

I open a window.

The air is good. Clean. When we move forward, I'll wake you up with my mouth. I'll kiss you on your Beckinsale. For now, the best I can do is give you a little love.

"So, first things first . . ." I channel you. I am you. "I hope you're feeling better. Second things second. It's my favorite kind of January New York night. Reminds me of being a kid. We had a clothesline, and my mom would hang up her bras out there and, in the winter, they'd be all stiff and crunchy. My mom . . . She had her problems, but this one time, this one winter, I got sick. Like nasty sick. Fever and all that. Anyway, I was in bed shivering and my mom brought all her frozen bras into my room to cool me off. And she said this was the thing about not having a lot, like if we had a dryer or whatever, those bras would be hot, but they did the trick. The wire and the nylon . . . My fever went down. And I was always happy we had a clothesline. Anyway. I'm just thinking of you, Vail. I'll see you in a few hours."

13

Thanks to a Xanax I bummed off a customer, I slept like Tom Hanks in his granddad's boat. I reach for my phone because that voicemail was my best work yet, and . . . Nothing. You didn't call.

Okay. That's okay. Seriously. I won't panic. Last time I panicked, I was wrong. You love my voicemails. You'll call soon and I'll tell you about the sleeping Virgo on the floor and maybe you'll put her in your sitcom.

But two hours into my shift . . . Nothing. Radio silence. Worst silence.

We are supposed to fuck in a bowl of frozen hot chocolate in a matter of hours and did I wreck it? Was the clothesline too much? No. *Stop it, Joe, stop it.* Everything is fine. It's still early, and we have plans to meet at seven. Ish. I keep you in my back pocket and you don't call, but you are having the week from hell. Or maybe not. Was it too much? Did I turn you off with my mother's drippy ice-cold lingerie?

Lunchtime. Mooney and me. Two ham sandwiches. No cheese.

No voicemail. Were you wrong about food poisoning? Was it something worse?

I want to call you to see how you are, but I can't. Our game is ping-pong. Back and forth. I can't go back if you don't come forth, and it's 3:12 P.M.

Are we on? Are we eating frozen hot chocolate and fucking our brains out?

I leave the shop without your Amy Sohn—I am slipping on the slush—and it's been twelve minutes and eleven hours since I let you in on the clothesline, since I (maybe) killed us with frozen bras. Or is it about your voicemail? *Drumroll, please.* Is that what this is about? Are you mad that I blew off your drumroll? I am just about to lose my fucking mind when you emerge from the shadows like a white knightess riding my black Motorola.

I pick it up on the first ring. Fuck it. I love you. "Vail!"

"Joe! Omigod I'm so sorry I've been MIA, but work is out of control."

Relief and no mention of bras, drumrolls, or my mother. "That stinks, baby."

The *baby* was maybe too much, and you cough. "Anyway, Barry is a mess over this big scene coming up. A party with six thousand extras in costume in our most important episode ever *and* shooting with a baby now that Miranda had Brady and—"

I AM SICK OF YOUR FUCKING JOB.

"Sounds like someone needs some frozen hot chocolate."

You didn't like that, but Christ. Aren't you thirsty? Don't you want me? "I'm sorry," you say. "I'm a mess. And I think you left me a voicemail, but in the craziness, I think I deleted it."

SCORE ONE FOR HANKS. "Oh, that's cool. It was nothing. Just checking in."

"Anyway, I have to be downtown for work, but I was thinking . . . I am so not up for going out-out, but would you wanna watch *Hannah* at my place? I have it on VHS *and* DVD."

"Of course you do."

"Ha. So how about we meet at the Beanery at like seven?"

YOU WANT TO FUCK ME YES YOU DO. "I will be there at six fifty-nine."

"Well, I will be there at sixty fifty-eight."

I am a man of my fucking word.

At 6:56 P.M., I open the door to the Beanery. My messenger bag is loaded. I have your scarf. I went back to the shop for your "signed" Amy Sohn, and I got you another book too, the script of *Hannah and Her Sisters.* I drop my messenger bag on a chair and wait my turn.

Dick nods. "'Sup?"

He said that like he's the Piven to my Cusack, and I do the same thing. "'Sup."

I look good for you, Vail. Second-first-date kind of good. I am *Romeo in black jeans,* and I open my Motorola. 7:02 P.M.

Dick hands me a coffee. Black. "So, how's it going?"

"Good," I say. "Vail's on her way over, and we're gonna hang out."

He winces like this is bad news—he is insane—and he walks off to grind beans. It's 7:09 when he finishes, and a girl at the counter licks her lips. She stares at Dick. I am invisible. And that's okay—I want you—but it's 7:14 and where are you? Are you okay?

The girl bats her eyelashes at Dick after he delivers her a latte. Paper cup. No lid. She leans over toward the barista. "I have to know. . . . Are you a Sagittarius? Because I'm a Sag . . ."

It's yet another astrology slut with too much makeup, and I hope that's not the reason you're so fucking late. It's 7:21. You are perfect. You don't need that black shit on your eyes and neither does the *Sag,* and Dick claps back. "I'm an animal," he says. "No sign."

The astrology slut laughs like that was funny and come on, Vail. It's 7:25 P.M. Get here.

Dick goes back to work, and the Sag stays where she is, staring at his butt, at his shoulders, as if he seemed remotely fucking interested, and I check my phone again. Nothing. Dick cracks his knuckles. He cracks his back. Everything goes *crack* and at some point I have to deal with *my* crackhead overlord who called again today but not until I go to heaven with you. You. Where are you?

The Sag fluffs her hair, preening. Dick doesn't look at her. He looks at me.

"The fuck's going on in that bag, son?"

The barista doesn't intimidate me, Vail. He probably thinks the cool one in *Swingers* was Vince Fucking Vaughn. I show him my bag of tricks. He strokes his comic book chin. "Yikes."

"Well, we haven't seen each other in a bit. Me and Vail."

"And she left the scarf at your place?"

"She hasn't been to my place."

"But you've been to *her* place. As in you're banging this chick?"

Chick and my face does all the talking—it says no—and it's 7:36 P.M. "Yikes," he says. "So let me get this straight. She's blowing you off. She's not blowing you, and you . . . you're blowing money on her."

"No, it's not like that. The book was free. It's a galley. The scarf is hers, and the screenplay was on clearance. . . ."

Why am I explaining myself to this guy? I know why, Vail. Because you're not here. "Anyway," I say. "We said sevenish, but she's stuck at work. She'll be here."

He shakes his head like I am the kid and he is the adult, and I go with it, pleading my case, telling him about our voicemail and our plans for tonight. "Oh, and we also talk on IM."

"Instant Messenger?"

"Well, we did, but her boss made her stop."

It sounds dumb when I say it out loud, but a lot of things about technology are like that. Dick sighs. I can't tell what he's thinking. I need to learn to do that with my face, to make it unreadable. It's

7:48 P.M. and it's dark out there, and Dick kicks back. "And how long you been seeing this Vail chick?"

The Sag with the black eyes and the latte clears her throat. "Oh, excuse me. Barista . . ."

Dick winks. "Watch and learn, kid."

He saunters up to her like he's Tom Cruise in *Cocktail,* and he folds his arms. Big and buff. Not like mine. *Soft and snuggly.* The Sag asks Dick for another lid—*My first was too loose*—and he tosses a lid on the counter instead of handing it to her. She taps it like it's a diamond necklace. "So," she says. "I feel like I've met you before. . . ."

Dick spreads his legs and yawns like he's in line at the fucking bank. He looks out the window. Is that you out there? No. He shrugs and winks at me as he answers her. "It's possible. I get around. . . ."

The Sag sips her latte and smiles. "I'll bet you do. . . ."

I'm going to throw up and the lid is still sitting there. I am still sitting here. Where are you, Vail? Where?

Dick tells the Sag to have a good night and looks at me like *do you believe this chick,* but she calls him back like the horny bad business lady in *Cocktail.* "Oh, barista . . . One more thing."

He smiles at me. *Watch and learn.* Fuck that. I'm not Dick. I am Tom Fucking Hanks. I am your type, and you are my type. I adjust my Portnoy as the Sag writes her cell phone number *and* her work email *and* her Hotmail on a napkin. She gives it to Dick and says he can even call her right now if he wants, you know, so she has *his* number too.

"Yeah," Dick says. "Sure."

But then he doesn't do it. He doesn't call the Sag.

I have to stay calm. We're not like them, Vail. We've got *Mail*—8:14 is not late-late. It's just girl late, and cell phones don't work underground. Dick comes back.

"Look," he says, spinning the dog tag he wears as if he went to war. He didn't go to *war.* He tries to make little movies, and obviously, he's not even that good. "Joe," he says. "You're not asking for my advice, but I'm gonna give it to you anyway. Scram."

"Leave?"

"Skedaddle. Fuck off."

I would never. And he squares up like we're about to fight.

"Are you banging this girl?"

We won't bang. We'll make love. "We've been intimate."

He grins like he knows I got a half a hand job. "So when did you last see her?"

"I dunno, Sunday, I guess."

He scratches the back of his neck and where are you, Vail? Why are you doing this to me? "Joe, come on. Be real. She leaves you hanging in a *coffee shop*. . . . And you're sitting here with your bag of . . . Don't you get it? Even if she does show up, you're toast."

My hands are shaking, and Dick says he gets it. He's been where I am, pussy-whipped.

"That's not me. I'm not . . ." I don't use that fucking word.

"It's cool," he says. "It happens. Mine was this model from France. Never seen anyone hotter. . . ."

I feel bad for the Sag. She's reduced to pretending to read an errant *Voice* and her castaway lid is *still* on the counter and is that what I am? A *lid*?

Dick snaps his fingers at me. "Look," he says. "It's simple. It's girls. If you want any chance with this girl . . ."

"I do."

"Then you gotta leave *her* in the wind. Make her hope like hell that she didn't lose you, show her that you're the prize, the money, the catch."

Another girl arrives, just as hungry for Dick, and I look out the fucking window and my phone rings—finally—but it's not you. It's him.

Angus.

My legs do me dirty, *shake shake shake*, and the coffee girls are competing for Dick, and I look around the room, the white clean walls, the antique overstuffed chairs. Every girl in here, all the seemingly smart subway minxes with messenger bags and their novelty journals wide open, pens in their mouths as they nibble . . . Every single one of them is eye-fucking the barista as if he's the real deal, as if he's Tom Fucking Cruise. He's not even a bartender, and okay, he has muscles—*soft and snuggly*—and okay, he has a buzz cut—*I love your hair . . . so '70s*—but there's no denying it anymore.

He knows *something* about women.

It's 9:01 P.M. and I'm a loser. I'm back in the third grade, on crutches after an "accident" with the stairs at "home." Snow day. Not allowed to walk home from school. Not like this. Mrs. Pearson whispering to Mr. Calder.

His vile mother said he can fend for himself. Can you believe that monster?

I thought I was the monster, unlovable, and maybe I am. Maybe it's a stench I can't kick. Maybe I really do need a fucking father figure who's not a crazy old bookworm.

Dick hands me a napkin like I'm crying. I'm not. Am I?

"D.B.A.," he says. "Couple of blocks south. My buddy Schlitz is behind the bar. Tell him you know me. I'll see ya there in a bit."

"And if she comes . . . Vail?"

"Joe," he says. "Go to the fucking bar."

D.B.A. is loud, and my Motorola is so quiet it must be dead. But it isn't.

You don't want me. You don't see me as the Tom Hanks to your Meg Ryan, and I want a vodka soda, but Dick says I need hard stuff.

"Okay," I say. "I'll have that stuff you got at the Indian place . . . Jim Henson."

Schlitz doubles over—he's a blond version of Dick—and Dick elbows me. "It's called *Jameson*, son." And then he raises his shot glass. "To my long gone big brother," he says, kissing those dog tags while all the girls turn to mush. "First of the day, God willing. . . ."

"See ya tomorrow!" shouts Schlitz.

I'm a part of this now, Vail. Yep, I'm the butt of an inside joke that Dick says will haunt me to my grave—*It's called Jameson, son*—and next thing you know I'm one of those dudes doing *Jäger bombs.*

It's not the worst way to spend a night without you. The *bombs* hit hard, fast. The caffeine and the booze rev me *up* and how is this even legal? Schlitz and Dick aren't the best but they're okay. They're a little older than Dumb and Dumber, a little smarter, like they rolled off a superior assembly line where they got the muscles and dog tags, the fuck-you-tight white T-shirts. What can I say, *baby*? Your bad week turned into *my* bad week. I can't help it. Maybe I'm bombed, but it feels good that these cool dudes kinda dig me.

Dick drops a twenty on the bar. "I got this."

No one ever bought me a drink, and the bomb explodes and tickles the thing with the feathers. The more I drink, the more I tell Dick about the way our Missed Connections are pulling us closer. He says I'm wrong. "If she missed you, she would connect with you. The end."

I push back. We are romantic. We are Napoleon and Josephine. We are *Love Letters.* He says it again. "If she missed you, she would connect with you. The end."

I tell him about Cynthia, about your boss, about the night with Angus. His eyes pop out of his head. "A *hand* job? Wait. She didn't even suck you off?"

I don't like that phrase, and I'm not *that* drunk. I have to stop talking about you because Dick came here to get laid and Schlitz wants his *wingman.* I am of no use. These girls don't interest me, and that's okay. It's okay to be DOA in D.B.A. But then again, you blew me off. Are you like the girls in this bar? Is *soft and snuggly* a bad thing? It sounds like a bad thing, like a laundromat owned by Mr. Tongue and Mister Softee.

Dick downs a shot of Jim Henson. "Look," he says. "I'm not a dick."

"I know."

"I'm just trying to help you out."

A girl taps his shoulder. "Do you have a cigarette?"

Dick has a cigarette, same way he has a lighter. He and Schlitz are the Cusack and the Piven, and that makes me a third banana, as if anyone wants more than two. Dick just got another number, and he lifts that fucking comic book of a fucking chin.

"Kid," he says. "You gotta stop sulking."

I can't. I'm a drunk banana, a poor man's Piven, so fuck it. I tell them what you said, *soft and snuggly.* And Schlitz spits tequila—a girl bought him a shot—and Dick tells him to piss off.

"Look," he says. "You did mess up, but if you want this . . ."

"I told you. I want this."

"Then learn from the past, my boy. Look around. Women don't like 'nice.' Soft and snuggly? Dude, come on. They *want* to want nice. They're all high on rom-coms, but deep down, chicks want to be choked. Tortured. They can't help it, kid. It's in their DNA and no rom-*con* is gonna change that. So what do you do? Here's what you do. You erase the words *Tom* and *Hanks* from your vocabulary and grow a set."

He sniffs and wipes his nose, and oh, okay. They're not just high on bombs and Jim Henson. They're on cocaine.

Dick waves his dog tags. "Check it," he says. "Shit happens. But the shit gets worse if you want someone else to wipe your ass. Man up and wipe it. You want the girl?"

"Yes."

"You want a bump?"

"No."

"You want to know how to get the fucking girl, Joe-boy?"

It might be the Jäger bombs talking, but who knows? Maybe Dick has the keys to the castle. Maybe this is the brother that *I* never had. "Yes, I fucking do, Dick."

"First things first. Tomorrow, you get a buzz cut."

"But she likes my hair. She said so."

"Second things second, son. That's *why* you cut it. Fuck with her. Take it away. Third things third . . . A buzz cut is good because when you go down on her . . ."

I never did that, but I laugh like I get it, like I did do that.

He rubs the back of his head. "It's all about *friction.*" I never felt like my ID was quite so fucking fake, and he laughs. "You ever see *Magnolia*?"

Schlitz goes in for a high five, and the girls around us shake their tail feathers like hope is all they have, like Dick and Schlitz are all they want. A girl with red hair buys them a couple of shots (what the fucking fuck) and they don't say thank you and she doesn't get mad.

"Seduce and Destroy," says Dick. "It's all about Seduce and Destroy."

I Seduced you, but I do not want to Destroy you. "Okay."

"The trench coat vibe you got going on . . ." I am not wearing a trench coat, but it feels like my sweater just grew three feet. "Lose it, Joe. Man up."

He gets my *digits,* and he says there's more where that came from. He winks at the girl who bought them the shots, and that's my cue. I get it. I stand.

"Oh, and Joe. If she does call . . . fuck that shit. No contact. Zero. Make *her* come to *you.*"

On the way home, I stop at the only video store still open.

There are couples milling about, a few loner-sad stragglers like me. I pick up *Magnolia* and get in line, and my Motorola comes to life.

It's you. You're calling.

The guy behind the counter groans. "Dude," he says. "You renting that or what?"

I want to know where you are, how you are, but it's late. So late. Dick told me what to do and the clerk is impatient and the couple behind me is antsy. Everyone knows what they want, how to get it.

You are here but not here, and Jägermeister is a bad influence or a good influence—I DON'T KNOW WHERE JIM HENSON ENDS AND I BEGIN—and it's a fork in the road. I'm drunk behind the wheel and I am not Robert Frost, and the music is too loud—*If my train runs off the tracks, pick it up, pick it up*—and do I do it, Vail?

Do I pick it up? Or do I let my new friend Dick lead the way?

14

Life is confusing sometimes. Like with *Magnolia.* Tom Cruise doesn't have a buzz cut in the movie. He has long hair. He has a fucking *ponytail,* but Dick says we're not Tom Cruise.

So I did it, Vail. I shaved my fucking head. You don't know it, because we're on a break. I send you to voicemail every time you call, and it's not easy; it's fucking hell. I haven't listened to any of your voicemails, and Dick is right. Talk is cheap. This is a long road. As the man, I have to show you that I'm worth it. Teach you to respect me as I transform and begin to look like *I* respect me.

I'm not buff. Not yet. It's only been five days. And it goes without saying that lifting weights is not my thing. It's also not easy with Mooney and his cheap shots—*You look like a skinhead who wandered out of Auschwitz*—but Dick says that pain is the way you know you're doing it right. *Soft and snuggly* is why you ditched me. *Hard as a rock* is why I'll get you back.

"Excuse me."

Customer on the floor. A woman. This is practice, so I make like Dick. No eye contact. Let her look at *me.* "What do you need?"

"Do you know the *Amelia Bedelia* books?"

It hurts. *You* know the *Amelia Bedelia* books, but I push you outta my head and laugh at her like she's dumb. "Sure thing, whatever."

She tucks her hair behind her left ear. "I mean, thank you."

Dick says you girls like to be spit on, so I bolt to KIDS without checking if this *chick* is with me—she is—and I don't elaborate when she asks how I like working here. I swear, Vail . . . It's not like I don't feel guilty being such an ass (I do!), but it makes sense when Dick explains it. It's not your fault that I *taught* you that I think I'm not good enough. I'm the one who messed up and brought you to Angus's fucking house, so now I gotta get strong so I can teach you that I *am* good enough.

I am *growing a set,* Vail. You want me? You know where to find me. *The end.*

In KIDS, I flex what will soon be my *pecs* under my new tight white T-shirt. Hanes . . . for *men.* The customer bats her eyelashes the way girls do for Dick. "I don't want to bother you," she says. "But I can't reach it. Do you mind?"

Unreal, truly. She's at least five seven—she can reach the fucking book—and the rules of *Seduce and Destroy* are legit. Here I am, being a total dick, and here is this woman wanting *more more more . . . how do you like it . . . how do you like it?* I pick up the *Amelia Bedelia*s, and my customer covers her mouth with her hand. Dick says that's how we know you're *in heat,* when you touch yourselves. I don't want her, Vail. But Dick says that you're all connected. He says that if you sense a little competition, you'll throw yourself at me.

The woman looks at me. I mean, she fucking *looks* at me. "You're a godsend, Joe."

I laugh at her, and *she* laughs at herself, and her pelvis tilts my way. Dick is a genius, he is. I ring her up, and you do it again. You call me.

I do it again. I send you to voicemail. You need to show me your *face.*

Dick has my back, and it's hard, pushing you away, especially when you didn't leave a voicemail for me this time. I sneak outside to call him like I'm an addict, like he's my sponsor.

"This is good," he says. "She's mixing it up. You're getting in her head."

"Or she's forgetting about me once and for all. . . ."

"Drop and give me twenty, you fucking pussy."

He's not an asshole. He doesn't *really* expect me to do push-ups on the sidewalk, but it's his way of telling me to hang in there. It's a new word in my vocabulary. *Negging.* According to Dick, I didn't *neg* you, which meant that you didn't get to feel daffy and silly. Pretty. He goes to NYU part-time and he's a *film producer* and he knows so many people. I'm lucky that he has my back. And he's right. *Magnolia* is genius.

"Later, Dick."

"Later, Goldschläger."

And that's it. Another day without you comes to an end. I hit the gym. I joined Crunch; Schlitz had an in. This is where I punch things. Bags that let me pound them, bags that come back for more. I lift things up and put things down, and then I go in the locker room.

A few days ago, I did almost quit.

Dick was on a tangent about how girls are sharks and we are killer whales and Valentine's Day is *open season* on sharks. Then, out of nowhere, he pulled a black case out of his locker. I gave him shit, the way guys do. "You putting on your makeup there, buddy?"

"Nah," he said. "I'm *playing* with my makeup. The chemistry in *here.*"

He pointed at his chest, and then it was fast. *Bam* kind of fast, where you can tell he's done this every day for a lot of days. He pulled a needle and jammed it into a little bottle and then he yanked his boxers and jammed the needle in his ass. And nobody reacted! I mean, it's fucking *steroids,* but Dick laughed at me.

"It's just some juice, Goldballs. Chill."

I *was* sort of staring, but watching him stab himself made me long for you. Life is simpler with you. Plus I think the poor guy might be getting ripped off. You've seen him, Vail. He's not Mr. Universe or anything. And the gym isn't a bodybuilding *Rocky* kinda complex. It's fucking Crunch. They have dance classes!

He must've been able to feel me talking shit in my head, and he slammed his locker. "Laugh all you want, Goldboy. By this time next week, you'll be bugging me for a source."

It's pretty obvious that this "source" isn't a mystery. It's fucking Schlitz. And Schlitz is a twig! But then he slapped me. Guy to guy style. Like the way they do in war movies.

"Life is war, son. When you swim with the sharks, when you go to the club or pitch a big investor, you take a bump. You put you first. My brother was high as a kite when they raided Iraq. This country, every girl I bang, no guy slays an apex predator without a little *bump* of something. It's the American way. You do whatever it takes to get what you fucking want."

Sometimes things just make sense, Vail. And I'm luckier than Dick in the sense that I don't need drugs. It was the first time that I initiated the high five and it felt good.

"Bitches and pitches," he said. "Bitches and pitches all the live-long *life*."

I wouldn't use the B-word when it comes to you or any girl—I'll always be a little part Mister Softee—but the gym is good for me. It's easier to push bad thoughts away. You get kinda high, kind of above it all where you could *crunch* the living daylights out of anyone who fucks with you. Angus is calling all the time and do I give a fuck? No. I send that *bitch* to voicemail. My shoulders are squaring up and do you remember when you said you *liked* that I wasn't a gym rat? I get it now. That wasn't you at your best because that wasn't me at my best. That was just you trying to fight your own nature. Dick is right. Women want hard men. I see the girls in the gym, the way they glance and turn red. And a strong body is the home of a strong fucking mind. I don't snap a rubber band when you pop into my head anymore. I punch a bag. I sweat.

I'm still me. I *miss you like crazy* when I retire to my cardboard box and pull on my Portnoy. I come on your scarf and turn off my phone and fight the night. I toss and turn over things I want to tell you, things I'd never tell Dick, how strange I feel in my skin, how I tried to eat Indian again but got the runs even worse, how I miss my hair, your hands in my hair, how I might die of wanting to call you. And then the morning hits me like a sucker punch and it's fuck that namby-pamby shit. Let's *do* this. I turn my stupid phone on and I shower and I shave. I ignore Dumb and Dumber when they call me *G.I. Joe.* Fuck them and their astrology sluts. The astrology sluts are different now. They touch their hair when I walk into the kitchen, bare-chested in boxers. They adjust their bra straps and ask if I'm seeing anyone.

I drink milk on Dumb's dime out of the fucking carton and shrug. Am I seeing you, Vail?

On the street, I turn on my Motorola.

ONE NEW VOICEMAIL . . . from Mr. fucking Mooney. I hit Play.

"Christ Almighty, Joseph, I don't understand the point of that thing if it's never on. Do better. Alas, you have a *visitor.* A very pushy visitor. So, you best get here now. As in right now."

It's the best voicemail of my life. The reason God invented cell phones. You did it! You came to the shop. I can't get there fast enough, and I don't have to wait long. Valentine's Day is coming and Dick did say girls get antsy this time of year. Horny. I pick up the pace. I wonder if you're wearing a skirt. I wonder if you cried, if the people on your sitcom know that you couldn't take it anymore, the yearning. I should be cool, make you wait, but I'm in the best shape of my life and you need to see me. You miss me. You want me.

I yank the door of the shop, and Angus Kaplan blocks me in my tracks.

"So, how was your first summer in Maine, Jimbo?"

It's a little ironic, Vail, and I'd be laughing if I weren't so totally fucking fucked.

I'm jacked for the first time ever. I could kick Angus Kaplan's bony ass six ways to Sunday, but we're stuck in the back seat of his fucking limo, and his fucking driver could be a body double for the Incredible Fucking Hulk. Fuck.

Angus bites his Ray-Bans. They crack. Why? "It's a felony, Jimmy. I looked it up."

"I really am working on it, Angus."

He tosses his sunglasses out the window. "So where's my book?"

He rubs his nose and orders the driver to play that song, the one about stealing the wine and getting the girl, and I was wrong, Vail. As it turns out, there are things that *don't* fall through the cracks. Angus didn't forget about our deal. He marked his calendar—I NEVER SAW A CALENDAR IN THAT CRACK DEN—and I'm staying cool. Singing along and convincing him that I've got the money—I have no money; I owe Crunch a lot of money—and my guns are of no use in this town car. His driver eyes me like he'd kill me just for kicks.

Angus fires up something in a little square of tinfoil.

I try to roll down the window, but I can't. The child protective bullshit is in effect, and I am healthy now. I can't be near this toxic shit, and it won't stop hitting me. The worst part is that I haven't even gotten to dwell on it, the sad truth under this town car of a truck that ran me over.

It wasn't you in the bookstore. You didn't come for me. You don't want me. And I don't even get to curl up in a ball in my *Bell Bottom Blues.* We're rolling up to the gargoyles. Angus is pissing himself and WHY DID I MAKE A DEAL WITH A RICH BORED JUNKIE?

"So what is this?" he says. "Did you go to *prison* when I was in recovery?"

That's a dig at my hair and "recovery" is the road to relapse and the driver hits a button. I open the damn door.

In the elevator, Angus takes another piss and waves his thing around. He says he's joining the circus and he says the circus is joining him and he grabs a hat off my head except I don't have a hat. I grab his wrist (I have biceps) and he bites my arm (I am bleeding) and by the time we make it to the sinking fucking living room where Peter Frampton is alive and louder than ever, Angus has done the unthinkable. Pissed on Philip Roth and Edwidge Danticat, hawked a heroin-laced loogie on some choice Paul Fucking Auster.

He drops his mess of a body onto the butter and leather. I eye Emily Dickinson on a shelf. That's new. *Sitting like a princess perched in her electric chair.*

"So, time's up. Where's my Franzen?"

"I'm working on it, Angus. I told you. Money is tight."

He pulls a pipe out of his pocket. New robe. Red and silk. Stained as fuck. "Not good enough, Jerry. I want my *Twenty-Seventh Town.*"

The word is *City,* motherfucker, and could I rob a bank? No, I couldn't. I look at Toni Morrison. Only inches from Emily Dickinson. *Seduce and Destroy.* Don't think. Do. Angus hangs his head between his legs so the drugs get to his head a little faster, and I cross the sinking living room. I lift the flap of my messenger bag, and I pick up one endangered lady wordsmith, and then another. I'm not robbing a bank. I'm not even robbing Angus Kaplan. This is a rescue mission. But also yes, I robbed that *Boogie Nights* derivative do-nothing right in fucking front of him and *Damn, it feels good to be a gangster.* My heart pounds like weights at Crunch. Emily and Toni are safe now, and Angus is oblivious. He's even dancing, if you can call it that. It's a high. . . . Picking up books and putting them down in my bag. *Sensitive thugs, y'all need hugs* so I widen the rescue mission and grab my boy Philip Roth. Angus is on another planet and I'm a baller with a buzz cut so I scoop up my man Bukowski. And that's it. My bag is loaded. Better than a gun, because books are forever, unlike bullets that just kill you.

Angus sways and his eyes go limp and thin. "Did I ever tell you about Kelly Demon?"

After I throw up on the sidewalk, I walk to the subway.

I can't believe I did it, Vail. A week ago, I didn't have *a set.* I was a victim. A beggar. But I just marched out of that fucker's penthouse with rare, precious cargo. I'm not gonna wind up in prison. I'm not that scared little bitch, not anymore. I catch my train and I take a seat and I don't panic. I don't piss my pants. I lift the flap on my messenger bag and there she is. My princess, the amazing Emily Dickinson. Encased in plastic, pulling me back home.

Hope is the thing with feathers.

I grab her by the spine. I open her up and find my favorite parts, the ones that stick. I feel the girls on the train wanting to know who I am, wishing I would take my Polaroid Nikon eyes off Emily and look at them. Once upon a time, I'd be counting the seconds until I could go home and check Missed Connections. But that's not me, Vail. It's like Dick said at D.B.A. a few nights ago. *His boy is all growns up.* I get back to the shop, and I go to Craigslist and I pound the keyboard like a boss, because I am a boss. It's right there on the walls of my gym. *Crunch: It's a Movement.* The old me was weak. Softee Joe got pushed around by Angus. I'm stronger now. I saved great works by great women and now I will bail out the young scared boy I used to be, the helpless softy who let a spoiled-ass crackhead get the best of him and pull a gun on you. Those days are long gone and the subject of my ad is my version of a bump. It's my *juice:*

RARE BOOKS FOR SALE. CASH ONLY.

15

I'm about to go on my fifth date tonight, and no, I'm not cheating. It's my new side business, Vail. A solid way to make some bank so I can pay off Angus. I'm also putting some of my dough aside for us. I want to take care of you. *You.* You've stopped calling and it feels like the end. My side gig is a good way to cope. I'm a busy man. Buyers find me on Craigslist and we wheel and deal. I'm making more money than I ever did, and yeah . . . It's a little gross for my life to be all capitalism and Crunch as the city grows pinker by the hour, as Valentine's Day approaches. But Dick is right. I am building a better me, and timing *is* on our side. Girls always get hungry for the one that got away in mid-fucking February. And that's me. It has to be me. Right?

"Joseph!"

Fucking Mooney, and again, Dick is right. I do need a better job, but this is the one I have. And who knows? Maybe the rest of my life already started. Maybe my "summer in Maine" is so fucking profitable that I rent us a loft in . . .

Gently, Joseph. I knock on Mooney's door.

"Don't knock," he seethes. "Get in here."

Not a good start, and worse inside. He's on his feet, wrapped around the phone cord. He covers the receiver and growls. "Angus Kaplan will be the death of me, Joseph. Mark my words."

Not gonna panic. I'm a hero. I saved Emily Dickinson from the fire. Paper covers rock, and Cruise covers Cusack. I did nothing wrong. I roll my eyes. "What did that crackhead do now?"

Mooney shushes me and goes back to yelling into the phone. "I never sold you any Emily Goddamn Dickinson, and neither did Joseph."

My nerves do creep up on me because fuck fuck fuck. Is Angus onto me? Yes, he is, and Mooney slams slams the receiver into the cradle.

"All right, Joseph, I'm going to ask you this once."

Real men use their heads, not their words. I nod.

"Did you steal books from Angus?"

Real men don't answer questions. They *ask* questions. "Are you kidding me, dude?"

He stares at me, and he hates the new me, muscles and *dude* bombs. But I like the new me. Fucking Robin Hood minus the sidekick.

"Angus says he's missing Emily Dickinson, among others. He seems to think *you* are a thief in the night."

I do not break. Not for Mooney, not for Angus, not for anyone. "Well, that's bullshit, Mr. Mooney. I mean, c'mon. The guy's a crackhead."

Mooney says capitalism and crackheads go hand in hand and he opens an old ledger and no. I won't go down like this. I am so close, Vail. I have twenty-five Benjamins in my messenger bag. Dumb to carry, but dumber to leave it home with Dumb and Dumber. Point is, I can soon deliver *The Twenty-Seventh City.* I'm gonna do that after I find Emily a new home, when I save enough cash to snag both the *City* and a new pad for us.

I grab the ledger and slam it shut. "Enough," I say. "I'm not a thief."

Mooney doesn't hate *everything* about me. Mostly, he just misses me, the way he points at my bag. "Going somewhere, are we?"

Yep. Going to sell Emily Dickinson to a douchebag with a *loft*. "Just chilling."

He grunts (he hates that word, *chilling*) and I try not to think about Emily Dickinson in my messenger bag. It is the thing with feathers. Not just my hope but ours. I will not break.

Mooney lights a cigar. I don't like the way he doesn't offer *me* a fucking stogie. "Apologies," he says. "It is impossible to take you seriously with that getup."

It's not a *getup*, and I have to get out of here. I have to move Miss Dickinson before she gets me fired. I slap my rock-hard thighs. "I'm gonna head out."

Mooney blows his nose on a dirty napkin. "Off to see that hussy with the boots, are you?"

Dick says I talk too much (real men know the power of silence), so I nod. It's not easy, Vail. I feel bad for Mooney, I do. He's on my side. He trusts me, he misses me, but I have to put you first.

"Well, that's a shame you're unavailable," he says. "Martha made a meat loaf."

My dumb heart breaks. He had to go there, to the wife. "I didn't know."

"She wanted you to come by for supper, but you have other plans again. . . . That's your right, young man."

That's a first for my Moleskine. I'm not *boy* anymore. I'm a man. "How is Mrs. Mooney?"

He rambles in the roundabout, blogging-out-loud way that he does when he doesn't want to be alone. I don't mind him, and I do like Martha. She gave me my first Paula Fox, and she makes a killer meat loaf.

Oh no. It's happening. I'm backsliding and getting soft and no. I'm too close. It's almost Valentine's Day. Like Dick said yesterday, this is crunch time. *V-Day is D-Day, son. Every chick in this city is on a post-9/11 mission to lock it down. Vail will run back to you, and you gotta be ready.* I don't want to hurt poor Mr. Mooney, but a man's gotta do what a man's gotta do.

"Hey, I'm gonna hit the road, but thanks to Martha."

I expect him to snap at me to sit, but then he pulls a rabbit out of his hat. There it is, Vail. The pink fucking Polo shirt.

"Well," he says. "To each his own. Enjoy your pink blouse."

An hour later, it's game on. I'm climbing the subway stairs at the Throop and Gates, back in the old neighborhood. I don't call it *home* (it's just where I started), and the directions I printed off MapQuest are shit. Orange cones, dead ends, and more cones, but I'm the man, so I find where I'm going.

The buyer is a liar. He described the building as a "warehouse turned speakeasy," but it's just another shithole pile of rubble, the kind of place where perverts and junkies huddle in the dark.

I take out my phone to call my source, but oh, that's right. I don't have his phone number. I wish I could email him, but even the Motorola has its limits, and the building is scary. A kid in my fourth-grade class died in a place like this, but that wasn't me, and now is now. No lock on the front door, and the rats are already scuttling. Shaky. There's a staircase made out of rust that leads to what used to be an office. Lights on somehow, someway up there.

I take Emily Dickinson out of my bag. "Yo. You guys up there?"

"Come up, Kevin."

That's my fake name (I had to protect myself), and the lights in the hidden second story go out. My skin crawls. That voice again. "Come on up."

I channel my inner Dick. "Nah, you guys come down."

It occurs to me that Cusack had his Piven, that Dick has his Schlitz, and I have no backup and wait. Did it just get darker? I think it just got darker. I hold on to *Hope.* I remember the first time I read it, sitting on the stoop by my school and looking at pigeons, wondering what Emily thought of those birds, the only ones I knew. That's a story I could tell you, a story I will tell you, and a rat crosses over my foot. Is that an omen? No. I'm the man.

But I'm only one man. They come out of nowhere, two of them, maybe three. Something lands on my left foot and something else crushes my kidney and the third fist mashes up my face.

I hit the ground hard, and I let go (when you're done, you're done). All the punching bags I've been whaling on at Crunch didn't prepare me for this. Those bags that can't hit back, and I failed you and me and Emily Dickinson. The bad guys have her, and they're on the run. I am passing out and bleeding and I can almost smell the meat loaf, same way I hear the old man in my head, what he said when he locked me in the cage.

A little bit of hope can do a whole lot of damage.

I come to on the floor of the warehouse and I'm not gonna call the cops.

I wouldn't even if I could. This is on me, Vail. I came here alone. I thought book people weren't violent people. Well, I was wrong. They got my Emily Dickinson and all the cash I made off the other books. I reach for my groin, and yes, they got me there too. Back in the day, getting my ass kicked wasn't so bad. I was kinda chubby. I had a gut. Padding. Pain hurts more when you're strong than when you're weak.

I fumble in my bag. It's not a total disaster. I have my wallet. I have my cell phone. And there's a light in the darkness of my screen, a thing with feathers in the form of three words.

One new voicemail. From *you.*

Jackpot and I owe Dick a case of Jim Henson. Once again, he predicted the fucking future. You came back for me, and I *am* the one who got away. You miss me and you want me so much that you don't care about timing. You are openly chasing me down a few *days* before

V-Day. I am ready to receive you, Miss Lonely. I got jacked for you—wait till you see my arms!—and I got *jacked* for you—if that's not love I don't know what is—and gone are the days of jacking off over you. We're about to get real. I press the best button on the phone: Play.

"Joe, it's me. Vail. Look, this is ridiculous. We're adults. . . . At least that's what I thought. And honestly, I'm fed up. Okay? Okay. Ten voicemails and you ignore me and that's it. The end. Be at the Beanery at 8:30 tonight and please don't feed me a line about how you're 'busy.' I don't want you. It's over. It's like I've said for days now. I just want my scarf."

Click.

16

I didn't go to the Beanery. I couldn't go, Vail. You don't *really* want your scarf. And you're not done with me. You called me! I know the way you are. You miss me. You wouldn't come out and say it, and you probably think you're playing hard to get, preserving dignity or whatever, but I know you. I don't care about the stupid fucking words. I heard it in your voice. The yearning.

Also, I'm a little busy right now. The mugging was a game-changing setback. Angus won't budge—when the fuck did he get a calendar?—so I had to get creative. Yes, I broke yet another law. I stole Mooney's *Twenty-Seventh City* from the basement of the shop. I don't know how I'll get the money or cover my ass, but I have some time to figure it out. I am risking my life and my job, and that's the way of the world for a guy like me with no backup, no family.

I am risking it all for you, Vail. Love isn't blind. It's twenty fucking twenty. I know exactly what I'm doing and I'm good with every bit of it because all of it, in the end, is for you.

My subway car grinds to a stop, and it hurts. I'm sore. But on I go, climbing the *longest set of stairs in New York City.* The gargoyles don't get to me, not today, and Angus buzzes me up.

Right off the bat, something is off. Wrong. He's wearing sunglasses, the kind with mirrors. He grabs the Franzen, and he doesn't sway. There's no music today. He doesn't open the book. He doesn't tear out a page to wipe his ass. He just tosses it in the fireplace like it's a piece of scrap paper, and then he picks up a trash bag full of robes. "Walk me out?"

This isn't the Angus I know. This man is sober. Silent. He pushes the button on the elevator and in we go and it's hard, Vail. Hard not to stare at him. Hard to know how to be when someone you know turns into someone else. And then the sunglasses are off and who knew Angus had eyes, the kind that see things.

"So, who beat the crap out of you?"

"No one."

He holds his head high. Smiles like a child. "I'm going to rehab."

"Well, that's good, right?"

"I'm not as bad as you think, Joe."

"I never said you're bad."

"Eh," he says. "I'm too sensitive for this world. Kelly Damon is having a baby this week."

"I'm sorry, Angus."

"For what, Joe? Stealing from me or taking advantage of me at my weakest?"

I should say something, defend myself or deny it. But then the doors open.

On the sidewalk, the town car is waiting. Angus hands me his sunglasses. "Oh, and Jerry," he says. "I changed the code. So don't even try to get in there."

Two days later, and it's like the world is over. My own little private September 11, part two. Minus you.

I know. I guess I am kinda lucky in one way. I'm on basement duty until my face isn't *a grotesque crime scene.* And Mooney's gout is back, so I don't have to worry about him coming down here and realizing that his *Twenty-Seventh City* has gone missing. But it's hard to feel anything close to good. I stopped going to the gym. I stopped waiting for you to call. I know what I am. *I'm a loser, baby, so why don't you* . . . Nah. No one wants to see a guy with a black eye and a bloated jaw, let alone be bothered to kill the poor fuck.

"Joeeeeeey. . . . Honeeyyyyy."

And there she is. The new woman in my life. Farrah *Virginia* Carpenter: Astrology Slut Slash Bookseller. Quotes that Concrete Blonde song that made it even easier for shitheads in school to bust my balls. Mooney found her from some temp agency to cover the floor while I lick my wounds, the ones you won't lick for me, with me. God, I'm pathetic.

"What is it, Virginia?"

"I need you, Joeeeey."

That's what I want you to say to me but nope. Nope!

I trudge up the stairs, toward the woman who is not, never will be for me. Imagine choosing to be Virginia when you could be Farrah.

"What's wrong now?"

"You look so cute today, Joey. So cute that I forgot."

Her parents were reaching with both Farrah *and* Virginia. They should have just gone with *Vagina.* Never known a girl who just fucking *wants* everyone to stare at her. She pulls at her bikini top (it is winter) and she whines at me nonstop. *Joeeey* . . . *baby* . . . It is Joe. And this is a *bookstore.* The pilled pink triangles struggle to hold on to her wide, low-hanging breasts and the pigtails. . . . The knee socks and the cologne-soaked men's shirt, unbuttoned. Open. I can't, Vail. I won't. I want her to cover up and call a psychic hotline for help. I don't want her.

I want *you,* damn it.

"Don't kill me," she says. "But I lost the ledger again."

The ledger is on the counter, where it lives, *tied* to a fucking latch. She touches my back—stop it—and I pick up her fucking *Post.*

"Oopsie! My God, you're so smart. I never thought to look there."

I'm a loser, baby, so why don't you kill me and Vagina and the whole damn world.

I miss you, Vail. I hate that I miss you.

"Joey," she says. "Look at my arms. Goose bumps!"

No shit. It's thirty-two degrees and I can't take this, Vail. Her nipples that aren't yours. The sunflower tattoo a few centimeters above her vagina that she's always petting. Do you have any tattoos? Will I ever see you again? Is this hell? Vagina opens *Cosmo* and points at her *confession.*

"The real news is . . . I'm published, Joey!"

I follow her painted fingernail to a gross little story about the time a guy stuck his dick in her butthole. When he pulled out, there were Pop Rocks on his thing. *Pop Rocks.*

If we were still together, I could tell you about Vagina, and you could put her in your sitcom. But we're not. "Nice. Congrats. Your family must be proud."

"Do you like Pop Rocks, Joey? Because this time of the year . . . it's all I can think about . . . Pop Rocks and—"

"Allergic!"

She says that's impossible—*Joey . . . baby . . . don't get crazy*—and Mooney saves the day with a scream.

"Joseph!"

I am the worst kind of Cusack. I am *Better Off Dead.*

The old guy, as you called him, well, he can't get enough of me. The bruises, the idiocy, the way I whine about Vagina. I knock on the door, and he cackles. "The fighter returns!"

"What's up?"

"I meant to ask you, Joseph. Did that girlfriend of yours do this to you? Did she wallop you with those vaguely sapphic boots?"

"She's not gay."

"I told you, boy. Didn't like her . . . didn't trust her. . . . And don't pick at the scab if you want it to heal, damn it."

I take my hand off my face. "Sorry. How's the gout?"

He grins. He won't talk about the gout. "Did you see Virginia's top today?"

"Yeah, about that. I think we need to call the whorehouse."

"Temp agency, Joseph. Don't be crass."

"Okay, but half the time, she can't find the ledger, so the numbers are gonna be off. . . ." As in thousands of dollars off, in case he *does* go downstairs.

"The pigtails, Joseph . . . You could bone her, you know. And if you don't, well . . . The pigtails do suggest a certain desire for an older man. . . ."

I can't do it, Vail. I can't have that image in my head. Plus, there's his wife. What about Martha? What about *love*? I sigh like I get it, because what else can I do? "Okay, but for real, a few customers have complained about her. A mom said she felt uncomfortable bringing her kids in . . . the whole bikini thing, and Vagina was all over her husband right in front of her."

He grins. "A slip more Freudian I cannot imagine, Joseph."

I DIDN'T MEAN IT LIKE THAT, and he rubs his big fat foot and kicks back in his chair. "She is a bit Bukowski, I suppose. Makes you want to take a cold shower, or perhaps a long, warm steam in the Russian baths. . . . Donna Tartt via *The Best Little Whorehouse in Texas*."

"Vagina doesn't know shit about Donna Tartt. And Donna Tartt wears suits."

Mr. Mooney slams a drawer. "Joseph, you are grumpy. You will not take your anger out on me or our new young lass."

"It's not me. It's her, and you don't get it. You don't have to deal with her. Nabokov would've given up on *Lolita* if he had to fucking deal with Vagina."

I overstepped. *Lolita* is his motherfucking favorite.

"I'm sorry. Seriously."

He sighs. And then it's business as usual. Order more thrillers. Take inventory of the cage. Yeah, yeah, yeah. Soon I'll be back in the basement for the third day in a row, and *I'm a loser, baby, so why doesn't Mooney just lock me down there once and for all and throw away the key?*

I slouch. He snaps his fingers at me. "Stop wallowing, Joseph."

"Sorry."

I'm me again. *Soft and snuggly.* Already my gut is a thing without feathers, without butterflies or hope. I lost it all, Vail. Everything. I shouldn't have gotten so greedy. I should've gone to his place to eat Martha's fucking meat loaf.

Mooney hands me a plastic container. "Oh," he says. "From the wife."

Martha Mooney put a pink heart sticker on the Tupperware, and I can't cry. Not in front of Mooney. Not over leftover meat loaf. Not a few days before the most lonesome V-Day of my little almost life. "Thanks."

"Know this, Joseph. You are down because you chose poorly."

"Vail didn't do this to me."

"You could learn your lesson, young man. That serviceable trollop on the floor would suck you off in a heartbeat. It's a nice thing, being a young man, and you best not think youth lasts forever. Women are meant to flaunt their beauty. Stop judging. Start screwing."

With that, I'm dismissed.

I avoid the register because Vagina is throwing herself at a customer who asks if we have *Penthouse.* I've never been happier to walk downstairs and slam the door behind me.

"Hey, Hector. You hungry?"

The sound of my own voice bumps me. I haven't talked to Hector since we first met. The loneliness is getting to me. Kinda like that volleyball in *Cast Away* and that's me. A castaway. Minus the part where my girlfriend in *the States* misses me.

I take the lid off the meat loaf. Mold.

My cell phone rings. Dick.

"Where you been, G-Money? You alive?"

Am I? "Sorry, Dick. I got into a jam."

"You knock a girl up?"

"No. I got mugged."

"Well, shit, bro. You coming out tonight or what?"

I look at Hector—*Is this guy on crack?*—and Hector looks at me—*No, the crackhead is in Malibu.*

"Goldberg, you gotta come. Me and Schlitz are going to Passerby. Valentine's, my man; this is when it's hard to *not* get laid, and the Thursday-night pussy patrol is on."

They are the worst words in the English language, and I sigh. "I have a black eye."

A disgusted grunt. "So?"

"So, I got jumped. My boss won't even let me be upstairs. I can't go to a bar."

"Dude," he says. "*Fight Club.* Chicks love a wounded bird. . . ." He laughs, and I wish they never made that book into a movie. "A black eye is baller, son."

Amazing, how the word *son* means something different when he says it than when Mooney says it, and I say it a-fucking-gain. "I told you. I got my ass kicked."

"Sure," he says. "But here's my pitch. You tell the honeys who are all desperate to score before V-Day that you got jacked when you chased down a mugger to help a little old lady. Seduce and Destroy. The hero bit, kid. It's not like they can prove you're lying. You feel me?"

I'm quiet, too quiet, and Dick tells me that he's only playing, that I need to lighten the fuck up. "But, Dick . . . I can't go out there and lie to girls and . . . I don't know."

"You're not lying to these girls, Joe. They're lying to us. The makeup and the Wonderbras and the 'I never do this kind of thing' after they suck you off in a cab . . . Girls want to believe I'm a producer, so I tell 'em I'm a producer. That way, when I blow them off, they can really feel like they missed out on something. It's actually, if you think about it, it's the least we can do to give 'em a reason to get outta bed in the morning, you know?"

I'm not him and I never will be. I've never had *my* dick sucked in a cab, but he won't take no for an answer, so a few hours later . . .

I'm the third amigo at *Passerby.* It's sad, the way it's not dressed up for *V-Day.* Like they don't believe in true love, in *Serendipity.* Alas, it's a nice break from my cardboard box, what with Dumb and Dumber teasing me about getting my ass kicked while their astrology sluts ignore me because I'm soft again. I lost it, the swagger. Passerby was a mistake. Drunk people all amped up over the floor tiles that light up like *Saturday Night Fever,* and what a joke.

No one in here knows how to dance like John Travolta. No one is looking for love.

They buy overpriced drinks just to spill them and you like this place, and I *don't* like this place. I can't take it anymore. The noise. The way I had you one minute and didn't the next. The world has some nerve to just go on like everything didn't end for me. Even Angus is on the way to a better place, and Vagina . . . She'll be there tomorrow, and the day after that, and the day after that. The blue tile becomes red only so it can go back to being blue ten seconds later and do other people do this?

Do they sulk in public and live in their black-and-blue heads?

"Goldberg."

That's Dick. Annoyed at me again. "What?"

"Let's do a shot of Goldschläger. In your honor, my boy."

I say no, and Schlitz rolls his eyes. He's sick of me. These guys won't be inviting me out again because *I'm a loser, baby, and I belong in a basement with a typewriter named Hector.* The music isn't helping either. "Golden Years." Bowie's ode to love that lasts. Did you love me? Don't you want your scarf? Am I really that easy to leave?

Some motherfucker bumps into me and I hold my loser ground,

lodged behind Dick and Schlitz, hanging on like the third bloated, banged-up banana that I am. There's no denying it tonight. I'm a round peg, and the bar is like the world. It's like you.

A square fucking hole.

I don't belong here, and I don't belong in my home, and I don't want to read a book or scour the sidewalks for old typewriters. I'm ruined. The swarms of *girls, girls, girls* don't do it for me anymore. I want you.

You you you you you.

And this isn't me. I'm the guy who wants all women all the time and what happened to me, Vail? Why are all girls dead to me? Is it because of you? Are you a witch? Why don't I want the astrology slut eyeing me? Why can't I stop thinking about you? I can't blame Dick for telling me to stop being such a *girl* because he's right, on a level.

You are just some girl. You're not my girl. And like he says . . . What even was it? What was so great? Yeah, we hung out. A few cups of coffee, a little *rat-a-tat-tat* on IM, all that fucking *phone tag*. We had our 9/11 in the sinking living room. But it's not like we ever did it. We never shipped the boat out. I shouldn't be this down. There's a whole world out there, in here. People date. They sleep around. Dudes want to put it in this girl and that girl, in all girls, and I only want to put it in you. Girls, guys, everyone . . . People go out with someone a few times and they turn around and they go out with someone else. But not me, nope. I should jump off the boat and hit on that astrology slut and I should also stop using that phrase.

It's not fair. It's not kind. It's not the man I want to be.

And then I feel it in my gut. In the moldy meat loaf that won't quite go away.

I should leave New York. You ruined it, Vail. Everywhere I go, it's the same, every place is just a place where I don't get to see . . . Wait.

Someone taps my shoulder and I want it to be you and I turn around and Frampton comes alive. It's you. "Is that you, Joe?"

Yes! Yes, it's me and yes, it's you. You're here, in this bar. You gasp and yawp and love me with your eyes, with your hands. You take my chin in your hand like I'm the one.

"Baby, what happened to you?"

I am *not a loser, baby, or you wouldn't call me baby.* I tell you that I'm sorry. I tell you that I should've been there, at the coffee shop, and you tell me that doesn't matter.

"My God, Joe. What happened to you, baby?"

Dick clocks me and I do it. I *build me up, buttercup,* and spin a yarn about a fight with a junkie who was trying to mug a little old lady. And it's just like Dick said. You believe! You call me a hero and take me in your arms and *there is no other place I'd rather be.*

"Baby," you say. "I mean, I *knew* something was wrong. . . . It's not like you to bail on me and I don't know what happened, but I just . . . Oh, you poor thing. Let's clean you up."

You want to lick my wounds after all and we weave our way through the sticky cauldron of Cynthias and Vaginas. *Seduce and Destroy. D-Day is V-Day!* It was all real. You lead me into the bathroom, and the bathroom has a door that closes, a door that locks.

"God," you say. "I'm so bad right now, but fuck it. I missed you, baby."

You drop to your knees and go to town on my belt. You tell me that it killed you, waiting for me in the Beanery. My buddy Dick said I might be out tonight, so you came and I owe that guy a beer and you unzip me. POW! My jeans hit the floor and you're on the floor and the Bowie is blurry, and your mouth is wet. The thing with feathers. *Hope.* You take me between your lips, and Little Miss Tongue goes up and down, fast and slow. Tawna Birch in fourth grade eating a cone by a Mister Softee truck; my first hard-on, maybe. You are Tawna, you are every woman I ever wanted, with all ten thousand of your hands digging into my legs and I am not a loser, baby, but yes. You are going to kill me.

I tug your hair. *Mine.* You look up at me. *Mine.*

You get back to business and the Bowie fades into light, white Philadelphia-based funk and you . . . Wait.

"Why did you stop?"

You wink at me and tear a wrapper with your teeth and really, Vail?! Are we doing it in here? Are we fucking? You hold up the little packet. It's not a condom and you're not Vagina, so why the fuck are you holding Pop Rocks?

"Pop Rocks?"

"Trust me," you say. "It adds to the pleasure or something. It's even in *Cosmo* this month. Not that I read that magazine, but Cynthia does, so we can thank her later. You ready?"

No, I'm not ready. It's my Portnoy and you and your mouth are enough, same way I am enough. Am I?

"Can we just . . . You don't need to do that."

"Joe, come on. It's fun. And I'm like drunk but not that bad. I know what I'm doing."

I'm pretty sure the guy doesn't get to tell the girl on her knees what to do, so I give you the go-ahead. You dump a few Pop Rocks onto Little Miss Tongue and you come for my Portnoy and it's good it's . . . Wait. That sound and that snap, like Snap, Crackle, and Pop are having a party on my fucking Portnoy and that's my foreskin. My sensitive skin. *The pain, the pain.* You want this, you said I would like it, so I close my eyes and trust you like Miss Frascatore said to do and before you know it . . . Yes. The pain marries the pleasure and you . . . *You . . . you, you . . . you make my dreams come true.* I tell you I'm getting close, and you lap at my Portnoy like it's an ice cream cone. I feel your hands urging me—*Come, Joe, come*—and I heed the call.

I come, Joe, come and I lose my mind in the good way. You ate me. You killed me. You own me. And then you . . . spit me out.

17

In 1983, Prince wrote about a girl who moves too fast. You know the song, Vail. Everyone knows the song. "Little Red Corvette." The one where Prince concedes that he should've known a girl was trouble. There were signs. She parked her car like she was ready to run at any minute. She had a "pocketful of Trojans, some of them used." *Hint, hint.* But Prince fell for her; he let her take him to "the place where the horses run free."

That's track number 1 on the mixtape I'm building for you. I'm camped out at the Beanery, and Dick has to stop teasing me. I'm not "stalking" you. It's a free world and I like it here and he picks up the insert card of the Maxell jewel case.

"*Pop Rocks,*" he says. "Goldberg, no. You're not making that chick a mixtape."

"Why not?"

"Because it's Valentine's Day and you're alone in a coffee shop."

"Well, I might see her later."

"No, Goldberg. She spit and ran."

I grab the damn liner notes out of his cynical fucking hands. "Don't you have beans to grind, Dickwad?"

He nods. *Nice.* He respects me a bit more now, and okay. It's true. Technically, you spit me out and bailed on me, but that's why you need a Little Red Corvette. I'm not judging you for being fast. Hungry. The city turns pink and we all get a little hungry. And I hope you're not judging me. Sure, you were tipsy, you turned into an astrology slut on spring break. But I let you put *candy* on my dick, so I kinda think we're even. But we're at a standstill. You can't call me—you blew me in a bathroom—and I can't call you—you spit me out on the floor. We both froze up. You stood there at the sink before you fled, washing your hands, avoiding your own eyes in the mirror. You said what girls say, what Dick says you all say.

"I never do this. . . . Please keep it between us. . . . I mean, I never ever do this."

I played it cool and calm, smushing my seed onto the tile fucking floor. "All good, Vail."

Of *course* you've had restroom romps but that was a first for me, and yes. You should have swallowed me and invited me home instead of running back to Cynthia to help her through her *That bitch stole my purse* drama and yes, I should've poured those fucking Pop Rocks into the toilet. (I think that's why you didn't swallow.) And yeah, I am a little undone, but how the fuck could I not be? It's Valentine's Day and it's been three minutes and fifty-six hours since you walked out of that restroom, and that's another one for the mixtape.

Track number 2. "Nothing Compares 2 U."

Dick grabs my liner notes again. "Seriously, kid, stop it."

I grab the notes. "No, fuckwad, you stop it."

"Jesus," he says. "One lousy spit take of a blow job and she owns you?"

"It's just a mixtape. I'm not gonna go to her house and play it on a boom box."

I can't do that—I don't know your exact address—and Dick slaps the counter. "Stop it. This is about dignity, Golddog. Face it. You Seduced. But you didn't Destroy. If you destroyed, if that Passerby blowie led to a three-day, V-Day fuck-fest. . . . The end."

Finally, he goes back to work, and he's smart about stuff, but he doesn't get it. He wasn't there when you looked up at me, when you tore off my belt. I won't lose faith.

Track number 3 is "All I Want Is You." U2.

I have things I need to say to you. I know that you felt gross for being a Little Red Corvette. I'm sure you're worried that I think you're not marriage material. I mean, that's obviously why you turned into *Cynthia's* barmaid mother. Helping her find her purse, credit card, anything to avoid facing me because you were worried that you blew it.

Ha. Blew.

Rest assured, my sweet. *You walked in through my out door* and there is no going back.

Track number 4 is "Raspberry Beret." More Prince. Fuck it.

Track number 5 is also "Raspberry Beret." Twice in a row so you really *listen.*

The parallels, Vail. They're real. Prince works in retail—I work in retail—and the girl walks into the shop—you walked into the shop—and his boss is Mr. McGee—mine is Mr. Mooney. Prince has no regrets. He does everything right. He's in charge. The girl gets on the back of *his* Harley, and he whisks her off to the country and they do it in a barn under the rain and I'm the one who fucked it all up. The rain can't hit the roof of a meat market bathroom bar in the fucking *Meatpacking* District.

I failed you, Vail. I let you get down on your knees and pleasure me in a disgusting public place. I didn't whisk you away. And I didn't chase you and help you with Cynthia. Now you're curled up in a ball of unfair fucking girl shame and what a waste. I loved my bathroom *blowie* and you did it. You made me . . . Yes!

Track number 6 is straight out of the bathroom. "You Make My Dreams." Hall & Oates.

The coffee is too caffeinated and maybe I'm wrong. Maybe you're not ashamed. Maybe you're curled up with Ben and Jerry and Cynthia, venting about the pig who let you get down on your knees while you were clearly under the influence. It's a terrible thought but it's a reasonable one. Did I take advantage of you? Did I, Vail? Did I really fuck up RIGHT BEFORE V-DAY?

No. You wanted it. But I should've made you wait for it. I didn't put you on the back of my Harley—I don't have a motorcycle—and the horses don't wonder where you are—the bartender winked at me, Vail. As did Dick and Schlitz. I didn't tell those guys what happened, but they knew. Guys are pigs. Guys know, and I check my Motorola. Not ringing. I can't live like this. Wondering. Sitting. Waiting for you to do what you do every Thursday between 8:45 and 9:30 A.M. This is your slow day. Your day to dwell and sip your coffee, and I should say fuck it and call you. Dick says that *you* have to be the one to make the first call, but I'm the man. Can't I *Say Anything* to you? Dick wasn't there. He can't know that I fell into something new with you in that bathroom and I could burn this coffee shop to the ground when I think of how fucking stupid I was, tongue-tied. I just stood there and let you binge on my Portnoy but that's your power, Vail. You make me . . .

Go all track number 7: You "Make Me Lose Control." Eric Carmen.

Dick grabs at my liner notes again, and again I grab 'em the fuck back because no.

No.

"Jesus," he says, then he sighs. "All right, so you're . . . You're serious about her."

"I'm serious."

"You still want this even though she's a spit and run—"

"Stop saying that."

"Well, son, I don't get it but if that's how it is, then you gotta set another trap. And you do not set a trap with a fucking mixtape."

He steps off to deal with a customer who brought him a heart-shaped box of candy—I worry for all girls, I do—and I am losing my fucking mind. Literally. I am Pavlov's dog from eighth-grade science. Hell-bent like Dick said. *Climbing up on Solsbury Hill,* and yes!

Track number 8: "Solsbury Hill" by Peter Gabriel.

I'm cruising now—track number 9 is "Thank You," the Dido song from *Sliding Doors,* the movie you mentioned the day we met, the day you were so nervous you claimed to be an *Anglophile*—and Dick is wrong. This mixtape is the perfect trap. It's Valentine's Day and I'm on fire. Yes.

Track number 10 is "I'm on Fire." Bruce Fucking Springsteen.

I remember everything when it comes to you. It's effortless evolution, a new second nature. I know what you like, what you want. You moved to the city because of Woody Allen movies, and you love *Hannah and Her Sisters* even if you think you need to say you prefer *Manhattan.* On this day, *love* is the thing with feathers and soon it will be spring and yes. Yes!

Track number 11 is "I'm in Love Again." Bobby Short. As featured in *Hannah.*

Then the hairs on the back of my neck come alive like a bunch of Peter Framptons—I need to add him to my mixtape—and then holy shit. Holy Saint Motherfucking Valentine.

It's you. Dick looks at me. *Stay cool.* I am cool. Am I cool?

"Hey. Vail."

"Hey."

You can barely look at me—you are ashamed, you're in love—and you put your eyes on a safe place, a sexless place, you put your eyes on Dick. "Could I get an extra shot?"

Dick says he can do that, and you sneeze. I knock over the napkin dispenser when I reach for a napkin for you, and you laugh at me. "Aw," you say. "I'm cool. I have a tissue."

There was something bad in your voice. Something cold. Snide.

I should have fucking called you. *I WRECKED LOVE DAY.*

"Hey, well, here we are. I mean happy Valentine's Day!"

You look at me like I'm the nut who thinks Pop Rocks and penises go together. "You too."

You too is not *I love you* (I should add more U2), and I have to save this. Fix it. I feel your pain. I didn't chase you. I didn't call to see that you got home safe, and there is no going back. But it's not fair, Vail. You didn't do everything right either, and you leave me no choice. I need to get my power back. Hide the fucking mixtape and pull my heart off the counter and spit you out, the same way you spit me out but WHY DIDN'T I FUCKING CALL YOU? WHY?

"Yo, Dick. Can I get a to-go cup?"

You are huffy. Sniffling. "Well, someone has places to be. . . ."

"Nothing major," I say. "Gotta meet up with someone. . . ."

It feels bad to fuck with you, but that's the rule of women, of bodies. *No pain, no gain,* and Dick approves. He delivers your latte. Ceramic cup. As in *Joe is going places and you're just sitting around.* You avoid my eyes the same way you did in the bathroom, and I know, Vail. I'm in pain too. But did I spit you out? Did I burn your private parts?

"So, what's shaking, V?" Reducing your name to a single letter. Casually cruel in the way where you'd sound crazy if you acted offended. "How you been?"

You nod at your latte. "Good. Great, actually."

Actually doesn't feel good and Dick would tell me to neg you but I want to fucking hold you. "Cool," I say. "You have a good rest of the weekend?"

You look at me again. The horror. "It's Thursday, Joe."

"Right. So . . . Are you having a good week?"

You blow your nose into that filthy Kleenex. "You first."

Dick lifts his chin—*You got this*—and you cross your legs—I got this. I shrug off the inquiry, and you're on the edge of your seat. Literally. Dick is right. Love is war. This is war. You're nervous. Wondering if I took some other girl out to *Old Man Johnson's farm,* and I can't resist. You're too cute. I throw you a bone. "So, how's Cynthia? She seemed pretty wrecked the other night. . . ."

I did good. I broke the ice and you're a babbling brook, sounding off on Cynthia. Relaxed. Dick catches my eye again—*Well done, son*—and laughing about Cynthia is a way for us to talk without, you know, *talking*. You talk fast as an overheated Red Corvette. I want to hold your hand, calm you. You blame Valentine's Day for Cynthia's antics. It always makes her crazy and it's a stupid holiday, even worse than New Year's Eve and now you're on a new tangent.

"See, Joe, there's a reason we don't do holidays on *Sex*. . . . Never mind. I forgot. You don't watch my show."

You pop an Andes fucking candy. Nine A.M. You're a monster. A lovesick little monster. "Anyway," you say. "I have to help a friend at work and help get pinks out."

"Cool. Are pinks a Valentine's Day thing?"

Dead eyes. Sad eyes. "No. But then again, you don't exactly know much about my job."

I don't know what went wrong, but you are standing. No. You don't get to leave me again. You scrunch up your Andes candy wrapper into a little ball and grab my paper cup. You pour your coffee out of your ceramic cup into my paper cup and the quicksand is sucking me in and WHAT THE FUCK ARE PINKS. I look at Dick—he's no help—and I want to take you home. I should've taken you home.

I throw it out there. *Gently, Joseph.* "So what are you up to later?"

You look at me like I am crazy, like you aren't *making* me fucking crazy. "It's Thursday. I told you. I'm working."

It's not Thursday. It's *Valentine's Day.* Fuck Dick. Fuck the "game." I don't want to play with you. I want to be with you.

"Cool. So how about Serendipity later?"

Big swing and Dick might fucking kill me. You sip your coffee. He hides by the espresso machine. You didn't say no, not yet, and a lack of a no is the possibility of a yes. But then you touch your hair in the bad way. Flip-flip. "We'll see. Crazy day, what with pinks and all. . . ."

I'm an idiot. I should've stayed away from the *one* coffee shop where you know you might find me. I should've stayed glued to your side the other night. I should've called. I should've come here *with* the fucking mixtape instead of waiting until today to start making it. I'm losing you, and seriously. WHAT ARE PINKS? Silence is a weight, and I can't lift it, can't put it down. You fuss with your beret like you didn't suck me off on the floor of a Meatpacking District glorified fucking dive bar.

"Okay, boys. I guess I'm out."

Boys. No. I'm your man and this is my last shot. I flash my liner notes.

You smile. Girls are girls. You like stuff. "And what is that?"

"How about I show you at Serendipity?"

"You're insane if you think we're getting a table there tonight."

You grin like you want me, like it's finally *okay* that we both know the Pop Rocks were fucking stupid. "Well, maybe I am insane, Miss Gunderson. See you there at eight?"

"You're funny, Cusack."

DOES THAT MEAN YES? DOES THAT MEAN NO? "So is that a yes?"

Dick coughs because I sounded like a pick-me-up poster in Miss Frascatore's office. You gather your things. No. *Please don't go, girl.* I am frozen like hot chocolate. Impotent. I can't do what I want, because I want to knock you over the head and keep you here. I don't mean it like that. I stand because you stand and I trip and you laugh at me. "At ease, soldier."

No eye contact, just a little wave of your hand, and that's it. You're gone.

Dick grabs his scalp. He groans. "Goldberg, what the *fuck*?"

"What do you mean, 'what the fuck'?"

"You just asked her out on Valentine's Day."

"It felt right."

"I don't know where to start with you, kid. But I gotta say . . . you still don't know what pinks are?"

"And you *do* know?"

"Christ," he says. "Pinks are scripts. Revisions come in different colors, and that's code and like . . . that's a big part of her job."

"How do you know that?"

"Because I'm a producer."

BULLSHIT, HE'S A BARISTA. "Well, I'm not a producer."

"But you *are* trying to bang her, so you'd think you'd speak her language."

He rubs his forehead like I need a dunce cap and then he swings his dog tags. He had a brother. A brother is a teacher. "Buddy," he says. "Your girl works in production, yeah? She comes in here, that's what she talks about . . . work. Don't you guys talk about her work?"

"We don't talk about my work either. I don't expect her to know every author I like."

He grabs my liner notes with so much authority you'd think he's the manager of this bright white hellhole. "All right, kid. Time for a little test."

"Fuck you."

"First things first. She hardcore ditched you the other night, yeah?"

I say nothing. He knows the fucking answer.

"You good on hygiene, kid? You took a shower, yeah?"

No. Too depressed. "I'm not a pig."

"Second things second. Did you clean your junk?"

Did I, Vail? Do I know how? *It's so rare to see one in the States.* He tucks the pen above his ear (I hate that) and he starts doing push-ups off the bar, the kind where you *clap* between each one so that all the girls look over. "Did you give her a heads-up before you blew your wad?"

No clue. Can't remember. "Of course."

"As in you told her you were gonna come."

Fuck you, Dick. I speak sex. "Next question."

"Did you hold her hair while she was down there?"

I don't know and his cheapo body spray is too much today and is that my problem? Do you want me to smell like a Duane Fucking Reade?

"All right," he says. "Did you reciprocate?"

I look at him like he's crazy, because come on. He knows where we were.

"Oh, right," he says. "You kids never got outta the loo. Scale of one to ten, how was it?"

I will not rate our private life and I will not tell him about our Pop Rocks. "It was good."

"Good how? Did you tell her how Daddy likes it?"

"Don't be gross."

"It's not *gross*. Some girls are into that. You know what gets her off, right?"

I look at him like he's stupid. You and I haven't been in bed together. How would I know if you want to be *Daddy's little girl*. He sighs. "Relax. I ask because it was *kind of* baller, putting her on the spot about tonight. . . ." *Kind of* never felt worse. "But she spit and ran, and of all the places to wine and dine a chick on *V-Day*, you pick an ice cream parlor for little fucking *girls*."

"It's a thing with us. Serendipity. Frozen hot chocolate."

"You know you sound like a pedophile."

"No. It's just . . . we saw *Serendipity* the first time we went out."

"Huh?"

FUCKING MORON and I say it again. "The movie, Dick, the rom-com. *Serendipity*."

"Never heard of it."

"It's John Cusack."

"Now *there's* a pussy."

"He's not a pussy. She calls me *Cusack*. And Serendipity is the thing we want to do that we keep *not* doing."

"Kid," he says. "When are you gonna get it? If she wanted to go there, you woulda gone. First few weeks with a chick . . . they do what they want. Always. And you do what they want 'cause you're working on getting it in. That chick does *not* want to go to Serendipity."

I hate to say it, but it feels like the truth. Same way coffee always smells like coffee.

"All right," he says. "Let's say we were going to France."

This again and Love Day ends at midnight. "Can we cut to the chase?"

"If you wanna go to France, you gotta learn some French. You don't breeze into a foreign country expecting everyone to speak English. You have to learn the language, *her* language. Show respect, make 'em see you want in. I mean, I get it, kid. You haven't traveled. . . ."

We are back in India, and I might die at this counter. "Not yet."

"A woman is a country. You wanna get into Vail, you gotta learn her language, speak it."

I don't know your language. "I do, though."

"Nah, it's production lingo, the plots and references . . . No matter what happens with her, it's a good language to master, Goldfart. . . . Look around. Every girl in here is into *Sex and the City,* and your girl . . . With *any* girl, you gotta be able to talk about Carrie and Aidan, Big . . ."

"I've never heard you talk about these people."

"Aw," he says. "Our boy's got some learnin' to do."

I never felt so *Dumbest,* but he moves in for a high five and I remember why we're friends. Dick has my back. He did tell you I was going to Passerby, and maybe I don't make it easy. "And the mixtape," he says. "I'm just trying to help you, kid. A mixtape on V-Day for a girl who spit and ran and left you hanging . . . Mr. Big would *never.*"

"Who's Mr. Big?"

He grins. "Well, it ain't you, kid. Not yet anyway."

18

At ease, soldier. Those were your parting words. And you know what, Vail? Not so wrong. I am a warrior. I left the Beanery and marched down to Canal Street, where I bought bootleg DVDs of your sitcom. I bought scripts too. Neon covers with titles like "The Turtle and the Hare" and "Three's a Crowd" (really looking forward to that one). I got Vagina to invite Dumb and Dumber to an astrology slut gathering somewhere in the Lower East Side, and my home is all mine. As it fucking should be.

I have the TV and the DVD player. I bought a Moleskine to take notes, because this is the closest I'll ever get to cramming for an exam. It's not right, Vail. We aren't built to watch hours of TV in one sitting. We're humans. David Foster Wallace knows that. We need to breathe. Talk and fuck. Watch commercials and oh yeah.

Read.

But this is what it takes to learn your second language, and I am a soldier, *a soldier of love.*

Season 1: Your idol Carrie Bradshaw is not what I expected. She's a sarcastic cynic pontificating on "the end of love in Manhattan." Do you buy into that? Do you not understand that you are trying to end love in this city by fucking with my head?

I know. It's not time for questions. But Dick was right. I do like Mr. Big. He picks up Carrie and calls her out. He knows she's never been in love. She's so insecure that she goes mute and stares out the window. In the next episode, she gets insecure because she's not a model, and I make a half-hearted ham fucking sandwich.

I am tired already. Models? Whatever.

Big goes out of his way to visit Carrie at her coffee shop. He says he just wants to be with someone who makes him laugh. Such a fucking cool cat! He went to her. He opened up to her but *still* Carrie spends all her time picking him apart with her friends. She's holding out for him. She claims she wants "love," but she dumps another guy for being nice to her. (That episode was boring, not enough Big.) Next one is better. Carrie makes out with a random young guy with a tongue ring, and she SLEEPS with him and I'm . . . confused.

I thought she was so in love with Big. I thought you were in love with me.

Poor Big doesn't know she's sleeping around. They have casual plans to meet up for a "drink thing." Nothing serious. He's with *his* friend who just got dumped, same way she hangs out with *her* friends. But she throws a fit and stomps out. And still he likes her! *Still.* She's picking apart the young guy because he has a roommate, because he has no toilet paper and sorry, but is this your hero, Vail? Do you talk like that about *me*?

And would Big like her if he saw this snobbery?! Now Big is out with his buddy. She bumps into him ON HER WALK OF SHAME. Poor Big doesn't know she was just in bed with another guy. He invites her to join them—so cool—and she is super condescending about his crossword puzzle. Right in front of his buddy!

And still, he likes her! *Still.*

HOLY SHIT SHE JUST BANGED *ANOTHER* DUDE A RANDOM EUROPEAN GUY AND HE GAVE HER MONEY AND SHE TOOK THE MONEY WHAT THE FUCK VAIL SERIOUSLY?! Do I need an STD test?!

Next one is better. Carrie and Big have a date. She wears a naked dress. The one she wears on the poster that goes on the bus. Charlotte is right. Clearly, she is gonna fuck him. He picks her up in a limo, and she lets him fuck her right in the car. He's cool. He treats her like a lady and takes her to a Szechuan restaurant that looks really fucking good—I AM ORDERING SZECHUAN—and she's rude. She leaves Big to hug a random guy, and then she refuses to introduce them.

That was gross and the restaurant was fast. My Szechuan is here. Score!

Big and Carrie are a step ahead of us now. They're a couple, but she's still complaining. He glances at another girl, and she gets mad. He doesn't introduce her to random friends on the street and she gets mad. Hypocrite much?! Hello . . . the Szechuan place! By the way, if we do make it and you're reading this Moleskine because I just died of old age and you miss me, you should've been here with me. The Szechuan is good. We could've taken this journey together.

Next episode. Carrie "caught" Big on a date with another woman. Instead of being sad, she stomps out and tries to make him jealous. And still, he likes her. Still!

Oh, Big, I feel you, brother, I do. Every episode is the same story. Crazy Carrie gives up on Big for no reason. He's a punching bag with an old soul and a lot of suits who never gives up on her. I got to "Three's a Crowd," and my God, Vail. Carrie is now obsessed with threesomes. That's all she does . . . OBSESS. She asks Big if he had a threesome, and the answer is yes . . . with his wife. As in ex-wife. Who cares?! The guy was married. So the fuck what? She's a psycho, Vail. She runs around with random guys but *he's* the bad guy? Is that your goal with us?

It's getting worse. Carrie won't tell Big how she feels. She stalks his ex-wife and shows up at her WORK. Big finds out, and she blames *him* for making *her* crazy?!

And still, he likes her. Still.

Road trip episode. Carrie and *The Others* are going to a baby shower for a woman they all hate, SO WHY THE FUCK GO?! Samantha sticks up for Charlotte. Miranda kills it with her commentary. Carrie thinks she's pregnant. She tells her friends like they aren't all down in the dumps trying to recover from that shower at a dive fucking bar. And duh. Carrie's not pregnant.

I'm surprised that she didn't call Big and lie about *being* pregnant, and the calypso music in the opening credits is starting to get to me.

ARE YOU KIDDING ME WITH THIS ONE?! Carrie farts in bed. Big laughs because news flash: FARTS ARE FUNNY. She goes nuts, jumps out of bed, and runs away and is this why you're so obsessed with *Everyone Poops*? Big teases her with a whoopie cushion (love that guy, I do) while she's being pretentious about going to a *museum.* Sorry, but if you can't laugh at a whoopie cushion, you don't deserve a guy with a whoopie cushion. Now he's not in the mood, and she's paranoid. But when he calls, she sends him to her *answering machine.*

Been there, brother Big. But I get it now. Carrie is abusive and selfish. Deranged.

And still, he likes her. Still.

Big shows up at her place (such a cool cat), and she's MAD at him. He says he likes her bed and she pretends she hasn't been a voyeur staring at her neighbors as they fuck their brains out in front of a window. Where is this Manhattan?! Why no curtains? Is everyone an astrology slut except me? She's a pervert and a liar who lives off *The Others.*

And still, he likes her. Still.

Season 1 is almost over, and I'm feeling pretty fluent. Carrie spies on Big and his mom at church. She's a stalker and she is *jealous* . . . of his mother?! Poor Miranda is her wing woman (only sane one, no big look-at-me hat like Carrie), and Carrie drops a BIBLE. She blames Big for her psycho, stalking ways and . . . and . . .

And still, he likes her. Still.

So much that he wants to take her on a vacation. He's paying for it. She's packed and here he is with his town car—I want a town car—and are you . . . Are you fucking kidding me, Vail? She's dumping him?! She's dumping *him*?!

Season 2. My left leg is asleep. Bloated from Chinese. I farted. You missed it.

Carrie plays the victim, as if she got dumped. Throws herself at a new Yankee, and her picture is in the paper with the new Yankee. Nice, Carrie. Really considerate. She runs into Big and he's the coolest cat ever. He walks right up to her even though she dumped him, made him go on vacation alone and rubbed another man's jockstrap in his face. He tells her that she never looked better. She stays with her Yankee who she doesn't even like and she insults his intelligence while Big is hanging his head thinking she's moved on and . . . and . . .

And still, he likes her. Still.

You said there are no holidays in your show, but this one is about Carrie's birthday. Her friends throw her a party. She invites Big and he says he's gonna bring someone and she acts like this is unfair. Turns out by "someone," he meant a buddy, a Piven type. Carrie gets jealous when Big tips the belly dancers AS IF THE BELLY DANCERS DON'T DESERVE TO GET TIPS.

Yawn. Now she thinks all dudes in New York are freaks. Like she's not a freak for rummaging through a guy's stuff. Fucking psycho, Vail. I don't like the circus music either. None of these guys are freaks. Even the guy who doesn't leave Manhattan. A little disappointed in Miranda, stomping off like Carrie. Maybe cuntism is contagious, like the flu.

Now Carrie has a photo shoot for a *New York* magazine article about single girls. She knows about the shoot, but she stays out drinking and oversleeps. She's mad because she looks like shit in the photo. Samantha is right. Like anyone's gonna give a fuck in a few days, and now it's another holiday, sort of. Carrie and *The Others* are at a funeral for a fashion designer. They're all making jokes about the dead guy.

Are you that cold? That crass? She's doing it, Vail. She's calling Big. They're bowling. Just bowling but . . . Nope. She did it, Vail. She got him back. This is not a rom-com or a rom-*con*. This show is your bible, the reason you think you have to ice me out, spit and run to keep me in your orbit. Don't you get it? Guys like me and Big, you can drag us bowling. Lie and cheat. Wear stupid *capes.*

And still, we like you. Still.

She's being a shady bitch. Yawn. Lying to *The Others* about seeing Big. Would Big even like her if he knew she was ashamed of him, of them? *The Others* are sick of her shit. She barely asks about their shit, and when she does ask, she just starts talking about her shit again. Is that why you lost your best friend back home? Is that why Cynthia's a wreck? Don't you realize you don't need friends if you have a good fucking boyfriend?!

Big is a good boyfriend. He's going to a wedding with Carrie. She tells him he looks good. She's finally being nice to him . . . for about ten seconds. She's nervous and bent out of shape about writing a poem for the wedding (he was supportive, tried to help her write her poem, and she mocked him) and now they're at the wedding. She's reading her poem, and he gets a call. HE IS MR. BIG. BANKERS LIKE HIM LIVE ON THEIR CELL PHONES. Now she wants to dance. He doesn't like to dance when people are eating (I get it, my man) and guess what LOL . . . she's pissed again. I kinda wish he and Miranda could hook up, but Carrie wants cake. They're going home to eat cake in bed.

I want to eat cake in bed with you, Vail. The episode ends and it's Valentine's Day. You didn't call and we are not going to Serendipity.

Still, I like you. Still.

Carrie seems to realize she's a lucky woman. Cool Cat Big is making an ass of himself singing an old song to her in a restaurant where everyone knows him. He's cooking for her (he's making veal, do you like veal?) and Miranda calls. Carrie is standing her up (such a bitch), and I don't blame Miranda for being pissed. Big asks if everything is okay, and she lies and says it is. And wait . . . that's Steve. Steve the bartender! You mentioned him. Miranda likes Steve, and so do I. He digs Hemingway. But Carrie is a bad influence, so Miranda's not giving Steve a chance. Gross. Time for dinner (in the show; I already had my Szechuan), and Carrie gives Big attitude because he's not dressed up. It's raining and he doesn't wanna go out and she's pouting. She is a wimp, Vail. Now she's in a restaurant called Denial (ha) lying to *The Others,* too full of herself to admit she fucked up with Big. But . . . here he comes like *a cool cat . . . tapping on the toe with a new hat.* Miranda has an epiphany and runs after Steve and who says love is fucking over?

I know where the show is going. Samantha will get with Donald Trump or Rudy Giuliani (Would he do a guest spot? Is that the kind of stuff we're gonna talk about now that I speak your language?). Big will go to a shrink to figure out why he can't quit Carrie and fall for the shrink. Miranda will start up her own practice in Steve's bar à la John Grisham. Charlotte . . . Ugh. She's like one of those girls who thinks you can't read books and sell them at the same fucking time. A soldier has his limits.

I was wrong. Miranda's already blowing it with Steve, whining about his hours like she didn't know going in. Carrie's bitching about Big, and is this what you want, Vail? To talk about me with your friends instead of being *with* me? They're never happy. Steve is too poor and Big is too rich. He gets Carrie a purse and it's embarrassing, like your cape. But hello . . . that's her thing. Loud, ugly clothes. Carrie isn't brave enough to say she doesn't like the purse. She says, "I love you," and he doesn't say it back, and hello, why should he?

We're the men. We say it first.

Now she's at a party with Big and holy shit. Even for her this is bad. She's smoking with a waiter and now she's leaving with the waiter, she's waking *up* with the waiter. Poor Big calls because that's what poor Big does because she made a fool out of him; she threw love at him because she was too weak to say she didn't like the stupid purse.

And still, he likes her. Still.

It's getting old. It's only season 2. This time, Carrie is mad at Big because she left her stuff at his place, as if he's psychic, as if he knew she did that on purpose. Anyway, sometimes I get it. Carrie can be a cool cat now and then, like when she flings her panties at him, and he says they'd better be clean. For once in her selfish life, she laughs and lightens up and who knows?

Maybe sometimes gold can stay.

Nope. Big got a job in Paris, and she is going crazy because it's always about her. Nothing he does makes her happy, and now she's drunk on cosmos. At least they're finally showing how women can't drink this much without getting drunk. She calls him to scream at him while he's in Paris trying to sleep. Oh boy. Actual psycho. He's home. She got a beret. She got McDonald's AS IF MCDONALD'S IS FRENCH. She tells Big she can visit him and they can have *les phone sex* and he's squirming. . . . HELLO SHE DRUNK-DIALED HIM LIKE A POSSESSIVE FUCKING NUTJOB and did she . . . Yep. She threw McDonald's at his TV and dumped him. Poor guy. Did anyone ever try so hard to put up with someone? I really don't think so, Vail.

Season 3 and I want a TV in *my* fucking kitchen. I pop an Advil. My back hurts.

The girls are in the Hamptons and Charlotte is lying about her age and Carrie is making a list of everything wrong with a nice, sheepish doctor. But ooh . . . Big is back and he has a new girlfriend. She's pretty. *Sarah, Plain and Tall.* Carrie is puking on the beach, literally green with envy. Now she's calling his house and hanging up because *the stick figure with no soul* picked up. I'm a little scared for Big. It's his engagement party and Carrie is skulking around and Big leaves his beautiful plain fiancée to go talk to Carrie.

Big is better than that, and poor Natasha rolls down the window like "Where's my man?" Carrie touches Big's hair like she owns him. Like she didn't make this mess. I'm tired, Vail; I have to put my pen down. I'll write more when I'm all caught up.

Okay, I'm baaack. And I made it to the present. I know where we are.

I think I know why you fear the end of love in Manhattan, Vail. Big lost everything because he couldn't let go of Carrie. He cheated on Natasha in their *bed.* Same way Carrie cheated on her dull, cigarette-hating boyfriend Aidan. Big's wife broke a tooth. It was all gross and it's all on Carrie. She's not a tube of red lipstick like Samantha. She's not a string of pearls like Charlotte or a hot slice of rye like Miranda. She's all show, all capes and sequins. Big is the opposite. A still water that runs deep. You once told me you're afraid of not having a dream. Because of *Sex,* you think the road to happy is paved with crazy obsession. On our first date, you warned me that you couldn't tell me about the fate of Carrie and Aidan. It kills me that you believe there was ever any chance of those two sticking it out. Two matches can't start a fire. They need the book, the charcoal, the friction. Same way a rowboat without oars just sits in the Central Park Reservoir. You need me to be your Big, and yesterday I turned into Aidan on you. A pathetic, aspiring heart-shaped candy of a man. Well, those days are over, my peanut M&M. I'm gonna get a suit or, at the very least, a blazer. I need an umbrella. I need my hair to get thick again, and I need to make reservations and talk a little slower, use fewer words. More biting my lip and raising my eyebrows. I stand here in front of the mirror like some doubtful loser in a movie and love is supposed to be a Billy Joel ballad where you love the person *just the way they are,* but I'm hooked. Invested. I just watched hours of fucking *television* for you and learned a language and . . . and . . .

Still, I like you. Still.

19

Sex is in my skin, in my blood, in my ears. I can't call you. Not like this.

I try to get my brain back. I open *Franny and Zooey.* I cut the cosmos and the cupcakes with Salinger, but now his name makes me think of the one about the guy who came too fast with the cool mom who said *Salinger used to get me high.* Did I come too fast?

I toss the Salinger aside. My *Sex*-athon killed my brain. It's no better at the shop. I'm slapsticking left and right, and Mr. Mooney says this "punning phase" of my life had better end soon. I leave the shop and hear that tinkly calypso theme music when I *strut down Fifth Avenue.* I walk into the Beanery and unconsciously scan the room for my buddy Steve. We would be friends in real life, but there is no Steve in real life. In real life, Steve is *Schlitz.* I hit the men's room and flush the toilet, but even here, I am altered. Brainwashed.

I look down at the bowl and *can't help but wonder* where it all goes, the shit.

I sit at the counter, and Dick wants to know what's wrong.

"I did it," I say. "I speak *Sex and the Fucking City.*"

He high-fives me, and I talk to him like he is a Steve, a bartender. The Big of it all (oh, shut up, Joe!) and the way you creamed your panties when you thought I had a fat pad on the Upper West Side. You want to be Carrie, and I wanna go Big for you. But do you know how much it costs to buy a nice fucking umbrella in Manhattan? Who has that kinda dough?

Dick sighs. "Goldberg," he says. "You need to chill. Those chicks are in their thirties. It's not about the money. It's . . . *Seduce and Destroy.* Anyway," he says. "You back at the gym?"

"No."

He frowns and did I get fat overnight? Am I a puffy third banana, the worst of all the men in that fucking show . . . Am I . . . "Dick, do I . . . do I look like Aidan?"

Not yet, according to the barista, but who am I kidding? I'm not Aidan. He's a furniture designer—WHY ARE THEY ALL SO RICH—and he has a dog and he doesn't own a hairbrush and he got dumped in Serendipity. In theory, this is a good thing. Carrie doesn't love Aidan. How could she with those my-family-went-to-Jamaica necklaces? He's a barn jacket of a man. Ick. But then the truth hits me like a Magnolia cupcake sugar bomb from the West Fucking Village. I am in the Beanery because of the off chance that you will walk into the Beanery. I live for you. I dwell on you and am I . . . Dick hands me a coffee. I can't help it. "Dick, am I a *Carrie*?"

"Decaf, son. You're scaring me."

"You're the one who told me to do this."

"Yeah," he says. "But can you ever just take it down a notch? It's not . . . it's not literal. You learned the language. Do your thing. Call her up."

He makes it sound so easy and he ditches me to flirt with some girl and *just like that* . . . it's official. I am Carrie Bradshaw. Obsessive. Needy. Annoying. My phone rings. It's Dumber. He lays into me about jacking off in the shower and the Szechuan I spilled on the sofa.

A Big (oh, stop it, brain) reminder that I don't have a doorman or a California king or multiple hotel-grade bathrobes or a driver or a town car. It's hard to respect yourself when you live in a cardboard box, when you can't even jerk off in the shower without your roommate calling to bitch about it.

Dick is back. He wants to go to Chaos later, to a party for *Details* magazine.

"I know that place! They go to Chaos in the pilot. Samantha goes home with the guy Charlotte was into, and Charlotte doesn't get mad at her. I don't know if she finds out about it."

Dick gives me the finger, and I can't blame him. I do this. I go all the way. This one time, I almost drowned because I didn't come out of the water and the lifeguard wasn't having it. *Why did you stay under? Were you trying to test me?* That's what I am, Vail. I go under. I stay under. I think I met you for the same reason you met me. We cannot become Big and Carrie on our own. We can only become Big and Carrie through each other.

Dick scratches the back of his head. "Joe," he says, and you know it's not good when he uses my real name. "Go home."

Not possible. Not with Dumb and Dumber scrubbing Szechuan off the sofa that belongs to them. I miss you. I go on a walking tour. I see Sushi Samba and I go to Magnolia Bakery, but I do not stand in line. I buy a vintage coat in a thrift shop. Do I look silly? Is this me? I go uptown to Big Town and waltz into a cigar shop for some Cubans and I wind up on the corner of Seventy-second and Madison coughing up a lung. I feel lost and broke. Stupid. There is something wrong with me and I know it, same way Carrie knows she's off. People are always telling me what to do, Dick and Mooney, but it's worse, Vail. I am always *asking* people what to do, like Carrie and *The Others*. After a while, the cigar smoke settles. My lungs aren't so full of Pop Rocks. A tall model type passes by and bones me with her eyes and *just like that* . . .

I am him. I am the man. I am Big.

I call you because I feel like it. Because I want to.

You pick up on the second ring. Desperate. Carrie. "Well, hello, stranger."

"Hey, kid."

That was my first *kid,* and it felt natural. You chuckle. Do you know? "Sounds a little funny coming from you, my friend."

That's what Carrie calls Big when she's gun-shy and sarcastic. *My friend.* "So, what's shaking?"

"Oh, you know, working around the clock and trying not to kill Barry. . . . I kinda thought I'd hear from you sooner. I feel like things got weird for no reason."

Less is more, and I sigh. "I wasn't sure if you wanted to hear from me."

You are quiet and you feel it. . . . There's a new Joe in town. "Wow, well, yeah, okay, that helps. . . . I wasn't sure either, but now that you're calling, I mean, can we just decide that V-Day made us lose our little minds?"

It was never this clear, Vail. You want the back-and-forth, the up and down, the breakdowns and the fresh starts. But what about the good stuff? The in and out. I know. We'll get there.

"So, I hear you guys are shooting a big Fleet Week scene, yeah?"

"Wow. How did you know about that?"

Gently, Joseph. "I saw something in the *Post.*"

"Well, look at you, reading about me. . . ."

"Don't flatter yourself, baby. I picked up that rag on the way home from Chaos the other morning."

I can hear the wheels turning in your head. The horror in your heart, me in a bar full of models, models who kept me up all fucking night. It's easy now. You crave pain, the possibility that I don't want you, not the way you want me. It's a joke (I want you!), but I can do this for us. Fuck with you to win the honor of actually, you know, fucking you.

"Anyway," I say. "How's tricks?"

It's another Big line. *How's tricks?* "Aw, tricks are for kids."

That was pure unadulterated Carrie Fucking Bradshaw and the conversation flows and before you know it we are equals, fluent. You're bubbling about the Fleet Week *pinks,* and it's easier to talk to you now that I know Carrie and *The Others.* I end the call abruptly without so much as a goodbye. I shut my phone off. On the subway, I just sit there smiling. What a change! I learned your language, and I owe Dick a bottle of Jägermeister or a case of Jim Henson. Does Big do shots? Whatever! Who cares! The world is on my side. Dumb and Dumber aren't home, and you called my Motorola *and* my landline. I turn on some more *Sex* and hit the Mute button and I give you a call.

"What happened?"

"Not a lot," I say. "Just life."

You're chatty like Carrie. You drop hints about the night ahead. You're getting off early. . . . You're *dying* for a drink and if I'm not sure about Chaos . . .

"Hey, pussy, that's not your TV."

I clamp my hand on the receiver and no. Not *now,* Dumber. You're asking what's wrong, and he's grabbing the remote and he hits that damn Mute button—FUCK YOU, DUMBER—and the volume is way up—FUCK YOU, TV—and you hear that telltale heart, that goddamned *calypso.*

I slam the door of my cardboard box that isn't a real door. You laugh.

"Wait. . . . So that's what's different. You're watching my show!"

I am self-conscious like birthday girl Carrie turning thirty-fucking-five. "Ha. No."

"Joe, come on. I heard it."

"My roommates, Vail. Their girlfriends are watching it."

"Oh, well, just so you know, if you did take an interest in my favorite show, which also happens to be my work . . . I mean, that would be a sweet thing, and I might even kind of like it."

That's the right kind of *kind of* and I KIND OF LOVE YOU TOO, but wait. Aidan is sweet, and he's not the one. I go stoic. Silent.

I will kill Dumber and bury him and the remote in the back fucking yard, but this is New York. We don't *have* a back fucking yard.

"Anyway," you say. "Have you ever heard of Il Cantinori?"

That was a test. A trick question. Carrie and *The Others* go there. I didn't break. I told you I didn't know it and you told me to be there at eight and I'm here first.

It's not the best table, but we're not rich and old. I cobbled a suit out of some more thrift store finds, and you're being the Carrie, as if I'll only love you if you're late and—

"Wow."

I rise to greet you. You're naked. Not actually naked. But your dress . . . It's Carrie's dress, the one she wears on the bus in the show. The naked dress. The one she wears the first night she fucks Mr. Big. You peck me on the cheek. "Why, thank you, sir. You're not so bad yourself."

No combat boots tonight. Heels. High ones. "I'm enjoying the new shirt, Joe."

It's a white-collar shirt. A Mr. Big kind of shirt. "I had a meeting."

"Since when do you have meetings?"

"I always have meetings, kid. I just don't necessarily tell you about these meetings."

You know the scene, it's season 1 or 2. Big refers to Carrie as his *girlfriend* and she goes wild, and he says he calls her that a lot, but he just doesn't say that to her face. We are doing it, Vail. We are becoming the people you want us to be. This is it, in that Rod Stewart *tonight* kind of way, where the spaghetti is spicy and the happiest people in the room are the ones at the worst fucking table. You tug at your dress and bend over to rub your foot, your poor *lovely bones* trapped in that caustic Blahnik. You are a girly girl and I am a manly man and the birds and the bees came alive for us, for the butterflies at play in our bodies.

You don't go on and on about your job. Carrie loves her work, but she loves Mr. Big more. I sip on scotch. You guzzle *cosmos.* We laugh a lot. I ask you if you lost your boots in actual fucking combat, and you ask what time my rent-a-suit is due back.

You tell me to be nice, and I raise my fucking eyebrows. "Baby, I'm a lot of things, but nice isn't one of them. And those boots really do have to go. . . ."

The fireworks stop cold. We aren't them anymore. We are us. You pull on your cardigan.

"Vail, wait. I was just kidding."

I've never seen you like this, actively trying to find where you end, where Carrie begins, telling me that I hit a nerve. "You don't know anything about fashion, Joe. Already I feel fat enough next to the girls at work, in the show. I don't need this."

"You're not fat, Vail. You're just not a beanpole."

"Gee, thanks."

Be the Big man. *Cool cat.* "Baby, come on. You know I love your boots."

Your hands are shaking. The white tablecloth is stained, and you're all Big-ged out. You gulp. "Sorry, I just . . . Joe, I don't know how to tell you this."

You love me. You can say it first. "There's nothing to worry about, Vail. I'm here."

You want me to get under the table. I comply. Am I supposed to go down on you like Samantha's awful fucking frenemy? Do you think I have a fucking foot fetish?! No. Your hand lifts the tablecloth. You make a little fist and you let go and then . . . And then . . . You pull off a stiletto and . . . Holy. Fucking. Six. You have six toes on your left foot. Is this how you felt when you first saw my Portnoy? I plant a kiss on that extra little piggy—you can do that in a dark New York restaurant—and I slide your special foot back into her high-heeled cage. I come up for air, for you. The first word out of your mouth is a good one—*wow*—and you bubble on about your armor, your go-to tights and your boots.

". . . And the last guy I dated was so cold, constantly teasing me and not in the fun sexy way, more like he was trying to get me to hate myself but you . . . That was pretty perfect."

Perfect has to lead to sex. "Just being me, baby."

"And it's especially . . . *wow* . . . because I was such a bitch to you on V-Day. I'm always snapping at you or being 'sensitive.' I mean, that's been an issue for me in the past. . . ."

"It's not an issue with me. You had every right to be pissed, Vail. I should've called."

"And I shouldn't have ditched you right after the Pop Rocks. Sometimes I think I'm allergic to good guys."

I take your hand. It's you and me. I say nothing. I know how Carrie needs Mr. Big to be quiet sometimes. You wipe away what might be a real tear or a crocodile tear, and I don't care. You smile. "I like tonight."

"Me too, kid."

You giggle—that's my last *kid* for a while—and we're good. You say that Sarah Jessica Parker lives in this neighborhood and it's easier now that I speak the language. You can't believe I kissed your toes, and you sip your cosmo. "What is it about you, Joe?"

"Hell if I know."

"Well, whatever it is . . . I do like tonight. I also like you tonight."

You move the tip of your bare special foot under my slacks and you wink and, oh God, we are going to do it, aren't we? Yes. We are those in-your-face fuckers making out in the dining area and it's the best it's ever been. We're gonna make love until our bodies turn into Magnolia banana pudding and the waiter intervenes.

"Here's your *check*. As it seems like you might be ready to leave."

We die laughing and I pay the bill, and you can't really walk in those heels and I can't really afford this but WHO FUCKING CARES?! I sweep you off your feet and we look like we just left a benefit where we saw Charlotte and Trey and there is no back-and-forth, no *where should we go*. Not tonight.

Tonight, you want me. You pull on my lapels. "Take me home, baby."

You want me to kiss you, but more than you want it, you want me to make you wait for it. I grin. "Abso-fucking-lutely."

Your eyes. The lump in my throat. I didn't just channel Big. I quoted him. A word from the pilot. *Abso-fucking-lutely.* It's twelve degrees on the street, but it's a million and a half degrees in my heart—*Sometimes a girl needs a half*—and was it too much? Are you mortified? Time doesn't slow down. It stops. It ends. The Magnolia Bakery goes out of business, and I can't take it back and you know. You know what I did. You know what I tried to do.

You lay your head on my shoulder. "You watched it for me, huh?"

"Guilty."

"No," you say. Your hand slides under my jacket and down my torso. "Innocent."

You kiss me and you are *ComelyCarrieSluttySamanthaShyCharlotteMatureMiranda* and I did good. Very good. We're in a cab and you can't say it enough—*I want you, I want you*—and I tell you what you want to hear, what you need to hear—*I want you, I want you*—and we are better than Big and Carrie because they were actors. Only pretending. This is real, Vail. Those are your teeth digging into my neck and your home is not Carrie's. It's a two-bedroom shithole in a six-floor walk-up. It smells like incense and strange men—fucking Cynthia—and there are movie posters taped to the walls. No frames. Dirty panties in your overflowing laundry basket and my Portnoy comes alive. We're surrounded by love stories. Posters. *When Harry Met Sally* goes to *Manhattan* to meet *Swingers,* and when I close my eyes, it's just you. Your sweet skin. That wisp of hair that gets caught in my teeth. You close your door and lock it.

"I mean, I know it's messy, but it's mine."

"I could say the same of you."

You lunge at me with your husky, musky little body. You tease my foreskin—I am special, *rare*—and you are as shy as Charlotte, feisty as

Samantha, cute as Carrie the way you call it *my lovely boner.* I am clumsy (I have a little Steve in me) and you are awkward (you are part Miranda). You bite me too hard; my touch is too gentle for you, but in time, we get there. I went to boot camp and I am ready for the battle and it's about to happen.

You pull out a condom and wrap my Portnoy in latex and roll over and I enter you all at once and is that . . . Are you looking at me? You are looking at me. Is that good? Bad?

"Slower," you say.

"Faster," you say.

"Wait," you say.

"Go," you say.

"Right there," you say.

"Not there-there. Right there. Sort of there . . . Okay, Joe . . . Okay."

I follow every command—I will beat Mr. Big—and you make a new sound, and your fingernails dig into my skin and is that . . . I'm done. "Wow," you say. "I really needed that."

I roll over and stare at Harry and Sally. *Wow* can be a bad word, flat. Something is off. Wrong. "Me too."

My mind is in overdrive and why? We did it. You trembled. You gasped. If it sounds like a duck and walks like a duck . . . But Miranda faked it for that lovable ophthalmologist and is that what you did? Did you fake it? Did you come, Vail? Did you? Do girls finish first? You don't hug me like you want more of me, but maybe that's because you really *didn't* fake it. Maybe you are satisfied and spent. Then again, you're breathing evenly and you're not as sweaty as you were at first. I wish I was one of those guys who blacks out after he comes. *I really needed that* is not *That was the best sex of my life.*

I think something's wrong with me, Vail. My brain won't die the way a dude's brain should after he gets laid. I don't want to be this guy, this Woody Allen worrywart. I wish we had Saltines or cigarettes. I say it out loud. "I wish we had Saltines or cigarettes."

You don't laugh. "Ha," you say. "If only."

You don't sound like a woman who had the best orgasm of her life, and I don't feel like the man who gave you one. Did I? Did you? You yawn and roll away from me. Wait. DO YOU THINK I CAN FUCKING SLEEP RIGHT NOW? You're out cold—Is that a good sign?—and I stare at the walls comparing myself to Billy Crystal and Vince Vaughn—Go away, fuckers—and eventually, the sun comes up. And then you.

"How'd you sleep, Joe?"

"Great!"

You pick up an old *New Yorker* and I feel like a guy who lasts one fucking episode. I was so bad that you're gonna *read*?! Was I supposed to sneak out of bed and make you breakfast? You don't look at me when you sigh. "So whatcha got going on today?"

Is that a hint? "A lot," I say. "Which is why I should get the hell outta here."

You flip a page and huff. "Well, okay then. Don't let me stop you."

You are not Carrie and I am not Big and was it all just *role-play*? At the gym, in the locker room, Dick once said that most girls *can't* get off the first time you bang them. *But then you give her that morning wood, Goldbitch.* I can't do that—I am soft—and did I fuck up? I fucked up. There's a way to leave with you wanting more, but I can't find my way in this tiny bedroom. I stub my toe on your stupid *New Yorker* nightstand and you don't ask if I'm okay and I hate myself for wanting you to ask if I'm okay.

"I'm okay," I say. "Barely hit it."

"Yep," you say. "It's not the best bedroom, but it's mine. . . ."

I remember when *mine* was a sexy thing. "Yeah, I hear you. I need a new place."

You fake a yawn like an aunt or a teacher or an old lady on a bus stuck with a crazy person and did you fake your orgasm too? You close your *New Yorker.* "If you want to move, the best way to find a place is just kinda walking around. That's how me and Cyn found ours."

Nothing ever sounded better to me than a walk through the city with you, but I pull up my pants like a douchebag in your *Swingers* poster. "Oh yeah?"

"Yeah, you make a day of it. You get a feel for a neighborhood, you go into one of those internet café places and hit up Craigslist . . . It's kinda fun. It's like hunting."

It feels like you want to do all that with me and I want it too, but you won't come out and say that, and I *can't* come out and say it. I pick up the only book in this room.

"Ah," you say. "That's my favorite."

'Scuse Me While I Kiss This Guy. The title alone . . . Like you want to be Carrie, close your eyes on real love to be the make-out queen of Manhattan.

"The book is famous song lyrics that we all get wrong in real life. Like it's not ''Scuse me while I kiss this guy,' it's ''Scuse me while I kiss the sky.' " You pull your hair over one shoulder like you're in a bar trying to pick up a stranger. "It's good for small talk, you know?"

No, I don't know and did you fake it? I fake it. "Sounds great. And who doesn't love Jimi Hendrix?"

You bite your lip like I said the wrong thing, like you have no feelings about Jimi Hendrix and maybe we have nothing in common. "Well, it's not about him. . . . It's more about misunderstandings, Joe. Things we hear and mishear and don't even know until . . . I love that kinda stuff. Miscommunication, and reading into things. You think you know the song, the world, a person and then whammo . . . you've been wrong all along."

"Whores de var."

"Huh?"

"That's how I used to pronounce *hors d'oeuvres.*" SHUT UP, JOE, and did I really just say WHORES in bed? I don't know how to relate to you. I don't even know if you came. I just know that it can't be a good thing, the way you go back to flipping through your old *New Yorker.*

"Anyway," you say. "I got it at Urban Outfitters. You can borrow it if you want."

You offered me a book. It's not fiction, but it's something. I should wrap you up in my white button-down shirt and carry you out the door. That's how a bill becomes a law, how a night becomes a life. We keep it going, drift down your stairs into the sea of less fortunate busy bodies rushing to start their dumb long days. We're that new couple moving slow as molasses. Holding hands while everyone on every *single* sidewalk smells it on us, the sex. Then we pop into some restaurant we never noticed that was clearly built for us, for today. We devour eggs and pancakes—so good, best ever—and talk about maybe going to see a movie. Obviously, we don't do that. We go back to your place for another round and become the couple we're supposed to be. Night falls and we both know that I don't need to find a place. We have your place. Before you know it, Cynthia's moving out and I'm moving in because you love me, because I love you.

But then you close your *New Yorker.* "Shit. I have to go pay my phone bill."

Sex doesn't "complicate" things. It destroys them.

I toss *'Scuse Me* on your nightstand and I lean over your mysterious little body. I peck you on the forehead. "Do your thing, kid."

When I turn my back on you, you don't beg me to stay. You flip through your *New Yorker,* the one from March 2001, the one you keep there for moments like this, when you realize that *Sex and the City* is just a TV show, that you are not Carrie Bradshaw, that men are Mr. Big in the bad way. Dickheads, all of us. The way we just walk out the fucking door a couple hours after making you orgasm. Or not. Did you?

"I, um . . . I had a really good time, Vail."

You don't look at me. Not even a little. "Later, Joe."

20

Two days is a century is an ice age is a long fucking time.

You don't call me and I don't call you, and Dick asked if I tended to your *devil's doorbell* and I said yes but what the fuck is a devil's fucking doorbell? He said to forget about you for now. He says that I *can't* fucking call you and he wants me to set a jealousy trap in the shop. Yes, Vail, it's more Destruction and Seduction. He says Vagina is the key. I've told him about her, how she climbs all over me, pawing at me, licking her *lips* at me. And apparently, this is just the kind of thing that will drive you nuts, so it's on me to let Vagina think she has a shot with me. Women only want guys if they pick up the scent of another woman.

But still. What is a devil's doorbell?

I would go back in time and let you smother my Portnoy with Pop Rocks if it meant avoiding a future that involves the hell of having you and then not having you. I'm staying away from you so you can yearn for me, but what if there's no point? What if I was a Big letdown? Or what if you really are allergic to good guys? What if I have it backwards and I was *too* good? Maybe girls don't scream when they come in real life . . . Yeah fucking *right.*

Vagina gooses me and I scream. She giggles. Vagina, a creature so devoid of subtlety or nuance that she could never even pop up in *Sex and the City* and I'm doing it again. Thinking like Carrie. Carrie, who would be mortified by Vagina's outfit. A tiny little black dress with spaghetti straps. No bra, no panties—*Going commando makes me so horny, you know?*—and I wish there was a way for me to know where you are. I wish I could tag you like a dog and I know. That's a sick fucking thought. But that's how it goes in this cage. That is my life without you.

Am I weird? It's only two days, I know. But two days isn't nothing when you love someone, when you know what it feels like to be in bed with them. And the way you don't call me makes me wonder if you liked being in the bed with me.

Dick says to be confident, but Dick doesn't know about my Portnoy. *So rare to see one in the States.* He swears that you'll storm the gates one of these days, and I go outside and call him. He's sick of my whining, but then he's never spent two double shifts in a bookstore with Vagina.

"Relax," he says. "You can't care so much. They smell it."

"But when is she gonna call or show up?"

"Dude," he says. "You should just get with that Virginia chick."

"I can't."

"Is she fat?"

Fuck you. "No."

"Ugly?"

AS IF DICK IS GEORGE FUCKING CLOONEY. "She's not my type."

Vagina knocks on the glass. I raise a hand—*one minute*—and she pulls her shirt down—one tit—and maybe she and Dick will get married and produce emotionless little horndogs.

"Anyway," he says. "This chick that *I* banged last night . . ."

Ten minutes later, I'm back in the trap, putting *Sex* books in CLEARANCE. Vagina's lips hit my ears—*Are you thirsty, Joey?*—and I run away. I climb the ladder to hide in HISTORY, but before you know it, she tugs on my jeans—*Need a hand, Joey?*—so I go in the back to bitch to Mooney. He cackles and calls me a pussy, and I can't live in a cage, in a trap.

I hate cages. Cages are for people who need to learn a lesson the way I did back in September, and I *learned* my lesson. I walk out of Mooney's hideaway, and Vagina walks right into me. She brings a *peppermint fucking latte* to my lips. "Taste it, Joey."

I want to fucking puke.

She hops on the counter like we sell porn, not books. "Check this out. It's a one-bedroom, and it sounds super cool."

It's the worst part, Vail. You wanted to help me find a place, but now *she's* helping me, circling ads in the *Voice*. I should've called you, I should've stayed with you and your devil's doorbell.

I don't feel good about Vagina either. Every so often, her shy, nervous smile reminds me that there is a person in there, a person who likes me. And I'm the bastard who's encouraging her. She licks her finger and flips through the *Voice* and what if September 11 happens again right now and you die thinking of me as that classic *SATC* one-episode jerk who never calls? Will I ever see you again? Do you love me? Hate me?

Vagina leaps off the counter to help a guy in HISTORICAL FICTION. Maybe the worst part about this trap. She thinks she can make *me* jealous, and it's nails on a chalkboard, Vail. She watches to see if I'm looking at her and WHY CAN'T YOU WALK INTO MY TRAP?! Karma might be real. Are we stalling like a new car with a bad engine because of what we did to Angus, because of the wine you stole, the books I "rescued"? Look at Carrie. She fucked Big in his wife's beige bed and a guy stole her Manolos.

Ugh. I have to get *Sex* out of my head. I feel like Samantha after she told Richard that she loves him when she was high on ecstasy and is this why you don't call? Do you *sense* me in this store having such unthinkable fucking thoughts? I didn't tame your cunt (your orgasm feels faker by the hour) and you don't respect my cock (you didn't put your lips on my Portnoy the other night). I want to buy you a new *New Yorker* and take you for pancakes and the door opens—is it you? It's not you, it's never you—and I know. Dick says it's like anything in life. *No pain, no gain.* He swears you're in the same boat in your own way, brunching and barhopping with your girlfriends to analyze every little thing about our *fuck-fest.* But was it a festival? Felt more like a classroom—*Slower. Faster. Not there . . . There*—and Dick might be too broken to advise. Gordie Lachance got over losing his dead big brother, but that's a Stephen King story. Dick is real life. He doesn't want a fucking girlfriend. For all his gym shit and his steroids, he's weak when it comes to girls. *Seduce and Destroy* isn't real. It's a thing Paul Thomas Anderson made up for a *movie.* It's a joke. I'm not a *playa* like Dick. I want the agony and *I'm a survivor; I'm not gon' give up.* I will wait and worry until I have no nails left on any of my fucking fingers and—

"*Joey . . . honeeeeeeey?*" Vagina shoves a *Voice* in my face, and maybe I will die right now. "Check it out, Joey. One-bedroom . . . Alphabet City."

"Mmm," I say. "I really think I'm better off with a studio."

"No. You gotta level up. You dress for the job you want. . . ." I guess she wants to be an extra in *Cocktail.* "You pick a home you can't afford so that you work your tail off. My last boyfriend got a two-bedroom when he didn't even have a job. He's now killing it on Wall Street."

It's the longest day of the ice-cold winter that is my fucking life, and I go back to dusting books. I messed up. I went too far with my Mr. Big act. That's another well-intentioned but misguided Dick trick. Learning your language backfired, didn't it, Vail? I turned into a silent stoic *Dick*head. I didn't do what I wanted—I wanted to spoon you, I wanted to stay—and I never should have listened to Dick. I never should have been so optimistic. A fucking *jealousy* trap. What a waste.

Amelia Bedelia never learns, and neither do I.

Vagina props herself up on the counter and crosses her legs as if that turns me on (nope!).

"Can you not sit there?"

"I know where you could sit, Joey . . ."

STOP IT, VAGINA. "Ha. I just need the ledger."

She shifts and lifts, forcing me to reach *under* her ass, and the next time she asks if her skirt is too short, I'm going to say yes. Get some fucking pants. I need a new job *and* a new apartment and a new HOW TO GET A GIRLFRIEND playbook and she's doing it again. She's trying to touch my neck.

I back off. She giggles like this is a game. "So does it hurt?"

It's another thing. You left a love bite on my neck. I thought you were marking your territory, but if that were the case, you'd be here, like how killers go back to the scene of the crime. Did I compare you to a murderer? I am losing it. *Slower. Faster. Not there . . . There.* I was so bad that you had to give me DIRECTIONS and maybe you didn't bite me in the throes of passion. Maybe you were just mad at me for being bad at a natural fucking act.

Vagina dangles a little tube of Neosporin, and I shake my fucking head.

"No, thanks."

"Well, you know, Joey . . . hickeys *can* hurt. . . . Did I ever tell you I almost *died* from a hickey?"

I act like I want to know more, and I wish I could put Vagina in the basement. Not in a sick way. Not lock her up and starve her to death. Just force her to be alone so she can realize what a moving, living, un-tantalizing fucking mistake of a woman she is being.

"*My* hickey guy . . . his name was Peter. . . ." Like Peter with the pepper mill dick in your show and is it that simple? Is my Portnoy not a pepper mill? "Or maybe it was Patrick." Patrick, as in the alcoholic who Carrie dumped for wanting her too much. "Anyway," Vagina carries on. "He tells me he's a vampire and he's so sexy that I believe him. . . . He was in this band that played at Don Hill's and they were pretty big in Belgium. . . . Ever been there, Joey?"

"No." Everything takes me back to you, Vail, and even Vagina has gone places, *places I have never traveled.* I miss you. I don't know why I walked out on you. I only know that I really did that. I left. Vagina's mouth is like my brain. It won't stop. Ever. She pouts and I promise her I'm listening (I was not) and on she goes.

"So, we get together and he bites me like a lot. . . . Like a *lot.* And the next day I'm dizzy and my roommate is like omigod, Virginia, your neck is turning blue. So, he picks me up . . . I don't weigh that much but it was still so sweet. . . ." Her roommate was a guy, and all her stories are like this, full of men who touch her as if I'll catch the drift and follow suit and WHY THE FUCKING FUCK DID I LEAVE YOU?

The window is closed. I can feel it. If I did call now, you would tell me to piss off. Right?

Vagina points to her neck. No scar. No hickey. Nothing to see here, folks. "Right there," she says. "Peter-Patrick bit me so hard that he clogged an artery. I mean, he almost killed me, Joey."

That's what you did. You killed me. You bit me. And then I hear my name. "Joseph!"

I trudge to the back of the shop—I will live and die in Mooney's, I really will—and he scowls again at my love bite. "This is a *bookstore.*"

"I know. I can get a scarf." Not a red one, though. Not a scarf like your scarf.

"Do you not own a turtleneck?"

"I'm sorry."

"Don't be sorry, Joseph. Consider Virginia. That sort of scar makes a lady uncomfortable." My jaw hits the floor. "Stop it," he seethes. "You are in no position to judge, boy."

"I know."

"What is it that you know?"

"I know I should've worn a turtleneck."

He motions for me to sit down, and that's unusual. Lately, he doesn't talk to me so much, but then again, lately I pun around in starched white button-down shirts. I don't know who I am, Vail. I don't know a devil's doorbell. It's like Samantha when she says she caught monogamy from *you people.* I caught something from you. Self-doubt. Stupidity. *'Scuse me while I kiss this guy.* Speaking of which . . . still can't read. I'm like the model in season 1 who brags about reading a whole magazine cover to cover.

Mooney glares. I forgot where I was. "Well?"

I missed it. Same way I miss a lot of things these past couple of days. "Could you repeat?"

"Have you really gone that soft, Joseph? Do you think I have nothing better to do than repeat myself?"

"No."

"Go home."

"I need the hours."

"Oh, you do?"

"I've been spending a little too much lately. . . ."

He kicks back in his chair. It swivels. I used to sit in that chair when I first started coming in here. I loved that thing. We didn't have anything that swiveled at home or in school. Once, I asked him to spin me around. He said no. I never asked again.

"Joseph," he says. "In Israel, all teenagers go to war before they go to college."

"Okay."

"Meaning you're eighteen years old, boy."

Seventeen, but who cares. "Okay."

"When I was your age, I had my own apartment. I was a *father.* I was a *man.*"

True, but his kid died in childbirth, so does that even count? Fuck him. This is my life. Our life. "Bet you also knew what to do with a devil's doorbell."

He looks through me. "Did you ever read the Neil Postman as I suggested?"

No. "Of course."

"Then you know that childhood and adolescence are invented concepts."

I nod the way I do with Dick, and I wonder if this is it for me. Maybe I'll never become my own Big and will live out my days turning to others for advice, to guys who don't even know each other, guys who would fucking *hate* each other if they met. Something is missing inside of me, and there's almost no family on *Sex and the City.* Carrie never calls her mother. She almost never talks about her dad. Is that why I'm like this, like her?

"I've had it up to here with your fluctuations of late, Joseph. The haircut, that *shirt.*"

"I know."

"No, you don't know."

"Sorry."

He pounds the desk, and I'm an idiot. Can't even delete the s-word from my fucking vocabulary. "Don't be sorry, goddamn it. Be a *man.* Call it a fucking *clitoris.*"

Three minutes and two hours later, I'm in the basement with *Our Bodies, Ourselves.*

I'm doing a skim read and a deep clean and did I ring your devil's doorbell? Did I touch your . . . Still not used to that c-word and I want to cry but I don't cry. *Boys don't cry* and when Carrie asks Big if he cried while they were apart, he says no. *But I sure did listen to a lot of Sinatra.* I stab the floor with my broom. This is what I am. I don't have my own thoughts. I used to live in books, and now I live in *Sex.* It's all the same.

Mooney is right. I'm not a man. I'm a mug. Empty. Real men pour their knowledge into my empty head but I trip on my own two feet and burn myself, then I'm empty again. Thirsty.

Footsteps above and the door opens. I wipe the tears away. Fucking crying. Didn't I *just* say I wasn't gonna do that?

The lights switch off and on, and that's Mooney code for *get the hell up here.* I trudge up the stairs like a child. I remember when I had that Beck song in my head. I thought I was a loser. Little did I know that I was about to become a *Sex* fiend who can't even make a woman come. I button up my shirt. It doesn't hide the hickey. And it's not a love bite if you don't love me, which you don't because how could you love me? There is no me to love. I make promises in my head.

No more quoting Carrie and the girls. Or their men.

No more coffee at Dick's.

No more letting Mr. Mooney treat me like shit.

I'm gonna get another job. A real job.

I'm gonna get my own place. Somewhere on the East Side. Or the West Side.

I'm gonna take a break from people.

I'm gonna read until my eyes bleed out and the right novel tells me where to go, who to be, what to do with all these white fucking shirts. I reach for the doorknob, and it's the worst thing about love, about you. The second I feel charged up about becoming my own fucking person and figuring out who I am, all I see for myself at the end of the road is, well, you. It's like Mikey in *Swingers.* You are the pot at the end of the rainbow. But I won't get near the pot until I forget about you, you and your naked dress and your six-toed left foot. Carrie never got this dark or morbid, and here it comes again, the words that feel like truth.

There is no me to love. Never was.

On I go, dragging my feet into the deserted floor of the shop. Too bright, too dusty. A mother reads *Strawberry Shortcake and the Winter That Would Not End* to her mini-me little girl. I feel a sneeze coming on, and it's a relief, to lose myself for a second, to sneeze and come a little close to death.

"God bless you, babe."

I turn around and YES! "Vail!"

You're laughing at me—I am loud—and fuck yes, I am loud. I don't *need Our Bodies, Ourselves* or Dick the Damaged or Mr. Fucking Mooney to know that this is it. You're here. And you wouldn't have come if you hadn't come. I did it. I rang your devil's doorbell, and you're holding two hot Greek cups of coffee and one of them is for me. You came. You're here. I take the cups and put them down and I pick you up and I do not put you down. I will never let go, never again. You hold me tight as eyelids on eyeballs. It is you. *You.* We stay like that, wrapped up as one, and I take it all back, Vail. Every last word. Especially the worst part, the part where I said that you can't love me because there is no me.

I was wrong. I am a person. You do love me. And God bless *Sex and the Motherfucking City.* God bless Dick.

"I missed you, Cusack."

"Me too."

"Ahem."

I put you down and uh-oh . . . It's Vagina. You mad dog her in a way that proves Dick is a genius. The jealousy trap . . . It worked. I make introductions. Short and sweet. Vagina, Vail. Vail, Vagina.

"Huh," you say. "I didn't realize there were two of you on the floor."

That sound in your voice, that heat in it, you don't just like me. You need me. I *did* make you come. "Yeah," I say. "Mr. Mooney wants two of us because of shoplifters and stuff."

"Aw," Vagina coos. "Am I your little secret, Joey?"

You didn't just not like that. You fucking hated it and you might haul off and smack her. The look on your face—Carrie Bradshaw would *never*—and you take a deep breath like an orderly is coming at you with a syringe. "Quite a dress," you say. "It's so rare that you see an LBD in the middle of the day."

Vagina pulls at her spaghetti straps and touches her body all over, and I wonder if you're going to kill her. "I know, right? Poor Joey, though, it *is* a bit distracting. . . ."

Your body is trembling, and you don't blame me, you blame *her.* I didn't know a jealousy trap would work, let alone work like this and the bookstore is a boxing ring and it's the best day of my life. You two spar. A verbal catfight, a duel between two women gunning for me and my Portnoy, and the digs just keep coming. Vagina says your boots are *cute* and look *so, so comfortable* and you say that when *you* worked in retail you never wore stilettos and Vagina says she's a dancer so she's *used to being elegant in heels* and you say it's a shame that dancing alone doesn't pay the bills—meow—and she says that you have a little spinach in your teeth and you say you didn't *eat* any spinach today and she says it must have been something you ate last night, as if you don't brush your fucking teeth and I wish I had this on tape, Vail.

You sigh. She sighs.

She picks up the cup of coffee that you brought for me and oh boy, oh shit. That's an illegal hit. She sips your coffee, and she's the trampy younger barmaid who had eyes for Aidan and you are the calm, cool, semi-collected Carrie. But then she spits that coffee out and wipes her full glossy lips with the back of her hand. "Ew."

I hope you don't kill her, Vail. I don't want to visit you in prison.

Vagina shudders and hands me the coffee as if sipping from this cup won't get me killed. "Fair warning, babe . . ." Suddenly, I am *babe.* "Your little friend forgot the Equal."

You huff, and you puff, and you blow her house down. "Joe hates Equal."

Vagina fixes her eyes on me like you're some idiot customer. She says it's *adorable* that I didn't mention I was dating anyone and you say that I'm a *classic gentleman* who didn't want to make Vagina feel *ill at ease.* The two of you are going to cut me in half with your talons and your tongues, and I am home. This is home. I feel new pathways forming in my brain. I am loved. Treasured. Hunted. I had faith in Dick and Tom Cruise and I had faith in you, didn't I, Vail? I wrap an arm around you—I can't keep you in that jealousy trap forever—and you stroke my arm—you won this round, you did—and the doorbell chimes—it's a customer—and Vagina leads the way to the front of the shop. I can feel you hating her for the way she feels up her hips to scratch a make-believe itch.

You elbow me. *Whore.*

I smile at you. *Madonna.*

The customer's a browser and he doesn't want our help, and Vagina grabs the *Voice* and rolls it up and smacks my ass.

Again, you might kill her. Again, I dread the idea of you in a cage.

Vagina tries to make you jealous. She talks about our day, how she was helping *me* look at apartments. You are so green, so flustered and is that . . . Is that smoke steaming out of your nostrils?

She looks at me, not you. "You gotta see this place I found in the *Voice.*"

I've never seen you like this, Vail. Reduced to little noises. High-pitched yelps that reveal how much you missed me, how much you want me. "Whoa," you say. "The *Voice* . . . Old-school."

Vagina looks at me like it's us against you. "Aw," she says. "It's the only way to find a good place in this city."

"Huh," you say. "I actually do better with Craigslist. That's where I found Joe. Right, babe?"

And just like that, we're back.

21

I didn't think it would happen this fast, but that's life. That's magic. We're a thing. An item. Carrie and Big in the sweet spot, after the second breakup when he cooks veal for her. Steve and Miranda and the night of the full moon. Joe and Vail holding hands as they walk down Broadway after yet another delicious date night. We climb the six floors to our abode—I mean, I've slept here four nights this week; it is ours—and love happens fast. Habits too. When we climb your stairs, I cup my hands on your bouncy J.Lo peaches. It's our thing, and you get a kick out of it, to say the least. Last night, you said you wish it was a *twelve-floor* walk-up, and I kept my mouth shut, but there it fucking is.

Love is wanting a steep, tedious climb to last a little longer.

We're like a little fucked-up family. I love it when Cynthia comes in smelling like a Long Island iced tea and groans. *Just what I need . . . the happiest couple on planet effing Earth.* You love it too, the way you kiss the back of my neck and remind me to lock the bathroom door because of her. Last night, she was drunk, whining. *I love you guys, but do you always have to be so effing happy? Why don't you have a big brother for me?* You whispered in my ear: *There could never be another you. They broke the mold with you, babe.* And you're breaking it again, making me into the man I am meant to fucking be. You possess me. You hate the idea of any other woman seeing me. You Carrie me to Big new places with your smile, with your Gollumy little scowl when my phone rings, when I slip out of the room to take a call.

It's equal parts you want me and you want everyone else to stay the fuck away.

I come back and you run your fingers through my hair. So much is so good. You know what to do with your eyes now. You are free to stare at me, to take me in.

"So who was that?" you ask.

I hold your eyes. You are mine. "That was Virginia."

You make like a cat and hiss, and it's fun having a girlfriend! That's what you are. I mean, I assume that's what you are. Do I have to ask you to go steady? Do people do that? No. I don't need to do that. I kiss the side of your thumb, one of your many oddly erogenous zones. "Relax, Vail. She was just calling in sick."

"What did we say about that word, Joe. . . ."

I like the way you help me about stuff like that. Girls don't like to be told to relax, but I only do it to get a rise out of you . . . which gets a rise out of me. And it's not just the sex. It's this too. You fit in my arms. We go together, like lovers in a movie poster, all wrapped up for consumption. I've never had that with anyone, and you haven't either.

I wasn't "eavesdropping." It's a small apartment and Cynthia is loud. ☺

You snap a picture of me with one of your disposable cameras—you're *obsessed*—and I tell you I'm gonna take that fucking camera and it's on. I chase you around your tiny little apartment and you squeal and gurgle and Cynthia says she's going to jump out the window if we don't stop being so cute (ha!) and you lead me back to your just Big enough bed.

I pin you down. You are breathless. We don't need that stupid camera, not now.

After the second fuck of the morning, we hop in the shower—we shower together—and you get down on your knees—you really *can't* get enough of me. Then I cook a mini-breakfast for you and Cynthia—I am better than Big; I am me—and your bare feet feel good on my lap, like a pet I never had.

Cynthia pushes her eggs into the ketchup. "So do you have any friends, Joe?"

I don't like that and I don't like her. "My best friend Jeremy just moved to San Francisco."

You choke a little and pet my arm and now I am the pet. "Babe, she just means anyone you could fix her up with."

I'm not gonna go exposing Cynthia to Dick and Schlitz. Our life is good the way it is, with boundaries like those TV dinner plates where the mashed potatoes don't touch the meat.

"All right," you say. You wiggle your toes. I squeeze all eleven of them. God, it's so easy with you. "Shall we?"

"We shall!"

Off we go, leaving Cynthia and your cabinets full of SnackWell's. We get dressed for the day—I'm done with white button-downs, you like me in sweaters—and I help you into your cape and you smile at me for no reason.

"You know she didn't mean anything by that, right? I mean, she's just lonely."

Amazing that you think I care about your roommate, who, as you say, is not even your true friend. And I smile. Because that's all I do now . . . smile. "Oh, man," you say. "This nonstop happy thing, right? I'm so fucking cheesy that I might . . ."

"Might what?"

You smack my ass and wink. "Maybe later."

You lead the way down the stairs as I lay my hands on your shoulders and you call it the *magic touch.* I know it's true because you know everything about everything. You knew to trust Craig and his list—we are sending that man a fruit basket—and he hasn't come through for us just yet, but we will find a new home for me . . . a home that we both know just might be for us.

On the street, we linger, and we kiss like those couples I used to want to kill.

"I'll miss you," you say.

"Me too."

We are gooey as fucking teenagers, me, the kid I never got to be when I was young, and you, the girl you didn't think you could be until me. "I can't do it, Joe."

Same thing every day. You won't leave me, and I can't bear to leave you. "I know."

You shiver and glisten and there's no such thing as moving too fast, not when it's like this, when it's right. You breathe in my scent. "Okay," you say. "You first."

As the man, it's on me to walk away, to let you stand there and watch me and worry about all the Vaginas in the city that might pull me away. But that's where I come in. I look back to show you that I care. You bite your little lips that feel so good on my Portnoy, and that's all you need. A look. A wave. A promise.

Work is a drag and a blast all at once. I have a girlfriend and I am a boyfriend, and the bookstore is a beautiful place, a happy place where I say things like *My girlfriend loves that book* and *My girlfriend and I ate there last night* and I'm so good with people, telling this customer dude that you *too* have a tattoo . . . for my eyes only. He laughs like we're bros—we are Red Bull and Jim Henson—and the greatest part about saying these things now is that they're true. I think. I mean, of course you're my girlfriend. Right?

"Joseph!"

Ugh. Mooney. I know what you'd say, Vail. *It's time to leave that jerk and find a new job. A boss who respects you!* Mooney's been good to me, but I don't need anyone barking at me, treating me like a little bitch. Yesterday, he asked about the last great book I read. I told him about *'Scuse Me While I Kiss This Guy.* He sneered at my "descent into drivel," and yeah, it is *kind of* true. I really don't read anymore. But I think you're right. Life is seasonal, like a tourist trap island or those old couples in diners with nothing to say to each other. How could I read a book when all I wanna read is you?

Mooney eyes the door. *Shut it.* I shut it.

"Sit."

I sit. Something's off. His glasses are on the desk. His shirt's a little damp.

"You okay, Mr. Mooney?"

"Have you found a new home?"

"I'm seeing something later. Vail's got a lead."

"That's one," he says, and I don't get it. One what? "Where is this abode, Joseph?"

"I'm not sure exactly. Vail has the address. She found it on Craigslist."

He grins and holds up two fingers, and I get it now. He doesn't like it when I say your fucking name. "Joseph," he says. "I am happy that you appear to be content."

Only Mooney would put it that way, and I laugh. *Content.* "I know you're not a fan, Mr. Mooney, but she really is a great girl."

"Irrelevant," he says. "That you'd choose that *caped* little Philistine over a tits-out broad like Virginia . . . Bygones. In any case, you've been doing well these past few days."

"I've been feeling it. I mean, I just sold that Bukowski that's been in the window for years."

He nods like he already knew this and he slaps a check on the desk. A check made out to me. My first bonus. I don't know when it happened, but in the jizz-soaked haze of the last few days, I learned to fucking whistle. Kind of. Almost.

"Whoa," I say. "This is five hundred bucks."

"You've earned it. And you'll need a deposit for your new quarters. As in, don't spend it on *anyone* with an extra hole." He shudders, because he just has to be a dick. "Be careful with that one, Joseph. Beware the women who go by the name of a place. Dangerous as the men with two first names or, the worst of all men, the ones with *three* first names."

Whatever and I'm outta there.

Later in the day, you ask me to meet up on one of those SoHo blocks that makes you know the city is slowly turning into a mall. I show up to find you standing there like a goddess. Scratch that. You are God. No *ess.*

You beam at me. The sinking living room rises every time I see you and God, if you ever leave me . . . *Stop it, Joe. Stop it.*

I kiss you. You kiss me. You squeeze. "You ready to be blown away?"

I like the way you said that, and you wave a set of keys. "Barry for the win!"

You are proud. Puffed.

You found me a home, a *SoHo* fucking home. I normally don't even look at apartments around here because they're all so fucking expensive. Alas, you told *The Others* at work about me and Barry knew someone who knew someone and that *has* to mean that I'm your boyfriend. I kiss you. On the way up the stairs you are bubbling. You told everyone I need to move, and Barry thought I'd like this place because of the bookshelves—you're my girlfriend, you are—and of course there are disclaimers. It's only temporary and you're worried that I won't like the wide open space, the *art gallery meets warehouse* feel of it.

"Vail," I say. "I can tell you right now, it's perfect."

You hand me the keys. "You first. I mean, it is *your* home."

You have to say stuff like that—it's too soon for you to ask to move in—and I know it before I know it. *I know it the way you know about a melon*. This is home, Vail. I carry you across the threshold and deliver you to the giant couch where I kiss your face all over and tell you I love the couch.

You run your hands along my head how I like. "Technically, it's a sectional. But the best thing is behind this white curtain."

You leap up to pull a white curtain and yes. Yes! It's a big fat California king. Just like Mr. Big's.

We christen the bed and the *sectional*—you are always teaching me, always—and we order Chinese and loaf around until we have the energy to go again. We christen the shower and we christen the kitchen and it's too good to be true and you pull your hair into a ponytail.

"Okay, it kind of is too good to be true."

The first scratch on the CD in a long fucking time, but I don't panic. I pull my sweater on. I make like Mr. Big. "Speak."

"Well, like I said, it's not, you know, forever. Just a sublet for six months and then . . ."

You look to the left and blush a little, and I know, Vail. I know you want to move in together and I know anyone would tell us it's too soon to think about that.

"Vail," I say. "You never know. Things change. Maybe it *will* be forever."

Oh, you liked that and I have you right where I want you. Wrapped around my little finger, a finger I never knew I had until I found you. I aced it, the Seduction and the Destruction . . . It's second nature to me now. I don't smother you. I don't ask when I can see you again and I don't take the bait when we walk downstairs and you ask if I'd rather live farther east, *closer to Virginia*.

Girls are funny and I have to laugh at you. "You're kidding, right?"

"Well, I don't know. We haven't talked about stuff and . . ."

"Vail, I'm not interested in Virginia, or any other girl."

You look down at the ground like *I'm* too good to be true. I can barely hear you above the street noise, but I can hear enough. "Oh, Cusack," you murmur. "You really are the sweetest."

Yes, I fucking am. You have to go to a *night shoot* and I lie that I have to get back to the shop. As always, it's not easy saying goodbye. There are models and modelizers all around us, and it's fucking scary to fall in love in a place like New York. But we are there, in love. I mean, hello . . . What "stuff" is there to talk about? You found me a home!

"Okay," you say. "Time to get back to the real world. Call you later?"

"I'm sure that I'll call first, Vail. I mean, you got me a fucking house."

You laugh a little and you blush a little and I get it. This was a first for you. You put yourself out there in a Big way and that's a big deal for a girl. We part ways and I do the thing we always do where I turn around to find you already waiting for me to see you.

This time is different. You're not there.

The old me might've freaked out. Not the new me. They talk about this in books, in songs. Things that get too good too fast tend to crash and burn. Girls get scared when they give a guy a lot. You made a grand gesture and it's my turn. The best grand gestures are sometimes small.

Fuck it. I call you. You pick up right away. "That was fast. Is everything okay?"

"It's the nicest thing anyone ever did for me, Vail. I wanted you to know."

The quick call was a good call, and of fucking course it was. *I'm a cool cat . . . tapping on the toe with a new hat.* RIP Amelia Bedelia. Mr. Big does everything *right.*

22

It's been three weeks, and you basically live with me. It started one night when you called me, exasperated, something about crabs and Cynthia. I told you to come over. I think you were lying—Carrie and *The Others* had a crab attack in the Hamptons—but who cares! You showed up with a backpack and a toothbrush that you stashed in the cup next to *my* toothbrush. I'm not Mr. Big. I didn't pack up your stuff. I love your stuff in my place! I love using your toothbrush too. It's soft. Last night you got a little testy when you found it all wet, but I saw you smile. You looked like Carrie when Big lends her one of *his* toothbrushes. And real life is supposed to be messier than TV. More saliva, less money. Everything clicks. You slept over and we're about to part ways and I tell you it's bullshit, the way we have to care about anything besides us.

And then you wince. Too much? Too pathetic?

"No, Joe. You're adorable . . ." I'm adorable. "It's just . . . it's a little early but there's no way to not tell you. . . . It's my birthday on Friday."

I know about your birthday. The other night, Cynthia spilled the beans while you were in the bathroom. I think I know what I'm gonna get you. "Cool."

"If you're busy, it's okay. . . . I feel like I'm sucking up all of your time as it is."

I wink at you and smile. "And then some."

You lick your lips. "So I'm having a tiny get-together at Botanica at eight in that back room. It's nothing major, just a quarter-life crisis hen party I planned before we . . . I'm such a Pisces and I *hate* my birthday. There is truly nothing worse than being the center of attention. And I'm not putting any pressure on you."

I *knew* you were part astrology slut and it's almost refreshing. Like all girls might be the same seeker underneath. I laugh. "I get you."

"Joe, seriously. You don't have to go. And I don't expect you to get me a present and I'm not trying to like . . . you know . . . I know you're not my boyfriend."

It's the best worst thing you ever said to me, and I can already see you bouncing off the walls in a sexy little slip dress, clocking me as I walk into the bar with a dozen roses, a mixtape called *Pop Rocks* and a *raspberry beret.* I will charm your friends, but I won't be *too* charming—your Vagina envy is real—and I can't wait for a new kind of sex . . . *birthday sex.*

"We'll see how it goes," I say. "I'll try to stop by."

I played it cool because you play it cool but of *course* I'm your fucking boyfriend. Fact: The other day, you begged me to play hooky. I caved, as good boyfriends do, and we watched a few episodes of your show. You love it when I yell at the TV like it's sports. I was Mr. Fun Boyfriend. I put on *my* show for you, playing the dumb guy who thinks Big is the problem. *Man up, Big! Stop dicking her around!* You peed your panties, you were laughing that hard. Would I do that for you if I wasn't your boyfriend? Would you hang your panties in my shower and wear my sweats if you weren't my girlfriend?

It's in the writing on the walls, literally. You bought me a calendar.

You said adults have a calendar. You're right. Even Angus had a calendar. You also bought me a snow globe like the one in *Sex* and I told you that it's me and you in there.

"The Twin Towers? Joe, um . . . it didn't work out so well for them, ya know?"

I lifted the globe and shook it. "It did in here, though."

You kissed my hand and called me *sweetness* and you knew what I meant. Love is a hermetic seal. And come on. Would you be helping me turn my house into a home if you *weren't* my fucking girlfriend? I don't think so, baby!

I test the water. I call in (love)sick and dare you to do the same. You do it, and we go to the movies to see *Crossroads*. Side note: I've never seen so many movies in my fucking life. *Ordinary People* and *Good Will Hunting* and yeah. That's some boyfriend shit right there!

And I know what the people around us see as we sink into our seats, Vail.

They see a hot, happy couple. Of *course* I am going to your fucking birthday party, the one you mention six hundred thousand times during the previews. You call it a "glorified girls' night" that's "no big deal." You swear that you have no expectations of me, but I want expectations. I want the fucking pressure. The lights dim. We are holding hands in the dark, sharing plain M&M's. By the end of *Crossroads* I am crying, and a couple fucking couples are giggling. You elbow me, gently. "Relax, Cusack. You know I love that you're so sensitive."

That's what a girlfriend says to a boyfriend and now we're walking to Benny's. You run off to the ladies' room, which is okay because I know what you want at our burrito place . . . because I am your boyfriend, me.

I know more things about you every day. I know about the ski trip your family took in sixth grade where you fell on a black diamond, the time you accidentally stole a pair of diamond earrings from a Macy's only to find out they were cubic zirconium. It's not just the facts, Vail. I am happy when you want to come home with me even after all the hours with you. I listen to you walk me through your life, the life that made you into the woman you are, a verbal free spirit with her bare feet in my lap, steering the boat as we travel down the river that is you.

"Tell me something I don't know about you, Joe."

I squeeze your little feet. "You first."

"No," you say. "We always talk about me. And it's partly because of the quarter-life crisis thing where I'm hyperanalyzing every tiny thing, but I . . . I wanna know about you."

Sometimes I can't argue with you. You do that thing where you pull your eyes away and lock them onto something far away, the end table or the framed cheesy college girl Picasso that was here when I moved in. I go blank. Everything that pops into my fucking head is a fucking *no.* I look at your feet, at the freckle above your extra tiny toe. Most of my life is like that. It hurts to say it out loud.

"Vail, you kind of . . . You kind of know all my stuff already."

"Not possible. C'mon. Tell me about your first kiss."

My neighbor, the drunk older redhead. "This girl named Serena. In the cereal aisle at my bodega."

"Adorable," you coo, and I am doing it again, lying, but does it count? Is it bad? Carrie doesn't do this to Big. She doesn't drill him about his fucking past and that's why I like *Sex and the City.* Nobody has old friends or fucked-up family, and everyone has a nice home like mine.

"It's a compliment, Joe. You should be flattered that I wanna know more about you."

I am good on my feet. Fast and creative. I rip off some shit from Roald Dahl's *Boy*—this is where opposites attract, where it is *good* that you are not much of a reader—and I feed you tales of my *adorable* childhood in Bed-Stuy until you seem satiated.

The next day, it's my lunch break at Mooney's. Good day, aka no Vagina. We're dead in March, so lunch is me and my Moleskine and a nice cold slice. I can't wipe the smirk off my face and I don't want to wipe the smirk off my face. I love having homework. I gotta write down all the stories I told you in the Moleskine in case you want to hear them again. Girlfriends are like that. They want their boyfriends to tell the same old stories over and over.

Mooney storms the invisible gates, disgusted. "Joseph."

I drop my slice and close my book. "Hey, Mr. Mooney."

"When you're done writing in your diary I need you to clean the bathroom."

The old me would drop my *diary*. The new me has you. Confidence. "I checked it earlier. It's all good."

"I did not ask you for your opinion, Joseph."

"I know," I say. "But I'm giving it to you anyway."

It's weird, Vail. Weird the way he doesn't lash out at me or threaten to lock me up. Even *he* gets that I'm not the same guy, that I have a woman in my life. I'm growing, I am, and he doesn't like it. He says there was integrity in the cardboard box. He says I'm different since I moved to SoHo, because SoHo is *poison*. Last night, in bed, you said I won't be in the shop for much longer. I mean, why would you say that if I wasn't your fucking boyfriend?

A boyfriend who's got things to do!

I pop into Bloomingdale's where I find the perfect *raspberry beret*. It's soft and cashmere and you'll love it and fuck it. Mooney said my bonus was for me, not you, but it's my life, not his, not anymore. I go home to finish my *Pop Rocks* liner notes. We'll listen to it after birthday sex—we'll call it our mixtape; CD is a bad acronym—when you are wearing nothing but the beret, thanking me for the best birthday of your twenty-five-year-long little life.

And I get where you have to be so cautious with our titles. You work for a machine that teaches women to think men are incapable of *being* a fucking boyfriend. But you feel me, Vail, don't you? You feel me doing things for you, preparing for you. That's why you called twice today. Once to bitch about Barry—*I am not a location scout, location scouts get paid!*—and once to say you miss me—*What are you wearing right now?* I like you like this. Wanting me to walk through the day with you. Torturing me by spending the night at your place instead of mine. *Girls need alone time or we stop looking like girls, my dear.* Ah, you're adorable. And in the morning, my bed is too big and I miss you but that's okay. It's okay because it's *fun* to exit my loft in SoHo and feel tourists eye me like I must be special. Amazing, the way strangers who don't matter have the power to make you realize you do fucking matter. I spend an hour picking out a hot pink gift bag in a dainty little stationery store, and Mooney has a point, he does. Fucking SoHo, fucking tragedy, what it used to be, but at the moment, fucking useful.

The girl at the register hands me the receipt. "Wow," she says. "You're the world's best boyfriend. I never saw a guy spend that much time and look at that much stuff."

I laugh at her because of you. *I know you're not my boyfriend.* Ha. And then I thank the girl and run before she can put the moves on me. I'm feeling myself, and Mooney's Benjamins are burning a hole in my pocket, so I glide into Marc Jacobs and buy a soft black sweater. A birthday suit for me to match your raspberry beret, the birthday suit I got for you.

My Motorola rings, and I forgot about the world. About people who aren't you.

"'Sup, Dick?"

"So he *is* alive."

I let Dick ride my ass about being *pussy-whipped* and before you know it he's talking to me about all the boring shit in his lonely life. The indie movie he's *maybe shooting* and a disease Schlitz caught off some girl. The poor guy is jealous and how could he not be?

"Fuck," I say. "STDs . . . bad dates . . . I'm glad I'm done with that sleeping-around shit."

He laughs. "Right, Goldballs. Sure thing."

I slip on a scab of ice, and Dick cackles. First time in weeks that I'm not a *cool cat.*

I cling to my precious cargo. He's like Mooney, just jealous. "I slipped is all, I'm fine."

"So there's a rave where every prep school chick in the city is looking to get *down.*"

Gross under any circumstances, but I humor the poor guy. "Ah, were that I was single."

"Don't be a doormat, Goldbitch. You're not married. . . . I hope."

"No, but I am out shopping for birthday presents and she did invite me to her party so, ya know. . . . It's like that."

"Huh."

I stop in my tracks. I don't like that sound, that silence that follows. Does he know something, Vail? Did he see something? Did I miss something? Did you *do* something?

"Kid," he says. "I think you'd better get down here. I think we gotta talk."

23

I was good, Vail. Wrapped up like *Pop Rocks.* Safe with you, sure of you, us. But now I'm climbing the subway stairs and again I hit ice—fuck you, Manhattan—and I have to calm down. *Gently, Joseph.* You're my girlfriend. You called me twice today. That's textbook girlfriend shit. Things with us are good and real. *Perfect.* But there it is again.

I know you're not my boyfriend.

I bust into the Beanery, and Dick makes a face. "No caffeine for you, son."

I sit at the counter. I sweat. "What did you mean? What did she say?"

"Have you looked in a mirror, kid?"

"I was in a rush."

"Yeah," he says. "That's some truth right there."

I drink my glass of water and give Dick the update on our sleepovers and here it comes. Another fucking lecture. He says I can't give myself away to you. He says it's a turnoff for a girl, the way I'm always with you, never with anyone else. Open 24-7 like a fucking bodega.

"I'm not an idiot, okay? It's not like I told her I love her or anything."

"But she told you she doesn't want a commitment."

"Not exactly, and you know girls . . . They have to say that."

He eyes the pink bag. The Marc Jacobs bag too. I grab my stuff. *Mine.*

He says a girl he was *actually pretty into* once gave him the heave-ho because he bought her a Brita water filter. "I keep telling you, kid. It happens to all of us. You like her too much and she knows it, so where's the challenge for her?"

I know you're not my boyfriend. You are holding back a little bit. Two phone calls in one day is not two *fuck-fests* in one day. I can't lose you. I just can't. "So, what do I do?"

"Well, you can't put the toothpaste back in the tube. Your only move now is . . . Seriously, what's in the bag?"

"I didn't go crazy. Most of it's for me."

"So what's the plan? Did you make reservations and shit?"

"I told you. She's having a party."

"Ouch."

"No ouch. She invited me and it's just a few friends getting together at Botanica. She and her roommate planned it before we got serious. It's cool."

"Well, there it is."

"There's what?"

"Goldballs," he says. "There is no fucking *way* you are going to that party."

He says a terrible thing like that and then he disappears to make lattes and is he right? He's always right. I have you because of him, because of *Seduce and Destroy.* And here it comes again, a nick from a bad rusty razor that bleeds when I pick at it, when I think of it.

I know you're not my boyfriend.

Dick comes back swinging, as if he *wanted* to wipe the smile off my face. "Dude," he says. "I told you to stop it with the mixtape. And you sure as hell can't *give* it to her. Not yet."

"But things are good. She practically lives with me."

"Does she have a key? Does she pay half your rent?"

Grrr. I look out the window, and he grabs the bag from Bloomingdale's and pulls out the beret. Are his hands clean? "Dude," he says. "Are you *trying* to get a restraining order?"

I. HATE. EVERYTHING. I need to keep things to myself. Mr. Big doesn't go to his *friends* for advice. Maybe your birthday will be a new start for me too. No more nay-saying know-it-alls. No more Dead-Eyed Dick and Misanthropic Fucking Mooney. "I gotta go, Dick."

"Goldboy, don't start crying."

"Then don't make it sound like I'm crazy. It's not like I'm gonna march into Botanica with a dozen roses or some shit. It's a mixtape and a beret." And maybe a dozen red balloons, like Big got for Carrie, but at least I know not to say it.

"Real talk, son. You're getting laid by now, yeah?"

None of his business. *None.* But also yes. "Duh."

"You meet her friends?"

"I've hung out with her roommate a lot."

"Roommates don't count, son. She told you you're not serious, so don't *you* get serious. You're not 'with' this girl. You're banging her. There's a difference."

He pours a cup of coffee like we're all done with me and starts to brag about some fundraiser for his *film* that will never come to pass. The last days with you are the best days of my life. You found me a home. You can't walk away from me without dying a little.

Dick groans. "Christ. Are you still thinking about your little mixtape?"

"I did it all, just like you said, okay? I played it cool. I still do. I don't pick up every time she calls. The Vagina jealousy trap? You were right. I set that trap. Worked like a charm. But we're past that. I have to go to her party, and I'm telling you, Dick. She wants me there."

"Vagina," he says. "That's what you do. You bring Vagina to the party."

"I have a *girlfriend,* asshole."

"No," he says. "You want to know what it's like to have a birthday girl girlfriend?"

Yes. "Does it matter?"

"You gotta make impossible reservations at some place they just *have* to hit up because they saw it on Page Six or in some fucking magazine. . . ." You don't want to eat alone with me. "And after you shell out the dough for dinner, because of course that's on you, she's your *girlfriend.* Well, then it's on *you* to carry the cupcakes you bought at Magnolia. Because for sure she told you to get the cupcakes . . ." You did not ask me to get the cupcakes. "You gotta hold her hand in the cab on the way to the party, because chicks go apeshit on their birthday, son. She's not walking in without her boyfriend. Especially when she invited every guy she ever met."

"She said it's mostly girls."

I wish I didn't say that out loud, but at least he lets it go. "Kid," he says. "You do *not* have a girlfriend. And you won't ever have a girlfriend unless you learn to back the hell off. You're the catch. When it comes to Joe Fucking Goldberg, it's all or nothing. Go broke or go home. Teach her that she doesn't get the milk without the cow . . . However it goes."

I don't know how it goes with the milk and the cow but Dick might be right.

"Don't be a little bitch," he says. "Okay, I'm getting an idea . . ." He rubs his hands together and spreads his legs, but he's not about to do those annoying standing push-ups. He claps. "Interior, Botanica bar . . ." I knew this would happen someday. Fucking film people. "Wide shot. The birthday girl holds court. Her gal pals know she's banging some guy but it's early, it's new . . . Whole night, she's watching the door, waiting. CUT to . . . midnight. She's drunk. She told everyone about this *great* new guy, and this great new guy . . . Cut to the door. He's a no-show. Midnight turns into one, and one turns into two. Cinderella's fully fucking wasted. Not elegantly. Just wasted. Drunk-dialing, making zero sense. Four A.M. Interior, the bathroom. Vomit in the toilet. She looks in the mirror, sees a drunk, obsessive, clingy, desperate chick who's old, getting older. She knows she fucked up. She hates herself. Exterior, Houston between Mott and Mulberry. Our hero Joe gets out of the cab. He walks into the bar. The music swells. The high-pitched scream of the girl who thought she lost the guy, the guy who knew that she needed to think she lost him. She runs across the bar. Jumps him as we fade to her bedroom, where she rides him like there's no tomorrow because all she wanted for her birthday was . . ."

"Me."

"Boom. That's a wrap, my boy!"

He grabs my head and gives me a noogie, and it's my first noogie. My first real-life buddy. He pounds his chest and becomes middle-of-the-night wasted Vince Vaughn in the middle of the fucking day. It's *Swingers,* Vail. It's right there on your bedroom wall.

"My boy is all growns up! My boy is all growns up!"

Dick is making a scene and the *girls, girls, girls* are amused and giggling. It's the bar mitzvah I never had, the graduation day I deserve. I'm getting better at this how-to-take-advice thing, Vail. It's not all or nothing. I'll make you wait for me, but I'm not waltzing into Botanica without a bouquet of red balloons. When Carrie turned thirty-five, her fancy birthday dinner got fucked up and *The Others* dragged her to the coffee shop. They said that they are her soulmates—HAHAHA—and Carrie went along with it—such bullshit. But *The Others* didn't see what I saw, what you saw, what we all saw. Carrie's face only *really* lit up when Mr. Big surprised her with champagne and . . . red fucking balloons. It's the reason we're here, to find that one person who fits, and I think I'm gonna add a little Wham! to your mixtape. It won't be a happy birthday unless you know that *Baby, I'm . . . your . . . man.*

24

We're off to a great start, Vail. You wanted *birthday eve girl time* with Cynthia last night, so I gave you "space" and called you first thing this morning to say happy birthday. You didn't pick up (no hard feelings), and I sang to you.

I'm not a singer, and I can't wait for you to tease me about my skills, and it killed me, waiting for it to get late, waiting for your quarter-life crisis to fucking end so that our full-blown happy life can begin.

But we made it. I'm walking into Botanica at 2:11 A.M. with a dozen red balloons and my hot pink shiny bag. And it's . . . a lot like Dick's screenplay. Your *get-together* in the way way back of the bar is . . . not a fucking *hen party*. That is a *party*. Thick with jerks. What the hell, Vail? Did you invite the whole city? I expected something small, a little coven of girls (plus a few guys from Cynthia's bed) squished around a table. And I'm not nuts. I expected something small because you prepared me for something small. Yet this is . . . *Big*. You have friends. The only one you ever talk about is Cynthia, but these mysterious friends bought a banner and hung it above the entrance to the back room of Botanica: *Happy Quarter Century, Vail!*

The balloons were a mistake, and I run outside and watch them float into the black.

Back in the bar, I make a beeline for the rear, and there's no air in here, only smoke. I'm bumping into jerks with jobs who jerk each other off like it's not Friday fucking night.

Jerk 1: Do you work in the mail room at Condé Nast?

Jerk 2: More like Condé *Nasty.* I'm at *EW* now.

Jerk 1: Amazing. I'm at Hearst and I couldn't be happier. So how do you know Vail?

Jerk 2: I don't know her. Does anyone ever know the birthday girl at these things?

They're not even here for you, and okay. I need to breathe. You did say you're in crisis and I'm late. It's late. But I'm here. I maneuver my way to the back room, a tobacco-scented, airtight colosseum. It's not late-late, not for Friday night in New York, and I can do this, find you, please you. I walk under the banner and enter the war room, but it's even worse in here. The people, your people . . . debauchery and douchebaggery. This isn't a party room. It's a performance space. Stacked stadium seating. Awkward as a high school fucking cafeteria and who *are* all these people bragging about their jobs, their conquests? *Gently, Joseph.* Girls do this—they hoard—and you're in here somewhere, but I don't see you. I'm casing the joint, peering into the bouquets of Dunhill Carrie Bradshaws and half-shirt Samanthas and the men . . .

Terrible. Sleazy. U of M baseball-cap-on-backwards dolts mixed with pompous *media* men, all of them unfit for a two-episode story on your fucking sitcom, let alone you.

I plunk my ass on the indoor bleachers. Two sweater-set-style Charlottes glare at me like I'm the problem, interrupting their heart-to-fucking-heart about their *careers.* I butt in. "Hey, have you guys seen Vail?"

The answer is no, and they don't want me, and I don't want them, but it would be nice to be wanted right now. There are too many men in here. Do you know them? Do you . . .

Gently, Joseph.

I am not that bitter prick. I am Big. Cool. Calm. Unbreakable.

The Charlottes ditch me to flirt with bespectacled snobs who cross their legs and drone on about Jann Wenner and *semantics.* You're not with them and you're not with the Dick-ish baseball-cap bros in the corner, rating the Carries and turning their backs on the Mirandas.

"Dude, you looking for anything?"

It's a beady-eyed snake in a Ramones shirt (oh, come *on*) and did you hire a drug dealer the way a mom hires a clown?

I can't find you, so I look for Cynthia but the walls of people are closing in on me. You're not here. She's not here. I don't belong and I am late, too late. A girl flips her hair, and the hair slaps my face. She looks at me like I'm Mikey in *Swingers.* Like she's seen my fucking bank statement. "Can you move?"

I move. I walk and I wonder what your true friend Anj would say about this collection of unbearables. A tickle in my throat. A death in my heart.

I know you're not my boyfriend.

Did you mean that? Did you want a night off from me? Did you go home with someone else? I dip my finger into the remains of your birthday cake. I clock the box. *Magnolia Bakery.* Who carried that cake into the taxi, into this room? Was it Cynthia? Was it a man?

A tap on my shoulder. Is it you? I turn around and no. It's not you. "It's a private party."

"I know. Where's Vail?"

"Who are you?"

"I'm her boyfriend."

The girl makes a face and she gives me the hand. "Oof. See ya, wouldn't wanna be ya!"

I'm not the bad guy—I am holding a fucking mixtape—and the

Bowie is foreboding—*Twenty-five . . . Don't wanna stay alive*—and is that you, Vail? Did you run off to end it all because I didn't show? FUCK FUCK FUCK. I won't let go of hope and I shove my way through the satin astrology sluts and now it's Fatboy Slim. "Praise You." I can't praise you. I can't love you and the song is from *Sex*. I am Carrie on the beach when she learns about Big and Natasha and there's no one who's gonna hold *my* hair back if I puke and no.

Don't fucking puke.

But my stomach is rumbling. The techno and the flashing bulbs on the disposable cameras, not Nikons, not Polaroids, no *greens of summers,* just cardboard one-off cameras that wind up in a landfill. Is that me? Did you throw me away? Did I throw *you* away? I spot a box with a sign on it. That's your handwriting, proof of your participation: DROP YOUR CAMERAS IN MY BOX. There are nine cameras in *your box*. My box. *Mine.* I push my way through the monsters of Botanica—bad name for this bar, no flower would survive—and I walk outside. I call you. Nothing. I call Dick. Nothing. One of my red balloons is caught in a fence across the street. You love me and I am late. I will not panic. Dick got it all wrong.

Interior. You in that back room, waiting for me.

Exterior. Me on the sidewalk, the asshole who stood you up on your birthday. *End scene.*

Or maybe not. Girls drink when they get sad, and it's a dark bar. I was in such a rush to get to the colosseum that I didn't check the main floor. The thing with feathers is alive in me again, and I walk back into hell. Two bartenders on duty. A woman who wishes she were anywhere but here and a guy with a wifebeater and a mohawk. I choose the guy, an anti-Steve who would notice a birthday girl in a plastic fucking crown.

A lot of guys would have noticed, especially those *New Yorker* assholes. *Grrr.*

"Yo, dude."

"What'll it be?"

"Have you seen the birthday girl around?"

"Ha. She was pretty toasted. Split a while ago. . . . You trying to buy her a shot?"

I picture you falling off the *Titanic* with an incompetent fake Leo. "Did she leave with anyone?"

He laughs and says he's so happy he's single and can anyone ever just let it be about *me*? "Are you drinking, or what?"

I toss a ten on the bar. I am not Big. I am small. A ten isn't a Benjamin, and I know what I look like. Little boy lost carries *hot pink gift bag* around a crowded bar after midnight. I check my Motorola and nope. You didn't call me back, not yet. I hate myself. I know better. I *knew* better. You *are* my fucking girlfriend. The proof is in the Magnolia banana pudding you fed to me the other night and how could I be so fucking stupid? I need to see you, Vail. I need to know what you did while I was home torturing you with my absence for no good reason. I need to know what I fucking missed. I make one last trip into the colosseum. I shove my hand in your box. I grab one of these cardboard plastic cameras and a screaming, semi-Charlotte shouts, "Hey! That's not yours!"

Oh yes, it fucking is, and New York was built for nights like this.

4:12 A.M. and the one-hour photo place by the bookstore opens at seven. I walk and I walk, and I buy coffee for myself, for the homeless. I help a drunk girl get into a cab and slip the cabbie a twenty to make sure she gets home safe. I am a good man. Lovable. Loving. I won't jump to conclusions, and I won't look back.

Yes, Dick was wrong. People who are right a lot are wrong at times.

I should've showed up at 9:31. I shouldn't have been singing into my Motorola at eight A.M. I get it. What a fucking tool, right? I bet you woke up, puked in your pillowcase, and played my voicemail for Cynthia. I bet she got in your ear, in your head. *Wow, that is not a cool cat. Does he think you guys are married or something? I mean, give a girl a little space.*

Deep down, I knew it, didn't I, Vail? I was wrong to call you this morning when I wanted to see you, be with you. I should've shown up at your place around eleven A.M. with my pink bag and my balloons. It's your *birthday* and you weren't pushing me away. You were daring me to make a *real* grand fucking gesture and I failed. F minus. I knew that *you* wanted me to go to your party. And if I really was *all growns up* like Mikey at the end of *Swingers,* well, come on.

An adult does what he wants. A pupil disobeys his teacher. A boyfriend comes *through.*

At 7:03 A.M., a scrawny guy with an Adam's apple the size of a McIntosh unlocks the door to the one-hour photo place. "Whoa," he says. "I haven't even had my coffee."

A business that opens at seven should be prepared to do business at seven. "Sorry," I say as I slip him the garbage camera. "I didn't mean to come in all hot."

I lean against a wall and wait for the fifty-eight minutes to pass. Like it or not, I will hold on to your first birthday with me and without me forever. This place. The dust particles and the light and his Adam's apple and the clock on the wall that ticks. A clock that takes me back to school, to Miss Frascatore's office. Is this what that is? Did you run out on me because I ran out on you?

Adam's Apple hands me an envelope. Twenty-four photographs inside. Gulp.

Opening a package of photographs is like starting a new book. It's a ritual. It matters, where you are when you read the first page. I exit the shop. I breathe. In air, out dust mites and chemicals. I'm only a couple of blocks from the shop, so I walk to the shop, down to the cage.

"Hi, Hector."

He's a typewriter, so he doesn't say hi back. He can't, unlike you. You could call me back. Will you call me back? It's early, I know. You were up late crying. *Why doesn't Joe love me? Why did I pretend I don't want to be his girlfriend?* I pop our mixtape into the CD player. *Pop Rocks.* Eric Carmen helps. It's fine. We're fine. It's just a birthday. It's not like your mom died. I can make it up to you. And you're older than I am. Of course you know more people. Girls hoard friends, and those guys in that Urban Outfitters colosseum . . . Oh, come on. That was all for me, wasn't it? A *Big* fat jealousy trap. You were trying to impress me, your new boyfriend who was supposed to waltz into that colosseum and kiss you and show the world that he belongs to you. Yes, in an ideal world you wouldn't have fucked with me and tested me. But I can't blame you for being Forever 21 at twenty-five. You learned from watching me.

I turn on the library lamp at the big desk. The green glass always makes me smile, *makes me gain control.* I set the hot pink bag on the table. Eric Carmen fades into Prince, and God, I made you a good mix. Every song on this baby is like a picture. It tells a story, if you read closely, if you listen.

I pull the envelope out of the hot pink paper bag. I pull out the photos. Warm and sticky, like my mom used to say about my blanket after I did the bad thing in my bed. *Not now, Joe. Stop it.* Deep breath. The top photo is a blur. Drunk people and cameras . . . If you paid for all these fucking disposables, my dear, you made a big fucking mistake. The next one is a blur and the one after that is a blur but . . .

Number five is a keeper. There's your cake. Hot pink icing. HAPPY BIRTHDAY VAIL WE LOVE YOU.

We is good. We is not *I.*

Your friends bought you the cake, whoever they are. I'll meet them soon enough, and then we'll find new friends. Better ones.

The next picture is a jolt. It's you.

A plastic silver crown on your head and wow. You got your hair done and your makeup too and it wasn't for me but then again . . . yes, it fucking was. I feel *warm and sticky,* and Peter Frampton comes alive, bringing shadows and calm into this cage.

Picture number six is not so nice, and I kill the fucking *Pop Rocks.*

Picture number six is what Carrie never did to Big. It's you. You're inebriated and barefoot. The dark side of Cinderella. One missing shoe is romantic. Two missing shoes is danger. Your extra toe exposed in real life, in glossy print. But that's not the problem, not really. It's your birthday, I know. You did one too many shots and your friends are jerks, which is why you never talk about them. All of that is fine. Good, even.

The bad thing is what lurks beside you. A man in a yellow hat with his arm slung over your shoulder. You know him. You trust him. Is he the guy from Jake's Dilemma? The one who called you *Gundylocks* the night Angus bulldozed our momentum? This is not some guy you just met. This is someone you wanted to see, someone you're happy to see, someone who makes you laugh. The whole-body, punch-buggy *intensity* of the laughter. Your toes are curled up. Your eyes are slits and your cheeks are flushed, and him.

Him.

The dark side of Aidan Fucking Shaw. His sweatshirt screams DALTON and his jeans are filthy. He wears Vans. He didn't dress up for you. He doesn't dress up for anyone. He's not your Mr. Big and did I blow it?

I push Play on *Pop Rocks.* Can't be alone, not now.

Is it over? Did you decide that I'm not Big enough for you? The waves *crash, crash into me,* and I forgot I added that song. I feel stupid. I'm the good-on-paper dorky doctor, the one who offered his home to Carrie when Charlotte had crabs in the Hamptons. You don't love me. You don't miss me, and your feet hang there so close to his. Dangling like dust mites in a one-hour photo. Do you love him now? The *Pop Rocks* burn a hole in my chest, Billy Joel turning on me like a bad burrito. It's all there, in your smile and your eleven exposed toes. You love him just the way he is, and where does that leave me, Vail? Where does that leave *us*? I tear the picture into a million little pieces. I stare into the trash bin, but his eyes survived my thrashing. Beady and blue.

I grab that little scrap of photo paper and tear it again because no. No, that fucker doesn't get to look at me, and then I see another piece of the picture. Your bare, beautifully deformed little foot. Why did I tear up the picture? That's not what I want. I want to be *in* the fucking picture, and I want to put it back together and replace the man in the yellow hat, but I can't do that, Vail. I broke it. Us.

25

I am back in my loft in SoHo because it's 8:48 A.M. and *Do you know where your children are?* No! I don't know where you are. I can't call you. What would I even say? I'm not the bad guy here, not really. You were drunk on your big day in your silver crown. You claimed that you hate being the center of attention, and I believe you, Vail, I do. But that's why you should've walked out of that bar, onto the sidewalk, and wobbled there for a spell and said fuck it. *I'm calling my boyfriend. I want Joe.* Drunk girls love calling boyfriends to bitch them out or beg for mercy. I would've picked up. You would've been blunt and slurring. *Baby I love you where are you ahahaha you're my boyfriend I don't know why I'm so stupid can you come please come okay yes come now.*

But you didn't. And of course you didn't.

I am the asshole who didn't show up. Sitting here wallowing in *Sex and the City* with new sad eyes. They should've called it *Who's a Bigger Asshole? Big or Carrie?*

I turn off the TV. Fuck Dick for getting in my head. Fuck Big for getting in my head, and fuck little Miss Carrie Bradshaw for getting in *your* head, convincing you that all men are so afraid of commitment that you have to be the first one to push them the fuck away.

I grab my coat.

I'm a reader and that picture of you and the man in the yellow hat told a story: PREP SCHOOL CAD MAKES DRUNK GIRL LAUGH.

But I don't know the whole story and I jumped to conclusions. I assumed he charmed your skirt off and got into your pants, and for all I know, you threw up on him before it even got to that. You told me I'm not your boyfriend. I listened to you, as if any girl in Manhattan who thinks love is obsolete can be trusted when she's on the verge of becoming a little less Forever 21.

I'm out the door and a dude talking to a plastic bag laughs at me and okay. You probably *are* in your bed that feels like mine with the man in the yellow hat.

Note to self: If she invites you to a party, you fucking GO.

I care about you, Vail. And I am better than Big. Did he ever walk nineteen blocks in the iceberg wind and make a right on the corner of 22nd and Fuck It? Would he ever stand on the corner pacing? Figuring out his next move? I don't know what to do. Do I show up at your place empty-handed? Do I buy you a coffee? Do I sit on a stoop and wait for you to emerge in brunch gear with the man in the yellow hat?

I sit on a stoop. Everyone is lazy and cozy in this wasteland. Ides of March. March madness. What a terrible time of the year, and my thoughts are little black ants marching all over me, all over each other. I am the asshole who didn't show up to your party. But you are the asshole who told me not to come to your party. Sitting there in your crown, letting the man in the yellow hat make you laugh, but then again . . . What else could you do? Your boyfriend stood you up on your birthday. But then again YOU TOLD ME NOT TO COME. But then again I sang for you, to you. But then again you got a lot of birthday calls.

Did you even listen to me sing? If I was bad, don't you get that I was trying to be funny bad like Big in the mafioso-esque fucking restaurant?

I stand. I can't do this to me, to you. Can't collapse into full-blown Carrie Ranting Bradshaw. I have no business being on your street, same way Carrie had no business showing up at Big's church. I am trying, Vail. I am here. I tore up that picture and it's gone, but I can't get it out of my head. It does tell a story. It tells the story of a birthday girl in a crown and the man who made her laugh. And it matters, the laughter. It's right there in episode 2 of season 1. Big walks into the coffee shop where Carrie sits with her hair in pigtails. He slides into the booth and says it: *After a while, ya just wanna be with the one who makes you laugh. Know what I mean?*

Carrie knows what he means, and *I* know what he means. I check my phone. It's 11:11 A.M. and fuck it. I'm me. I'm your boyfriend, the guy who rubs your feet in my SoHo loft, the home you found for me because again. I am yours. You are mine.

The end of the dwelling. Time to *act.*

I start with your home phone. It rings and it rings, but that's girls. Girls screen their calls. And that's what makes us boys into men. We speak into the machine knowing that you might be standing there listening, rating us like there's an Olympics for fucking voicemail.

I clear my throat. "Hey, Vail! Hey, Cyn! Hey, happy birthday! Sorry I missed you last night . . . long story, but maybe I can take you to brunch or something. I hear birthday girls like brunch. . . . Maybe Eleven Madison? Or we grab and go from Magnolia? Or Veselka?"

The machine cuts me off because WHY THE FUCK WOULD IT LET ME KEEP GOING WHEN I AM NAMING RANDOM RESTAURANTS? I picture you and the man in the yellow hat camped out on the sofa. No. I have to stay positive. I call your cell phone and there you are but aren't.

You went to Vail and all you got was this lousy voicemail.

I do a couple of high kicks so the nerves won't come through in my voice and again I offer to take you to Eleven Madison. I crack a joke about how I can't afford Eleven Madison after the money I blew on your gift, and I laugh. "Just kidding. . . . But also not. See, I did get you a gift or two and . . ." DID YOU FUCK THE MAN IN THE YELLOW HAT? "I'm sorry."

Your Motorola cuts me off and I am going to find your cell phone and destroy it so you can't listen to that message, but I can't do that. Your phone is with you, Vail. Where are you?

I sit again. I wait for you to walk outside, to sense my presence, to feel me longing for you. I miss my old apartment. I miss Dumb and Dumber and my cardboard box and the way things used to be. I hate that you have two phone numbers, which means you got to reject me *twice.* A person is a person. One body, one soul, and there should only be one way to reach you. Seconds turn into minutes and you're not calling me back but of course you're not calling me back. When Big upsets Carrie, she hooks up with her version of the guy in the yellow hat, that artist slash bartender who sang Three Dog Night and drank too many margaritas. I have to have faith.

Carrie didn't kiss the artist with the stupid tattoo. She didn't have sex with him.

The one she really wants is *Big.*

I hit up the bodega and spring for a sack of daisies (*the friendliest flower*). On the way back to your place I ditch the daisies and run back to the bodega and buy roses (the sexiest flower). I'm good. The roses prove that I'm in this for the long haul, that I'm not going to freak out if the man in the yellow hat is in there with you. Your building isn't fancy—you don't have cameras—and I feel better already. I can do this. You're going to hear my voice and rush to get dressed and order the man in the yellow hat to stay put until we're gone.

I hit the buzzer, but there is no God in Murray Hill. The buzzer is broken. I push buttons again as if I can fix the call box—I cannot fix the call box—and I call your cell again but you don't answer. I call your landline again but I get your machine. Did you break the fucking call box to keep me away? *Gently, Joseph.* Ditch the roses. *'Cause you're a cool cat.* Relax. You had a late night and it's Saturday fucking morning. New York is yawning. Slow. For all I know, you're alone, sleeping it off.

A girl in last night's clothing walks out of a nearby building with a naughty smile and this is good. It's the witching hour, when one-night stands turn into walks of shame. The man in the yellow hat has not emerged from your building, but then again, the man in the yellow hat has not emerged from your building. I stare at your front door. I am going in circles and standing still at the same time and there it is again, in my head. *I know you're not my boyfriend.*

"Beep, beep."

A woman with a stroller and two bags from Key Foods is trying to get in. I know her, but I don't know her. She lives in your building. There are cans in that bag and cans are heavy and I'm a gentleman. A New Yorker who doesn't think twice when he sees a woman with a stroller navigating subway stairs or apartment stairs. I grab the bag. She unlocks the front door. I'm not "breaking in." This isn't like Angus Kaplan and the gargoyles. I'm simply helping a put-upon Murray Hill–adjacent mom. She doesn't thank me with words, but her sad eyes say it all. She closes her first-floor apartment door and locks it.

I am in. Close.

It feels good to climb your stairs, to be your Prince, to take it one step at a time. No roses. No clue what I'm gonna say or do, but this is how you know you love someone, isn't it?

I am not here because I want to be here. I am here because I *have* to be here.

And now I am here. Sixth floor. Your floor. Approximately twelve steps from *The Last House on the Left.* Why am I scared to knock? Why do I feel bad being here when I've been here, when I'm yours? I tiptoe. *Gently, Joseph.* The goalposts move and now I am here as in really here. Eye to eye with your peephole and why can't these peepholes be two-way streets? Who's to say everyone on the inside is so good? Is he there, Vail? Are you alone?

I can't see things, but I hear things. Calypso music . . . *Sex.* Not actual sex. It's your show. I smell something burning and what if there's a fire and no. *Ding.* That's an overcooked Pillsbury Toaster Strudel—it is cherry—and it feels weird, Vail. Knowing what I shouldn't know. Being where you shouldn't be and being where you belong are not supposed to be the same thing.

I raise my fist. I should knock. I am allowed to be here. I am *dating* you.

I can't knock. I am not your boyfriend. It is before noon on a Saturday.

I will knock. You invited me to your birthday.

I can't knock. I showed up late. You had already left with the man in the yellow hat.

I have to knock. Big was here, in a way. He had to tell Carrie that he knew she stalked his ex-fucking-wife.

I can't knock. Carrie was here, in a way. She had to hang her head and cop to stalking his ex-fucking-wife.

While I was in my head, something happened. No more calypso. Silence.

I hold my breath and who designed us fucking humans? Why can't I choose to stop breathing for a few fucking seconds? Is this trespassing? Is this love? The quiet is that kind of quiet where I question my own memory, the sound of the Bible hitting the floor of the church.

Thunk.

Fuck this shit. This is us. You and me. I bought you a beret and I made you a CD and there are eleven red balloons in the sky, soaring. You're my girlfriend, even if you say you're not my girlfriend. I have every right to be here, and if you are in there with the man in the yellow hat, then it's not my fault, not your fault. It is our fault. We're allowed to mess up. I should've insisted on taking you to Pastis, and you should've told me what kind of cake you wanted from Magnolia. I raise my fist, and my knuckles are sharp. White. Wait.

What was that sound?

It's the absence of sound, the feeling that someone on the other side of the door is holding her breath. Quiet in that intentional way where you hit the Mute button because you feel the mouse in your house even before you spot the little whirling dervish. Is that what I am? Am I the mouse? Do you smell me out here? I want to knock. I have to knock. There is no scarier sound than silence—just ask Simon and Garfunkel—and a real man is fearless. A real man raises his fist and connects his knuckles with the door and—

26

I didn't do it, Vail. I didn't knock on your door.

See, I never had a Nintendo, but I had a neighbor that had one, and sometimes he let me come over to play *Super Mario Bros.* A skinny older guy in his thirties or some shit. Stefan. A Nordic dude who was always talking about his visa running out. I was young. I thought he meant his credit card. Anyway, my dad didn't like him. Called him a *creep.* He was pasty and nervous and always squinting because he couldn't afford new glasses. My dad, my booze bag, screaming vicious dad, he thought he was better than Stefan because he had someone to fight with. Stefan wasn't creepy. He was just alone. But it's a thing about the world, isn't it? When you're alone, people assume it's because you can't get anyone to be with you.

That's why I didn't knock, Vail. I felt too alone in the hallway and it's kinda like Mario and the princess. One time I told Stefan I was sick of the game. He said that's the point: "You don't get to be with the princess until you beat all the bad guys."

It's the same in your rom-coms. And it's the reason I am on East Eighty-ninth Street across the street from the Dalton School wearing a Dalton ID and a Big white button-down that looks good under the blazer I picked up at Goodwill. The ID isn't the best, but it's still kind of cool what you can do with a laminating machine at a fucking Kinko's.

It's almost three o'clock, almost go-time. I toss my hacky sack like a carefree boy just back from Turks and Caicos and I'm on the move. I spent a couple of hours watching these kids and I think I'm a pretty good mimic. I know how to contort my face, how to hold my head back like the world is mine, the street, the front door of the Dalton School, the girls in plaid skirts passing by, playing a dangerous game of Who Would You Rather?, but wisely choosing David Letterman over Rudy Giuliani.

I know, Vail. You have a crush on our former mayor. Yawn. But I swear, there's something about that guy. Something I don't trust.

And here we go. The first level of the game. The front doors of the Dalton School.

It's a little scary to be trespassing, but a little scary is good for a guy. That's how you save the princess. And I did it, Vail. I *waltzed* in here and breezed by a nervous-looking teacher who probably lives in a place like yours. She didn't card me. For a school that's so hard to get into, it's pretty easy to get into, and I'm not dumb. I know the man in the yellow hat doesn't go here anymore—he is older than I am, same way everyone is older than I am—but he was wearing that Dalton shirt, wasn't he? If I can dig up his yearbook, I can learn his name. I'm sure his parents bought him an apartment when he graduated from college and I'm sure the apartment is in the actual fucking white pages and when I hunt him down . . .

MAYDAY.

There's an adult coming my way, a real *all growns up* teacher type of guy and he's flagging me down and I'm freezing up but then it happens. . . .

The bell tolls for me.

The hallway fills up with kids out of *Kids* who make me feel old and young all at once. I take a second. I need a second. I can't pretend to be one of these pricks if I don't walk among these pricks. They're all so relaxed, Vail. They're going to the Meadow or they're going to *KK's place because her parents are in Rome,* and me . . . I'm going to the library.

Level 2. My next obstacle is the librarian. I have to channel Angus's entitlement in order to get past the watchdog, to make it to Level 3. And I can do it. After all, if I really were one of these kids, would I let some librarian who makes $30K a year get in my way? I open the door, and the librarian could be your age, maybe a little older, and for a moment, it bumps me the way a video game will do that.

You really are older than I am, Vail. I'm a long way from twenty-five.

I nod the way Angus would, like she's beneath me, and the librarian seems sick of it, her life, and who wouldn't be sick of dealing with the likes of me, but she doesn't stop me, and hell yes, I'm on to Level 3. God bless librarians!

Already, I feel better. Hunkered down in the stacks, surrounded by great works of literature . . . as well as ALUMNI READS. My school barely had a library, let alone a section like that, and I feel good, Vail. Full of purpose and pride and there they are, the fucking *yearbooks,* and you graduated high school in what—1994? '95?

Much as I hate to admit it, girls tend to like *older* guys—*I would so do David Letterman*—so I grab the '94 yearbook. Except it's not a yearbook. It's something better that must only exist in rich kid schools. The cover says it's Dalton *Faces and Names.* Kinda like a phone book with addresses accompanied by something you don't see in the white pages: *pictures.* Game on. I sit down at a table that's nicer than all the tables in my school combined. It doesn't wobble, and it isn't *warm and sticky.* I turn the pages and confront the faces of all these kids who hit the jackpot before they were even born. Some look like assholes, and

I'm sure they are, but some of them . . . I dunno. Some of them don't look so bad, and it makes me worry. What if the man in the yellow hat is one of the good ones? Is he? Could he be? I move through the alphabet, and he is not a Broder or a Calder. He is not a Souther, and you probably had sex with him last night. For all I know, you could be having more sex with him right now and he is not a Tester or a Von Feller and what time does this library close?

I assumed the man in the yellow hat took advantage of you and your perfectly imperfect little foot. I assumed you felt so guilty about the sex that you chased it with *Sex* on TV, but what if I'm wrong? What if he really *is* one of the outliers in this *face*book? One of the few who doesn't look like a total fucking date-raping douchebag? What if *I'm* the douchebag because I let you *go down on me in . . . the bathroom* when you were wasted on cosmos and Pop Rocks? Me, the guy who stood you up at your birthday party. What if you prefer his chopped-up Portnoy over mine and what if he's so big that you realized I'm *not* Mr. Big and—

Gotcha. Level 4 unlocked.

Harris Wesley Walker IV is a total fucking date-raping douchebag. I can see it in his eyes, in his three last names. Dick and Schlitz are all talk. They would never, you know, actually do that to a girl. But the monster who occupies the upper right-hand corner of page 87 is bad to the boner. And I hate it, Vail. I hate this for you. His *pooka shell* necklace and his rumpled fucking hair and his upturned collar and a smug, uneven smile like he knows how to save the princess, like his daddy gave him a secret illegal playbook. That aristocratic streamlined dildo of a face, even clearer in this photo. He looks like he has forebears who pillaged with abandon. He looks like he uses that word, *forebears.* Baby-soft brown hair—no lead in *his* fucking lunch meat or his pipes at home—and I am sure of it. I'd bet my life on it.

Harris Wesley Walker IV is a prick. A prick who took advantage of you. Better yet, my love, Harris Wesley Walker IV will pay for what he did to you. He will pay because of me—my forebears were ragpickers—

and by the time I'm done with him, his face will be a rag. Bloodied. Torn. I swallow and flinch. Would I? Could I?

It's funny, Vail. A lot of authors touch on the fact that hostage negotiators will say the name of a hostage because it humanizes the hostage, because it makes the kidnapper remember that the hostage is a person.

And as it turns out, authors don't know everything, because sometimes, sometimes when you say a name, when you know a name, sometimes it makes you want to kill them even more.

27

Don't worry, Vail. I know I can't "kill" Harris Wesley Walker IV. My dad didn't go to Dalton, and in the event of a trial, I'd be stuck with some hapless public defender. Besides . . . Murder? Not my style. I wouldn't want to kill him or anyone even if *Daddy* could get me out of it.

But I am going to find the fourth-generation fucking knockoff. I am gonna get to the bottom of that yellow fucking hat. I wish I didn't have to work today. Mooney is in a mood. He just lit another cigar—ugh—and it's not fair. I don't belong here. Not anymore. I don't need books or advice or a smoke trap. I need to leave. I need to hunt Harris Wesley Walker IV.

"Joseph," he says. "You can relax."

Nope. Not yet. "Okay . . ."

"I am not mad at you. I'm not your *father,* Joseph. I am not 'disappointed.'" He leans forward. "I am disgusted."

Does he know about Dalton? "Okay. Okay, sorry. I can explain."

"Impossible, Joseph. Unless you know what you did. . . ."

Uh-oh. I didn't fucking "do" anything. I walked into a school. I didn't steal. And no one can punish you for killing a family of dick-heads in your head. "I know I fucked up."

"Language, Joseph."

I do not say sorry. I am fighting for my life.

"I received a phone call today, young man."

Can you go to prison for going to a library? Am I fucked? "Okay . . ."

"I received a phone call from our friend Angus Kaplan."

Wait. Angus? "Okay . . ."

"Joseph, do you think I am a stupid man?"

It feels good to tell the truth, to be direct. "No. You're the smartest guy I know."

"Well, you don't know that many men, now do you, Joseph?"

I hang my head. You know a lot of men, Vail. You know Harris Wesley Walker IV. I know four men—Dumb and Dumber, Dick and Schlitz—unless you count Mooney, which I don't, not right now. "Mr. Mooney, whatever that Philistine said . . ." Pause and give the boss man a second to remember that Kaplan is an asshole. Someone we *hate*. "Whatever he said, I can explain."

He spits in his ashtray, and all the trash trucks in New York City take a dump on me. He is crying. I made him cry. He doesn't do that, he doesn't cry, and what the fucking fuck have I done? "I'd like to see you try, Joseph. I'd like to see you try to defend stealing from me, running a business behind my back, stealing from a customer, and breaking into said customer's abode to have sexual relations with a woman who doesn't even like you, let alone love you."

Oh fuck. The cat clawed its way out of the bag. "I can make it up to you."

"No, dear boy, you can't. I have taken you under my wing. Your actions reflect on my person, my business. This is the real world, young man."

It's another fucking loss. A hit when I'm down. I can't lose my job, and I'm not on my knees begging but I'm close. "Mr. Mooney, please . . . I'm sorry. I can apologize to him. I can work for free, and I can . . . I know I screwed up, but that's on me and I can fix it."

A single tear rolls down his left cheek, and it may as well be blood. The old man really did think of himself as my father. He trusted me. All you adults, you and Mooney, you're the same. You say the opposite of what you feel. There's no way around it, Vail. I killed him, the man who gave me a job, the man who tried to teach me everything he knows. I want to bring him back to life and I want a world where Mooney doesn't cry and then the door opens and oh no.

Oh shit.

It's you.

You don't look happy to see me and you can't be here. Mr. Mooney hates you, and you can't see him *cry*. He rises out of his chair. "Get out of this office, woman."

You ignore him like that's allowed and I reach for you and you push me off like I'm bad news, like I'm Harris Wesley Walker the Fucking Fourth. "Outside, Joe. There is no way I am having this conversation in front of that monster."

Mr. Mooney cackles, and you don't get it. You can't see him cry. It would be better if you walked in on him jacking off. "I will meet you outside in five minutes, Vail."

You balk, and Mooney pounds his desk. "You will do no such thing, Joseph. And you . . ." That's to you. "You are not welcome in this shop, young lady."

"And you are not welcome to speak to me like I'm your fucking child." And then you look at me. "Let's go. Let's go right now or else."

"Joseph," he says. "Beware the woman who gives a man an ultimatum."

Your face pops like a kernel. "Excuse me, but you need to step the fuck off, old man."

The two of you are fighting over me in the worst possible way—*Who gets to kill Joe first?*—and if I look at you, I'm not looking at him, and if I look at him. . . . I am being torn in half, and this must be how you know you're an adult, when two other adults are pulling your arms and legs off your body with their eyes. Miss Frascatore is not coming to my rescue. I am not a kid. I am not a victim. I'm a grown-ass man and I fucked the fuck *up.*

I have power but I don't know what to do with it, with him, you.

Begging feels right, so I go for it. "Vail, please, give us like five minutes."

Your cape is dirty. Stained. "No. I'm not waiting for you, Joe, not after what you did."

Mr. Mooney cackles. "Says the broad who broke into a customer's house with you and didn't suck you off for *weeks.*"

You gasp—this is bad—and I tell him to stop. You spit. "Fine, Joe. Stay with this old man pig. I only came here to tell you that I do not mess with effing *stalkers.*"

Effing is a Cynthian word—I knew she was a bad influence—and Mr. Mooney cackles and ARE YOU FUCKING KIDDING ME? I am not a stalker. I am your BOYFRIEND whether you like it or not and I can't say that out loud because it doesn't even sound good in my head but come *on* already. Come *on!*

"Vail . . . I don't know what you mean by that, but if you just give me a minute . . ."

"Cynthia saw you, Joe, okay?"

I don't like that. I don't want to be seen and you are waiting for me to say something, but what?

"Ah, the silent treatment. To be expected, I guess, given that you're a child, and a stalker."

No. "No."

"I'll spell it out for you, 'Joseph.'"

Mooney gnaws on his cigar, and you're so mad you don't even react. "Cynthia was home, Joe. She was there by the door . . ." Oh no. Please, no. "She saw you, sicko. She saw you lurking in our hallway and trying to look in the peephole and—"

"I love you. Don't you get it? I went there because I was *worried* about you."

"You love me? You love me so much that you stood me up at my birthday party?" NOT FUCKING FAIR. "What gives, Joe? Were you scared to meet my friends?"

"You told me not to go."

"I told you to do what you want, Joe. And apparently, you wanted to make my birthday about waiting for you to show up . . . and then stalk me the day after. Cherry on the cake, truly."

You are stabbing me incessantly with the word *stalker* and I can't breathe, I can't keep up. I pull my fucking hair. "Jesus Christ, Vail, will you stop? I am not a stalker."

Mooney grunts. I reach for you. You back off like I have STD fucking cooties.

"Don't touch me. Don't stalk me. I mean it, Joe."

"Vail, you're right. I'm sorry. I should've shown up. And the day after, yes . . . I should've knocked on your door. I just . . . I got scared. I didn't know what to say."

"How did you even get into my fucking building?"

"Language, young lady."

You flip the bird at the *old man* and you don't get it, Vail. He could lock us in the cage, if he wanted. Does he? "Answer me, Joe. How did you get in?"

"The door was propped."

"Nope," you say. "That's a lie. See, I know my neighbors. Molly in 2A told me how you played the good guy and quote-unquote 'helped her' with her stroller."

I did not "play" the good guy—I AM the good guy—and Mr. Mooney puffs on his cigar. Disgusted. "That extra hole, Joseph . . . Lying to a woman is a dangerous thing to do. . . ."

Your eyes pop out of your head. " 'Extra hole.' Did you hear that?"

That's to me, and Mooney said that, not me, and I don't control what comes out of his mouth and I am freezing up, fucking up. I don't speak your language. I speak no language. I don't have a mouth.

"All right," you say, and now there are tears in *your* eyes, as if the tears in him ran off to be with you. "That's it for me. Follow me, don't follow me. Whatever."

You are calm in this way where there is hope for us yet. *Whatever* means you want me, and Mooney clears his throat as you walk out the door, as you leave the door open.

"Joseph," he says. "If you exit these premises, there is no future for you in this shop."

He breaks eye contact. That's how I know he means business. You are close by, pretending to search for something in your purse. That's how I know you mean business.

No dog can have two masters. I can't be his bitch and your boyfriend at the same time. I don't say goodbye. I don't even have the nerve to look at Mr. Mooney.

I turn my back on him. He mutters, "Pussy-whipped."

He doesn't mean that, but nobody likes to be left in the dust. And this is it, this is my grand gesture. I leave Mooney Books and call out to you. I'm on your tail and if I was really "stalking" you, you wouldn't slow down. You wouldn't want me to catch up with you. But you do.

"Nice try, Joe, seriously. But you're wasting your time."

The nice, sweet, loving girl I know is gone. You are angry. Angry and loud as if I didn't just WALK OUT ON MY JOB FOR YOU. As if I'm the one who stained your fucking cape. And it's the worst kind of angry. Your hands are in your pockets. You walk like a cop or a mom who's mad at her son for shoplifting. You are loud, screaming about the *best birthday ever.* Sarcasm is not your look and today is not your birthday, but that's girls, as if the word is *birthweek* and not *birthDAY.*

I grab your arm. Mistake. You pull away. "No."

"Vail, I'm sorry, okay? You know I'm not a stalker, and we both know you're just mad that I didn't show up for you on your birthday. And believe me, I'm mad at me too."

You stop in the middle of the sidewalk. "Don't tell me why I'm 'mad,' Joe. And I'm not 'mad.' I am simply reacting to what you did to *me*. Creeping up on Cynthia . . . I mean, come on."

"I should've been at your party."

You roll your eyes and tell me I'm insane. "I don't give a shit about my stupid party. . . ."

Oh yes, you fucking do. That extra hole is a black hole where all truth goes to die.

"I told you, Joe. I am 'upset' because you stalked me and scared Cynthia to death."

CYNTHIA WHO BRINGS MULTIPLE STRANGE MEN FROM PASSERBY INTO THE HOME YOU SHARE WITH HER. *Gently, Joseph.* I do that thing Cusack does when he thinks he lost the One. I hang my head. Sad Joe. Bad Joe.

It works. "What now, Joe?"

I shrug. "Nothing. I just . . ." It's like passing a hot potato. I have one shot to turn the tables. "I wish you'd just asked me to go to your party, ya know? I wish you'd let me take you out for dinner and at the very least just . . . I get where you felt rejected, like I don't want you, so you come in screaming about me stalking you . . . If there's some other guy, I get it, Vail."

The man with the yellow hat didn't make you come—I can see it in your skin, not so shiny—and your hands aren't in your pockets, not anymore. You rock back and forth. You like the attention we're getting as *that fucking couple*. "Look, Joe, I know you're not a stalker." YES. "And I'm not gonna call the police."

THEY WOULD LAUGH IN YOUR LITTLE PERFECT FACE. "Okay."

You pull your hair back into a ponytail, but you don't have anything to make it stay. You let go. You shrug. "Okay, yes. Turning twenty-five made me think about things, it made me think a lot. And I didn't know how to say it, but . . . Sometimes I think I'm too old for you. I'm in my life. . . . I'm in my career. And it feels like the only thing you want is . . . I mean, I can *feel* you wanting to be with me but you don't know what you want beyond that and you just . . . You don't know me well enough to want this or . . . Whatever."

"You always say you don't know what you want. We both have stuff to figure out."

"Yeah, but that's the thing. I'm figuring it out. I'm learning and growing. I had my party mostly to get some job leads and you're . . ."

"I just got fired for you."

You rub your forehead like you don't know what to do with this kid, like you're gonna ship him off to military school. "Yeah. Okay. The birthday. I . . . I messed up."

I knew it, but I'm not so fucking young that I say it out loud.

"Joe, you just . . . You have no idea how it felt. I told everyone I'm seeing this guy, this *hot young guy,* and then it gets later and later and you just . . . Why did you have to hurt me like that?"

What I say here matters. No. What I make you feel here matters. That poster in Miss Frascatore's office where the sun smiles at the cloud. I have to make you feel good. I have to make you remember that *I'm* good. Meaning I have to remind you that you hurt *me.*

"Did you get my voicemail, Vail? The one where I sang to you . . ."

"Yeah, and I would've told you how much I . . . Well, you didn't show up at my party. So the voicemail . . . I mean, that's really all you wanted to give me on my birthday?"

I need a new plan. I could blame Dick. He's the one who filled my head with his bullshit fucking theories, but then I'd have to *tell* you about his bullshit fucking theories. "Vail, you do remember that you directly told me that I didn't have to come, right?"

"No, Joe. I told you there was no pressure. You blew it off. That's on you. And maybe if you were a little older you would get that but I . . . I wanted you to read between the lines."

"Well, much as I may like to read, I can't read a book that doesn't exist."

I have you where I want you, in front of a Cosi full of businesspeople and their businesspeople salads. People who would be on my side if they knew what I know, if they knew about Harris Wesley Walker the OH WHO FUCKING CARES.

"Here's the thing, Vail. You don't know how it feels to be me trying to make sense of you. We're practically living together, but your birthday comes around and you treat me like some random dude you just met. I didn't know what to do, okay? You told me not to come."

Love is war and you are tongue-tied. I am winning. "Vail, I wanted to be there. Hell, I made you a *mixtape.*"

You look at me and I did it. Got you.

"You made me a CD?"

"Of course I did. Yeah, I'm 'young,' and this is new for me but I also know you're . . ." The only two words that can't take a man down. "I'm sorry. And you can have the mixtape, if you still want it."

Dick would be proud—my mixtape Seduced; it Destroyed—but you're fighting the urge to love me, jump me.

"Joe, I can't believe that and . . . I'm young in my own way. I don't know what I want sometimes, and I know it must've felt weird, me being all casual, but I've had some pretty bad birthdays when it comes to guys, okay? You think he cares about you and you let your guard down and he *uses* your birthday to show you he doesn't care."

"Well, that's not me, Vail."

I forget it sometimes. The simple math of it all. Your heart is a weathered thing. It's been around, and your feathers are battered. You say that I must think you're crazy and pathetic and immature. "You're over me, Joe. Just say it. I messed up. I would be over me and everyone gets bored of me 'cause of shit like this and wow . . . You made me a mixtape, and I'll never get to hear it. Sounds about right for my life."

"I'm still here. And I like doing things for you."

You shrug. Words are not enough. It's your birthweek. You want presents and I want you back. I need to give you all my gifts, even if it means giving fuel to the "stalker" fire.

"It's not just the mixtape. I did something else . . . I went to Dalton for you, Vail."

"You went to what?"

"Well, I went to your party and stole a disposable camera because I was late."

"Wait, wait, wait. You showed up after I . . . You stole one of my cameras?"

Your pupils are dilating. You like this. I stormed the castle for you. I stole for you. That's me. Me! I can't stay mad at you; I love you. You want to be wanted and courted and I want you. I court you. You!

"I stole the camera and I stayed up all night so I could be at the camera shop first thing. Most of the pictures were blurry, but I saw you with the Dalton guy and you looked . . ."

You cover your face. "Drunk. Believe me, I know."

You are too quick to shame—I brought you shame when I let you down—but this is how we fix it, by making you realize you are loved. Worthy. I tell you about sneaking into the school to dig up old yearbooks. I exaggerate a little—you are visual, you need to see me scale a fence—and you are awestruck.

"But why . . . I mean, what was the goal of your Dalton fence-breaking heist?"

Heist. "Well, you were vulnerable, last spotted with this guy. I couldn't reach you and if you disappeared, I wanted to have a name for the cops and the mixtape, the heist at Dalton, it's all the same . . . I'm into you, Vail. And I'd do it all again in a fucking heartbeat."

A commuter lady from the '80s in Reeboks jabs you with her bag. You don't even feel it, do you? You see me, Vail. You are not stalked. You are just not used to being loved.

You throw your arms around me. "Wow," you say. "Wow."

I pull you in for a kiss, but you flinch. Seriously?

"Joe, wait. I have to ask you something."

This is not a time for questions. We are in *love, love, love love . . . crazy love you* but the Van Morrison between us fucking scares you. Then again, reaching the last level of any video game to capture the princess is always a fucking trial.

"Okay, Vail. Ask away."

Your eyes zero in on me, and they kill Van Morrison. "How old are you, Joe? Truth."

I answer the question with a question. "Who is Harris Wesley Walker the Fourth? Truth."

You pluck a banana clip off the strap of your messenger bag and pull your hair up. It stays put. You seem different. Bereft or something. Like you're only just now realizing that you want to make Van Morrison songs with me for the rest of your life. You know what love is. It's the CD with your name on it. We freeze up in front of all the businesspeople and their business salads. The air is polluted. Could I forgive you for cheating on me with the man in the yellow hat? Will you dump me for something as stupid and out of my control as my age?

Are we really gonna end it in front of a fucking Cosi?

You take off your banana clip, and are you trying to distract me? You tap my shoulder with your banana.

"I asked you first, Cusack. How old are you?"

28

I'm still playing the whole scene in my head because wow. I have never gone from so scared to so happy so fast. There we were in front of that damn Cosi.

I jumped out of the plane knowing I might die. I went first, yes. "I'm seventeen."

After the longest two or three seconds of my life, we landed safe. You smiled. "You're a teenager."

"I got a fake ID after we met."

You arched your back and shook like you were about to fucking come. "I am in . . . I mean, holy shit. My . . . my boyfriend is in *high school*. Wait, you're not . . . Were you homeschooled?"

"Does any of it matter?"

"Your name is Joe, right?"

"Ha."

"So is this like . . . are you into older women? Did you get expelled because you seduced some sexy math teacher?"

Girls are insane, they really are, and I laughed. "No, Vail. It's just about you."

And then we started walking. You said you knew I was younger, but seventeen is . . . You beamed. "Just don't call the cops on me, okay?"

And then it was your turn. What a moment, what a win. I wasn't even scared to hear about Harris Wesley Walker IV—you just called me your boyfriend—and what a relief, the way you laughed.

"You mean that picture of me and Dubs? He's one of Cynthia's boy toys, and I was mostly begging him not to mess with her head. But he is pretty funny; you'll meet him if . . ."

I wrapped my arm around you. No if. Just us.

We walked and talked and wandered into one of those midtown Irish bars where nobody knows your name and never will. You were excited to watch me flash my fake ID.

I did hit a nerve when I teased you about being a pervert, but then I fixed it.

"I don't think you're a pervert. I think your impending quarter-life crisis made you realize that life was passing you by, that you needed to do something different, which is why you posted that ad on Craigslist and convinced yourself that I was a twentysomething."

You murmured in that sheepish please-stop way. "Interesting theory, Dr. Goldberg. Very Judd Hirsch in *Ordinary People* meets Robin Williams in *Good Will Hunting*. I like it."

I knew I was right. I also knew to leave it the fuck alone.

And then you elbowed me. "Only you would get a fake ID with your real name."

"Hey," I said. "If it ain't broke, don't fix it."

We toasted to my coming out of the age closet, which almost got us kicked out of the bar.

Yes, Vail, it's another one for the Moleskine. We survived our first fight. I brought you home to SoHo and you put on your raspberry beret and we had makeup sex with *Pop Rocks* in the good way. On my CD player, not my dick. And we had yet another first!

I sucked on your tiny extra toe. And then you gushed. *Best orgasm ever.*

We're on a roll. Best week of my life. And you're right. Life should never be *all* good, so it's kind of perfect that I wake up in heaven every day only to go to hell.

I still can't fucking believe it, Vail. I can't believe how far I'll go for you, for us. I can't believe I work at the Virgin Fucking Megastore in Times Fucking Square.

I love you so much that I put on a red shirt and talk to people about NSYNC. Dick thinks I'm insane for working here, for dating you. *She has all the power, Jailbait. You gave up your job and your home for this chick, this chick who's old enough to be your mother.* Not true, and sad that Dick doesn't get it. We good guys go to hell for love. I needed a job, and you wanted an employee discount, and speak of the devil . . . it's you. Breezing into the loud, dumb madness.

I smile. "Welcome to hell. How may I assist you?"

You plop your booty on the counter by the register. Two Woody Allen DVDs and a book, *Fast Food Nation.* You lower your voice. "Don't worry, babe. Barry has some feelers out. You won't be here long."

I don't have a care in the world and I know you and Barry won't let me die in this plastic fucking hellhole. "I like your beret. Where'd you get it?"

"Isn't it great? My boyfriend gave it to me. . . . He also made me the best mixtape. . . ."

"He sounds like a keeper."

You hold up *Fast Food Nation.* "Wanna go to McDonald's?"

I love being in hell with you, navigating the human bumper cars, holding the door for you as we approach the golden arches. We get burgers and fries and a side of nuggets, and I tell you that you're insane—you like Sweet 'N Sour sauce and you hate Tangy Barbeque—and you tell me that I'm insane—I got a strawberry milkshake.

"At least I have a reason to be insane."

You dip a fry in Sweet 'N Sour. "What do you mean, babe?"

I rant about the new woman in my life, my evil boss *Petra,* about capitalism. You laugh, and I pause. "Yes, my dear."

"Nothing, just sometimes, Joe . . . Sometimes I'm like . . . there is *no* way this guy is seventeen. He's a grumpy old man."

"And sometimes I think there's no way you're twenty-five, but I digress."

You ask if I'm almost done ranting, and I give you a nugget. You smile. "Go on."

"No self-respecting *bookstore* has neon fucking signs. People are lazy, so lazy that they want the bookstore and the T-shirt store and the junk store to be in the same place, and Petra . . ."

You elbow me and giggle. "I love her for you."

"You're just happy that she's into girls."

"Well, yeah, babe. I mean, I don't miss Virginia, but you . . . Never mind."

I know you well enough to wipe my hands and avoid another misunderstanding. "Vail . . ."

You turn a little red and close your *Fast Food Nation.* "Okay. The thing is . . ."

You need a second, so I give you a second. For a girl, you're not that good at talking, but this is how we are now. Open and honest. Direct. "Okay," you say. "I know what I mean when I tell you that there is no way you're seventeen."

"Because intellectually and physically I am at my peak. Thirty-five."

"Ha. Okay, but the real thing is . . . When you say there is no way I am twenty-five . . . I just . . . What do you mean by that? Do you mean I seem older? Younger?"

I don't know. "I don't know."

"Right. . . . That's the thing, Joe. You can't . . . Don't mirror me. I know you're into me. And when you say things just because I said them, as if you want to match me, I'm trying to say . . . I am *so* twenty-five. You are so *not* seventeen. Do you get what I mean?"

We're not in McDonald's. We're in heaven. I can't help it. I have to say it again. "I love you."

"Me too, babe."

I said it first like three days ago and you haven't said it, not the words, but *me too* means you love me so much that you're afraid to jinx it.

"So are you still good for tonight? The comedy club?"

I must do something funny with my face, because you laugh. "Oh, come on. One night at Caroline's won't kill you."

"Unless I have a heart attack and die from pretending to laugh."

"Dubs is actually pretty funny."

I remember that picture of you and *Dubs,* the way he made you laugh. But it's okay. Cynthia's with him, and you are with *me.* You sip my strawberry shake.

"All right," I say. "I'm in."

"And if Dick and Schlitz or any of your friends wanna come, Cyn can get a bigger table."

Friends. Dick and Schlitz are not my friends, and they're not yours either. Dick referred to you as *an old maid* and told me I should bail because *all older girls do is get older.* Schlitz . . . I forgot he exists. "Nah," I say. "Honestly, I'm taking a little break from those guys."

You chew on my straw. "Oh, okay, well, if there's anyone else, then . . ."

There is always a little crack in the ceiling of heaven, a little room for Satan to slip in. I can literally feel you thinking that the business guys to our left who belong at Cosi are normal just because there are four of them. You want me to be more like that. Crewed up. Walking in slow motion with my *bros.* Fuck it. I need to give you what you want. Or at least a version of it.

"It's a shame my buddy Jeremy moved to San Fran. He loves stand-up."

"Oh yeah! Jeremy. You have to show me his blog."

I can't do that—it's like him, it doesn't exist—and I dip a fry in BBQ. "I'll find it. He's coming to visit soon."

You light up and smile. "Yay! When? I am just dying to meet someone from your world who isn't the man we do not speak of, you know?"

It's the sugar and the chemicals and the human feces in the food. I am high on you, on bad things, and I can't help it. I have to make you happy. "Actually, I think he's coming soon. And he's bringing his girlfriend."

And now you are on fire. You want more. You cannot *wait* to meet Jeremy and his girlfriend. You are the opposite of unsettled Carrie Bradshaw, so content to be at a little plastic table sharing a little plastic meal with your one true love, better than Big, me.

"Ooh," you say. "Before I forget. Would you ever work at *The View*?"

I am a man. No. "Of course. I love that show."

You frown because I am lying, but this is the good kind of lie. "I mean, it's not a great job and you don't need to lie. This guy I know works there and he says there might be a PA gig. It's not a lot of money, but someone like you . . ." Don't call me an *assistant.* "Well, we know the ladies of *The View* will see your potential."

You are my girlfriend, my human resource. You have to work, and I have to race back to hell. You give me a little kiss. Sweet and sour strawberries. "Caroline's at eight."

"You do know you're sending me from one hell to another. . . ."

You gasp. Sarcasm and sex appeal. "Ah yes, but you do know that I know you would only run from one hell to another for meeeeeee."

See, there it is. You don't need to say the words. You love me.

"This is true, my dear."

I watch you disappear into the throngs of people who are not you, and I'm not back in hell for two minutes when Petra calls me out. Buzzkill. "You're late, Joe."

Poor Petra. She needs to get laid. Held. Loved. "Sorry."

"I need you to set up the *SpongeBob* display."

Hell finds new ways to be terrible, and I am dragging a giant cardboard fucking cartoon character to the front of the store. I miss Mr. Mooney, but you're right. I deserve better. I have potential. Within weeks, I might be Barbara Walters's right-hand man, and I won't let Satan win. I won't tear SpongeBob in half and set this place on fire, and I won't jump on the table and pound my chest and tell everyone in hell that I love you.

Hours later, we're settled into a wobbly, tiny table at Caroline's Comedy Club of Horrors. I'm the (unofficial) opening act and you're busting a gut laughing at *my* SpongeBob hell schtick. You are all over me, and I like it. Gentle and warm. Showy.

"The thing is, though, my dear boyfriend, we are *supposed* to be in hell in our twenties."

I look at you like you're crazy, and you smile.

"Oh," you say. "Fuck, I almost forgot. I didn't tell Dubs and Cynthia about your age yet. Is that okay? I didn't want you to feel weird, and you do *seem* older. . . ."

I love you for lying to them, and I feel a little better about my imaginary buddy Jeremy and his girlfriend. "All good, dear."

Cynthia slams her briefcase on the table. She groans. "Stop being the perfect couple until Mommy gets a drink."

You ask her what's wrong, and I tune it out. Miranda Hobbes and Carrie Bradshaw were right. Comedy clubs truly are the modern-day equivalent of hell, and I am a *little* nervous. Dubs is older than I am. His name was outside, on the marquee, like he's important. And you're always not quite you when Cynthia's around. I feel for you, the way you go her way, the way she never goes your way, and it's a relief when the lights get low. He walks onstage, and you scream, Cynthia screams. It kills me a little, but I do it too; I scream. He starts his "act" and there's a little light at the end of the tunnel that is a five-minute "set." The spotlight is harsh. Dubs is not as good-looking in real life and he *is* "actually pretty funny." He's speaking *my* language, going off on karaoke, about this girl who made him do "Father Figure" as a duet. It's hard not to nudge you and remind you that I am *just* as witty. But I hold back. No pain, no gain. And it's okay. It's enough for me to make you laugh. I don't need a bunch of drunks howling like a giant collective clitoris under my clever, knowing thumb. I'm lucky. Dubs will ditch Cynthia the second he gets a big break, and he will break her heart, but you're not going to break mine. Your hand doesn't leave my leg during his set, and when he wraps up and walks offstage, you squeeze my leg before you fall in line, before you rise to hug him.

He shakes my hand and looks me in the eye. "Hey, Joe. Thanks for coming to hell." *Wink, wink.* "You want a cosmo?"

The joke was on me, but in the good way where you touch my arm and claim me. "Sorry, babe, but I told our friends how much you *love* comedy clubs . . . and *Sex and the City* . . ."

Dubs elbows me like a buddy. "Fuckin' A, Joe . . . I might have to riff on you in my next set, if that's cool. The only guy in New York who watches *Sex* . . . You might be onto something."

I say that's cool and you whisper that *I'm* cool and I'll tell you what's cool, Vail. Me. The waitress asks if we want another round. I am first and fast: "Abso-fucking-lutely!"

Now *I'm* the funny one, and the night is in full swing. "Ooh," you say. "Let's play pointers."

Pointers is a drinking game. I didn't do this kinda shit in college like you people, but I know better than to ask how it works, and you are kind and sensitive, explaining the rules, in case anyone "forgot." It's simple. We go around the table and ask a question. You start with something banal: "Who's had the most sex?"

Now, as you say, we all point at the person who's had the most sex. We all point at Cynthia, including Cynthia, and she laughs. She drinks.

You tap my arm. "You go, Joe."

"Who's the best kisser?"

You point at me and I point at you and Dubs points at Cynthia and Cynthia points at you, and damn, if I'm this good of a kisser at seventeen, imagine how great I'll be in my twenties!

After the show, the four of us share a cab and go downtown. Dubs is a step up from Dick and Schlitz. He pays for the cab even though his parents cut him off when he turned down a job at Lehman Brothers to pursue stand-up. He's like the good version of the younger comic book guy that Carrie dates in season 2, and when I say that, you laugh. Cynthia laughs. Dubs laughs.

I am the funny one, so I keep it up as we walk through the Village, riffing on the Virgin Fucking Megastore. Dubs says I should try stand-up, and you say the perfect words: "Joe would *never.*"

The line at Sweet and Vicious is too long, so we dip into a speakeasy that Dubs knows about, and I could do this, Vail. I could grow older with you in clouds of cigarette smoke. You tell me that *I* should be the one working on your sitcom as we hold hands in the dark and Dubs and Cynthia disappear while you and I are making out.

The way I performed tonight, I know you can't wait to get me in bed, so we head outside.

"See, Dubs is great, right?"

"Very great."

"I can give you his number if you guys want to hang out."

I can't help but laugh because come on. Me and Dubs? No and no. I hail us a cab and open the door and I do a Big voice. "Your place or mine, kid?"

You *close* the door of the taxi that I hailed and the cabbie takes off. Are we here again? In the bad place? You kiss me. "Look, Joe, I'm not . . . I'm not pumping the brakes on us, but . . ." You lay a hand on my chest, a brake pedal of a fucking hand. "Babe, I just . . . I need some space this week, a little time to do my own thing, you know? Do my hair, get into *Fast Food Nation,* and just kinda . . ."

Live in a world without me. "Whatever you want, Sitcom."

You look into me and smile. "Honestly, Cusack, we're good. This is not me freaking out like I did before my birthday. I just don't want us to get sick of each other."

"I could never get sick of you."

"I know, but . . . Joe, I think you need to do some check-ins, you know? Call Jeremy, see how he's doing. Maybe go make things right with Mooney."

"But you hate Mooney."

"But you *don't.* And that matters to me. I know you left things bad with him. I feel responsible . . . See me getting all neurotic? This is why I need some alone time!"

It doesn't feel good to hail you a cab, but I do it. And I'm not worried as I close the door of the cab.

You roll down the window. "Can I be crazy?"

"Of course."

"For all my 'alone time' and my very sincere intentions to read that book and finish it . . . I also reserve the right to call you in the middle of the night if I get, you know . . ."

I give a thumbs-up to the cabbie. "You know where I live, Vail."

"Oh yes, I fucking do, baby. See you soon . . . sooner than you think, no doubt."

29

Fifty-one hours later, I am wasting away at the Beanery like a gigolo with no place to go and what is *soon*? Is soon tonight? Is soon never? I'll tell you this much, Vail. It's not sooner than I think! Are we done? Is this because I don't want to drink beer with Dubs? Dick groans.

"You need to chill, Goldie."

"I am chill."

He smirks and who the fuck could chill? I tell him your parting words again—*Sooner than you think, no doubt*—and how do I do it, Vail? How do I chill when you're trying to kill me and INXS is too fucking loud. *Live, baby, live*? More like *Die, baby, die.* Dick taps away on his suddenly ever-present laptop. What the fuck does he do on there all day? Is it really that hard to make a movie you're never going to make? No. I won't be that asshole, Vail. I won't blame him for the things *you* do to me. He smirks and says they're all "nuts," and he closes his laptop. Good riddance. Computers should not be fucking portable. Coffee shops are for talking!

"All right," he says. "Here's the truth, Goldbitch. Seems to me like she still doesn't want a boyfriend. She wants a dog. Do you want to be her dog? Obey every command?"

"Woof."

He rubs his eyes. "Well, then you have to let her train you."

"You mean like when Carrie told Aidan she wanted space and then freaked out when she couldn't get a hold of him?" I have to stop doing that. I *will* stop doing that. "Sorry."

"Go home," he says. "Two days is nothing, and I'm warning you, Goldboy. No girl wants to be your whole fucking life. And yes, she put you in the doghouse because you wouldn't hang out with that Doug guy."

"Dubs."

"Whatever. Don't sweat the 'soon' stuff. Forget about her and go to a strip club or hit some fucking golf balls. Whatever passes the time so you have something to fucking say when she hits you up and that's the other thing. No calls, Goldbitch . . . Let her come to *you*."

I do it. I *live, baby, live.* I pull doubles in hell. I eat at McDonald's and think about how to check on my typewriters back at Mooney's. I don't "make things right" with him. I don't know how to do that. I call Vagina to say hi. I don't go to her "modeling agency" parties, but I do get invites. After another long day in hell, I go down to Union Square and hit the bank and blow a hundred ones on random buskers, a Black guy with drums, a willowy young blond girl with a cat on a leash and a guitar, a voice that haunts me on the walk to Veselka, where I order six different kinds of pierogi, all of which I rate in my Moleskine.

See that, Vail? I have a life. And maybe I need to invest in it. Girls seem to like the way Dick carries his *laptop* and the computer at Mooney's isn't mine. Fuck it. Overtime in hell is pretty good, so after Petra liberates me, I go to Circuit City.

And now I have a laptop. I walk home to SoHo, and *soon* is a short word, a long time. Where are you? Dick is probably right and I should've just had a beer with Dubs but it's not like I did something terrible. The silent treatment is a bit much and I'm not a dog, not completely. I log onto IM for the hell of it and holy shit it's . . .

Me: *You're up late.*

You: *Omigod JOE! HI! HII!!!!!!!!*

You owe me more than a "hi," and those exclamation points hit like acid-laced daggers. *Gently, Joseph.* You are trying. But I can't ask you if you miss me, or how many hours it takes for "soon" to fucking end. I have to be a cool cat. Hard to get.

You again: *So really how are you Joe? What's new?*

Me: *Nothing. Barry let you back on IM?*

You: *No lol we have a night shoot so I'm holding down the fort. Yawn. But yay for good timing! Work is crazy and Cynthia got me a Giuliani poster lol you will die when you see it.*

Oh, joy. Yet another older man on the walls in your bedroom. GREAT! But also actually great because you invited me back into your bedroom. Can I come now? Too soon?

You again: *Are you there?*

Me: *Yeah. Kinda hungry. Might go to that diner on 23rd Street.*

The minute I let those words go into your laptop I know I fucked up.

You: *Cool! Who with?*

YOU, GODDAMN IT, I WANT TO BE WITH YOU.

You again: *Well don't let me stop you. I mean if you're hungry you gotta eat. Ha.*

Ha and I nod like you can see me, but you can't.

You again: *I'm actually kinda starving and I do love their spinach omelet.*

Me: *Oh yeah? You gonna wrap soon? I can wait if you want.*

I *sooned* you, and I get silence. Is that bad? Do you want me? It's 1:12 A.M., and my heart races like Aretha Franklin is inside of me howling, hoping. You said you want me to see your Giuliani poster and I want to tear it off your wall and what the fuck am I doing? Hunched over this laptop when you specifically told me that you want space. You need to learn your lesson—I'm a fucking catch—and for once in our relationship, I have to be the teacher.

I close my new Dell laptop. Let *you* drown in the *soon.*

I don't go to the Twenty-third Street diner, but I do eat six Fruit Roll-Ups. I think I sleep. Maybe?

In the morning, I don't need to ask Dick for per-fucking-mission. I earned the right to call you, and you know it. You pick up on the first ring.

"Joe! I thought you got kidnapped or something."

"Ha." That is payback for *your* fucking *ha.* "What's up?"

"Are you by chance hungry again? I have a little time."

I am always hungry, but it's too *soon* to reward you. "Not just yet."

"Ah."

"Ah?"

"Well, I mean, if you don't want to see me, you don't want to see me."

"Vail . . ."

"Seriously, Joe, it's fine." WHY DO YOU SAY IT'S FINE WHEN IT ISN'T FUCKING FINE. You grunt. "I mean, I'm cool."

"Vail, I'm sorry. . . . Fuck it. I miss you . . ." *Who let the dogs out?* Me. Me. "And I don't mean that in the needy clingy way but . . . Where do you want to eat?"

"Shit," you say. "Work is calling. I'll let you know when I'm free, okay?"

After you hang up on me, I call in sick to hell. I can't go to the Virgin Fucking Megastore. I am in my empty loft shaking our snow globe likes it's a Magic 8 Ball when Dick orders me to report to Sweet and Vicious.

He takes one look at me and orders two Jäger bombs. "Fuck. That. Slut."

"I didn't even say anything about her. And she's not a . . . Never mind."

"You don't have to say it. You look like hell . . . again. And fuck you too, Goldskin. I warned you. This is what happens when you give a girl a mixtape."

I hate Jägermeister even more than I hate Jim Henson and I hate Sweet and Vicious, but there is nothing that I hate more than me. Two bombs in, he tells me to forget it, you. "Girls like Vail . . . Do you get it now? She's a head case, kid. And honestly, I'm psyched for you. You put your foot down. Any girl who puts you in the doghouse isn't fucking worth it . . . You're free."

"But I don't want to be free. . . . Do I call? Even if I just ask for Dubs's number?"

He's aloof. Things never change. He's rating the six girls eyeing him and he knows things, how to make women want him just by sitting at a bar with his laptop in a bag like he's a big shot. I didn't bring my laptop. What's the point of it when I can't IM with you?

And then he deigns to speak to me. "You should go to the cops."

I stare at him. The cops?

"Bro, come on. . . . Technically, it's statutory rape. For all you know . . . You should get tested."

He gets loud like that to make the girls around us think I'm the young dumb one, but he fusses with his brother's dog tags and it's hard to feel anything but pity. "She's clean, Dick. Trust me."

"When a chick blows you off, she's probably blowing someone else, Jailbait. Make her pay. Picture it. She's at work. . . . The cops show up, that hottie detective from *SVU,* and they ask questions and she's banging a minor and . . . Where is your self-respect, kid?" He elbows me, pulls me so he can whisper. "She gets jammed up, you get over it and you and me hit up some high school dances or some shit."

I don't choke him out with his dog tags because he says he's "just kidding," but this isn't fun for me, Vail. I miss you.

He groans. On to the next order of business, a manila folder stuffed with headshots and résumés. "So many actors . . . so little talent."

"Are you finally making your movie?"

"Nah. I'm just being the fucking hero. Helping this kid cast his short, but the actors . . . Someday I gotta learn to say no to people. This kinda thing is below my pay grade. . . ." HE IS A BARISTA, VAIL, A BARISTA! But I'm lucky. If you don't have a big brother, you can't lose a big brother and turn into a dick. "This kid is casting off Craigslist because . . . Whatever. My brother, may he rest in peace . . . I get it from him. Some kid comes to me for help and ya know . . . I'm Mr. Yes Man."

None of that was true and none of it was for me. He says that kinda shit for the girls at the bar, some of whom probably believe that he's a big shot. It's kinda funny and kinda sad and kinda . . .

I throw a twenty on the bar. I can't get outta there fast enough. Dick shouts, "Don't call her, Goldberg! She belongs in jail!"

I pump my fist and fly out the door and how did I not think of this sooner, Vail? You know how to get what you want. Once upon a time you went on Craigslist to look for NYC Bookstore Babe. Craig delivers. Always. The man can help a person get anything from a devoted boyfriend to a rape fantasy three-way to . . . I don't want to jinx it, Vail.

But I have a hunch that I'm about to make some friends. Literally.

30

Here's a story I would've probably told you this week if you didn't need "space," if you knew the definition of the word *soon*. Once I saw Spike Lee in a Key Foods. I was in eighth grade, old enough to know that you're not supposed to say hi to famous people, but young enough to realize that the city is an equalizer, a boss that sends us all underground and then up into places like Key Fucking Foods. Anyway, I followed him around for a bit. I watched him pick up a box of linguini and I tried to decide how to play it. Did I tell him my name? Did I ask him to adopt me?

And then he turned around. I froze. Did he know I was following him? Was he freaking the fuck out? And then I blurted.

"I like the way you call it a *Spike Lee joint*."

He laughed, and I thought I had this whole new life where Spike Lee was gonna teach me how to go fishing. "Thanks," he said. "But I got bad news, little man. I'm not Spike Lee. I just look like him."

I'll never know if that was him, but it doesn't matter, because the best part was the lead-up to the meetup, the part where I *believed* I met

Spike Fucking Lee. You've made it clear that you want to *believe* that I have a life. I do have a life. *I'm a slave 4 U* because *nothing compares 2 U.* But your heart wants what it wants, so here I am set up in a midtown fucking Starbucks. I am here to produce *A Joe Goldberg Joint.* As in I am producing my fucking *life,* the one you want me to have, the one you need me to have.

My first step is to build Jeremy's blog. The first entry is easy. Jeremy complains about his system crashing, how he lost his *entire archive* of his work. ☺ The second entry is about the guilt that comes with leaving New York so soon after 9/11, and the third entry is about his heroes, the kings of September 11, as he calls them, David Letterman and Rudolph Giuliani.

My Coldmail heats up ten minutes after I send you the link: *I loooove Jeremy and I can't wait to meet him and you can relax, Cusack. Rudy G is too old for me, I like em young, as you know. Miss you.*

I don't fall for that. I don't tell you I miss you, and I don't nag you about getting together. But I *do* tell you that my boy Jeremy and his girlfriend are getting here on Thursday.

I'm a cool cat, I really am. ☺

My next step is to write an open letter, a casting call:

> *WANTED: Male, early twenties. Jeremy Piven type. Good sense of humor. Solid and sober type to play "the best friend." Woman, early twenties. Girl-next-door type. More Molly Shannon sidekick aura. Less Kate Beckinsale beauty queen. One day. Non-Union. Meals covered. A JG Joint production.*

It's Day One of casting and I am camped out in a midtown Starbucks. I didn't give out my full name. Actors scare me a little. I'm a private person. I can't imagine wanting everyone on the planet to know who I am, but here comes my first potential Jeremy, and he's . . . a bit of a letdown. The Alan Schweib in the headshot looked young and short, and this guy is a thirty-five-year-old beanpole. I take his photo and résumé. Dinner theater in Delaware. A Tide commercial two fucking *years* ago.

"All right," he says, once he gets his Americano. "What are you shooting on?"

"Well, I'm not actually shooting."

"So, it's performance art?"

"You'll be playing my buddy Jeremy."

"Do you have a script?"

Stay in your lane, Alan. "It's pretty simple. I'm the John Cusack, and you'd be the Jeremy Piven."

Alan sighs like *he's* the Cusack. "What's the setup? Meaning what's my motivation?"

"Well, my girlfriend wants to meet my buddy Jeremy, but he . . ." DOES NOT FUCKING EXIST. "He's out of town and you're, like, stepping in to play him."

"And you've already cast your girlfriend?"

"No, my girlfriend is my girlfriend."

"Meaning your girlfriend is playing your girlfriend. . . ."

"Meaning my girlfriend in real life wants to meet Jeremy in the flesh. So you'll, you know, you'll be the Jeremy. . . ." I save the best for last. "And you can pick your Sarah."

He's too snide to sell Tide, and he sneers. "Meaning this is not acting. . . . This is fraud."

"Buddy, I'm just trying to make my girlfriend's dream come true."

"By lying."

He snatches his headshot and goes off about his professionalism and tells me I'm gonna wind up behind bars. I resist the urge to make a dig about dinner theater in Delaware, and Carrie Bradshaw was right, Vail. It really is the end of love in Manhattan. My next potential Jeremy is from South Jersey. Too pretty, too tall, and, once again, too cynical. I thought actors were short. I thought they were in the business of *dreams,* but after four rounds of *You need help . . . This is fraud . . .*

Will there be an orgy? I'm starting to panic. I told you that Jeremy and Sarah arrive today and my buddy Craig is letting me down. New York is letting me down. The fucking *judgment.*

A businesswoman in business attire glares at me. "Do you need that chair?"

Starbucks brings out the worst in people with a menu that encourages people to be really fucking picky and I should've done this downtown.

"Joe?"

Right off the bat, there's something different about Carl Casey. For one thing, he's not taller than I am. He's a ginger, nervous, and a nice guy who thanks me for the opportunity. And he's Pivenish! Jumpy and caffeinated. He had two lattes today and he has no résumé, not yet. He's doing extra work and improv classes. I tell him I get it, and when I tell him about my production, he says the magic words.

"This is like something out of a movie. Talk about romantic!"

It's been a rough day, so I'm still hesitant. "Yeah?"

"What can I say? I'm that guy . . . total sap. I love love. Romcoms . . . Woody Allen . . . *When Harry Met Sally.* This is why people come here, to run in the rain and get the girl!"

"Thank you, Carl! You get it!"

"One day when you guys are old and gray, you tell her what you did, and she'll think it's the most romantic thing in the world."

I did it, Vail! I found my Piven. Carl doesn't judge me. Carl doesn't like Starbucks—he applied for a job, and they never called him back—and he has a friend who tends bar not far from here. He says she's the perfect Sarah and we're on the move to check out the bartender slash actress when he stops short by a hot dog stand. I ask him if he's hungry. Producers do that kinda thing, they spring for lunch.

He smiles. "I'm good. When I was at NYU, before I dropped out, I had a crush on this girl. . . . She was graduating, and she was a poet. I showed up at her house with a tape recorder and told her I was an assistant at *The New Yorker* doing research for my boss Alice. We didn't stay together, but we did get together. It's Shakespeare, my man. All the world's a stage. . . . You gotta stop and smell the hot dogs."

And then we're walking again. The potential Sarah slings Jägermeister in a waiting-for-my-train, vaguely Irish tavern. Carl's "friend" is named Betty, and she *is* the perfect Sarah. A smiley ginger in a tight white turtleneck who would totally stop and smell the hot dogs. Her hair is in a bun, and her face is a blank canvas that breaks my heart a little. I can already see her playing a corpse on *Law & Order* and failing to parlay it into a career as she realizes that she belongs with Carl. Yes, it's obvious. He has a thing for her, but that's good with me. I too *love love.* Maybe we'll even visit Carl and Betty one day when they're shacked up in Hoboken, running an Irish bar and popping out little gingers and . . . *Gently, Joseph.*

"Joe," he says. "Meet the best actress in all of Manhattan."

"And bartender," she squeaks. "Don't forget my other talent!"

By the third beer, it feels like I've known Carl and Betty my whole life.

Betty is from Wisconsin. She was Beth when she moved to New York, but she changed her name to Betty because she loves Bette Davis and all things retro. They've been *sort of* seeing each other for a couple of weeks. Carl came into the bar for six nights in a row to woo her. Betty doesn't like to give out her number, so it took some time. Meaning they get it. Me. They don't think I'm "playing with fire." They don't see me as a manipulative phony bound for prison.

"You're trying to *start* the fire," says Beth turned Betty. "It's very Bruce Springsteen."

I hire her on the spot and you call me—yes!—and I send you to voicemail. See that, Vail? I have a *life.* I wrap things up with my actors. Tomorrow, they'll begin their "research." They'll go to Mooney's. After all, that *is* where Jeremy and I met. I'm high and maybe a little tipsy when I leave the bar, and it's time for the first scene of *Joe Goldberg Has a Life.*

It's okay to call you because you called me, and you pick up on the third ring. Trying so hard to be a lady. "Hello, hello! How's Jeremy? Did they get here okay?"

"Great," I say. "I really can't wait for you to meet them!"

"I'm free tonight."

"Oh, man, I would say yes, but Jeremy wants some catch-up time."

"Totally get that. See, isn't this better, Joe? We went out with my friends. We do our own thing for a bit, and now we're gonna go out with your friends. I'm excited to meet them, but I'm even more excited that you guys got to catch up on your own, you know?"

Fuck no. "Yes, I do. And I gotta run. I'm finally going to Mooney's to make things right and maybe get a slice of his wife's famous meat loaf."

"Really?"

No fucking way! The cage. The cage! "Yep!"

"Ooh, Joe, I meant to tell you that my friend at *The View* says it looks promising with that PA gig."

No dice. *I'm a producer, baby, so why don't you blow me.* "We'll see. But no pressure there. Jeremy might also have something for me."

"Okay, now I *really* like the sound of him."

My stomach is rumbling, and no wonder Dick is always so worked up. Making a movie is nerve-racking. Can I do it? Can I pull it off?

Three . . . two . . . ACTION.

Here you come, walking down Eighth Street, and this is it. The first scene is a quickie. Just us. Smooth sailing thus far—KNOCK ON WOOD—and you hug me. You missed me; you don't have to say it. I feel it. We reenter India on Eighth Street for THINGS I LEARNED HOW TO PRONOUNCE. You know, a redemption tour kinda thing.

We are first to arrive, and our asses are planted on green velour pillows. I've been practicing, training my stomach the way I trained my muscles. You look good, like you care. You wore your cape and my raspberry birthday beret, and I brought TUMS. I'm not gonna get the runs tonight and you want beer, so we get beer and you rub your hands together and clap.

"So how have you been?"

I'm too nervous to say much, and I can't tell you about my auditions. "You first."

You're nervous too, so it's good for you to anxiously talk about your day with Barry, even if it is hard to pay attention. This is dangerous, what I'm doing, and the city is a character, the one I can't control. What if you know Carl? What if you've been to Betty's bar? I showed them a picture of you, and they swear they've never met you and they wouldn't lie to me—I like those actors, I do—but what if you saw them? Betty told me to remember the bottom line. *This is what we do, Joe. We met in an improv class. Do not worry. Love always prevails!*

You put your hand on my arm. Love prevails. "I think that's them."

The curtains open wide on the Dinner Theater, a Joe Goldberg Joint.

I knock back a shot of Jim Fucking Henson. A good director stays loose. Ready. *Action.*

Jeremy is a hugger, and he looks like Piven. Blazer over a VICE CITY T-shirt. I'd believe he's a blogger and he jokes about the last time I was here like a real friend. You can't *believe* I told him about that, and Sarah says Jeremy and I talk about *everything.*

They sit on their green pillows and we sit on our green pillows and the little bowls of THINGS I CAN PRONOUNCE start to fill up our table. The conversation flows. You love Jeremy. You say it so many times that I'm having yellow hat flashbacks, and I'm relieved when he steps away to take a call on his cell, when Betty slips off to the bathroom.

"Well," you say. "What can I say, Cusack? I fucking *love* them."

That's an A-plus from a Lisa Schwarzbaum movie review, and I am *good.* "I know, right? Like you said . . . Dick and Schlitz, not quite my speed, but Jeremy and Betty . . ."

"Who's Betty?"

JIM HENSON BE DAMNED, and I choke. "Shit."

"Are you okay?"

No. "Yes, just went down the wrong tube. Betty is Jeremy's ex."

"Ah," you say. "So, you don't know Sarah as well?"

"Well, Betty was a bartender, and we used to hang out with her at her bar a lot."

"Which bar?"

No no no no no no. "Oh, it closed. Some dive on the Upper West. No great shakes."

You nibble on your naan and Jeremy trots back to the table. "Sorry. That was my agent."

Everyone is a liar, a dreamer, and you whistle. "Wow," you say. "I feel stupid, but I didn't realize that bloggers have agents."

OH THAT'S RIGHT AND FUCK YOU, JEREMY CARL. I cut in, as the director has to do in a jam. "Well, Jeremy is also writing a novel . . ."

He gets it. He opts out of another shot and nurses his beer and says he can't talk about the novel until he *finishes* the novel—you hear that, Angus?—and you say that sounds like *Fight Club* logic and Betty is back from the bathroom and you don't miss a beat.

"Sarah, have you read Jeremy's book?"

Betty blinks in that way where you can tell she's an actress, new to the game, the gig. "Did I read what?"

I was wrong—I *am* going to get the runs—and Jeremy laughs. "Ouch. . . . *Ouch.*"

They really *are* good with improv, the way Carl feeds Betty the intel about his novel, the first few pages of it anyway. Betty plays with this new information like it's an old toy, entertaining you with tales of his angsty late-night brooding back in *San Fran.* They have me convinced. They have you convinced, and much as I like them . . .

I will *never* trust a fucking actor. Ever.

Betty wraps up a tale of her own little quarter-life crisis, the way she might apply to grad school but for what, who can tell. You sip your beer and smile. "Sarah, I hear you so hard. I thought hitting the big two-five would make me chill out, but my level of lost is that I borrowed my roommate's camcorder to tape an audition for a cohost job on *The View.*"

You turn red and everyone laughs and it's just the kind of thing you never would've told me until tonight and now I get it, the reason you needed "space." You touch me. "Don't worry, Joe. If I get on that show and you're a PA, my first order of business is to give you a promotion."

You will never be on *The View* (that's a compliment) and I will never work at *The View* (that's a fact) and it doesn't fucking matter! All that matters is now. Jeremy and Sarah are perfect. Encouraging, as in they can see that for you. Sarah says there is too much pressure in the city. She only figured things out when she moved to San Francisco, when she had space and sunlight.

You touch your heart. "I could never leave New York."

We all felt it. By New York, you mean me. I kiss the back of your hand. "Big did."

And now it's time to talk about *Sex*. A relief, because more food arrived and the pressure is off. *Sex* doesn't require me to lie or keep track of every little detail. I'm able to focus on small bites. I don't sweat or get the runs, and then it's a wrap on this scene! We split the bill as Carl and I joke about that time we drunkenly accidentally dined and dashed at Veselka—give this man an Oscar!—and now it's our MONTAGE: HANDSOME COUPLES TAKE ON MANHATTAN.

We leave India, floating through the East Village like Harry and Sally and the other two. We point at funny T-shirts and crazy shoes, and it's all so natural, the way Carl and Betty drift ahead of us, the way you lean your head on my shoulder.

"I really do love them. Maybe sometime we can visit them in San Francisco."

"Yeah," I say. "Maybe we could do that."

"Maybe soon? Barry doesn't have an episode in April. I could get away for a few days. . . ."

This is not possible, Vail. Jeremy and Sarah do not exist. "Well, that would be great."

"I know I'm a hypocrite with the *let's take it slow* and then . . . *let's fly to California*."

Indeed. "Never."

"You're probably like, 'This little old lady is going from zero to sixty,' and I just . . ."

Jeremy looks back at us to see where we are, and he sees us having a moment. Paid friends are the best friends. I look at you. The new you. The new you as in the one who sees the full me, the loved me. "Vail, it's a cliché for a reason, okay? Age is just a number."

"Sarah's really pretty."

That is bait. I do not bite. I do better. I kiss you. "And yeah, Vail. It would be fucking fun to go to San Fran, maybe even move there. . . ."

You ask me if I like hills and rice as we laugh and realize we don't know *shit* about San Francisco. We're more equal than ever and you're afraid that you want me too much, afraid that I will back out the second you jump in. "I gotta say, Joe. I was nervous, but this . . . this is nice. And it means a lot to me, meeting your friends, and they're so settled, you know? They make me feel like I'm gonna figure out stuff in my life. I love that."

The tables are turning. You are the young one, despite your age, your world-class family travel, and your college degree. "Well, they love you, Vail. And if we wanna go to San Francisco, we can go to San Francisco. We can do whatever the hell we want."

Your lips quiver. "I lied to you."

THAT IS NOT IN THE SCRIPT and I fucking hate improv, I do. "Okay."

"The reason I haven't introduced you to Barry . . ."

"Vail, that's your work. I don't need to meet your boss."

"Well, Joe, I have to say it. . . ." He has a big cock. "He's my uncle, okay?"

You don't seem to get that this is *good* news. "Ah. He's your Uncle Angus."

"No, Joe. I make it sound like I'm a part of things on the show. I'm learning the ropes, but really I'm just . . . I'm a professional niece. Everyone I work with knows it, I'm only there as a favor to my ritzy uncle, so last week . . . I can't."

"It's okay." And necessary. I have to know why you iced me out. *Learn, baby, learn.*

"I went to this temp agency, and the woman was so mean. She was like, 'Do you have pantyhose? Do you have references that aren't family? Do you know Excel?' "

"Fuck her."

Sometimes it really is that simple to love someone. A simple, strong *fuck her.* You kiss me. "Thank you, Cusack. I guess your friends are just so . . . Together."

I hold your hands, both of them. "I believe in you. And if you want me to kill the lady from the temp agency, I'm game."

The gallows humor only works because I am me. Gentle. Devoted. The scene doesn't need more dialogue, not right now. I hold you the way you need to be held. And then you pull away. You tilt your head. Uh-oh. "There's one more thing."

NO, VAIL, I ALREADY CALLED CUT. "Okay."

"The whole San Francisco thing . . . I can't . . . I can't promise you the *we* when I barely have the *I.*"

I laugh it off, I am somewhere between Big and Steve. "Vail, come on. You know when Miranda sees Big show up for Carrie in Denial?"

"Who *are* you, Joe Goldberg?"

I am a producer. I am the man. "I'll say it whenever you need to hear it . . . I'm here."

You look at me like you wish you could take off all my clothes. "Mm-hmm."

Been a while since I got an *mm-hmm,* and I keep at it.

"I don't wanna play games, and I know I can be a little clingy . . ."

"No, last week . . . that was totally about me and the temp agency."

I needed that; you knew it. "So what next? Is it gonna be *Live! With Regis and Vail*?"

You're laughing—I am funnier than Dubs—and you don't say that no guy's ever been this good to you. You don't need to say it. It's in your eyes, in your shoulders below that silly cape. I check on our friends and give a *two minutes* hand signal. I wish this were all on tape. You take me in your arms and bring me home right here on the corner of Fifth and Sixth. We form an invisible statue that will be here for the rest of time. We hold on tight. We don't let go. We hold on to each other in a way we never have, and this movie is the kind that changes lives. It's like when Steve called Miranda late at night after she was at her worst with him, when he responded to her darkness and self-loathing with his best. He gave her the fucking moon, and so did I. I was wise to make a movie for you. That's how your brain works, and you really did need to see someone *else* believe in me. I feel the Carrie leaving your system. Same way I spit out my Big. We're not perfect. But we were never realer than we are right now, and reality doesn't bite, and sorry, Mr. Mooney, but hope isn't always the stairway to hell. I took a leap of faith and I landed on my feet, in your arms. I win.

31

Heaven is this bed. It's a place on earth. You're asleep and I'm awake. Buzzing. I'm too happy, too proud. I did it, Vail. I proved the cynics wrong and I saved us and I can't *sleep*. I need to do a victory lap. Strut my stuff and mark your place with my scent.

Gingerly, in honor of our new best friends, I leave our nest to go into your shared "living" space. Oof. You and Cynthia are *effing* slobs, but you always have good snacks in the fridge, even if I *do* have to check the expiration dates. I wonder if I'll move into your place or if you'll move into mine, or if we'll go and find a new place together. What a thing it is, Vail. To plant my bare ass on your couch and eat the rest of your Tasti D-Lite with a melted, dented spatula. Who does that? Who saves fake ice cream in the fridge?

Girls.

God, I love you. And it's another first. No more *Gently, Joseph.* Tonight, you wanted to be the big spoon—you really fucking *love* me—and I am buying you a new spatula tomorrow. I don't have to worry anymore. You needed to meet someone from my past who isn't a dick like Mooney, and I gave that to you. I'm still hungry so I get off your icky sofa and open the freezer. It's an igloo. You and Cynthia don't fucking defrost it the way you need to with old appliances, and again I have to laugh.

Girls.

The Lean Cuisines are expired—that's a long fucking time to hold on to powder-based Alfredo—but there's a pint of Ben & Jerry's in the back. No lid. The word *CYNTHIA* scribbled on the label and a fork stuck in the Phish Food, or rather the frostbite that *used* to be Phish Food.

Girls.

I take my second dessert to the six-by-six cell you call a living room—we will get our own place—and I kick back on your sofa. We'll get something better, softer. Pigeons are fucking in the air shaft, and one of Cynthia's shoes is stuck in the cushions. I pull it out. Gum on the heel.

Girls.

And there's more in this old couch. Errant quarters and half-smoked cigarettes and receipts and you have a junk drawer in your kitchen. Do you really need a junk fucking sofa?!

Girls.

The ice cream is gonna take a century to become semi-edible, so I collect the coins and the butts and the receipts and the crumbs. I like doing things for you, and one day, when we have kids, we will have a cleaning lady. Or maybe we won't need one. Maybe you'll stop being a Miss Lonely/Miss Piggy when we live together. Better yet, *I'll* do the cleaning. It's addictive, especially when you're naked. I love the idea of you waking up tomorrow and realizing what I did for you. It keeps me going as I scrub your kitchen floors and line up Cynthia's shoes by her bedroom door and stack the *Vogue*s and the *Time Out*s on your sad, wobbly coffee table. You don't own a screwdriver, but I tighten the legs with a butter knife, and that's when I realize the cushions were the tip of the iceberg. There is a literal field of junk *under* the fucking sofa.

Girls.

I grab your broom—I am surprised you own a broom—and I sweep up the tampons and the maxi pads and the coupons. I can already hear you gasping come morning. *Oh, Cusack, you are such a prince!* Your floor is my next project. A sea of *Village Voice*s, which is insane. It's free, Vail. They print a new one every fucking week, and time passes. Events come and go. I go to dispose of obsolete *Voice*s and why is there a bra in your microwave?

Girls.

Back to the sofa, where I'm on Skittle patrol. So much candy. Too much candy. And what's that in the back corner? Is it an electric bill? A phone bill? I reach. I strain. I get there. And here's my prize in the box of Cracker Jacks. It's pictures. The envelope is heavy and of course I have to have a look. Of course I want to see you. I open the envelope and see . . .

Dick.

Okay. That's not what I was expecting. It's fine. My heart needs to slow the fuck down. You don't like Dick. He third-wheeled on our first dinner date, and he's your barista. You knew him from the Beanery before we met. So yeah, he went to your birthday. So what? I'm the one who told him about the party, and he thought I was going and he *is* that horndog who would show up to hit on your friends and bogart the disposable camera to shoot his own fucking face. Whatever. I won't get my boxers in a twist. It's one stupid photo and I toss it aside so I can see you in the next one except that's not what I see.

Again, it's not you. Again, it's him. Dick.

I'm sweating. Is it from all my hard, selfless labor? Or is it from the sight of Dick, camped out on the steps of the colosseum at Botanica? There's something I don't like. No Schlitz by his side playing wingman. There's a fresh drink to his left, his *I'm so important* messenger bag with his laptop to his right. His legs are spread and his tongue is hanging out of his mouth and he's winking at the camera. You are *my* girlfriend, not his, and who took this fucking picture? Did you take this picture? Why didn't he call me. *Yo, Goldbitch, get your ass over here.* My heart thumps. I was in heaven. I was your spoon. We're still there. Nothing has changed. I *am* your spoon. So he didn't mention going to your party. So what? He's a guy. Guys are stupid and forgetful. Guys are not Jeremy. Even Jeremy isn't Jeremy.

These are pictures of the past. And we have a future.

I know what to do. Close the envelope, put it where it belongs, finish off that Phrostbitten Phish Food, and go back to bed. I do it. I close the envelope.

I remember my mother yelling at my father. *You can't leave a gallon of Rocky Road in the freezer, because I can't sleep until I go down that road and hit the dead end!* I am my mother's son. I want the ice cream. Fuck it. I pick up the envelope but no. I am *not* my mother's son. I have willpower. I have you. So what if Dick went to your stupid birthday party? So what if there are pictures to prove it? Disposable cameras are what they are. Things that wind up in the trash half the time. But you are all out of trash bags. It's fine. Dick is my buddy. He didn't go to your party to see you. He went there to see . . .

Girls.

He probably left five minutes after he got there with some Condé Nasty cold fish that you half know who wanted to be *Seduced and Destroyed.*

I take a deep breath. Fuck it. You're mine. Nothing can change that. Nothing.

I dive back into the Botanical birthday time capsule and my balls crawl back up into my body. The next picture gives me what I want. It's you, finally, but it's like the Phish Food in the microwave. Corrupted. You are not alone, my princess. You are with him.

Dick.

It's ugly. Worse than the wart on my mother's thigh. Worse than the skid marks on Mooney's tighty-whities. My hands are shaking. Bad picture, very bad. Dick holds a big fat birthday candle and you suck the frosting off his finger. You make eyes at him while he makes eyes at the camera and wait.

Are those his fucking dog tags? Are they nestled between your pushed-up fucking tits?

Not good, Vail. Not good.

Your fingertips rest on his dirty asshole of a hand, and I'm on my feet. I can't stop now. The pictures are a flip book from hell. I thought it was bad when you were sucking on Dick's finger in front of all your half friends, wearing his dog tags like you won them in a contest. But now you're in the bathroom with Dick. Dick, who holds the camera because you can't hold the camera.

You are on your knees, dangling a prop. A prop that is a kick to my nuts, a slap on my face, sandpaper on my Portnoy. You hold a little bag of Pop Rocks.

The urban legend is no myth. Pop Rocks are dangerous; they can make a man explode. I am done. Dead.

I drop the pictures and they splatter all over your floor and my body sinks through the living room, crushing everyone below us. My balls drop, my soul drops. Your living room isn't sunken, but it's getting there. Is this just fucking life? Is it the way of all living rooms? Relationships? I sit on the sofa and take in the evidence of the crime scene. The pictures are all exposed and now they're out of order, but the story is there.

You really did this to me, Vail. You traded your plastic birthday girl crown for Dick's fucking dog tags. You got down on your knees for him. You put him in your mouth. You let him take pictures of you and no. That's not you. Not Miss Lonely sleeping in your bed fifteen feet away, dreaming of baguettes with me in France.

Okay. I gotta find the light, the space to breathe and go on.

There is context. It was your birthday. You were drunk. I know Dick. Dick is a dick. And I may as well have set the two of you up by *standing* you up IN THE MIDDLE OF A CRISIS. Turning twenty-five made you crazy, and I'm crazy. I never should've opened the fucking envelope. You would die of a shame-induced heart attack if you knew I found the pictures. You care about me. Now is now. *Be here now.* But still my heart beats. The lion in the cage that won't be tamed, can't be tamed. You can't unsuck Dick's dick, and I can't unsee the Dick pics. I could tear them up or dump them in the East Fucking River or shred them and eat them, but they would still be here.

Kinda like his dead brother's dog tags. Some things just never disappear.

Think, Joe, think. I clean up. I gather the Dick pics and shove them back into the envelope, back under the sofa. I close my eyes. Still I see them, you and him. Pop Rocks. I want to scream but I can't scream and I don't scream for ice cream. I'm a Talking Head; I *Stop Making Sense.* There should be a way to get out of your own head, an escape hatch with a button that you push when you need to not be you for a few fucking minutes. I pick up your little book of misunderstood song lyrics because something needs to take me away from all this, but "Bennie and the Jets" don't do shit.

Nothing can help. U were a slave to Dick, and he betrayed me and you betrayed me and is it me? Am I just not a real fucking person to anyone in this real fucking world?

Here come the tears and no. Fuck that. I won't play the victim. I messed it up, Vail. I failed you when I followed Dick's advice instead of my own fucking heart. *I know you're not my boyfriend.* You drove me nuts with that shit and then I drove *you* nuts. I am the reason for the season. The blame is on me.

I slap my own face. Bad Joe. Dumb Joe. How could I do this to you? I rejected you in slow motion in your colosseum at the peak of your crisis in front of all your jerk friends. You were waiting for me to waltz in and take you away from *semantics* and tequila shots and theories on Jann Fucking Wenner. You were hurt and half-dead. Too insecure to call me. Too unsure of us to believe in us, to put yourself out there. If I hadn't been such a pussy, Dick wouldn't have had a chance to be such a dick. Do you ever do this, Vail? Am I weird? I put myself into your combat boots without even knowing what I am doing, but do you do that for me?

Do you put yourself in my shoes?

You murmur from the other side of the door, the place formerly known as heaven. "Joe?"

I am your dog. I come when called. I climb into the bed with you. There is nothing for me to do or say. Talks like this can't happen in the wee hours. You roll over, and I comply. I am the big spoon again, the one that holds on to the little spoon because it just can't fucking help it, because even after what the filthy, wounded selfish little spoon did—you cheated on me, you abandoned me—well, even after all that, the spoon still fits. That's love. It's inevitable when it's real and my sad arms are too limp to hold you properly tonight.

You wiggle. You squirm. "Babe," you say. "Not so tight, okay?"

32

I didn't sleep. Lasted in the bed about five minutes and went back into your living room and found your bleach. I did your floors, same way you did Dick. I am atoning . . . but also, I am testing you.

Things always look a little clearer in the morning, and yeah . . . You should've been stronger. Carrie resisted the caterer slash artist. You should've had *faith.*

You emerge from your chambers. Sleepy-eyed and soft in my mother's Nirvana T-shirt. You rub your eyes, you sniff. "My oh my, what did you do?"

I didn't blow Dick on my birthday. "Nothing. I couldn't sleep."

You ooh and you aah and you are bashful like you don't deserve a guy like me, a guy who pulls an all-nighter turning the house you've lived in for a long-ass time into a home. You are *amazed* by your squeaky-clean apartment. You prance around like a princess and you call me the best. I go with it.

"Well, it's for me too. I like a clean house. I told you. I couldn't sleep."

You pick at a hole in my mom's shirt. "Ah. So this is just like . . . You just were antsy."

Watching your heart break a little is a thing that breaks mine. I might hate it, the way your sadness wins. Without even deciding to go to you, I do it. *Love love love love crazy love* doesn't allow me to stay mad at either one of us. I put my hands on your shoulders. "No," I say. "This was for you, Vail. Just for you."

It works. You perk up and pour expired pre-ground coffee into the machine that needs to be cleaned. You tell me stories about the way you used to be so neat, so obsessive with your Cabbage Patch Kids, lining them up and making everything just right. "Something happens when you get to college, you know?"

No, I don't know, and you should know that, but maybe you don't carry me the way I carry you. "Sure."

You go on, and I am not on your radar, not right now. "It's probably a form of rebellion or something. This fear that if I go into happy homemaker mode, I'll get stuck crocheting a bath mat or something and never figure out what I really want to do, you know?"

OR MAYBE YOU'RE JUST A LAZY AND SPOILED COMPULSIVE FUCKING DICK-EATER. Sorry. I didn't mean it. Soft as a butter knife: "Do you have an ice pick, Vail?"

You gawk at me. "An ice pick? Like in *Basic Instinct*?"

I am not going to let one drunk blow job get the best of me. But I am also not gonna put up with any more fucking movie references at this moment in our life. "Yes."

You don't have an ice pick, and I need to get away from you, from the bleach.

I leave.

Outside, the air is fresh. No hot dogs to smell, not just yet. I walk to Third Avenue, and Dick is somewhere in this city. Dick whose dick was in your mouth. I enter the nearest hardware store, and *I can't help but wonder* . . . Did he enter you later that night? Would he defrost your freezer while you were sleeping? I buy an ice pick.

The flirty clerk who's pushing fifty smiles at me. "I love that movie."

Maybe all women are all part girls giggling over dirty movies. Maybe they all see a young guy like me as a toy. Maybe they never grow up, not fully. Does it matter? Do you love me?

I walk back to your place and climb the stairs. Full-blown Best Boyfriend Ever. I climb like Dick isn't in there, exposed for all eternity under your filthy fleabag of a sofa.

You open the door. Are you blushing? "I should give you a key."

YOU SHOULD GIVE ME YOUR HEART. "Yeah, cool."

You are you. Too nervous to ask me what's wrong, choosing instead to babble about *Basic Instinct* and erotic scenes and Al Pacino in *Sea of Love* and some story about how Sharon Stone is a genius and some bullshit you read about in *Entertainment Weekly*.

I am an idiot. A tool. But at least I am a tool with a tool. I tune you out.

I open the freezer and toss the expired frozen things into your kitchen sink. And then I begin the real work. There's nothing like that moment the ice finally weakens and an actual chunk of it hits the floor of the freezer. A war is a bunch of battles, and I am in it. An all-day fucking endeavor. You go to your sofa, *sitting like a princess perched in her electric chair,* and you do God knows what on your laptop. Soon enough, the noise bothers you.

"I feel so Carrie when Aidan was doing her floors, you know?"

That is your way of trying to tell me that you know I'm mad, that you're trying to reconnect with me through *Sex*.

"Sorry, but there's no way around it. Defrosting a freezer that's been neglected for this long is a loud and long endeavor."

You rub your eleven toes. You're still in my mother's Nirvana shirt like you know I might leave you. "Well," you say. "You don't have to do it, Cusack. You already did so much."

"That's me, though. I started. I have to finish."

You tell me you don't know what you did to deserve me, but the words are carnations that die the day you get them. You peck me on the cheek. "Back soon."

You're off to a coffee shop or maybe to suck Dick's schlong. No. That was one time. One night. It's better like this. Alone on your turf. Breaking what can be broken. Stabbing ice so I don't stab Dick. The more I sweat, the smaller the pictures feel. A one-off accident you would erase if you could.

"Fuck."

My hand slipped off the ice pick because my grip was too firm. *Not so tight, okay?* I cut my knuckles on the cold wall, and my blood is hot. It stings like Pop Rocks on my Portnoy, and you're not here to wash my wound. I drive the pick into the wall of white. I sweat and I stab and I bleed as minutes turn into seconds into the word for something smaller than a second. It hurts to be alive. I stab because the ice is still there, because you are still there with Dick in my mind. My arm is thumping and sore, but on I go like a machine. A robot. Sometimes I am stabbing Dick. Sometimes I am stabbing Cynthia, the one who makes sucking dick in a bathroom seem like a good thing to do. And then what a joke, right? I am the tool with a tool. Sometimes I am stabbing myself.

The thing is, there is one person I am never stabbing.

You.

Love is a brick wall. A block of ice. You are not the problem. The ice is the problem. Dick is the problem. Implacable. The way he's fucking out there, lodged behind the counter of that Beanery. Heartless. No dog (tag) in this fight, in any fucking fight. I know, Vail. He shouldn't have messed with us. Especially you, vulnerable you. All the times you sat in there talking to him, all the times I sat in there talking to him, being his friend, taking his advice. I know what he would say to me were I to get him in a choke hold. (Could I?)

It was one night, Goldbitch. And I warned you about that girl. She told you she's not your girlfriend, kid, and who cares? No pain, no gain. Bottom line is, son . . . You got what you want. You locked it down. Girls do shit like this.

Think of me as her bachelorette party. Be here now. You Seduced. You Destroyed. It's always good when they hate themselves a little for doing you dirty. It means they wanna get clean for you. Also, she was wasted. She might not even remember it, kid.

Weird, how I don't need him anymore because it's reached that point where I know what he's going to say before he says it.

Your freezer is like new, and I did that. Not him. I wash my hands with hot water (you need to buy soap) and I reach under the sofa. I take the pictures. Mine now. Not yours. *Mine.*

I call you and you answer. First ring. Is that guilt? Boredom? Love? Is there any fucking difference? "Hey, you. I miss you."

"I'm done. Your freezer is a freezer again."

"Aw, you're my hero. Thank you, Joe!"

You were too perky. Too polite. "Are you alone?"

"Me? Of course."

"Beanery?"

"Nah, I'm kind of sick of that place. I'm just around the corner and I just . . . I still can't get over it. My place has never been so clean and you just . . . You gave me a freezer!"

"I guess I did."

"I want to do something for you. Wanna eat?"

You ate Dick's dick. "Maybe."

"Pick a place. Anywhere you want. It's on me. I mean, me and Cyn have been swearing we're gonna deal with the freezer for months and, like, I owe you."

I don't want you to owe me. I want you to love me. I can feel some guy listening to your side of the conversation, some random dude thinking we have the best relationship ever. Do we? Is this as good as it gets? Is this the best you can do?

"You there, babe?"

"I'm here. And it's really not a big deal, Vail. I did this to our freezer growing up all the time."

"Aaah."

Girls: All they want is history. Ammo. *Insight.* "Anyway, Jeremy and Sarah had a fight."

You gasp like a girl who doesn't suck Dick's dick in a dirty bathroom bar. "Oh no."

"Apparently, she's been stepping out with some guy. He's pretty down, so you know . . ."

"Joe, no, this is awful. I love Sarah and . . . Are you serious? She cheated?"

"He's pretty rattled, so I gotta be there for him."

Your voice is lower now. "Of course you do, because you're the best."

Yesterday that would have meant something. Today it just makes the Dick pics hurt even more. "Look," you say. "I know you don't need my help here, you're so smart about stuff. . . ."

I am the stupidest man alive. A tool with a tool. "Okay . . ."

"Well, it's just, I barely know them, and I know you know them way better."

They don't exist. "Uh-huh."

"But I felt that instant kind of . . . Well, please tell Jeremy that I said that Sarah does love him."

"Okay."

"Joe, she raved about him. And if she messed up . . ."

She did not suck Dick's dick. She never would, but is that just because she isn't real? Because true love is a thing you can rent but never own? "Okay . . ."

"Jeremy should know that she loves him. And if she did step out . . . Again. Every chance she got, she told me how much she loves him. People make mistakes. So maybe remind him of that, you know?"

Jeremy doesn't exist, so I don't go meet up with him.

I'm alone. Can't call Mooney. He hates me. Can't call Jeremy 'cause . . . Yeah. Nothing exists. Nothing but me and the Dick pics. I am Woody in *Hannah.* Walking through my own blues, all the way to the East Fucking River. I tear up the pictures. One by one. I tear his face in half. I tear your face in half. Off they go into the wind. Shards of confetti at a funeral and I need to snap out of it. I need to do something. I need to know how deep it goes with you two.

I forgot about real life, Vail.

I became so dependent on Craigslist that I forgot about who I am. I don't need anyone. And the good thing about having such a crap childhood is that I'm all good with the golden rule: The only person I can truly count on is me. You are different. *You Can Count on Me,* but I can't count on you. You're a girl. The world is harder for girls and them's the breaks and that's okay.

I dip into an internet café that smells like pineapples—why—and I sign up for a new AOL account. It's pretty amazing, Vail, how easy it is to build a whole person. I like this kind of production more than my movie. Less stressful. No actors in a fucking Starbucks.

I name the girl LucyGoosey87. She's a *silly soph* at the Dalton School, the kind of teenage girl who only exists in porn (I hope). Lucy met Dick at the Beanery; she asked someone else for his *deets* because she liked what she saw.

I'm a good director. But the question is, can I channel a teenage girl in a fucking chat?

LucyGoosey87: *Whatcha doing hot stuff?*

DickHead111: *lol who dis?*

LucyGoosey87: *Extra hot latte three Equals. People say I look like Britney lol I heard I could find you here so here I am. I have a free period and I was thinking about u . . .*

DickHead111: *Ha. Same here. What's up?*

LucyGoosey87: *Meeee cuz there's a rave in Bed Stuy if u wanna come my parents are away hint hint heehee*

DickHead111: *whoa someone's really begging lol u alright there kid*

OH FUCK YOU, DICKHEAD. But I know Dick.

LucyGoosey87: *You are so funny omg are you like hot AND smart?!*

Dick is in, so I give him the address of that warehouse where I got jumped. Criminals aren't the only ones who return to the scene of the crime. And then I remember part two of my mission: the computer. I need him to bring his precious laptop.

LucyGoosey87: *can you bring your computer? Mine broke* ☹ *and in the morning I have to do homework*

DickHead111: *You coulda just asked me to sleep over but yeah kid all good* ☺

It's on! And I got a lot of shit to do before the big rave! I buy a ski mask at a We Sell Ski Masks and Empire State Building Trophies kinda joint. Then it's off to a sporting goods store for shitty black sweatpants, you know, kinda like the shitty black dress that Miranda got for her mother's funeral. I score some juice off a guy who sells at a Crunch downtown, and I hightail it to the East Village, where I buy coke and *rocks* off a kid who dropped out of school the same week as me. There's a woman on the sidewalk selling candles. I buy a candle—it is dark in that warehouse—and I feel smart, Vail, like the person who invented the disposable fucking camera. It only takes an hour for some stoner to turn that piece of plastic into twenty-four glossy pictures and then poof, it's in the trash.

I made a girl! I have a backpack of customized weapons!

I get out of the subway and I love it when night falls while you're underground. The air is crisp. I am here in Bed-Stuy, walking into the rat-infested warehouse. I never felt like more of a baller. Large and in charge, what Dick wanted me to be. I blew you off both times you called—you shouldn't have called, you know Jeremy needs me right now—and I'm hunched in the back of the warehouse, just like the guys who mugged me. I almost don't even hate them as I sit in the dark waiting for Dick to show up. And then . . .

He is here. Dick. Messenger bag included.

This is so obviously *not* a rave, but he is idling, horny. Tossing his bag and flexing like he thinks he's about to get jumped in the fun way.

"Lucy . . . Come out, come out, wherever you are."

This is it. My big moment. And I know. In an ideal world, violence is never the answer. But this is for you, for all the women on this fucking island. I mean, the more I think about it, the more Dick *needs* a good ass-kicking. A little tough fucking "love." He joked about putting you in prison! He came here to have sex with a fifteen-year-old *girl*. If you think about it, I have a moral obligation to emerge from the shadows in a ski mask and kick this predator in the fucking balls. Those guys who jumped me needed the money and they did whatever it took to get it, and I need Dick's computer and he goes down easily. My fist connects with his right kidney and it feels right to kick him when he's down.

And then he's out cold. Perfect. I'm shaking, but all first times are like that. You get nervous. You fumble. First things first: I tie him up with cuffs I bought at a sex shop by Crunch. I *lift him up and put him down* into a broken freezer and I tape his legs together.

I'm not a monster, Vail. I am the good guy. And good guys care. I love you too much to shame you. I can't ask you about your birthday. I can't ask you if it was a one-night stand, a mistake you hid under your sofa. It's possible you're just a slob. Possible you never even opened that envelope. Possible you don't remember what you did to me. (I hope.)

You can't defrost a freezer without blood and sweat, tears and time. And that's what I'm doing in this warehouse. I am here to defrost our misguided, malevolent "friend" Dick. Chip through the ice to get to the steel walls, to see what, if anything, went down with you two, and, I hope, make him *want* to stop being such a, well, *dick.*

It's a lot on my back, yes. I am sore from cleaning your floors, putting your Skittles where they belong, and bloodying my knuckles to serve you for the second time in a matter of fucking hours while you're probably at home shoving a boot into your sofa. I say it again.

Girls.

My senses are in overdrive. Every little thing I do is magic. Even sitting in a chair feels like action, like the first time. I keep looking up to make sure he's there, to make sure I did this—he is; I did—and I take his laptop out of his messenger bag. There's a blue Post-it taped to the underbelly of his bag.

> *PROPERTY OF DICK PALMER*
> *DICKPALMERRULEZ@HOTMAIL.COM*
> *AOLIM PASSWORD: #1DICKIZTHEMANNN69*
> *HOTMAIL PASSWORD:*
> *#1DICKIZTHEMANNN69*
> *MOM EMAIL:*
> *MAMAPALMERRRRR@HOTMAIL.COM*

I sigh.

Men.

33

Dick is still sleeping it off and that's a good thing, Vail. He has *seventeen* AOL IM chats open in his fucking laptop. There's no internet in here, but that's okay. I don't need access to the internet to see the women trapped in *Dick's Web.* He is trying to fuck all these girls, which is sad, but even sadder . . . they're trying to fuck him. My heart bleeds for all of them.

I'm moving through the white boxes, and I doubt you're in here. The blow job was probably an isolated incident. A quarter-life crisis right up there with auditioning for the fucking *View.* I tap and scroll and am I gonna catch an STD from putting my fingers where his fingers go? Or wait. Did you give *me* an STD with your fingers?

No. My Portnoy is fine. I am fine.

But the girls pining for Dick . . . How did they get here? Where are their mothers? Because yes, some really are in fucking high school. They buy his bullshit excuses about why he didn't call, and they come back for more. They want to be Destroyed by this dick who doesn't even bother to Seduce. To look into this icebox of emotions is to know that what Carrie said in the first episode of *Sex and the Godforsaken City* is at least a little bit true.

"No one had told her about the end of love in Manhattan."

But that's not you. You're not *GailForceWinds* and you're not *LaurenIsBored.* Every time I close a white box, I brace to confront *VailInTheCity* in the next one. When the box isn't yours, I get a high. I'm thrust back into your place, breaking a patch of white ice, one step closer to resurrecting the fucking freezer. You don't *chat* with Dick. You are safe. *Mine.* If it was one stupid blow job on one stupid night, I can do it, dig a grave for your filthy past and put it behind us. Dick is a horndog. A taker who wants any woman, every woman. You were in the right place at the wrong time, vulnerable. You're not dopey like *HeatherFeather,* who says Dick deserves a Purple Heart for keeping his brother's memory alive—OH COME THE FUCK ON, HEATHERFEATHER—and you're not *CarrieComeLately,* who forgives Dick for banging the girl's cousin because the girl was "begging for it" and he "couldn't let her down." *And, Dick, I know it was a hard day for you, the anniversary of your brother's death . . . That has to HURT.*

ARE YOU KIDDING ME, LADIES?!

I make that box disappear and there are no words for what happens when the next box is revealed. My eyes aren't playing tricks on me and I can't make it go away. That's your name on his screen in a little white box you share with him. I knew this was possible. It still hurts. The sky is falling and I am falling and the *calliope crashes to the ground* under the weight of this heavy white box.

And it's not that you talk to him online, Vail. It's that you talk to him a lot. You talked to him . . .

Today.

VailInTheCity: *Well, hello you. Stalker boy is now also my house boy lol long story. What's shaking? Last night I had a dream about you. I never remember my dreams and . . . I have to tell you in person. You will die lol I died.*

I die. I cry. You were with me, dreaming of him, and I know you. You never dream. You told me that in the sinking living room on the

Upper West Side. I told you that you are normal, that most people are exaggerating their stupid fucking dreams, that you will dream when you aren't so exhausted, so on fucking call. You said that made you feel good, but here you are chasing Dick, baiting him with fake fucking dreams.

A computer is not a photograph, and I cannot tear it into pieces.

I put my finger on the little felt clitoris on the Dell fucking laptop. I push and I push and I will my eyes into their sockets so I can't read the words as I scroll and I scroll. The conversation becomes something long. It's a book. The worst kind of time machine, still going.

My heart is the Hulk—it is pumping like a motherfucker and shredding the cotton that is my thin, nice-guy skin.

I cried at *Igby Goes Down*! Don't you know I can't handle this?

I try to read, but it's like that first spicy Indian food on my weak white boy belly. I can't digest. I catch things here and there—*uncut frozen hot chocolate child*—and I am a reader, Vail. I won't skim. I started on the last page like Harry, Property of Sally, but I'm going back to the beginning, to page fucking one.

Yes, this book is beneath me, it might be a waste of my time and my heart, but it's a book, Vail. And reading is the only thing that brings me peace.

Dick coughs. "Hello? What the fuck is this?"

I almost forgot he was here. I can't face him, so I turn around to read while he screams and swears like a little fucking *boy*. I can't focus with him having a fucking tantrum, and I know. I should have closed his mouth *before* I tied him up, but what can I say, Vail?

I'm not a psycho. I pull his boot off. I take his stinky white tube sock and shove it into his mouth and I fix it good with some duct tape.

He's still shaking, *waaah waaah waaah,* and those dog tags are *clink clink clinking.* He is not fit to wear them, so I pull them off his fucking chest and wave them in his fucking face.

"Your brother would roll over in his grave, you piece of fucking shit!"

He has things to say, but I can't hear him. It always feels good to solve a problem. To defrost a freezer. To silence a dick. I punch him in the head so this place'll feel more like a library, and I get back to my computer.

My hand hurts, but it's nothing compared to my heart.

Page 1. Your first chat.

March 12, 2001, and what the fucking *fuck,* Vail? You go back with him, far back, *farther than I have traveled,* and I'm imploding. You've known Dick for a long time. Is our life a lie? Are you a lie?

You: *So it's me . . . the birthday girl . . . lol that was crazy and it goes without saying . . . I am not that girl blah blah blah . . . did I tell you I work for Sex & the City?*

Dick: *Ha yeah no biggie*

You: *Nice big reference*

Dick: *?*

You: *I can be a little Samantha . . . Especially on my birthday but also like NICE TO MEET YOU and PLEASE DON'T JUDGE ME IT WAS THE WHISKEY AND THE SHOTS AND . . . OMIGOD I HOPE THE POP ROCKS DIDN'T HURT YOU*

Dick: *Haha that was a first*

You: *omg I am your first yeeeeee lol YAYAYAYAY*

Dick: *Calm down kid*

You: *So what's up!? How are you? When did you leave? I was kinda hopin you'd still be in my bed but figured you are busy with your movie. Anyway! Wanna get food later? I am sort of dying for pizza. I miss Detroit pizza. Did you ever have Detroit pizza?*

Dick: *It's a plan stan*

You: *All cool. . . . what rhymes with cool lol I'll think of something by tonight. I'll call you to see where and all that later, yeah?!*

So you hooked up at Botanica . . . on your twenty-fourth birthday.

At least now I understand why you are so fucked-up about your birthday. It's not really your big day unless his dick is in your mouth.

Anyway, it's obvious that he bails on Detroit-style pizza. You've never talked to me about Detroit-style pizza. Two days after he stood you up, you shoot another shot.

You: *Hiiiii I saw this doc about vets and I thought of your brother. It's playing downtown and I would totally see it again if you were into that.*

Dick: *lol sorry shit got crazy. My buddy fell off his bike. Fuckin taxis*

Once you told *me* that Cynthia got hit by a bike messenger. Is this where you get your excuses? The best worst books are like this, Vail. You want to stop. You can't stop. I don't stop.

You: *Oh no! Is he okay?! Are you okay? Can I help?*

Dick: *All good yeah took him to the hospital and all that no biggie*

You: *Spoken like a real hero . . .*

Dick: *You still want pizza?*

You: *I always want pizza*

Dick: *Haha I'm broke a dollar slice at Joe's or some shit unless your flush*

You: *I like all pizza . . . I am working.* 🙂

Dick: *Mm-hmm*

You: *Mm-hmm*

I thought that was an us thing, the *mm* and the *hmm,* and I am waiting for myself to hate you. But I'm not that kind of guy, that kind of reader. My feet are in your combat boots, and I will see where this story goes. You are the heroine. I know you, I love you. My pain is your pain and is that what's wrong with me?

Anyway, you did it. You took Dick to a ritzy Italian place. You fucked him again.

I did things for you. I gave up my cardboard box for you. I gave up Mooney for you. I'm a *slave . . . 4 U . . .* and I too am wrangling a boa. I can't kick Dick in the balls and put an end to his life. I am what I am. A reader. And I can't put this one down.

You: *Coming into the Beanery but I'm not stalking you I just genuinely love the coffee.*

Dick: *Free country*

You: *It most certainly is mm-hmm*

Nothing. And you kinda knew it, which is why you did the *mm* and the *hmm.*

You: *So how are you?! How did your meetings go?! How go the plans for your brother's memorial?*

He ignores you, and I go into speed-reading mode because, Christ, this book is tedious. I skim through the same scene over and over. You beg him to go to an engagement party with you and he flakes. You beg him to go to a wedding with you. Dick loves weddings. *Best place to pick up chicks.* Open bars, *Goldschtick!* You fuck him at the wedding. Him and a bridesmaid.

You: *I mean thank you, right? You are the best date and everyone LOVES you.*

Dick: *You're not pissed? The girl jumped my bones nothing I could do*

You: *Oh please. I go kinda crazy at weddings too as you saw . . .*

Dick: *Ha. She's cool. Were going out next week*

I know you. That *had* to hurt. But you block it out.

You: *Adorable and omg your dancing . . . I will never hear Backstreet Boys ever again without thinking of you ahahahaha what a BLAST you are my fire my one desiiiiire we should go do karaoke yeah?!*

You Again Because DON'T YOU GET IT HE DOESN'T LIKE YOU: *Don't mind the babbling. Pretty sure I am still drunk. Anyway how's work? Big day?*

You Again AND DON'T YOU REALIZE YOU ARE TALKING TO YOURSELF?!: *Random but my friend Joan and her boyfriend wanna do something this weekend. This super cool underground karaoke place. Zero pressure lol it's not like it's another wedding!*

You Again AND NOW YOU'RE DRUNK AT NIGHT: *asakjn the squirrel heart spaear botanical hmmm baby dance askjdakj hiiiii*

You, the day after: *someone might have had a wee too much to drink last night. howru*

You, sober and stubborn: *Okay you were right. Raising Arizona is art. And I might have an investor for your film, this guy who asked me out a couple nights ago . . . I mean I could go out with him and bring you and kill all the birds with one stone . . .*

It makes me cringe, Vail. I know what you did there. You tried to be the Caring Girl, asking about his dead vet brother. You tried to be the Fun Girl. None of it worked, so you set a jealousy trap as if Dick wouldn't see that coming a mile away. You think you're clever, but you can't put the zookeeper in the zoo. Did you ever read a Russian fucking novel? Didn't you at least read some Dickens in high school? You can't nail a Dick with a dowry.

There's a break, as if you had temporary sanity. And then you lost it.

You: *So I think I have to move back home. Long story and I'm okay but I got mugged and just . . . No thanks New York. Anyway maybe I'll see you before I go. Already told my roommate so if you know anyone looking I should help her find someone.*

Classic. You're playing the victim, the princess in the castle, the girl tied to the railroad tracks. Don't you understand that Dick is not me? He is not Mario! I am Mario.

Dick: *In Canada on location. You can't leave New York, darling. You got mugged. You're a New Yorker haha see you in like five or six days when I get outta this fuckin tundra.*

You: *OMG CANADA I AM SO SO STUPID AND DUMB. You TOTALLY told me about Canada and oh my brain . . . Stay warm I'll keep New York toasty for you* ☺

At long last, there is a *fuckin'* plot twist. Four days later, Dick is the instigator.

Dick: *Vail*

You: *What? What do you even want?*

Dick: *Vail*

You: *?*

Dick: *I didn't lie to you. I was in Canada. I was gonna call.*

Ah, so you bumped into the lying horndog. This should be the end. It should matter that he lied to you. And I like you like this. Disgusted. Terse. How you are with me when *I* mess up.

You: *Right. Sure. Whatever you say Dick.*

Dick: *We wrapped early and it was a mad fuckin rush to get back to town. And yeah I'm a piece of shit. Shoulda called yada yada. What can I say? I suck. You can delete my digits*

I'm guessing that didn't happen. I read between the lines, between the days that passed and it's pretty clear that you called him. A lot.

You: *I'm sorry I'm calling so much . . . I just miss you and I know you want things to be chill and all that and I do too honestly lol but I really do need my scarf.*

My Portnoy twitches. It's stupid. I wanted to be the first guy who held on to your scarf.

Dick: *Been busy. Got fucked over on that Canada job. I'm a piece of shit. Can't talk now.*

You: *No you're amazing, Dick. You are a great line producer and the idiots on that film are the pieces of shit. You do everything and you deserve more.*

Dick: *Ha. Sure. At least I'm not a total fuck up. I do have your scarf.*

You: *I'm on my way*

Dick: *Haha it's at the Beanery so you can pick it up whenever.*

I need a break. I am sick for you, Vail. You won't be stopped. You are a train and you rolled off the tracks, but you're the one who's gonna get run over. A few days later.

You: *Look, Dick fuck it. No more games. I like you. I want to see you. Like see you see you. It's not just 'cause of the wedding or that you know all the words to I Want it That Way and love Sex & the City. I want to go out with you. And if you don't want to go out with me, you need to say it because here I am . . . And I am hitting send. Send.*

For twenty-six hours, you probably sat there welded to your laptop. And then he threw you a bone.

Dick: *Do you like Indian food?*

I need a TUMS and a barf bag and was *anything* between us our first? Is there one fucking cherry that I popped? India wasn't spontaneous. It was a code word between you and him, yet I believed you when you said it was all random. Something happened for the two of you in India. Or you read some article in *Cosmo* or got a lecture from one of the *Sex* writers. Anyway, you put up a wall, blew him off after the trip to India on Eighth Street.

You: *Hey sorry I missed your calls. That Indian place was sooo good and thank you for spoiling me! And the travel bug is a thing. Totally. And yeah we should go to Costa Rica. It's insane but let's be insane lol I deserve some insanity cuz this job is killing meeee*

Dick: *Ha I feel ya brb*

Oh dear, oh, Vail, don't you get it? He is laughing at you, still.

You: *I could do November or December or January. And I shouldn't say this but like . . . everything I want to do in CR is couple stuff. Not that we're a couple, but I really wanna go*

Dick: *I'm so fuckin broke*

You: *So would November work? Gives you time to save*

Dick: *Hang on fuckin Schlitz is hitting me up*

He leaves you hanging, and this book is bad. Monotonous and depressing. I skim the next few *chats.* You push him about Costa Rica and karaoke and he does not *Seduce.* He *Destroys.*

And then, after all his nos, you get a yes. He agrees to be your plus fucking one at the VMAs. You made it sound like you were with friends, and no wonder you rewrote your fucking history. It appears that our enemy Dick went home with someone else.

You: *Just so you know, I'm not mad. I feel sorry for you, Dick. Delete my number. Go away. I really do hope you grow up and learn that women are people too. I wasn't trying to "lock you down." I wanted to dance with you and during Slave 4 U . . . It's a song, dick. I meant I loved the song. Not fucking you.*

He respects the boundary but we all know what happened a few days later, the day the towers fell, the day Dick rose to the occasion.

Dick: *I tried calling and I'm coming over to see that you're okay are you okay?*

You: *Come over please I am losing it*

Dick: *On my way*

My veins can't hold my blood. They're not wide enough, not strong enough. When New York got hit, I was in Mooney's cage. Oblivious. Meanwhile, Dick was plowing through the dust, the human particles. Warring his way through the closed-off streets of the city, using the tragedy to get to you, to own you. You held on to him, and he held on to you. You told me you were lonely on the sofa with Cynthia and some guy and that's a lie. Dick was your person. You went through that together, the haze of not knowing where the world went now. You thought *Sex and the City* would never shoot again. He thought about joining the marines, like his brother. (Oh, please.) You became obsessed with Giuliani and Letterman. You had Dick by the balls, and he played your hero, supporting you through an anthrax freak-out, a bomb scare by your apartment. The two of you walked on eggshells together and I have to face facts. You might never stop loving him. If some girl rescued me while I was in the cage . . .

Alas, Dick is Dick. I gulp and I swallow. My character is about to show up. It's December, right after your first trip to Mooney Books, you head home to Beverly Hills to be with your family for Christmas. Dick stays in New York and after one too many nights at Passerby, he brings a girl home. And not just any girl. A teenager.

Dick: *I'm sorry I am I have PTSD from losing my brother and it was just one girl*

You: *You're lucky I don't call the cops.*

Dick: *She wasn't THAT young*

You: *I trusted you.*

Dick: *The girl's dad was in Tower One so yeah*

You: *Right. Sure. That doesn't sound at ALL fabricated or made up or whatever.*

Dick: *Sorry I'm human sorry I'm not a hero all you talk about is cops and firemen and fuckin Rudy Giuliani and David Fuckin Letterman sorry I make coffee not movies and I probably never will make movies. Never gonna get out of the coffee shop. Never gonna make a film. Sorry I'm not my dead hero brother and I'm gonna move back to Chicago or some shit. Fuckin serves me right treating you the way I did but I hope you get everything you want kid. You deserve so much better you do*

I love you for ignoring that message. You really did ice him out. You slammed the freezer door and didn't look back. He keeps trying to talk to you. You ignore him, and I like this part of the book. I won't get ahead of myself, but it's starting to feel good, Vail, like you—

Fuck.

You: *Okay I can't not tell you about my life lolol*

Dick: *Look who's back hi sexy whats up*

You: *I know! Sorry I was just busy. But omg so a few weeks ago I go into this bookstore to pee.*

Dick: *I'm hooked*

You: *And this high school boy like practically comes in his pants*

Dick: *Ha*

You: *And then he puts a Missed Connection on Craigslist I mean he's like OBSESSED with me.*

No. THAT. WAS. YOU. You put the Missed Connection on Craigslist. You threw the bottle into the ocean and you were obsessed with *me.*

Dick: *Creepy*

You: *Right?! And I'm no better cuz the girls at work read it and I . . . I might have gone to the movies with him yesterday. NO JUDGMENT.*

Dick: *Oh shit. You locked up in a basement right now?*

You: *Not yet. But if I am, I know who to call* ☺

I scramble up to my feet, but my legs barely work. I know what comes next in your trash fucking book. Dick was the ex who "dragged" you to bookstores, the reason you were on antibiotics when we first met—*You should get tested*—and you probably never even auditioned for *The View.* I puke on old newspapers and rat shit. You lied to him. You lied about us. About you. About me. I hawk a loogie, and it lands on the pile of vomit. Perfect. I could stop now. Leave it there. It was early. A lot of true love starts with a lie and I fucked up. I reached under your sofa, into your past. Maybe I was never supposed to know this, any of it.

But I do know it and I can't write it off as a fucking origin story. You just talked to the bastard . . . today. Your book is a work in progress, and I go back to my character's point of entry.

Dick: *Bring the stalker in so I know who he is in case he really does kidnap you or some shit*

You: *I dunno. He's awfully young and handsome. Might even make you jealous . . .*

Dick: *Haha*

And then you did it. You lured me into the Beanery to meet the Dick that got away. And then you went to him to talk about me. Innocent me.

You: *So?*

Dick: *So you're gonna break that poor kid's fucking heart*

You: *lol just having fun*

Dick: *Cut him loose. That high school chick I got with? Fuckin slow play low key attempted suicide. Don't fuck with the youths*

You: *Well maybe he just needs a strong older man to guide him . . .*

Dick: *I do kinda miss my brother*

You: *You're adorable*

Dick: *You're a pervert*

You: *I miss your dick*

Dick: *How's his dick?*

You: *Pleading the fifth and keeping my legs crossed for now*

Dick: *Tease*

You: *Slut*

Dick: *Come over*

You didn't like me and you probably didn't have your period and it wasn't about your extra fucking toe. The night I took you to Angus's, you didn't meet up with Cynthia. You ran to him, to Dick and his dog tags. *Cundylocks*. Of course.

You: *So that was crazy. I mean I never have three orgasms*

Dick: *Ha. You were just freaked out by the dude's gun you were scared as fuckkkk*

You: *Or freaked out by how good you were . . . my hero*

Dick: *Ha how's stalker boy taking it?*

You: *Might be time to cut it loose and find me an older man . . .*

Dick: *Shit gotta run*

It's a pattern. The book gets worse because I'm in it now, only not. You paint me as a stalker, an incompetent pussy who puts you in danger so Dick can step up to the plate to save you. It's *Super Mario Bros.,* but you are not the princess, and how do you not see it? I have access to the truth, to the unabridged book of us that lives in my mind, in my Moleskine. You are the same but you choose to lie, to play. Dick is now becoming my "big brother," telling you about training me and you are telling him he could be a trainer in *mental gymnastics.* We're about to get to our first semi-time together, to the bathroom at Passerby, to Pop Rocks. And then we do.

You: *HOLY. FUCKING. SHIT. I can't believe I did that lol*

Dick: *I can* ☺ *And I'm psyched for my boy. Kid needed a blowie haha*

You: *Okay but . . . um I shouldn't but I have to omg Dick he's . . . it has a little hat lolol*

Dick: *LOL MY BOY IS UNCUT*

I would rather be marooned in a fucking comedy club in the Times Square Virgin Fucking Megastore while Vagina *riffs* on her love life than in this fucking warehouse. I didn't know anything about hell on earth, and now I do. And I can't even tell you about it. Which is easily the worst part.

You: *I almost have to sleep with him to see what it's like because who knows when I'll have the chance again right?*

Dick: *Damn that explains a lot*

You: *How so?*

Dick: *There's something off about him a little freaky no deaky*

You: *I know but I kinda like being mommy. I got him out of his shithole apartment and his weird job. Honestly social services should have something like this, women in their twenties help the boys become men . . . Maybe I could start a business . . .*

Who are you, Vail? You are not this way with me. You are sweet with me. You have morals with me. It is him. He is the problem. The poison. I saw you, Vail. I saw you light up when you found me my apartment and I saw you turn green when you met Vagina, when you were jealous, jealous because you want me, because you love me.

But you just can't quit Dick.

And I don't get it. He doesn't love you. He doesn't love anyone, not you or his hero brother or his wingdick Schlitz. He doesn't even bother to bring closure to his sentences half the fucking time and he sure as hell doesn't care about me.

Dick: *Schlitz is kinda over it not so into the big brother shit lol but I bring the kid around cuz he has no bros and I don't think you get it Vail. The kid wants you bad. Kinda weird*

You: *I don't think it's reeeeally so weird for a guy to want me lol*

Dick: *You know what I mean he's a loner and you can't trust that shit*

You: *Aw, are you trying to protect me?*

Dick: *Don't invite him to your birthday*

You: *Ah, so you don't want him messing with our anniversary*

Dick: *Ha right*

You: *It'll be fine. He digs his own grave like he booked a VACATION for us in Bermuda for my birthday lol . . . I killed that, I mean wtf right? But he's still bringing up my bday every thirty seconds to the point where I had to say that he's not on boyfriend duty. Why don't boys get hints? I know I'm good lol but dude . . . Back off. We're not married.*

LIES LIES LIES WHY WHY WHY

Dick: *It gets worse. He made you a fucking mixtape*

You: *No he did not. Oh my heart.*

Dick: *Also I'm thinking Costa Rica in June if you could swing it minus the kid*

You: *Are you serious? Like that feels like a birthday slash anniversary present . . . And what do we do with our boy? Do we ask Schlitzy to babysit LOLOL*

Dick: *Ha. Don't sweat it. I'll make him bail on your b-day. Kid does whatever big bro says to do. Kinda fuckin cool honestly*

You: *Ha. Good luck with that. He's obsessed with me and I warn you he'll be there at 8:01 with Pop Rocks so you better get there first* 🙂*. Don't want to get locked in his basement!*

So there it is. You two put me in a no-win situation so *he* could go to your birthday. He "let you" suck his dick in the bathroom. You came running back to me the way you always do when he puts you in your place, which is to say no place. When you pushed me away, it wasn't your fucking *job* crisis. It was because Dick reneged on Costa Fucking Rica. How are you so smart and stupid all at once and what does he have (aside from his chopped-up penis) that I don't have? I want to bash the computer over his head, but I can't do it. I'm a reader, Vail. I have *compassion.* You're not the two-faced girl you play on AOL IM and I'm not the stock character bully who flies off the handle and kills Dr. Evil. Dick is not "evil." The bad guys in books are always the way they are because of some unresolved childhood bullshit. Dick is punishing anyone who tries to love him because he doesn't think he deserves to be alive. Dead brother guilt is a thing.

Yes, even after what he did to me, what he did to us, all I want to do is help him. I feel . . . sorry for him, Vail, same way I feel sorry for you.

You were so intimidated by my sincerity and my decency that you went behind my back and pretended to stab me. But that doesn't change the way we were in real life, in private. You prepared me for this moment, showing me *Good Will Hunting* and *Ordinary People.* Stories where lost dicks get schooled by super-ass-smart good guys. Robin Williams didn't write off vicious Will Hunting and Judd Hirsch didn't put whiny Conrad Jarrett out of his misery. You see Dick's pain and think it's your duty as a female citizen to let him take his shit out on you. But that's not how it works, my dear. Only a *man* can fix a man. And come on. This is New York Fucking City. The towers hit the ground and *we bounce* up *like round ball.* We chin up like Carrie Bradshaw, and we take care of our own. We help the mom with her stroller and yes! Yes, we help the bald, guilt-ridden leftover lesser fucking brother.

I peel the duct tape off his face. I feel like God. Reading; it really does elevate the soul! Dick spits the sock out, kinda like how you spit me out . . . No. I won't go there. Love is all or nothing and the novel that the two of you co-fucking-wrote is like those forgotten teenybopper books from the '80s where the Hardy Boys teamed up with Nancy Drew. It's in the trash, obsolete. Gone. I'm the lucky one, Vail. You and Dick need two faces to get through the day. I only need one. *Yours.*

"Goldfuck," he says. "What the fucking fuck?"

I roll up my sleeves. Dr. Goldberg in the *hizzy.*

34

You know that Beatles song about how you get by with a little help from your friends? That song always kind of annoyed me. I dunno, Vail. I like the Beatles better when they sing about holding hands and long, winding roads and taking sad songs and making them better.

Look at Dick, look at you. People with a lot of friends and big fat families are usually the *most* fucked-up, if you ask me. Dick's laptop has a million pictures of Dick being loved and adored and he's never alone but he *is* alone.

He never learned how to carry his brother's death and do his friends fucking care? Not even a little bit. From the look of his pictures, I'm the only real friend Dick ever had. You tried to help him, but Sally's Harry said it: Men and women can't be friends. True friends like (fake) Jeremy are rare. They see you suffering and they toss you in the basement. Tough love is real love and I'm picky about people because if it ain't Piven and Cusack or Carrie and *The Others* who stand by no matter *what,* why fucking bother?

I light a candle—thank God I brought a candle!—and our "friend" Dick screams, totally misreading the candle, same way you misread song lyrics. He cries for help and pledges that he's going to kill me, that he won't put up with my *satanic cult bullshit.* Don't worry, Vail. I remain calm, centered. And then it's my turn to lead.

"I'm not here to hurt you, Dick. I'm here to help you. It's kind of like a memorial."

"You're a dead man, Goldberg."

"No, but that is why we're here today."

"I'm sorry, asshole. Is that what you want? 'Cause I get it, kid. If I found out my girl was stepping out I'd lose it. But now you know. So you're welcome. We're good. You can go ahead and let me the fuck out of here."

People are fascinating. He really thinks I'd drag him here out of revenge? "Are you religious, Dick?"

"Jesus Christ, Goldberg."

"Me neither. But I always did like the sound of *shiva.* Do you know about shiva?"

"I know I'll make a shiv and cut you if you don't undo this fucking . . . She's a *slut.*"

I won't dignify that—you're a lady—and it's not your fault. He Seduced you. He Destroyed you. You work very hard to keep it all a secret from me, and you wouldn't do that if you didn't love me. Dick calls me crazy. But that's what people drowning in guilt and self-loathing do when faced with true love. I sigh. Back to brass tacks. "I lit the candle because that's what you do at a shiva. It's a mourning ritual. You cover the mirrors. You don't shave, you don't shower. You shut everything out and you do nothing but honor the dead for seven days."

"You're insane."

"Oh, don't worry, Dick. This won't take seven days. But we are going to mourn your brother David so that you can move on, you know, so you can stop being such a fucking *dick.*"

He throws back his head and screams. "Aaaaah!"

I run at him and do the same thing. "Aaaaah!"

Primal screams feel like they belong in a shiva, but he just stares at me. "You need help."

"Yes, I do, Dick. I need you to help me. Tell me about David."

"You don't know shit about me or my family."

"I went on your computer, Dick, so I do know a little."

Poor Dick claims he's been violated—ha—and says I'm *gonna pay for this*—I am already paying; I'm here—and it's tempting to lecture him about teenage girls, but I can't save the whole world at once. He's scared of me, Vail. I'm pretty sure he'll tread carefully from now on. So if you think about it, I already saved a fuck-ton of misguided horny young girls!

"All right, Goldfuck, what the hell do you want from me?"

I pull up a metal folding chair. I straddle it. I am the man. "You want to know what I didn't see in your computer, Dick? I looked through all your pictures but someone is missing."

"You and Vail aren't married or some shit. She is not worth this, buddy. Seriously."

"I didn't see your brother David, Dick. Did you erase every photo of him?"

The truth is like duct tape; it shuts his fucking mouth. Yes!

"I thought so, buddy. You do that. You erase your brother and block every girl who gets too close. I don't need to go to the Palmer family house in Chicago to know that your parents probably turned David's bedroom into a shrine . . ." His eyes are bulging; I hit a nerve. "I'm guessing he died when you were fifteen or sixteen, right? You thought it shoulda been you. I bet David was one of those larger-than-life kinda guys. The firstborn motherfucking *soldier* and you try to sleep but you can't sleep. You still hear the screaming of the lambs, the sound of your mother crying over his pillow, wishing it was you in the ground."

It's the longest Dick has ever gone without talking and holy *fuck* I am good at this, Vail. I could make a career out of it.

"You guys went to Turks and Caicos. Felt like the kinda trip the family takes after a horrible death, yeah? I saw the pictures. I bet you had a few illegal fruity cocktails and went to your mom to beg her to love you. I bet it hurt like hell when she shut you down. I know you hate yourself, Dick. I know you want everyone around you to feel what you feel, the pain. Tell me. Was he a David? Davey? Does he haunt you at night and beg you to stop being so bad to girls?"

He's about to break and move over, Judd Hirsch. There's a new shrink in town.

"I see you, Dick. Choking yourself with his dog tags, grabbing at them every time you feel happy. Let it out. Let him go. I've got your back, same way you tried to have mine."

It's the first time he looks at me and my skin crawls a little bit. The deadness in his eyes. "Can I have a bump?"

I was hoping he'd start talking on his own, but people drink wine at funerals, so what the hell. I give him a bump. He twitches a little and he laughs. "I can't fucking believe this, Goldberg. You're crazy. You know that, right?"

"No one's watching, Dick. We're not at the Beanery. We're not at the bar. If you think it's crazy that I'm trying to help you say goodbye to your brother . . . I'm sad for you."

He hangs his head. I don't want to get ahead of myself, Vail, but is he crying? I think he's crying. His shoulders are jerking and he's hiding his face in his hands. This is going faster than I expected and yep . . . He's crying. I can't see it but I can hear it.

"There it is, Dick. Yes! Let it out. David Arnold Palmer is gone, but you're here. You deserve to be happy. You deserve to be loved and then I promise . . . You won't have this urge to be such a fucking . . . You can be Richard, Dick. I promise you. It's never too late."

It's like an exorcism, the way he shakes, burying his head so I can't see him cry. I knew this would work if I gave him a chance and would you look at that, Vail? It's working.

"This is good, buddy. Let it out. I'm not here to judge you for the seventeen chat boxes. You were just lonely. I know there's a good guy in there, and your brother . . . You gotta know that a guy like that, a soldier . . . He above all people would *want* you to be happy. The Seduction, the Destruction . . ." The betrayal. "It's all just survivor guilt and I know that, Dick, I do."

He's shaking like a coked-up fucking jumping bean and I wish I had this on tape.

"Let me ask you this. What would you say to David right now if you could?"

He lifts his head and I'm a miracle worker, Vail. Dick is a changed man. Raw in the eyes and red in the face and I think . . . yes, those *are* tears. I grip the edges of the metal chair. I am a teacher and a rabbi and a priest and a shrink and the next fucking coming of Miss Frascatore.

Or . . . Wait. Am I?

Dick turns into *Shining* Jack Nicholson and grins. "Are you serious, Goldbitch?"

I don't talk because I can't talk. I don't like this. Dick staring at me like his cooler-than-thou crap works on me. Laughing at me in this way that makes me get off the chair and stumble. He's not *crying.* He's laughing so hard that it *looked* like he was crying. I am not Judd Hirsch in *Ordinary People.* I am not Robin Williams in *Good Will Hunting.* I am just me, *Goldbitch.*

"Goldberg," he says. "I just . . . Are you really that fucking gullible?"

The skin on my arms turns cold, and the blood in my veins runs hot. Fool me once, shame on you. Fool me twice, FUCK FUCKING YOU.

"Kid," he says. "The dog tags aren't real."

"I don't know what you mean."

"Oh, Goldberg, come on. Don't you get it? I don't have a dead brother."

The plane is going down and I don't know how to save us. "What do you mean?"

"Have we ever fucking met? Kid, come on. You saw my computer. Fuck . . . There are no pictures of my brother 'cause I never had a fucking brother and the dog tags . . . Can't you feel it?"

I am holding the dog tags and I can feel the dog tags. But obviously I can't.

"Joe," he says. "I got those stupid dog tags at a *bar mitzvah.* Got my first handie that day too, but that's another story. You got another bump?"

The plane hits the ground and there are no survivors. Only quicksand. I give him a fucking bump. It's better than using my voice. I'm not sure that I still have one.

"So it was a *Top Gun*–theme bar mitzvah. Ya know . . . theme party. Ray-Bans and leather jackets and fucking . . . They had some guy making party favor dog tags but the dude screwed up on mine. He put David Arnold Palmer instead of Richard Arnold Palmer."

"I don't . . ."

"Few years later, my freshman year, my roommate's little sister visits. She's not hot, maybe a six at best . . . Anyway, she goes through my stuff, she finds the dog tags and she's like, 'Oh no, did your brother die in war?' and I'm all 'Hell yeah.' Next thing you know . . . Chicks love that shit, Joe. They love it when we're all 'emotional' but what *you* don't get . . . I still can't . . . You *fell* for that shit . . . You're not supposed to show 'em your *real* 'feelings,' ya dummy. Are you really that . . . Christ. Gimme another bump. I don't even. . . . I can't."

I give him *another bump* because I don't know what else to do. He's not scared of me, Vail. He talks like we're still friends, like it's *cool* that I got all *macho* and knocked him out. He thinks this is a joke and he thinks life is a joke and DAVID ARNOLD PALMER HOW COULD YOU DO THIS TO ME?

Dick whistles—he can whistle—and he wants more coke and I give him more coke and HOW COULD *I* DO THIS TO ME? He's higher by the second. He doesn't seem to care that he's cuffed in a freezer. I didn't plan for this and I couldn't plan for this—FUCK YOU DOG TAGS FUCK YOU—and I shouldn't be pacing but I am fucking pacing and he whistles and we get it, Dickwad.

You can whistle. You want more blow.

"Goldberg, it's cool. I'm not gonna like . . . I told you. You stepped up and manned up. We're cool. If the shoe was on the other foot, if I saw you and her on my laptop, you'd be six feet under in a Hefty bag. We're good, bro. I'll back off Vail and you . . . Fuck that."

"Fuck what?"

"Obviously she's dead to you so let's blow this Popsicle stand and pick up some hotties."

Am I not a man? Am I not the key master and the one in fucking *charge*?

"Tell me something, Dick. Did you take Psych 101 in college?"

"Joe, come on. We're good. I won't tell anyone about this or how you're the first dude who bought into the dog tag bit and you . . . You're free. It's over. Slut's outta the bag."

I can't let him out into the wild like this; he's too dangerous. I have to tame this cunt, I do. "So, Dick, if you had taken entry-level psych you would've learned that lab coat types lock up hamsters to learn about punishment and rewards and stuff like that."

"Happy to finish this conversation in a bar over some *Jim Henson,* bud. Come on."

The *Henson* reference was a failed fucking neg, and I am back. "First, you put the hamster in the cage. You feed it every three hours. Hamster's happy. All good."

"It's not hamsters. It's *lab rats,* Goldberg. And I get it. You're pissed. You'll get over it."

I'm pacing in the good way now. Dick can eat my fucking dick.

"Once the *hamster* is adjusted to the feeding schedule, you skip a feeding. You fuck with it. Hamster's going hungry, going crazy. *What did I do? Where did I go wrong?* It blames itself."

"Let me outta here, Joe. This isn't funny anymore."

"You feed the hamster. Hamster is happy, but hamster is confused. *I got a treat! I must've done something good! What did I do right?*"

He bangs his head against the freezer wall and I am better than Judd Hirsch and every rabbi-priest-Frascatore-guru combined. I wait for him to stop making noise. He stops.

Good dog, and I give him the treat in the form of a bump. He sniffles. "I'm good."

Like I give a fuck and I smile. "So! Our hamster is officially fucked. It doesn't know when food is coming and how could it? It's hungry. Confused. It looks inward instead of calling out the lab coat. The hamster . . . It blames itself."

"You got another bump, kid?"

I pull up a chair. I smack his fucking face. "Do you get it, Dick?"

"Yeah. Mommy never got you a hamster. Gimme a bump."

"Vail is not the problem. You are the reason a *lot* of girls in this city are what you call 'crazy' and 'needy' and 'slutty.' "

He smiles ever so slightly and I smack the grin off his face ever so harshly. "You put Vail in your cage and string her along. It was one thing when I thought you lost your brother. But nope. You have it all handed to you on a silver fucking platter in Turks and Fucking Caicos and *still* you're an ungrateful shitbag of a dick."

"So kill me."

I smack him again and doesn't he get it? He laughs like this is a joke and cocaine really is a terrible drug. I give him a bump and you never know, Vail. Maybe he'll overdose. But then sometimes you do know. He laughs. "The dog tags . . . You dumb fuck."

I smack him upside the head. "I'm a *nice* fuck. What the hell is wrong with you?"

That last jab got him and whaddya know? There might be something like a soul in there after all. But then he lifts his chin. "You're not just a little bitch, Goldberg. You're a hypocrite."

"Bullshit, Dick. Nice try, though."

"*You're* the asshole when it comes to girls, Goldass. Hell, I'm bad sometimes but you . . . You just compared your so-called girlfriend to a fucking hamster."

I did but I didn't and I sink to his stupid level. "Fuck you, Dickwad."

He eyes me like he has access to his hands, his fists, and if I could have that ego for an hour. I cling to his stupid bar mitzvah fucking dog tags. If.

"Buddy, Joe . . . it's cool. We're cool. You got your revenge and I get it. I overstepped. I'll back off Vail, I'll lay off the high school girls, and it . . . it really is cool. I been through worse."

I hate when people say things like that. Pudding is nothing without proof. I run this town. Not Dick. I raise my fist and he flinches. I drop my fist. I win. "What have you 'been through,' Dick? Enlighten me."

"You saw the IMs. I tried to push Vail off before she started up with you and she's. . . . stage nine. The cling is real. I stopped going down on her like the second time we hooked up, told her she tastes funny. I told her to get that rank-ass toe chopped off. She drunk-dialed me the same night, begging to come over."

And still you like him. Still.

"So if you really don't want her, and it was all just Seduce and Destroy for kicks. . . . I mean, what do you want? Why do you have to be like this?"

He shakes his head, and it's sad. It's scary. "Gimme a bump, son."

I give him a bump. He shrugs. "You gotta stop reading into things. Shit's not that deep."

"But you chased Vail. You went to her on September 11. You talked to her *today* and you expect me to believe you're not in love with her?"

"Everyone shacked up after 9/11, kid. None of it was real. It was just really easy to get laid. And Christ, dude . . . Are you stupid? Don't you get it? She comes . . . back . . . to me."

I wish the DARE to stay off drugs campaign didn't work so well on me because I don't like this, Vail. I could use a *bump.* "Well, just so you know, she lied about stuff, about me."

He grins. "Oh yeah?"

"She posted the Missed Connection, Dick. That was all her."

"No shit, Goldberg. Everyone lies when they're trying to get laid. Dog tags, or you know . . . *age* . . . "

Will I ever have the upper fucking hand? "I wasn't trying to get laid. I was—I love her."

"Enough with the love crap. We all lie. It's nothing to freak out about. It's like when the chick in the office sends herself flowers so all the guys think she's taken."

"Excuse me if I never worked in an office."

His phone rings; it's his mother.

"Man," he says. "You're telling me that no girl ever took you in her basement to watch *Clueless* while you finger-banged her on a mangy plaid sofa?"

I don't know how to get out of this, Vail. Everything turned upside down and I'm the victim, cornered into feeding him bumps off his dog tags. I have no plan—I wanted to sit shiva—and I am *Clueless* about him, about us. I never would've lured him in if I knew there was no dead brother and you can't teach a high young dog new tricks. You can't leave him, and *I* can't leave him—for very different reasons—and why is it so hard to walk away from people?

"All right," he says. "This is played out. And I need a beer."

I look at him. That smirk that is a stain, a spot out of fucking *Hamlet* . . . *Macbeth*? Fucking Shakespeare and I snap. "Why do people . . . Girls . . . Everyone . . . Why do people like you so much?"

Dicks love compliments, so he sighs. "Shit," he says. "I gotta call my mom back. Seriously, Goldbitch."

"Your *mother* can wait."

"You don't know everything about me, kid. My mom's a worrywart and when I don't pick up she goes into panic mode and calls the Beanery and if they don't know where I am. . . ."

He's lying, right? He has to be lying. There's no chocolate at the center of the Tootsie Roll Pop. He's just . . . a fucking dick. His phone rings again and it's you. You're doing it again, calling him when you should be calling me. I never should have let him get this close to us. Gym guys are bad guys, because the world is full of problems. Schools that need construction. Women tied to the railroad tracks who need saving. But guys like Dick . . . What do they do?

They lift things up and put things down.

"Dude," he says. "I'm not a threat. I don't want to be somebody's ball and chain."

"Everyone wants it."

"Don't take this the wrong way, but, like . . . what happened to you, Goldberg?"

I am the one with the keys to the handcuffs and *still* he has to *neg* me. Swing his fucking dick around. I won't let him get in my head, and there is nothing wrong with me. I am not the pervy pig on Instant Fucking Messenger. That's him.

His phone rings again; it's his mother.

"Joe, come on. Let's get a drink. You don't want my mom calling the cops."

"Why do you let these girls chase you if you don't want a girlfriend?"

"Because I can. Fuck, dude, why did the chicken cross the road?"

"To get to the other side, to find someone! And if you're really not pining for Vail or any of these fucking girls . . ."

"I'm not."

"Well, don't you . . . Don't you feel bad about hurting them?"

"Not my monkeys, not my circus."

I never went to the circus. "Huh?"

"I'm trying to get my career going and that's hard enough, and girls . . . It's an outlet."

"And you just plug in when you feel like it."

"Goldberg," he says. "Don't even try with bullshit feminism. Maybe it's 'cause you didn't go to college . . ." Where guys learn to be dicks and girls learn to obsess over dicks. "But girls want it too, the bullshit. And one of these days, Vail will . . . Gimme a bump."

I give him a bump. The phone rings. It is the Beanery. He is missed.

"The funny thing is, Goldberg . . . You don't even like Vail. You like the chase."

"Bullshit."

"It's true, kid. You're using her. She's using you. That's the game. So yeah . . . Save the feminism for another night. If you cared about women, you'd let me talk to my fucking mom."

"Who would disown you for good if she saw all these chats on your computer."

"Are you shitting me? She's my mom! First one to say that all these New York City girls are nowhere near good enough for her boy."

It's what Miranda said at the baby shower about the boy whose mommy told him he's *perfect*. Mr. Mooney blames my mother for my "issues," but is it *ever* on us?

"All right, Dick. If you don't want Vail, why did you go to India with us?"

"Huh?"

He doesn't remember and my God, to be a dick. "India. The first time we all hung out. Vail and I had plans, and you say you're going to get Indian food and we go with you. Why?"

"I was hungry." He laughs. "Goldberg, come on. You can't *still* be into that chick . . . Her face is all right, but the body . . . She needs to go to the gym, even if it's Curves. And she's so . . . in her head. You call that sex? She lays there like she's only doing it to tell Cynthia. And she thinks we're all so stupid, the whole 'I never show anyone my janky toe' act and 'the last guy I dated' bit . . . Don't you get it, G? She's not *capable* of anything real. Maybe in ten years but who cares . . . Those tits aren't the kind that hold up, kid."

I never talked about women in the locker room in school, and I won't do it now. I am losing my grip on him and his phone rings again. *You.* And somehow he just knows.

"That's another thing. The calls . . . the babbling. She can never just chill. And India. Picture it from my end. She's in my shop every day and I'm about to file a restraining order and then you walk in with your stinky flannel and your heart on your sleeves. . . ."

"Sleeve. Singular."

He rolls his eyes. "Dude, she didn't even put you on the Evite for her *birthday,* let alone let you fucking hang with her."

There was an Evite? "You don't know anything about us."

"Meanwhile she's harping on me about the party, calling me non-stop, all 'I didn't see your RSVP, are you coming?' . . . *Girls.* I told you, Joe. If she was into you, she would've wanted to eat cake with you, not me and fifty other fucking douchebags."

Memory Lane is too rough for me right now. I can't help it. I break. "You could've mentioned that to me, maybe told her you're not interested, maybe cut the fucking cord and come clean about . . . I'm a person. I'm a . . ."

I want to say more, but my voice is cracking, his phone is ringing. A 212 landline.

Cops?

"Your monkeys, your circus, Goldilocks. And you were right, what you said about girls . . . They *are* fucking hamsters . . ." I hate that I am the hamster who got a pellet, approval from Dr. Dick. "Not at first, though. You hit the bar and girls are wild. They're out on the town, bendy li'l monkeys with legs for days, grabbing at your banana. You take that monkey home but next thing you know . . . Meta-fucking-morphosis. That wild monkey . . . It turned on you and it's . . . a hamster."

"Bullshit."

"I know! Because what fucking kid wants a hamster? Hamsters aren't *fun*. They're just work. They don't play with you. They just shit in that cage waiting for you to come back and come on . . . We're supposed to *respect* that fucking hamster? That's what I meant, kid. This shit you pulled with me . . . I been through worse. It's nothing compared to the shit they pull on *us*."

I give him a bump and I guess I am a *little* hypocritical. Or maybe I'm just afraid of jail.

"We are guilty of *nothing*, Goldberg. We hook up with monkeys and then they hamster up on us. So no, I don't worry about Vail or any fucking girl . . . Not my monkeys, not my . . . Did you know I had a dog?"

I didn't. "We're getting off track."

"Roscoe was the best. . . ." Is he playing me? Are the cops on the way? "Roscoe was my boy and he loved me. Hamsters don't love you. They don't jump when you come home. Not like Roscoe. Roscoe was the bomb and I tell you this, Goldberg. I would sacrifice all the NYC 'hamsters' for one more hour with my good boy . . . You know what my mom said when she saw Vail? She said I'd be better off back home with a girl who's not stuck on a hamster wheel. I think she meant the rat race, but you get the gist."

I do get it. And that's when I do it: I knock his fucking lights out. One clean hit.

My hand is raw. Not bleeding badly but bleeding. I blow out the candle and I tape the stupid sock back in his mouth. Am I fucked? No. I'm not a criminal. He's the bad guy, I'm the good guy and you're . . . I picture you and Dick IMing a week from now.

Dick: *So then I spout off all this bullshit about hamsters and monkeys and the kid believes it. I'm coked out of my mind and this kid is listening*

You: *OMG our poor boy lol you knew how to play him you saved your own life I mean WOW DICK WOW and I still can't believe he compared me to a hamster. Asshole much?*

Dick: *I told you he was off. I mean you do understand why I had to call the cops on him. Dude is deranged enough to do that to me, imagine what he could do to a girl.*

You: *I'm just so happy you're alive, baby. What a long strange trip. I mean I'm happy we BOTH survived that crazy lil boy.*

Dick: *Me too. So. Wanna get married?*

Stop it, Joe, stop it. You're not getting hitched and the shiva wasn't a total bust. I know what we're up against now. An acid tongue. A carnival jackass charlatan who waves his dog tags to distract you while he steals your pride, your soul, your heart. I was wrong. He really *is* fucking evil and he's just gonna keep going, isn't he? Let's say I drag his veteran-disrespecting ass out of here. We laugh it off as a coke bender gone sideways. Where does that leave us? You and me. We're back to square one. You're plagued with guilt about pulling the Dick-stained wool over my eyes and you think you don't deserve a guy like me. You run around with him behind my back, casually breaking my heart as his acid piss rain corrodes our *greens of summers* in-fucking-definitely.

But if he died . . .

Gently, Joseph.

35

I need the World Wide Fucking Web so I'm in the back of an internet café with my back against the wall. I have Dick's laptop and a slice of pizza. Pepperoni. But I can't eat. How could I? You're still calling him and you're not calling me and you're sicker than I thought. I got into his email, Vail. And it was one thing to read your little chats with Dick, but to see you put words in my mouth—*NYC Bookstore Babe, you were so sexy in your cape*—I mean, this sucks. I HATE YOUR CAPE. You rewrote your Craigslist letter and reversed everything and I won't judge you—it's a cycle of abuse—but you're a monkey in his circus and I have to save you.

We can't have his mother getting in our way, so I send her a back-off-Mommy email. And then I can't help it. I have to taste the spoiled milk. I dig around to find your Evite.

He wasn't exaggerating. You invited one hundred fifty-six people to your birthday. Way more guys than girls. And you let your "friends" invite whoever they wanted. *Especially hot guys! All guys welcome lol wooh!*

So what do I do? Dick is alive, in the freezer, and I can't actually, you know, kill him. Is he hungry? He is probably hungry. I buy him a slice. But not from the good place. From a shit place closer to the warehouse. When I get back, he's still down and he's blinking, bloody. And for a moment, it looks like he is the victim. But no. I get my head together. I am the victim. I pull the sock out of his mouth. I slap his face and he comes to and I give him a slice. It's a dangerous thing, to be a man with no plan. That's how you wind up spoon-feeding pizza to an asshole. He burps.

"Nice left hook," he says. "See, that's something else I did for ya, Goldberg."

He talks like we're downtown, killing time before we hit up Passerby. He eats like I am a boy. Not a threat. And then he spits out the crust and sighs. "So, we done here?"

"No."

"Kid, it's all right. She was your first love. Everyone goes batshit with first love."

"She was not my first."

Not fair, Vail. Not fair that he can read me like Miss Frascatore.

"Look," he says. "It sucks, I know. You got your little heart smashed into a million pieces. You think some girl didn't break *me*? I told you. They get to us. It happens."

"That's not what happened."

"Maybe if I say it in your language . . . She's fuckin' Carrie, bro. She only loves guys who don't love her back. That chick will never, could never love you. I mean, dude . . . she doesn't even like your cock."

It's my PORTNOY and it's perfect. Is it? "You don't know that."

"Relax, Goldfuck. You'll rebound. And this . . . this is nothing. Let's go knock back a couple of Jäger bombs and forget she ever happened. Seriously. She's not worth it."

This again, and I can't let it go. "Yes, she fucking is."

His phone rings, and it's you again. As if even now, you are on his side. Leaving you becomes a thing I could do, and he knows it. I would delete your number and go *knock back Jäger bombs* with Dick. I'd have to hang with him, make him trust me. It's that keep-your-enemies closer bullshit and what? I'd just . . . never see you again? And he'd see you whenever he felt like it and I'd always kinda sense it when you two had a *fuck-fest* and—

"C'mon," he says. "Take inventory, kid. You're not walking away empty-handed. You got a sweet pad in SoHo. She really *is* trying to hook you up with a gig. You got me, you got the gym. Not too shabby for a—"

"High school dropout."

"You said that, Goldilocks. Not me."

I tell him to shut up and he shuts the fuck up and finally there is silence. He is getting to me, Vail. Maybe he's right. Maybe there was never a chance for us and maybe I should forget I ever met you and untie the fucker and go get Jäger bombed with him. You started this. You did this. You talked to *him* about me. He went with it. He's a shithead. But I wasn't ever in love with him.

I love you. I'm a *slave . . . 4 U.* Like it or not I'm Sam Cooked for life and I will *always be your slave till I'm buried in my grave.* I saw the white box. The history. The Evite. The pot of gold at the end of the rainbow might be a pot of shit. I am not "the one." We never even made it to Serendipity. You are ice, and my pick isn't sharp and hot enough to melt you. And now look what I did. I put myself in hot water.

"Joe," he says. "Remember the one where Big beat the shit out of his buddy who hit on Carrie?"

"That never happened."

"Exactly," he says. "Don't blame me about 'the end of love in New York.'"

"The line is 'the end of love in Manhattan.'"

"Blame that fucking show. Blame AOL. Blame the fuckers who blew up the towers when shit was just getting *fun* and girls were at their new millennium Forever 21 fucking best. I didn't do this, Joe. You want to blame me, but you can't. I'm your bro. Think of it this way. If you did this to some girl . . ."

"I would never."

"Well, no girl would ever forgive you if you lured her to your cave and knocked her out and locked her ass up in the icebox. We can't let them turn us against each other."

Maybe he's right. Maybe growing up means outgrowing you. You're not the only fish in the Central Park Reservoir. You mocked my Portnoy. I know for a fact that you didn't finish *Fast Food Nation* and I'm not all that experienced. Maybe you're *not* that good in bed.

"You know what you should do, Goldberg? *EuroTrip.* I did a semester in Manchester after I got pussy-whipped and, man. . . . It'd be good for you to get outta Dodge, seriously."

I set up a bump on a dog tag. He smiles and hoots, and I am what I am. It is what it is. I can't tell you that it's not good to see the fucker laugh a little, relax.

But then my phone rings for the first time in a long time and it's . . . *you.*

He shouts at me to stay, but I don't stay. The Eric Carmen blasts in the heart part of my head and I run to the door *and I step out in the street and the city's the color of—*

"Vail! I almost missed you."

"You sound so out of breath. Are you okay? How is Jeremy?"

I gulp heaps of fresh air and I close the door. Tight. "He's good. All good."

"Oh, thank God, because I have a question for you, Cusack."

Do you love me? Are you in bed with one hundred sixty jerks right now? "Shoot."

"Well, I'm starving and I want something sweet. . . ." Because your fingers got a workout calling Dick? "Do you . . . do you maybe want to finally do what we've been saying we'd do since the day we met? I mean . . . do you want to go to Serendipity with me, my dear?"

The answer is yes, and I can't get back onto the island fast enough. Fuck it. I hail a cab.

I did this. I made this possible. I put Dick on ice and I defrosted your cold, scared heart—your freezer was good practice—and you did it! You called me for frozen hot chocolate and steaming hot sex. I know it's hard, Vail, but you made the right call. And I hate that I ever doubted you. I look down at my hands. I do have to wash up, but then again . . . no, I don't. I fucked my hands up when I was defrosting your freezer! My hands are clean in the way that matters, all the better to hold your hands over a nice cup of frozen hot chocolate. Dick was wrong, and so were your bosses at *Sex*. It is not "the end of love in Manhattan." It's just the end of you and that low-rent Hardy Boy.

Life is good. The taxi driver is a talker in the pleasant way, sharing his story of how he got his medallion, how many years it took to memorize this city and every street, every tunnel.

"Driving a car into Manhattan never gets old," he says. "It's the opposite of going home to the wife, but don't tell her you heard that from me!"

We laugh together and I pledge my allegiance. I'm a lucky man. I can't imagine ever dreading coming home to you, Vail. I'm going to see you and I love a spontaneous cab ride. I love the idea of Dick tied up and crying in that busted-ass freezer. I never had anything to worry about, did I? If he breaks out of his cage—he will not bust out of that cage—I am fine. We're fine.

That's the upside of a simultaneously arrogant and insecure prick. That gym rat ice-hearted circus freak of a man would never tell a cop or a mother or a bored girl at a bar what I, the young, roid-free bookselling intellect, did to the big, bad globe-trotting dick.

You have to be very careful about who you lock up in a cage. I chose well.

36

But then we hit traffic on the bridge and the high fades as the truth surges like fucking cab fare. I wish the cabbie would shut up about his medallion and his wife. I'm not *safe.* And neither are you. You called me, sure, but it's not that simple. You only called me when you couldn't have him, and here I am, going to see you as if I don't know that. I know what I am, what I have.

I have stage IV cancer of the heart.

We make it into the city and I look out the window at all the pretty girls, girls who might be less deceitful than you. But they don't interest me. I can't see myself hand in hand with them. I love *you.* Can't stop, won't stop. Same way I was with that book, the one you coauthored in real time on *Instant* Fucking Messenger, and that's another thing I forgot to be mad about.

You told me you couldn't do that anymore. You just preferred to do that with him.

Am I Carrie with the whip? Am I *a masochist or something*?

Possibly, because here I am now, jumping out of a taxi and hugging you in your bad blue cape (the first red flag). You smell like you, and my whole body tingles. It's like I never read that awful fucking AOL IM book and love is crazy.

Stage IV cancer is crazy. A beast without boundaries that doesn't quit.

You request the table, the one from *Serendipity*, and we are in luck. It's available.

We climb the stairs in the wake of a hostess who thinks we are *adorable young romantics*, and you raise your eyebrows at me and the cancer spreads like wildflowers. I want you no matter what and I am Angus with his little crystals of meth and crack. This is all I ever wanted. It's the opposite of a fear of intimacy. You're safe with me, and Dick can fuck off. You're not a *monkey* and you're not a hamster. You're a woman. You wouldn't be here if you didn't want to cut him off. It's okay, Vail. You made it to Serendipity. And because you are safe, I can breathe. Relax. Dick won't escape. He only pushes himself when someone's around to see it. At heart, he's a lazy fucker. He's sure as hell not busting those cuffs while we eat our frozen hot chocolate and even if he does manage to get free . . . Who cares?!

I am the man, the motherfucking gunslinger.

I have Dick's phone in one pocket and I have my phone in the other and I have you in my crosshairs. You really don't know what I did for you today, and it's pretty fucking cute, the way you are still going on about your stupid freezer, my poor battered hands. Oh, Vail, if you ever knew about the *other* fucking freezer . . .

You raise your spoon, so I raise mine. "To the man who did the undoable . . ." I tied up Dick so he can't fuck with you. "To the man who brought my freezer back to life."

We click our spoons, and I can't stop loving you. I don't want to stop. Not here, not like this. Same way I didn't stop loving you when I saw the yellow hat. Or the night you left me alone with Angus.

Everything between *us* was fine then, it's fine now. Better, even. Which is impressive, when you think about what I've been through today . . . the IMs, the betrayal, the rewrite of our Missed Fucking Connection.

Yes, I ought to have my head examined, but there is no fucking point. Love is a disease. A cancer.

The waitress delivers our bowl of frozen hot chocolate, and you clap and shine and, God, there is a world in you. A disposable camera in your pocket because we just *have* to remember every second of this. I smile for the cardboard plastic camera and I should've stopped loving you in the bathroom at Passerby. *So rare to see one in the States.* But I didn't stop loving you then, and it is real to me now. *One True Thing* by Anna Fucking Quindlen.

I will never stop loving you, Vail. Ever.

"I'm sorry," you say. "But I'm like . . . This is good. I say we make it our thing. We go to every place from every rom-com."

We're on fire, back-and-forthing about New York City movies. I tell you that *Taxi Driver* is a rom-com just to fuck with you, and you say in that case, so is *American Fucking Psycho.* I ask if you read the book, and you flick a lovin' spoonful at me. Adorable. Creamy and wet. *You.*

"So," you say. "How is it going with Jeremy?"

I sip my water. *Think, Joe, think.* You used me to get to Dick. I built Jeremy from scratch to get to you. Your cancer is a thing we can beat, this thing you have for Dick. And I think my buddy Jeremy can help us out.

"Ugh," I say. "The poor guy . . . I dunno."

"Well, did you tell him what I told you about Sarah?"

"Yeah, but, Vail . . . it goes a little deeper than that."

"How do you mean?"

Gently, Joseph. "It's kind of a long story."

"My favorite kind, honestly. Lately I think I do prefer TV over movies because TV just goes on and on, you know?"

One day, you will become a reader, but that day is not this day.

"Okay. A few weeks ago, Sarah's boss threw a binder at her head. She had to get stitches."

"Jesus Christ."

"Exactly. Jeremy wanted her to quit."

"Understandable. That's physical abuse. She could sue him. Did she go to the cops?"

Did Dick get free? Did he go to the cops? No. "You didn't hear the whole story."

"Joe, the man threw a binder at a woman's head. He deserves to be castrated."

"The thing is, Sarah told Jeremy that her boss apologized. He was going through some stuff, having a hard week, and she's worked for him for two years and she swears by him. She says he really is a good guy."

"That's just the cycle of abuse. And the only way to end that cycle is for her to leave."

YES. "Agree."

"So why won't she go to HR or quit or kick him in the balls or whatever?"

"Well . . . there's a little more to it, Vail. Last night, she confessed. Turns out, Sarah was cheating on Jeremy with . . . her asshole boss. Poor guy was blindsided. He had no clue. And now he *really* wants her to quit."

You sigh. "I wish I could call her, but she told me she was leaving her family plan and said she'll have a new phone soon and will give Jeremy the number to give to you, to give to me, blah blah blah."

Betty Named Sarah and Carl Named Jeremy deserve Oscars, they really do. I nod. The waitress delivers a second helping of frozen hot chocolate. You lay a fresh napkin on your lap and it's exciting. You dip your spoon in and come all over it. "Oh God, fucking glorious. Why did we wait so long?"

Because of Dick, and I do the same. I come too. "Jesus Fucking Christ, this one is even better."

"Right?! God, I wish we could live in here, you know?"

For a minute, we're little pigs in love, pretending this is our new home as we push the whipped cream and chocolate shavings to make sure we're both satiated, to keep things fair. And then you put your spoon down.

"Okay," you say. "Sarah . . . I can't believe this."

"I know. I can't believe she cheated."

"No," you say. "People cheat. It happens. The real shitty thing she did is she went and told Jeremy what she did. That is so selfish."

I can't eat. Can't see. You're fighting it, us. Pushing off the medicine we need to get better, to be at our best. This is not who you are, and you are wrong. "You think cheating is okay if the other person never finds out?"

"Well, you know how it is . . . Sarah cheated. That's on her. That's her baggage to drag around. When you tell someone what you did, it's not honesty, Joe. It's cruelty. What is Jeremy supposed to do with that? I'm not confused here, right? Like, Sarah didn't break up with him."

"No."

"Sarah wants a future with Jeremy, and they've been together a long time. They're committed and solid. They moved away together. I mean, they're not . . ."

Us, and it hurts. But life is not a competition; we'll get there in time. "Yeah," I say. "They've lived together for a year or so, at least."

"If she really wanted him to love her and be happy and trust her, she had the perfect way out. The blood on her forehead, the stitches. She could've quit the job, told the boss to piss off, and taken it to the grave. But no. She did the selfish thing. She dumped it on Jeremy, so *he* has to drag around *her* baggage. Dating is nice. So is living together, but it's not married. You can't break a vow that doesn't exist. I mean, that's how I see it anyway . . ."

I never loved you more than I do as I watch you try to apologize for what you did to me. The person you need to forgive is yourself and you'll do that, in time. "Makes sense to me."

"It's funny," you say. "They almost remind me of my parents."

"I thought they were still married."

"They are, but that's what I mean. When I was like twelve, my dad came home from a business trip and told my mom about some stupid affair he had. . . . It ruined their marriage. My mom was never the same. Either trying too hard to be sexy, or paranoid and sniffing his shirts, digging through his pockets, blowing his head off about nothing. And my dad . . . he's not that guy, you know? He hated himself for the fling. He was going through some midlife crisis stuff, and yeah . . . he messed up. But he loved my mom. And if he never told her about his stupid crisis, if he had been strong enough to carry that on his own . . . I wish he'd never told her. They're not married because of 'love.' It's partly financial, but it's mostly this thing where she spends the rest of her life punishing him and testing him, and he stays because he thinks he deserves to be punished, tested. I think that's why we went on so many vacations."

You laugh and tell me it will be *so much fun* when I meet your parents. I stare at you. Your Beverly Hills soap opera of a family is almost worse than mine. "Wait . . . I'm confused. You really don't wish it were simpler? I mean, you don't just wish he never cheated?"

You call me sweet and dip your spoon into the frozen hot chocolate. "Oh, Joe. That's a waste of time. People cheat. It happens. And come on. We all know that guys are more sensitive than girls. If the tables were turned, if my *mom* cheated and told my dad . . . Men can't handle that kind of thing. You guys are so sensitive, and unlike us, you guys can't run to your friends and talk about all your shit. I love you, Joe Goldberg, so if we get super serious and I fuck up and fuck around, I will carry the guilt and the shame. I will protect you, keep it inside. . . . Okay?"

That's as close as you can come to saying Dick is dead to you without upsetting your *sensitive,* loyal boyfriend and yes. Yes! You dig the spoon into the last of our whipped cream, and you're about to eat it when you pull a fast one and give it to me, the man you love. It's a

Miracle on Sixtieth Street. You've rewritten the book, atoned for the past by painting our future, and I see things as you see them. You want to look out for me. I get it. You were terrible to me. You cheated on me. But you love me. You want me to join your family soap opera so we can spin off, out into our own little world. You want me to meet your sadistic mother, and your masochist father, and I did it. I saved you. You copped to your sins, and I am not your priest. I see you now. The childhood that scarred you, and maybe people just never grow up. I see the children nearby being scarred as we speak. Maybe everyone in this place, the spoiled kids and the high-strung adults, maybe we're all just sitting here trying to get over our stupid fucking parents.

You dab your lips with a napkin. "I need to pee. You okay?"

Off you go and I'm not just okay. I'm great. Never better, no sarcasm. Neither lonesome nor lonely. You lost a taste for Dick. I can feel it in my bones, in my Portnoy, and then my phone rings, but it doesn't. Mine is quiet. It is his phone, Dick's phone. I pull it out of my pocket, and I'm not used to having two phones, and there is another stage of cancer. Stage V: *You.*

You're not powdering your nose. You're calling Dick.

No. YOU JUST TOLD ME YOU LOVE ME. I shut off his phone. He doesn't want you and you don't want him. I have to be a *cool cat, tapping on my toe with the* . . . No. I can't sing my way out of this one. A dark cloud in this upscale fucking ice cream parlor. You really have been brainwashed by your rom-cons, by Carrie's never-ending chase and her lies. That shit with your parents . . . That didn't help either. But the enemy is not you. I trust my gut, the way I stand when you walk into the room. *I,* the gentleman who loves you, the one strong enough to endure you and your self-loathing, your inability to be loved, cherished.

"Aw," you say. "So old-school, pulling my chair and standing and all. I love it."

No way around it, Vail. It has to be done. I have to test you. I thought I cured you, but I didn't. And to cure you, I need us to share more than frozen hot chocolate. I need us to share the truth. "Random question."

"Random answer."

"Did you and Dick ever go out?"

You sip your water. "I don't know if I'd call it that. Why do you ask?"

Because you just fucking called him again. "I dunno. He's been a little weird lately. Even for him, partying a lot and jacked up on roids . . . You know that, right?"

"Sure. He and Schlitz . . . Whatever."

SO WHY DID YOU JUST CALL HIM?! "Mm-hmm."

You blink a little. "Joe . . . Where is this coming from?"

"Well, he's been talking about his ex and he never uses her name, which made me think . . . maybe it was you."

You laugh and you're a terrible liar and we're not your parents, Vail. We're not Jeremy and Sarah. We're better than that. I want you to tell me the truth. Tell me that what started as a joke to woo Dick turned into something real. You may *think* I can't handle it, but that's not fair. You've pushed me away again and again . . . and I'm still here.

And come on. You can't have Dick. You tried that. It was bad for you. No monkey in its right mind would choose that sadist fucking ringmaster over *me.*

You rub your belly. "Oof, two bowls was maybe a reach. . . ."

You still didn't answer the question, and I wave off the server. We're not checking out, not yet. "Maybe we just need to give it a minute."

"So," you say. "What have you got going on later?"

"Well, Dick and Schlitz wanna hang out."

"Cool, like a boys' night thing?"

The way you ask tells me that you still don't get it. I am not Dick. "Funny thing is, no. I'm gonna meet his new girlfriend."

Oh, your face, and I didn't need to fix him or lock him up in a freezer. I just need you to think he has a girlfriend. Someone worthy of his devotion, someone who makes you finally know what I know, that he's not afraid of commitment. He just plain never did, never will fucking love you. Your voice is fake as the little blue packets of fake fucking sugar. "Dick in a relationship . . . Really?"

"Sorry, I know you two . . . Well, you went out or something, right?"

"Eh, kind of. Honestly, I'm more like his therapist."

You run your fingers through your hair. I am a reader, and you are an open book. Visibly wondering why you are not good enough for him, as if being good enough for me is not enough for you. Fucking Dick.

"Vail, you can tell me if you guys hooked up. I mean, you know me. I'm not a child. I don't care."

"So who is she? The girl."

"Well, like he says, she's a 'dime.'" I shudder. "I hate it when he and Schlitz do that, when they rate girls."

"Oh, I know, and that's one of many reasons I never, you know, 'dated' Dick for real."

For real and is it really that easy to lie to me? "Vail, I wouldn't judge you if you did."

"Well, I would judge me. I mean, I work for *Sex and the City.* I think I know an unavailable cad when I see one."

Cad and it's all coming together. The day we met. *I am such an Anglophile.* I bet he told you about his *semester* in Manchester. I bet you turned British for him. He really fucking brainwashed you and you really do need me. I nod. "Okay."

"Okay."

A long silence, and then I break the ice, same way I did in your freezer. "So do you wanna come out with us?"

"And meet Dick's flavor of the week? I think I can skip that."

I hate to hurt you, but I have to hurt you. "Well, according to Dick . . . this is it. They might even go to Vegas and get hitched. He says he's never been in love. It's actually made me like the guy a little more, you know?"

Kids scream and giggle. Not you, though. "Married?"

"I mean, who knows, and sorry if this is gross, but Christ. He won't stop going off how it's the best he ever had, best sex, best . . . Never mind."

"What does she do?"

"She's a lawyer."

You roll your eyes and you will never want to set foot in the Beanery again or even walk down that block. "Right," you say. "He does this sometimes. Finds a mommy. It won't last."

"She's only like twenty-six. Some genius I guess who went to law school while she was in college. He worships her because she's so . . . together or whatever. But you're right. I guess she is kinda like his mom. She has her own place, and like he keeps saying, she's *all growns up*."

Oh, Vail, I know it hurts. I know you are comparing yourself to the imaginary lawyer and you think you are failing, but you need to quit this fucker. You need to see him for what he is, a pig in a freezer. Heartless and cold.

You tuck your hair behind your ears. "Well, good for him! And as a plain old twenty-five-year-old lost girl . . ."

"You're not lost."

"No, but Uncle Barry is all over me. He called while I was in the bathroom, and I gotta run some errands for him. We good?"

"We're great, Vail. *You're* great."

It's not a lie. We are good. You collect your purse and you reach for the cape, but you stop. It's not easy for you, I know. But maybe you needed Dick to fall in love, to set you free. Now you can really be with me, the man who makes you mixtapes and cleans your home and sucks your extra toe and loves you no matter what you fucking do.

I pay the bill—you're welcome—and we go downstairs, out into the cold, and we laugh about the nasty northeast wind, but it feels forced. Like we're doing it for cameras or something. I don't like missing you when you're right fucking next to me, and it's not me. It's you. Your teeth are chattering. I offer you my coat.

You pause. You resist my nice warm coat. "What about you, though? You'll freeze."

"Don't worry about me, Vail." It's not that cold in the warehouse.

"I can't take your coat, Joe. I can't believe I forgot my cape."

"We can go back and get it."

"Nah," you say. "I think it's meant to be. Let some other girl have it."

That's what I want to hear, and you are turning on Dick at ninety miles an hour. Again I offer my coat. "Vail. . . ." Let me love you. "You're not taking it if I'm offering."

You do it. You allow me to save you. I ease your arms into the sleeves. Your teeth chatter and it's not because of the cold wind. It's because of him, Dick.

Do you get it now, Vail? Dick bad. Joe good. Sometimes, it really is that simple.

You peck me on the lips. "Love you."

"Love you too."

When you round the corner, I turn on Dick's phone. A nanosecond later it is ringing and it's you. Oh, you are challenging me, and I am rising to the occasion. *No pain, no gain.* I feel your agony. You call again and again, and I'm sure you're still at it while I'm underwater, bound for Bed-Stuy, and it's infuriating. What is *wrong* with you? You are Sharon Stone in *Casino.* She marries the good guy who loves her and *still* she sneaks off to call the bad man, the pimp. If she knew how to be loved, if she wanted to be loved, she would have allowed herself to be loved. I picture you at home. I see you, *little colt.* You are crying in your pillow and whining to Cynthia about that *effing* dickhead bastard. And it's sad. I don't want you to be sad, but where is your dignity? I tried to help. I removed him from the equation. I got him a genius girlfriend.

And still, you call him. Still.

I make it back to the warehouse. I reach for the door, and the ghost of Virginia Woolf blows through me like the wind.

Some people have to die so that others might begin to live.

Dick is wide awake. Humbled. That's what sitting in a puddle of his own piss will do to a man. No more pride. *He's a loser, baby, so why don't I kill him?*

37

I can't do it, Vail. I can't kill him. I'm not that guy. But I also can't send him home.

I grab his laptop. He rubs his eyes. "I get it, okay? I was a piece of shit. I'm . . . I'm sorry, kid."

Too little, too late is a saying for a reason, asshole. "She deserves better."

"No," he says. "Fuck Vail. I'm talking about you, Joe. I dunno. Been sitting here like . . . She's not just a bitch. She's a witch. I cannot believe the way she roped me into this and I fucking . . . I am sorry, bro. You gotta understand, that wasn't me . . . That was me stuck under her fucking thumb . . . You know me . . . And if you want revenge on her, I'm right there with you. Shoulda said something sooner but . . . I know people, kid. I'm not saying she has to . . . you know . . . But she can't get away with this. She deserves to suffer and . . . We can do that, you and me."

He still doesn't get it, Vail. He still blames you, and it feels good to carry his computer out the door. Stupid, stubborn people shouldn't even *have* computers, and I'm feeling better about our trip to Serendipity. It's kinda like the Dick-napping. Not perfect, but productive. You passed the first test with flying colors. I came away with a better understanding of your warped take on relationships, all that stuff about your parents and *blah blah blah.* But I settle back into the rear of the internet café and I reconnect Dick's dirty laptop to the world and girls are IMing him within seconds—WHY OH WHY—and one of those girls is you.

You: *Baby you need to call me. Joe told me about this lawyer lady and I just . . . I need to see you. Now. You don't get it. I love you. And I do get it. You love me. So if that's what this is about and you think you had to go tell our little friend that you're running off to Vegas to get married . . . I mean come on. This is me. Us. I know you, Dick. I know you don't fall in "love" like that and if this is your way of saying that you can't do it anymore, can't watch me run around with the kid, well okay. Consider the kid gone and let's fucking do this okay? Do you get it now? Do you get that there is literally nothing you can say or do or no amazing prodigy lawyer lady who will ever make me stop loving you? Baby, enough already. Let's do this. Today.*

I log off and I just sit there. I sing the same old song to myself about how that's not you, how you don't really mean that and can't be held responsible for the things you type into that white box. That white box isn't real. Life is real. Frozen hot chocolate is real. *We* are real.

A girl taps on my shoulder. "Are you using the computer?"

"I am."

She is trembling in that way where you know she just broke up with some undeserving prick. "Well, the thing is, though . . . you're *not* using it. But you're taking up the space as if you are using it, and that means that I can't use it. And that's not right, because you're actually *not* using the computer. You're just sitting on it to stop *me* from using it when I am standing here ready with stuff to do, when I need to use it right now. See how that works? Do you see how that fucking *works*?"

I stand to offer the computer, but she bursts into tears and runs out the door.

On the subway back to Bed-Stuy, I can't get that girl out of my head.

She was so rattled, Vail, so pure. All she wanted to do was use the computer. And I was a dick, cockblocking it and why? Why didn't I walk away when I was done with it? Dick is keeping you on deck, in case he wants to use you. He plugged you up when he put his thing inside of you and left it there. There's nothing wrong with me—I don't have cancer; I am in love—but you are out of my reach. You can't let me in because he is still inside of you. And as long as he is on this planet with us . . .

It's time for me to be a man and surrender. I enter the warehouse, and Dick is . . . asleep. I stand over the man you love, the man you want when you go to the bathroom in Serendipity. The man you can't quit. Why? I know. He made you the way you are. He is the reason you can't love yourself, let alone me. He is the luckiest man alive, and here he is, snoring like he doesn't have a care in the world. It's insulting to you—you are still trying to call him—and it is insulting to me—scared hostages don't snore—and it's insulting to the dealer from my school.

Was there coke in that coke? How the *hell* is he sleeping?

My hands are shaking—this is illegal—but love is war. I can't choke now, not when you need me the most. I don't like needles and I looked away every time Schlitz and Dick shot each other in the *delts* but I know what a delt is and it's now or never and I need him to wake up.

I try for his delt but he gets in his own way and the needle winds up in his neck.

Oops.

It's all predictable, like a rom-com, the way he whines and calls me crazy, demanding to know what's wrong with me, like I'm the fucking problem. He goes into threat mode and he's gonna call the police (like he has his phone) and my heart starts to pound a bit, because in that rom-com way, it's ironic. If you could see me now, risking it all to take care of your evil one true downfall, well, Vail, maybe then you might finally realize I'm the one.

I pull up a crate. No more metal chair. I am not a shrink. I am Dunkin-addled, tough-love-dispensing Ben Affleck at the end of *Good Will Hunting.* Except my buddy ain't a genius. He's a bald fucking bastard.

He's stuck in you and I want him out but you want him to stay. I think I'm allowed to be a little critical. A little disgusted.

I slap his asshole face. "Did you really suggest we have her fucking killed?"

"I say a lotta shit when I'm high." Classic excuse and he rubs his neck. "You got a bump in there?"

I think I know why you like him. You are both in the same boat. He snorts cocaine to kill the love he withholds from you while you sit in all the bars guzzling cosmos to kill the love he won't let you give to him.

I load his dog tag with a big fat line. "So how does it work? The producers who hear your 'pitches' . . . They're connected? You gonna call 'em up to take care of your 'bitches'?"

"Just one," he says. "Bitch." And then he winks. "I'm kidding. It's a joke."

He does another line and then another and then he looks at me like it's my fucking fault. "You need to call 911, Goldfuck. I think my neck is . . . Call 'em. Right fucking now."

This is what you love. A selfish untrustworthy dog. They say if you love something, you set it free, and if it comes back, it's . . . Sorry, but Sting is wrong. If you love something, you keep it *safe.* You're in danger. One of these days this dog is gonna bite you, possibly kill you. I won't steal you away in the middle of the night and whisk you off to a world without feral dogs. There's no such place and you'd only howl at the moon. I tried everything. I built fences while you slept. You tore down every one and I went out there to build another. I can't change the way you feel about this feral fuckwit, but I can domesticate him, or at least try to anyway. You're lucky, Vail. Turns out my cancer is your cure. You love him more than you love me, and I love you more than I love myself.

I throw the dog a bone. "All right," I say. "Interior . . . Pastis."

"Fuck you, Goldberg."

"The young stud walks into the restaurant. That's you, Dick. You're the stud. The love of your life is in a booth and she's a ten . . . a total dime. She thinks you walk on water. She wants to be yours for life."

"I need a doctor. Or a bump."

"But there's something else waiting for you at the bar. A producer who can single-handedly change your life. It's Harvey Weinstein, and he's there to see you."

Dick does more coke. What else is new? "No," he says. "Harvey would pick a hotel."

Harvey, like they're equals, and I will not be distracted. "The woman waves. She wants you. Harvey waves. He wants you. Where do you go? Who do you pick?"

"How about you go fuck with Vail, kid? She's the one you're mad at, not me. Fuck."

I need him to focus and crackhead Angus did have a way of getting centered. I dig into my bag of tricks and load a pipe for Dick. He waves me off like he's too good for it, but five seconds later, I am lighting him up. *And just like that* . . . the dickhead is a crackhead.

I walk back to my crummy little crate. "Okay, Dick. Interior, Pastis. Who do you pick? The girl of your dreams or the producer who claims he can make your dreams come true?"

"My neck. I think you hit a blood vessel."

He sounds like Vagina with her hickey and I can't. "Dick, come on. You know how it works. Our protagonist is facing a choice. What do you want more? Love or money?"

He bangs his head against the wall of the freezer, and then he chuckles. As if *this* is a movie. As if this warehouse isn't real. "All right, fine," he says. "Interior. Pastis. Lightning-paced cuts from the babe to the producer and the producer to the babe. Harvey all the way."

I am the dog now, foaming at the mouth and calling bullshit. I really am rooting for you, Vail. Like Samantha clapping for Steve and his half-court-shot pipe dreams, I want Dick to realize what he has, what he *could* have. You!

"Oh, come on, Goldbars. I choose Harvey and the babes line up."

"But we're talking about the one. . . ."

"No such thing."

"Yes, there is. Vail . . . She's yours. Christ, you know this and still you . . . Do you get it, you asshole? I would kill for her to feel that way about me. But you . . ."

He says you don't love him and he says he doesn't love you, and I get in his face. I make direct fucking eye contact, Frascatore-in-the-guidance-office level of *direct.*

"If you realize you're the luckiest man alive, you walk out of here and you get the only thing that matters. You get the girl."

His eyes aren't eyes. They're TVs in *Poltergeist.* "Joe, you need help."

"You did it, Dick. You used me as a jealousy trap and it . . . it worked. She's yours."

He sticks his tongue out and laughs and you think *I'm* the child? I smack him.

"Dick, come on. Guy to guy. We know the deal. Love is the path to glory. If you would get with Vail for real . . . Harvey Weinstein would probably show up on your doorstep the next fucking day. The right girl, the girl who chooses you no matter what you do . . . You get that girl and everything falls into place. . . . Women *make* men, Dick. Literally."

For a minute there, I think I got him. But then he wants more crack. A movie, even an *indie,* takes years to come together and every baby, even those nowhere Serendipity brats in their Polo shirts who are gonna end up doing the same thing as their dull dads, *every* baby needs months in the womb before coming into the warehouse of the world.

Life is precious. And the man you love is throwing it away to avoid being with you.

That wannabe *Shining* grin again and I can't believe you love him. "This shit is good."

I rub my forehead. The fumes. The pain. "So, I took her to Serendipity."

"To what?"

Idiot. "We went to this place we've always wanted to go and we were happy. I mean, to me, that was us at our best. But then she left me. She left me to go call you. Do you know how that feels? You've got a hold on her and you don't care."

He laughs. I don't. He's *not a boy, not yet a man,* and I feel older than him, wiser. Like Britney at the end of *Crossroads.* He barks: "Gimme that rock."

Two hits of crack and it's *rock.* I load his pipe. "And you're so lucky, Dick. You're so fucking lucky that she hangs on to you, and you . . . Do *you* know what I would do to have her love me like that? Do you get that I actually . . . I meant every fucking word I ever said to you. And you had her, you could have her right now, and I'm not that guy who is gonna blame it on her. I am not that guy who says, 'If I can't have her, nobody can.' I am not a fucking sicko and I would never help you hurt her and . . . Can't you just be good to her?"

He licks the bulb of the pipe and I am trembling. On the edge of the cliff. No one pushed me. I slide off the mountain and my fingertips are raw. I meant what I said. I would let him have you and I would let you have him and is that what love is? You above me. Him above me. Everyone above me on their feet while I grope falling rocks and hold on for dear life?

I see it now. He's gonna have his come-to-Jesus moment and I'm gonna let him out of here and the two of you are gonna make babies and rub it in my face and I'm gonna have to move to *old Honolulu, San Francisco, or Ashta-fucking-bula.*

"Wowza," he says. "I can't believe I've been wasting my fucking life."

There it is; he wants you. I am gonna lose you, I really am. "Okay then."

"Fuck cocaine, Goldberg. Gimme that rock."

I can't do it, Vail. I can't spend the rest of my life knowing that I was the one who brought this dead phantom dick back to life and let him wrap you around his finger. I can't let you *linger* unloved and caged as you and Dick mimic the soap opera that is your sad-sack S&M parents. If you love a woman, and the feral dog bit her and is champing at the bit for more, if she is numb to her pain and oblivious to the blood trickling down her leg, then you do the impossible.

You don't set the dog free. You drag it into the woods and shoot it.

Mr. Mooney says readers hate books where people kill dogs, and Dick is not really a fucking dog. Dogs are sweet, even the wild ones that aren't meant to rely on us, lay down with us. Only a man can be wholly fucking vicious and I hope that all dicks go to hell, same way all dogs go to heaven.

I stick his party favor props in my pants pocket. I light up the rock. I know his limits; I don't need a gun. I watch him go white. Didn't know eyeballs could sweat like that. I see it in his neck. He was right! Blue and red. This is the rock that no paper can cover up. This is the blow that ends him and saves you and there is fire in his face. Smoke snaking through his lungs, pulling them in tighter. His eyes are not on the same head. Bubbles in the sky above the schoolyard. I can't catch them, can't see them. He's the kind of asshole who will probably get to hell and cry to all the pretty dead girls about his tragic suicide at twenty-five. That's what liars do. They lie to themselves first, to practice for all the lies they tell *The Others.* I bend over his body—it's a body now, he is going going gone—and I know the truth. I know it when I dig his wallet out of his back pocket.

Richard Arnold Palmer didn't overdose and wasn't a fucking accident. I killed him. I broke his dickhead heart.

And I did it for you.

It is quiet. I expected something dramatic. I thought the world would explode or something. And that's stupid, right? People die every day. I wait to feel heavy or hardened. I'm supposed to be a changed man. That's how it works, right? A solider is never the same after the first kill. But I'm not like that, I guess.

I feel . . . the same.

I was testing him, rescuing you, but now that he's gone I can admit it. I did this for me too, Vail. I wanted to know the depth of my devotion. Would I still kill to be in his shoes if he was dead . . . if being the one you love meant getting killed in a warehouse? Losing out on a future, a life? Would I, you know, *die* if that would make you love me? I stand over his dead body and I'm sure of two things. First, there was only one way to find out. Second, the answer is yes, Vail.

Yes, I fucking would.

38

Life goes on and we pick up the pieces and you know what I'm gonna say. I'm a murderer now—holy shit—but nothing's *that* big of a deal. That's the joy of being a reader. We book people will tell you that we go back to our novels, to our paperbacks, because a book is a friend. A light in the dark. As a reader who knows that the best work we do as people is the work that outlives us, as in the stories we tell so that others might read them and feel seen. Known. The one on my mind as I get cozy with a corpse for the first time in my life is Stephen King's *The Body*. You know the drill, the lost boys who have each other go on a mission to see a dead body. That one changed my outlook on people.

I went to school and looked at *The Others* in a whole new way, all these potential buddies. I put myself out there, tried to find a crew, build a team. The deceased man in the freezer is a solid example of why I never did find my crew. The truth is, Vail, most guys are like Richard Arnold Palmer.

Most guys are dicks.

And why did Mother Nature waste these thick eyelashes on Dick? I pull one out. *Snick.* A first for me, Vail. So many firsts that I can't keep up. My first murder. My first dead body. It's an honor, if you think about it. Because of me, there is one less dick in this city. He had his chance. Were I in that freezer, with some brave lone figure standing over me, I mean, hell. Who does coke at a time like that? Who tries *crack fucking cocaine* when they're trying to survive? When the love of their life is out there waiting, yearning?

I wish I could write the obituary. *Richard Arnold Palmer (no wonder he was an alcoholic) spent his charmed life abusing women, rendering them incapable of love. He pitched several hundred lackluster film projects to several hundred visionless producers. He did not like being rejected. Instead of giving up the nightmare when he realized the dream was never going to come true, he took his frustrations out on women. He was loved, but he did not reciprocate. Richard Arnold Palmer died at the hands of a better man who shall remain nameless, a man who provided "Dick" with time to heal, to own up to his missteps and speak his truth. One might say that Richard Arnold Palmer died of a broken mirror. He could not face himself. And so the glass cracked, shattering his body, which was already ravaged by years of compulsive abuse. In lieu of flowers, his mother requests grandchildren she'll never fucking have because of a man named . . .*

Is it weird that this whole thing feels kind of cool?

I'm not a sicko. I feel bad for the guy. But how do you watch someone act like life's no big deal and *not* kind of prepare for them to die? And come on. It's a big world. Dick got around. He was popular. He had plenty of chances and he knew so many girls. And it's me, Vail. I'm the last person who got to see him alive. The only person who watched him die.

I am the tree in the forest.

And it's normal that I don't feel guilty. I'm just a kid. He took advantage of me. He took advantage of you. What do they say about men who abuse women and children? They say that's a sin because we are the ones. *We are the world.* Dick tried to slaughter us. And what a waste. He used his last moments on this planet to beg for a crack pipe. I was the only real friend he ever had, the one who cared enough about him to call him out, to speak the truth. I know I was wasting my time, but that's me. I want to believe there's a good person buried inside every dick. I want to give every Gordie Lachance a chance. Now I think I get it.

Sometimes a dick is just a dick. Gordie is fiction. Dick is real. And the world is hard enough, right? Because of me, there is one less bad dick running around. Because of me, you are free and maybe, just maybe . . . Well, come on. I killed him for you. It's romantic. It's classic. I belong to you now. I bet you feel it too. Change is in the air. He's gone but I'm still here and maybe in a world without that undomesticated dog . . .

First things first. I gotta get him outta here. Say what you will about Mr. Mooney, but he's the kinda guy you can call when you're in a jam.

"Hello."

"Hey, Mr. Mooney. It's me."

Maybe the only person in my world who knows what it means to be me. "Well, hello. Are you in some sort of trouble, Joseph?"

Yes. "No, but I kinda need to borrow your car."

"Is this your not-so-subtle way of asking to return to work?"

I don't know how to answer that, and I hear Martha in the background, Martha making meat loaf. "Tell our boy we miss him!"

Mooney has my back. He doesn't punish me for leaving him hanging about the whole job thing. I leave Dick in the freezer and schlep out to Long Island. The keys to Mooney's beige beast are where he said they would be, on the left front tire, and there's a plastic case of meat loaf on the passenger seat. No mold this time. I am loved.

Driving is not my thing, especially under these circumstances. You're calling me and Dick is dead and the sun won't go the fuck down. I pick up. Gotta seem normal. *Cool cat.*

"Vail, sorry, I'm in the middle of something."

"Are you with Dick and his perfect ten?"

Dick is dead. There is no such thing as perfect, not when it comes to people. "Nah, he blew me off. I'm gonna catch up with Jeremy."

"Oh, well, did something happen with the perfect lawyer girlfriend? Why did Dick blow you off?"

The misplaced longing in your voice, the motherfuckers who cut me off. We need a win. "Sounded to me like they were having a fight or going to get hitched, but seriously, Vail, Jeremy's waiting for me."

"I'm sorry I was weird with you. Sometimes I just . . . I don't know what's wrong with me."

I know what's wrong with you, Vail. And I fixed it. "That's okay. Don't worry. Plenty of time for us to figure it all out, but right now . . ."

"You're a good friend, Cusack."

Your parting words were just the little boost I needed, Vail, and yes. I am a fucking saint. A lucky saint. The warehouse is still a ghost town. Nobody found Dick in a box. He's heavy, but I'm strong, and I manage to get him into the back of Mooney's Buick. And it's a good thing that some places never get gentrified, as if the city knows the world will always need dark corners like this, places where you can stash a dick in the trunk of your car. No cameras. Not even any vagrants or kids. I'm on the road, bound for the beach—Dick did love the water—and Long Island is pleasing at this hour, when it's neither winter nor spring nor summer but some mishmash of all three.

No birds chirping or eyeing me. No bird-watchers either. I am safe.

I forgot how much *I* like the water, and it feels good to park the Buick. To kill the lights and be alone with Mother Nature. I like her, Vail. She is fair. Indifferent to all people, unlike all the real mothers on this fucking planet. It's this John Prine song in Mooney's tape deck. *You want me to find what I've already had.* Some people get too much love too early, and it is possible to love someone too much, too hard. I'm lucky that's not me, and I remember what Dick said about his mother.

I wonder when she'll see that she went wrong, if she'll regret telling him that *no* girl is good enough. No one is above Mother Nature's Law—what is lifted must come down—and I wonder if Mrs. Palmer made meat loaf for her son and I wonder if his dad took him to some pier like this to go fishing and talk about the birds and the bees.

What a waste, if so, and I pop the trunk. "'Sup, D. You ready to go for a swim?"

I lift him up—he is heavy—and I put him down—he is dead. My muscles are tight. Throbbing. But I can do this. I leveled up at Crunch when I was a gym rat, but mostly I can do this because of you. You deserve your freedom, and he was never going to let you go. He is gone now, and I drag it—a body is a thing, not a *he,* not a *she,* it is an *it*—and I listen to the waves pound at the pylons. Dick was a reckless abuser. The kind of cocky faux artiste who came to places like this to get high and "think" about all the movies he was never going to make.

Mother Nature sends a few pellets of hail that bounce off what used to be his face. Yes, it's starting to rain. Icy. Cold. There is lightning followed by thunder and am I gonna get shocked? Killed? Is it safe to be in the open on a pier with a single soaring lamppost? For once, I wish a computer *did* fit in my pocket so I could Ask Jeeves if I'm safe. The hairs on my arms tickle me. Are they trying to tell me something?

Is anyone watching? Does anyone see me?

No. I am alone. I'm good at knowing when it's just me. I had a lot of practice as a kid, waking up on my mattress in the wee hours. I never needed to turn on the lights. I would just feel it, the absence of other hearts beating behind closed doors.

I toss Dick's computer into the sea. I don't hear it land, because of the wind. Next is the phone. And then I toss the *paraphernalia.* Some make it into the water and some do not. That word never made sense to me. *Paraphernalia.* It sounds like fun, not like this.

I would say a few words for our friend Dick, but I already wrote that obituary in my head. Honestly, I'm kinda mad, Vail. Frustrated that I'll never get to put any of these firsts in my fucking Moleskine. I'm not a bad guy. I don't kick him into the water. I'm not mad at him anymore. I take my time with it. I push the top half of his body and then the lower half, going back and forth and before you know it, he is home again.

He always did say there are plenty of fish in the sea. And now he belongs to them.

I sit on the dock by the last little crack pipe, and I do . . . I do kinda miss the guy. I guess that's what happens when dicks die. You can't help but think of the good stuff.

Mooney and his wife are asleep when I head back to their place. I leave the keys where I found them, like he asked. I stand there a minute looking at their place, wondering why they stay together, if there's any love in that raised fucking ranch, in any of these houses. It's getting light now, *too light to see.* I walk through the mist and I am not Woody in *Hannah.* I am not Elliot in *Hannah.* They never killed for love, and they didn't have what I have, what we have.

They also didn't have internet cafés. I pay up and rev up one of the loud, chunky computers in the back and I log in to Dick's AOL account. There you are. Available. Online. Desperate.

Me as Dick: *You up*

You: *I am always up for you Dick. Can't help it. And honestly if you made up some girl so Joe would tell me and make me jealous well good job . . . It worked.*

The muscle under my ribs needed that, Vail. The pain. This is not you. This is you on him. On the drug that is Dick. You were a lost cause, I know. Stuffed so full of the ghost of his assembly-line penis that you were incapable of letting me in there. But all that changes today.

Me as Dick: *lolol r u fucking high? enough's enough. Check it: u need to get a life. It is never, was never, will never be you. your tits are too small; your nose is too big. you're a stage-nine clinger and hate to say it but I guess you need to hear it, kid. joe told me that you were the one who went looking for him on craigslist and like . . . Relax. I didn't tell him I know whats up. But you need help. Get a shrink; get that janky toe fixed. Join a gym. Get it through your thick head (a little too big for your body by the way). you are not a lovable beautiful baby; it is not my job to take care of you lol I'm audi 5000 vail. C ya*

39

I didn't sleep. I'm guessing it's not easy to sleep after you see a dead body for the first time. Especially a body that you made, compounded by the idea of you reading the dead dick's last written words, tearing yourself to shreds and crying to Cynthia, too rattled to call me, too hurt. The pain of wanting to be there for you kept me up, pacing, knowing that I cannot be the one to bring you Häagen-Dazs and assure you that Dick is a dick.

My buzzer rings. Is it cops? Did I mess up?

No point avoiding the inevitable, if so, and then I crack the door. I hear your little deformed feet, those combat boots on the stairs. To the victor go the spoils and wow. Wow! I was right. You washed that bastard out of your hair and you lunge at me in your pajamas—you came here in pajamas—and my coat overwhelms you. I hold you, and for hours, it goes on like this. I let go to scratch my shoulder, and you tell me to come back. "Don't let go, baby. Not now, not ever."

"I am here, Vail. Forever."

We lie like that in my California king. Sleeping on and off. Our clothes in rumpled lumps on the floor. Peace in the valley, in the loft. No words from either one of us because transformation requires silence, bodies touching, mouths at rest.

And then you roll over. "Why are you so into me?"

"Why do you ask?"

"I mean, it's scary to me. . . . I haven't ever . . . You see I am so bad at this, and it feels embarrassing sometimes, you know, as the older one who's supposed to be so mature or something."

"I love you, Vail. Sometimes it really is that simple."

It's 11:17 A.M. That's when our new life begins.

You pull an Andes candy out of your purse and you worship me in a new way. Licking my toes, moving up to my calves. You come for my Portnoy and lick your lips.

"Truly so rare to see one in the States, babe."

"Is that a good thing?"

"Are you kidding? Maybe this will convince you."

Your mouth assures me that it most certainly is a good thing and it's different being inside of you, like his dick really was in there blocking me and overcrowding you. I have more places to go and I bend you like a pretzel. You last a long time and I last a long time and you scratch me and I bleed. You lick my wounds and shudder. This is a whole new you. The you that you were always meant to be, and I don't need to work on forgiving you for the past.

It is gone. Like it never happened. And if Dick is out there in the ether, if there is some way for him to see us, hear us . . . well, sex was his thing, Vail.

He hears you climax every time. He knows he didn't die in vain.

We get out of bed and get dressed so we can go to La Bonbonniere. You want to see the cat, and we get jelly omelets and make big plans and little plans. You don't mention the Beanery, and it feels like we won't be going there anytime soon. I test you, just the same. I ask if we should walk to the East Village, get a coffee.

You shrug. "I'm kinda done with that place. It's a rip-off, and the coffee's never as good as I want it to be, you know?"

Do I ever. You want to see a movie this afternoon. You call in sick to Uncle Barry and you won't be there long. You went for it last night, when you couldn't sleep. You applied for a fundraising job at the Carnegie Corporation, and they want to meet you, talk to you.

"You seem surprised."

"Well, I am surprised."

"Vail, come on. Who wouldn't want to meet you?"

What an honor, what a first. To bear witness to the blossoming of a young woman like you. You are happy to know that Jeremy and Sarah are back on in San Francisco, genuinely relieved that they are intent on making it work. You want me to blossom too. You tell me that I should forget about running around to pour coffee at *The View*.

"And, Joe, seriously. I know you hate that show, same way I know you hate working in Times Square."

Yes yes *yes*! "Oh, it's not that terrible."

"Well, just the same, I think you should quit. I'm not saying you should go back to Mooney's, but I don't want you working there just so I can get a discount. If anything, I need to focus on the books and movies I already have, you know?"

"I was hoping you'd say that, because I think I might have gotten fired."

"Well, good," you say. "And fuck that stupid store."

Jelly omelets and a whole new you and it just gets better! Like the third chapter of a really good book where the rhythm is kicking in, amping up, and you know you picked well. You want to go to Costa Rica with me, and I want to go to Costa Rica with you. You reach for my chin and wipe the jelly I left there on purpose. You lick your finger.

"Okay, I have an idea."

"I like ideas."

"It's an idea that honestly would be better off if it was your idea. . . ."

"Well, I have an idea of what this idea might be and I'm pretty sure we have the same idea, Vail."

"Mmm . . ."

"Hmm . . ."

And then we kiss. We are so cute that I want to kill us and I almost feel bad for the busboy. I hope he has what we have someday, and I hope he knows it doesn't come easy.

"Okay," I say. "Tell me about this idea of yours."

"You first, Joe."

I love that Dick's venom exited your system along with his ghost dick. You don't seem sad or wounded. You seem free. And I'm proud that I'm not some asshole who wants the credit. A little secrecy is good, especially with a new start in a new world as a new us. Dick was wrong and Woody Allen was right. *Shocker.* Girls are not sharks. *Relationships* are like sharks. They have to move or they die. (Are sharks feasting on Dick? Do sharks eat dicks?)

"No," I say. "How about *you* go first."

"Ooh. Bold Joe . . . I like it. Okay! And remember, you can say no. Because before I even say it, I know it's too soon. And also yes, I know I always say I want my independence, and I want to take things slow and do my thing while you do your thing and all that but we all have the right to grow faster than we kind of expected, and honestly . . ."

I am one step ahead of you. I didn't just buy tools for Dick at the hardware store yesterday. I got something for you too.

"Ta-da."

You take the spare key with both hands and you kiss me and the grumpy old waitress tells us to get a room and who cares?!

And what a day! We don't waste any time. It's what Harry says to Sally. You want the rest of your life to start *now.* I have come so far, and because of me, so have you. The world is ours. We part ways.

"Love you, babe."

"Love you, Vail."

You said it first—yes!—and I quit the Virgin Megastore and you tell Cynthia that you're moving out and she's relieved. She wants to live with someone like her, someone fully *effing* single. It's the best first yet. It's your first time moving in with someone. It's my first time moving in with someone. I go to your place and roll up your posters and I would never say it to you—I am a gentleman—but it's so much nicer when it's clean. Too late now—hooray!—and we fill cardboard boxes with your panties and your jeans, your movies and your very small "collection" of books. What a joy, going up the stairs and down the stairs. Halfway down, you stop on the stairs.

"Joe," you say. "I'm cheesy, but I have to say it out loud. I'm happy that you're the first guy I'm gonna live with."

"Me too, Vail. Me fucking too."

We are, at long last, the people we were always meant to be and *every little thing you do is magic.* You keep your pale pink fuzzy slippers by your side of the bed. Two little piggies that feel like pets. You are a milk fiend. I knew that, but I didn't know how far it goes. Because of you, there are always two cartons of 2 percent milk in my fridge. One open, one in waiting. I like living with you. You are prepared. You worry and you plan. You tease me about being a *neatnik,* and I tell you my name isn't Nick and I tease you about being a slob. It's playful. And you are what you eat, what you live with. I teach you how to use a broom—you grew up with a cleaning lady, and Beverly Hills, Michigan, may as well be in Cali-fucking-fornia—and you help me *take a load off, Annie.* I let my empty mug idle on the hardwood table. No coasters. Life is short.

Just ask Dick! Terrible, but what can I say? I'm happy.

We are there for each other. You fuck up your interview at the Carnegie Corporation, and I fuck up my interview at a bookshop downtown, but you trust me when I tell you it's okay, when I tell you it was the first step in the process. And I, in turn, trust you when you tell me I'll find my *Shop Around the Corner—same way you found me, Cusack.* I know you in a way I didn't before we lived together. You don't wash the tub after you shower and you wear the same panties for two, sometimes three days in a row. There are tampons next to my towels and you sleep in my mother's Nirvana T-shirt and sometimes you want to sit alone and stare out the window.

"Are you sure I'm not annoying you, Joe?"

"Not at all. It's perfect. I feel like reading."

"And you don't think it's weird that this is like my version of reading?"

It is weird, but I'm starting to understand that you meant what you said on day one. You are a visual person. And I think that's why we belong together. I am a words person. I need to turn the pages, whereas you need to see the world walk by. I know what it's really about when you sit in that puffy chair. You are Miss Lonely, wondering where you belong, and there is only one thing in that big, cold city that fills you with confidence.

You are waiting for the *Sex and the City* tour bus to go by. You never tell me that you see it. But I see you, Vail. You grab the arms of the chair and sit up straight. When you see that bus, you get a shot of adrenaline. You came here. You made that. So what if your uncle threw his weight around? You got in, you learned about *pinks.* You believe in yourself, and you remember that you did something with your life. Then the bus glides on by, and you go back to sitting like a normal, anxious twenty-five-year-old girl who shacked up with her *unbearably sweet* teenage boyfriend.

Unbearably sweet.

That's the way you described me to your mother. I didn't keep it a secret. I told you that I overheard you on the phone and it was *unbearably sweet,* the way you turned red and sputtered on about how wonderful it is to be with me, to know I'd never cheat.

You run your hand through my hair. "Who are you?"

"Joe Goldberg. Seventeen and twenty-one. Did you hit your head and forget?"

"Well, how are you this sweet? I'm serious, Joe. I'm curious. . . . Your mother is, like, so close and she never calls and you never mention your dad and I just . . . How are you so sweet with me when no one was ever so sweet with you?"

I kiss your hand, the one that was just on my head. "Easy. I have you."

And then I check my watch. We are late. One of your eighty zillion semi-friends is acting in a play a thousand miles off Broadway. They're doing *Closer,* and it's your favorite play, so we're going. I'm nervous, Vail. I like it in our cocoon. And things are so good. Do we really want to ruin it with a botanical garden of jerks in an undoubtedly small, smelly black box of a theater? And yes, we do, which is why I don't complain. I know you, Vail. I know how it is.

Girls.

I put on my Romeo jeans, the ones I was wearing on our first date, and you whistle at me.

I give you some golf claps. "Closer."

"Ha."

"No, I mean you almost did it then. You almost actually whistled."

You clap your hands and that's our little project this week. We are learning to whistle.

"All right, Cusack. Are you finally ready to blow this Popsicle stand?"

That was Dick speak—*let's blow this Popsicle stand*—but you'll stop speaking his language in time. You swat me with a new scarf. Black and white stripes. "Don't say it, lover boy."

"Then don't call me *lover boy.*"

"Okay, lover boy."

It's one of those nights where it feels like spring isn't a myth, so we decide to walk downtown. We pass a hot dog stand, and I tell you about Jeremy, how he likes to stop and smell the hot dogs. You ask about him and Sarah, and I tell you they're still good.

"I'm so relieved, Joe. Ooh, and I would love to call Sarah and say hi. I won't, like, tell her that I know about stuff. I just . . . I do feel like I could be friends with her."

The loneliness of the girl with a million friends she doesn't trust or know is real. The way you yearn to find your *Others*. The tragedy that I can't help you.

"I'll get her number from Jeremy, but part of their, you know, healing or whatever . . . She's trying life without a cell phone for a while. The guy she cheated with, her boss . . . She was always sneaking off to call him, and she and Jeremy both . . . Well, it was her idea."

You loop your arm through mine and lay your head on my shoulder. "That's kind of sweet. Maybe I'll ditch mine too."

You are neat tonight in your black on black on black. Professional. Honest. We go to the play, and then afterward we go to Veselka, and sometime after three, we leave a big fat tip that we can't afford and walk home together. We aren't spoons, not tonight. Tonight, we face each other. And it's a first for me, Vail, to fall asleep in your arms, with you in my arms, wrapped up in a way that shouldn't be conducive to actual fucking sleep. My left arm should be full of pins and needles, and your neck should be on fire. But bodies rise, don't they? Like souls. A few times, I wake up for a second or two. You look different tonight.

I'm pretty sure you're doing what I promised you would do eventually. I'm pretty sure you're dreaming. Your restlessness was never about work. All jobs are bullshit, to a degree, and you're back in REM mode because of what really fucking matters: love, as in me.

And then the nightmare comes all at once. I wake up alone. Bad. I like it when you're here and you're not here. And then from bad to worse. I hear you crying. You're out there. The loft never seemed this big and I can't get to you fast enough and I'll kill him, Vail, whoever broke in and did this to you. I can't do that naked so I pull on shorts and I tear the white sheet. You're alone, seemingly safe. Killing someone does have its consequences. I worry for you because of all the dicks still out there lurking in the shadows, picking locks on *SVU.* It's a relief to see you bent on the floor, down on your knees. Physically unharmed. Pages of the *Post* at your feet. I sink to your level, and you are scaring me, sobbing. We're the happiest people in the world and it's hard not to feel a little miffed. I didn't think you'd ever cry again.

"Vail. Are you okay?"

I reach for the cover of the paper.

DEAD MAN SWIMMING

40

The woman behind the counter at Magnolia Bakery has seen a lot of me these past couple of days. I recognize that strain in her jaw. She knows something bad happened but she doesn't know what the fuck to do with that knowledge. I've offered condolences to customers in the past. Retail is weird. You know a customer and you're not supposed to know a customer, but you do. And sure, you're on the clock, but you're a human. At some point, you have to do it, go there.

"Okay," she says. "Here's your change, and I'm not trying to pry."

"It's okay."

"Well, whatever's going on . . . I hope it gets better."

I thank the nice woman and walk home to you, the sad woman.

Will it get better? It doesn't *feel* like it's getting better. Dick's body was found three days ago. He dumped you on *Instant Fucking Messenger,* and you're acting like he was ever anything but a dick to you. It's getting scary, Vail. You haven't been out of the house. You sleep on the sofa. You don't mean to ice me out and I hear you when you say it's "not about me," but I miss you, Vail. The best night of our lives led to the worst night of our lives, and I could kill that prick all over again for rolling up to Jones Fucking Beach. What? Even the *sharks* didn't want him?

I climb the stairs in SoHo, and I knock on my door as if it isn't mine. A habit that began a day or so ago, as if I have to make sure you're not masturbating over your IM fucking chat history. "All good, Vail?"

"You can come in."

No shit, Sherlock, and I come in with my cupcakes. That's all you want. Cupcakes. You don't thank me for the loot. You grab it. You tear off the best part, the top part with all the frosting, and toss it on the table. Most people prefer the frosting. Most people confront death and want to fucking *live* and hello . . . It's not like you killed him and are scouring the papers paranoid about being caught. You have no idea, Vail, no fucking *clue* what this is like for me.

"So," I say. "How're you doing? You good?"

"Why do you keep asking me that? Jesus Christ, Joe, I am not good. I am not going to be good until I am good, and I will never feel good if you keep asking me like you just want to fuck me or something."

"I didn't mean it that way."

And then you're doing it again. Crying. This is how we don't break in half. You bite my head off a lot, but always, you crumble and fall apart, apologizing ad nauseam. And I like you better like this. Your body convulsing in my arms. Mascara-muddled tears drenching yet another perfectly good sweater. At least I wear black. And then the clouds pass. The storm is over. You are blowing your nose on a dirty tissue and lighting a pink Nat Sherman *Fantasia.*

Ours is an indoor smoking home now, and the snow globe you got for me is covered in a brown film, but that will change. Change is the only sure thing, like they say. Death and taxes and nicotine stains and change. You *will* get over this. But when?

"I just . . . I should've called him more. He was my friend."

No, he was not. He made fun of your special toe and he wanted you in jail. He called you an *old maid*. He used you. He didn't love you as a friend or a woman but I say the only thing a good boyfriend can say at a time like this. "I know."

"He was in so much pain."

Wrong again. He felt nothing for you or anyone. All semen, no soul. "You tried, Vail. And I know it's a shock, but if that's the case"—it is not the case—"well, maybe now he's at peace."

"Do you know this girl's last name? The new girl he was seeing?"

There was no girl. No one was as good as his fucking mother. "Nah, and honestly . . . he might've been exaggerating. I know he was just insecure and all that, but he did that sometimes, you know . . . He wanted to seem like a baller."

You sniffle and you shudder like I don't know him the way you do and hello . . . I killed him for you.

"Joe, I just . . . I feel like I should've known. Things were not going well with his work, and to think of him alone in the dark like that . . . I mean, I knew he messed around with drugs, but crack? Did he smoke crack with you?"

Yes. I held the pipe! "I don't smoke crack."

You tell me you want the truth, and I tell you it *is* the fucking truth. "I think you don't get that I really didn't know the guy all that well. Don't get me wrong, okay? I'm sad he's gone."

"I know."

"It's not like we were best friends or anything. Jeremy moved away and I met Dick through you and I dunno. . . . He was trying to big-brother me and stuff. And I'm not speaking ill or anything, but he . . . Yeah. He got into stuff. Steroids and coke, and that's just . . . It's not me."

It's not *you* either, goddamn it, and you twist your greasy hair. "But you guys talked."

And you guys talked about me. And then some. "A bit."

"Well, Joe, Dick and I talked a lot, maybe more than you realize."

I know. I read the IMs and that book is out of print and why the fuck didn't I bury him in the woods? "Okay."

I reach for you, but you don't want me. Not yet. "Sorry. I'm just . . . I'm mourning."

If you were the one washing up on Jones Beach he'd use the headline about your corpse to get a pity fuck at Passerby. Girl love is different from guy love, I think. There's a whole world in your head and truth is not allowed. So here we are. The Mourners. The clock ticks in the way it does now that we live in a sad house. I never noticed the fucking ticking until Dick's body washed up at Jones Beach. Now it's all I hear.

"Okay," you say. "I feel like I shouldn't say this, but I can't . . . I have to talk about it."

"You can tell me anything."

"Well, okay, yes, I slept with him a few times."

I know. "I kinda figured. And I get that, Vail. You guys had a thing."

"Yeah, but, Joe, it was more than that, okay? He talked to me about stuff. I mean, I *knew* him. The drugs and the whole 'baller' act . . . He was always trying to get away from himself."

BECAUSE HE WAS A FUCKING ASSHOLE. "Yeah . . . Yeah, I see that."

"Can I tell you something he told me in confidence? And you won't judge me for breaking his confidence?"

You don't seem to understand how death works, but you are sweet. "I would never judge you for anything, Vail."

"Well, the thing is, though, he explicitly asked me not to tell you about it."

Wait. Did he send you a telepathic message? Did he tell you I killed him or leave some ridiculous letter claiming the cops should look at me in the event of his fucking demise? "Okay."

You take a deep breath and reach for another cupcake. It's not easy. I know you're about to tell me the whole fucking saga. But it's a necessary moment for us. Let the demons out so they fly away home to hell. "Seriously, Vail, there is nothing you can say that will upset me."

You like that. You touch me. "Thank you."

You pick up the blanket. The one you brought all the way from Beverly Hills. "All right. When Dick was little, he was in an accident with a lawn mower, you know, a riding mower."

Not where I thought this was going, and I nod like it is. "Yikes."

"It was bad. He's, like, thinking about it all the time and I'm sort of the first girl he can talk to about it for whatever reason."

He is dead, but you talk about him like he is alive. This too shall pass. "Well, you're easy to talk to, Vail." Among other things, but no. I will not be that asshole, not even now.

"All right," you say. "So his dad was on the mower, behind the wheel, and I think that's why he was so . . . Well, of course he was so insecure around guys. Unresolved anger at his dad, I mean, you know about that anyway. The whole show he put on, the hypermasculine macho act . . ."

See that? Already it is passing. You speak of him like he's gone, which he is, because of me. "It could be a bit much."

"I know," you say. "And the nonstop womanizing . . . so embarrassing, right?"

You're smart and you see things, and we are safe in our snow globe. Free. I pat your hand and kiss it. "Agree."

"Anyway, the accident . . . Dick was just a toddler, just lying on the grass minding his own business, playing with his G.I. Joes, the poor kid . . ." I never had a lawn or G.I. Joes or a father who mowed the lawn, but yeah. Let's feel sorry for Dick. "And then his dad got distracted by a neighbor and he just . . . he ran over his own son . . ." My dad gave me cigarettes for breakfast sometimes. "It was bad, Joe."

"I had no idea."

"And he had to have surgery on his . . . you know . . ."

"Dick."

I don't buy it, Vail. It never came up once in your instant fuck-me messages. You're on your feet and okay. Even if it's true, if Dick had a bad dick. It wasn't *that* bad. It didn't stop him from swinging that thing into half the women in this fucking city.

"Joe, I'm just gonna say it. The surgery was bad. He couldn't come."

I saw the pictures, Vail. He can come. "What do you mean?"

"They call it *dry ejaculation* or something. He gets excited and he climaxes, but nothing comes out. Meaning he can never have kids. Meaning he ran from girl to girl so he could avoid telling girls about his issues. That's why I was so shocked when you said he has a girlfriend."

No. You weren't shocked. You were jealous. You called him. "I had no idea."

"Was she nice?"

HE IS DEAD AND SHE IS FAKE. "I don't know. I didn't end up seeing either one of them. Last time I saw him . . . I can't even remember."

"Well, anyway . . . I told him over and over that girls don't care, not *really*. And when he and I met . . . Well, part of the reason he told me was my job, you know? He wanted me to tell the writers so they would do an episode about him, so it would be, like, a thing girls know about, that some guys . . . some guys don't jizz."

A user even then, and it's starting to feel like it *is* the truth, but is it? "So what happened with the show? Are they doing an episode?"

You shrug and say it's not your decision, but the answer is probably no. *Too dark, too rare.* Now you're psychoanalyzing him and talking to me about those days after September 11, when he was crushed, confronting the reality that he would never be a father, not the old-fashioned way. And even though I knew you were with him, it doesn't exactly feel good to have this fresh fucking image. The two of you walking and talking your way through the city while I was in the basement of a bookstore. And it's hard, Vail. It is hard for me to leave the AOL IMs where they are, in the computer. Hard for me to accept that I only saw part of the conversation. Maybe I'm stupid or maybe stupid is code for young or male or Joe, but somehow I never let myself go there. You and Dick did what we do. You hung out together. Ick.

"Oh, Joe, if you could've known him the way I did, the real him . . . I tried so hard to lift his spirits, you know? And sometimes I made him come around. I would be like, 'Well, what if you met a girl and she couldn't bear children?' And he'd be like, 'We'd adopt. I wouldn't care.' And I'd be like, 'Okay, this is no different, your issue.' But then you know how it is. He'd get with some girl and turn into the same old douche, push her away before he let her get close. I showed him my foot. I . . . Remember when I came in and bought *Everyone Poops*?"

"Of course."

"Dick couldn't accept himself. So ashamed, so self-conscious, and like . . . Why?"

You didn't give that book to your cousin. You gave it to him. "You're a good person."

"No." And you smile at the floor. "Is this too much? Am I making you uncomfortable or anything?"

Yes. "Of course not."

"Thank you because talking like this with you . . . it helps. So many memories . . . Oh God, this one time, early on . . . he left his brother's dog tags at my place, I wore them to work and . . . Never mind. It's too embarrassing."

Did you find out they're fake? Do I tell you they're fake? No. A body in motion is meant to stay in motion. I nudge you. "It can't be that bad."

"Oh, but it is. I mean, he left before I was up and I find them in my bathroom. I squealed . . . Oh, I squealed. I put them on. Pranced around at work like he was my boyfriend . . . And halfway through the day he calls, which is a miracle. Usually after we hook up he disappears for a few days. . . . Anyway, he invites me to dinner with his parents and . . . This is *it*."

We will never have dinner with my parents, but I can come inside of you. "Okay."

"He says coffee shop at seven and I'm there at six fifty-nine, and he's outside waiting. I'm fluttering. It's so romantic, we're getting serious and then . . . he just wants his dog tags."

Asshole. "Shit."

"I told you it was bad!"

The only thing keeping me alive is your laughter. Tragedy plus murder equals survival. I'll get through this. I will. "Eh, it's cute. You're cute, and he could be a real fucking asshole."

"No, Joe, he wasn't a bad guy. We were babies. We just didn't know it."

You were a baby, and he was an asshole. But now is now. "You hungry?"

You touch your chest. "And then he wants me back, he's sending me the flowers and begging me for another chance . . . Total puppy dog mode. Remember that night we all went to the Indian place? Oh, the guilt . . . Also side note. I love how we can talk about anything, you know?"

Not really, Vail, and wait. Guilt? "I thought you were mad at me about my flannel."

"Oh, right, yeah, but beyond that . . . mostly I felt so bad being with you because, well, he was sort of obsessed with me. The drugs and the girls . . . I think he was just nursing a broken heart, you know? A little bit too sensitive for this planet, I guess."

I'M THE SENSITIVE ONE, YOU DUMMY. "I can see that, I think."

"So there I was with you . . . you can make all the babies in the world. I felt so *bad* for him. . . . You got sick and after you left . . . oh, he begged me to go home with him. . . ." I am in awe of you, Vail. Do you believe the horseshit that flows out of your mouth? Is there a Wonderbra strapped around your brain? I know why you rewrite history. You want me to see you as a lovable princess. Same way you told Dick that I was the one chasing you. I can't believe you are lying to yourself at this level. And for me now! It is progress and I accept you for the nervous little liar that you are. I love all of you. Unlike *some* people. You can show me yours all day long, build a world where Dick worshipped you in full. But I will never show you mine. I got my stuff. I killed a guy. I'm a sap. Gullible and forgiving. But my flaws are my business.

I think that's called compromise.

"Anyway, Joe. I'm sorry. I'll stop going on about him. It's hard to explain."

"It's okay. You had it bottled up and you're getting it off your chest."

And soon we'll never speak of the motherfucker again.

You're crying again. This time, it is a good thing. A *bye-bye-bye* style cry. You're scared that I won't love you just because *he* didn't love you. There's nothing to worry about, not anymore. I am the man, your man. I can give you children and pearl necklaces until the cows come home. And who knows? Maybe he was honest with you. Maybe he didn't jizz. I don't care. He is gone. He was using you, and I was right to remove him from the equation. You are not a therapist and you are not his sister or his mother. You are mine, all mine.

You pull away. Oops. My Portnoy got excited. "Not now. Not yet, okay?"

"Sorry. It just happened."

"I am not ready for that."

"I know."

You yawn. You want to take a shower and change into something cozy. I do not ask if you want company.

"I'm pretty fucked-up, Joe."

"Me too, Vail. It's what you say to me." And Dick, grr. "Everyone poops."

You leave to wash up with a singsongy *I love you.* I *me too* you and I sit in your chair by the window. There's a lesson in here, Vail. Dick had the chance to be honest with me, to tell me what he told you (if it was true). The more I sit with it, the more the no-jizz thing feels like the truth. It does explain a lot. Would I have killed him if he came clean? I tried. I asked him why he's fucked-up about women. If he told me the *real* reason he's scared of love . . .

There's the lesson. Speak the truth, or a lie can kill you.

Soon, you come back to me. Better now. Clean. All cozied up in . . . Oh fuck.

You're wearing my shitty black sweatpants, my murder pants.

Your hands are in your pockets, my pockets. Your lower lip trembles and the city doesn't quit. Sirens and Jane's Addiction from a scratchy car radio and a hot dog cart with a bad fucking wheel. *Jane says, "I'm done with Sergio; he treats me like a rag doll."*

"Vail . . ."

I don't finish my sentence. I can't. You've got *one hand in your pocket* and here comes the other hand and it's holding Dick's dog tags.

41

It's been *seven minutes* and I don't know how many centuries and you're still at it, still shouting. You didn't find a smoking gun; it's a set of dog tags. But you scream at me like you caught me red-fucking-handed. Most guys in my position would fight or fly away down the stairs, but I can't do that. I can't run out on my investment. I mean, come on, Vail.

I killed for you. I love you. We've been sitting shiva for sixty-something hours. I've taken care of you, tossed your frosted cupcake tops in the trash, assured you that you don't smell (you do). There are stages of grief, I know. I did feel like you were stiffening up a little—*Not yet, Joe*—like you *wanted* me to fuck up so you'd have a reason to lash out at me, tie me to your whipping post. And it's a first for me. I actually kind of . . . I want *want* to be whipped by you.

I must be blushing or some shit because you gasp. "Are you . . . This isn't a *joke*, Joe."

"I know."

"Why do you have his dog tags? I mean, what the hell did you do to him?"

You don't really care about him *or* his fucking dog tags. This interrogation is more like a Trojan fucking horse, a cover for all the questions you're too scared to share with me when you sit and stare out the window. *What am I going to do with my life? Why did I fuck up my interview at the Carnegie Corporation? Why do I want Dick when he treats me like shit? Why don't I feel like I deserve a rare hot smart sensitive prince like Joe? What the fuck is wrong with me?*

The answer is this, Vail: Nothing! Nothing is wrong with you. I mean, hello. If you were defective or unattractive or (perpetually) smelly . . . I wouldn't have *killed* for you. We'll be okay. You're mad at him, but you're mad at the world and it's the scariest thing about you, about girls in general. Why are you so *angry*?

"Hey, Vail, how 'bout I get you a coffee."

"A coffee? Are you insane. These are his dog tags, Joe! His *dog tags* in *your* pants and I just . . . I *knew* something was off. I knew it! What did you do, drag him to the beach and . . . and . . ."

You don't *really* think I killed him. You watch a lot of movies. If you thought that I murdered the guy, you'd do what all the smart survivor girls do. Be a cool cat and fake an excuse to slip out. Instead, you stomp around ranting as if I haven't been the most supportive boyfriend ever. I killed for you. (Sorry to repeat, but it's kind of a big deal.) You swan about our loft making your closing arguments like a lawyer on *Law & FUCK YOU JOE.* Not gonna lie. It hurts, Vail. I love you! Even if there is something squirrelly about you, the way you load all your anxiety and self-loathing into a gun and point it at me. Me! The guy who killed for you. But maybe I deserve it. The fucking dog tags. Pretty dumb and I hang my head.

You put your hands on your hips. Haughty and naughty. "You gonna answer me, Joe?"

"You're making something out of nothing. We hung out. That's it."

"You told me you didn't end up seeing him."

UGH. "I got mixed up."

"And he doesn't take off his dog tags, Joe. Ever."

"Well, he crashed here and he did."

"That's a lie. He doesn't take them off when he sleeps and he doesn't take them off when he showers . . ." You come at me like there's a wall between us, plexiglass and prison bars. "He doesn't even take them off when he *fucks*."

HE DID WHEN HE SLEPT WITH YOU but I'm not you. I won't hit you sixty miles below the belt. I don't mean to laugh but come on! You're being crazy. Maybe you're right. Maybe I am acting like "a child" but I can't fake scared. I love you, that's that, and you can yell at me *all day and all of the night* but you can't get to me.

Love is plexiglass. Love is prison bars.

You light a pink Fantasia. Ugh. "You did something to him, didn't you?"

Yes. "No."

You ditch your barely smoked cigarette in a castaway bottle of Evian that you can't fucking afford—*girls*—and out of nowhere, I am sad for us. Sad and yes, a little scared.

You plop into your chair and stare out your window. "I need to . . . Just let me sit here."

"Whatever you want, Vail. Take all the time you need."

You don't respond and that's okay. I need to catch my breath, prep for battle so I don't fuck up again. Remember those Choose Your Own Adventure books, Vail? Oh, who am I kidding. You didn't read those books. And honestly, I never did either. I tried, though. The first time I went to Mooney Books, I asked the boss if he had them, and he laughed. He said I seemed too smart for that *horseshit*. I said I saw two kids at my school reading them, that they seemed fun. One kid chooses to go one way, the other kid goes another way, and you see where you both end up. Mooney doubled down. *Horseshit*. "Storytelling is life, a series of choices. Any book in print is the result of the author's choices, good and bad. You don't rewrite a novel once it's out there, you can't erase the past, even if you would go back and do it differently. Actions have consequences, boy. It's physics."

A-fucking-men. I *chose* to put my life on the line for you, and you chose to wear my sweatpants. I think that's why we're both stuck in the mud right now. We made bad choices. And from now on we have to make *good* ones.

I am gentle as a husband with a Hallmark card. "Hey, Sitcom, you okay over there?"

"Oh yeah. Peachy keen. Who's next, Joe? Me? The guy at Starbucks who gave me the free croissant the other day? You gonna kill every guy that looks at me?"

I don't like you like this. Even crazy Carrie was never this nasty. But I don't like me like this either, I broke a golden rule. You kill someone, you dump the clothes, same way you dump the body. How could I be so fucking stupid?

You grip those dog tags, and talk to the walls about how I'll rot in a prison cell. What do I do? Guilty people say too much, and innocent people are quiet. I rise off the couch and you jump out of your chair and run to the door and block it. The sweetest fucking thing—*Please don't go, boy*—and oh, Vail. Don't you get it? I'm never leaving you. I *love* you.

"I mean it, Joe. You're not getting away with this."

"I would never leave you when you're upset, Vail."

Your shoulders drop, and it feels good to be coveted, possessed. You want me to be all yours, same way Mr. Mooney locked me up. I'm starting to see the pattern, Vail. People who care about me have this thing where they need to hold me hostage, probably because I was neglected or something and they think I need this extra dose of love.

You sigh. "Fair is fair." I don't know what you mean by that until you walk to the kitchen and pick up your cell phone. "I found evidence and I'll turn it over to the cops."

I make my choice. I fight for you. "All right, Vail . . . You got me."

You put the phone down and look at me. "You 'got' me. What is that?"

Girls do that. They pick one word and hold on to it.

"Look, I didn't do anything to him, but I lied about seeing him. I was afraid of . . ." Don't say *you*. "This."

" 'This'?"

"Well, look how mad you are."

"Oh my God, you are standing here telling me you killed him."

"Vail . . ."

Sometimes you say a girl's name in a way where you become her mother and her father and everyone who ever loved her all at once. You are stumped. Soft. "So what happened? You were out with him and he died and you left him there but took his dog tags? I mean, explain it to me, Joe."

It's a good time for me to shed a tear, and holy shit, my tear ducts rock. I shed a tear. "You feel guilty for not being with him, and I'm the opposite . . . I feel guilty 'cause he was on a bender. And I should've dragged him to a rehab or something. He got kicked out of the bar, he was doing I don't know *what* in the bathroom and by the time we got here . . . He puked on the floor and passed out in the tub. You were at Cynthia's and it was easier not to tell you. And a couple days later he died . . . What was I supposed to do? What does it matter?"

You look down at my area rug like a little Harriet the Spy. Our nice *clean* area rug. "Okay."

"I planned on telling him he needs help in the morning, but I woke up and he'd already split. He left the dog tags in the tub and yeah, I blame myself a little, but you know me. This is why I generally stay *away* from those guys. I'm not a party animal. I'm not a dog. And I didn't know *anything* about the stuff you told me today. I didn't know the way he felt about you, I didn't know about his . . . ya know, so gimme a minute to catch up here, ya know."

You do, but you're a girl, never wrong, so you purse your lips and nod.

"And Vail . . . I get it. You found the dog tags. Whoa. But also . . . you didn't 'find' them. They're right there in my sweatpants. I'm not *hiding* anything. I forgot about them because, yeah . . . I should've stayed up to watch out for him. And I have to live with that, I know."

I don't overdo it—I'm a man, a strong man—and you clutch his dog tags like rosary beads. I did it—I got *you*—and the earthquake starts in your shoulders. They jump up and down, and the rumbling spreads through your body, into your lips, your limbs. Are you going to explode? Release all that pent-up anger at Dick by riding me in our California king?

You wipe your nose on your sleeve. "So he stayed here."

"Yep."

"And he left in the morning?"

The *ridiculousness* and I say it again. "Yep."

You open the freezer and pick up the Grey Groose. "Well, that's funny because I know Dick *never* takes off those dog tags. And when he crashes at my house . . ." Oh, stop it. "He always takes my vodka on his way out. This bottle's been here a while, Joe."

FUCK FUCK FUCK FUCK FUCK and you're at it again, stomping around like a jacked-up conspiracy fucking theorist and *this* is why serial killers should never take trophies. Wait. No. I'm not a "serial killer." I killed one dirtbag, and I forgot about his stupid necklace. It's not a *trophy.* You're getting in my head, lecturing me like a fed-up teacher who thought being with kids would make her love kids even more, and every other word out of your mouth is Dick and how do you not get it? He's gone! Game over! I DID NOT CHOOSE THIS MOTHERFUCKING ADVENTURE. My pants are too big for you, and your history is too much for me. What would Dick do right now? He'd put you in your little fucking place. And maybe this is like that. Maybe I have to be a dick.

"All right, Vail. There is one other thing about that night . . ."

You throw your head back. "Thank you."

"The girl he was seeing, the lawyer, well, she sort of . . . I didn't want to upset you."

Girlfriend voice, like we're comparing long crazy nights out on the town. "I don't care . . . She 'sort of' what, Joe?"

My sophomore biology teacher's chalkboard. KISS. *Keep It Simple Stupid.* "She made a pass at me. And that's why Dick imploded."

I'm the man. Me! You fold your arms and that's right, baby. *You better be good to me.* "Huh. Before you said you didn't know much about her but now she's hitting on you. . . ."

I HATE LYING. "Well, what am I gonna say? I didn't flirt with her and she was probably just drunk but Dick broke *down.* And honestly I didn't get it then, but now I do. Clearly he was carrying a torch for you. Makes sense 'cause it felt like there was more to it . . . you."

You flip your hair and part of you will always be in middle school. "And why didn't you say anything?"

BECAUSE THE NIGHT NEVER HAPPENED. "Vail, come on."

I'm not good at lying because I'm not a fucking liar like most guys, but I get it. You're bitter. He had the last word. He dumped you over Instant Fucking Messenger. You can't tell me how good it feels to know that he got his, that the lies you told me are true. This is *teamwork.* I'm fertilizing the seed you planted, building a world where you are the princess.

"Anyway, he was cratering, and I know it's not my fault. There's nothing you or me coulda done. Sometimes that's how it is, and it's awful, it's sad, but that's all there is."

You touch the Grey Goose. "Maybe he was still drunk and just forgot. . . ." Relief! "But he *loved* his brother . . ." Ugh. "And he would never, *ever* walk out of this place without his dog tags. His *brother* was everything to him."

I was hoping it wouldn't come to this because I really *don't* like to talk shit about the dead, but there's no way around it. Drumroll, please. This will hurt. "You didn't know him as well as you think you did."

"Excuse me?"

"It feels shitty to tell you, like I'm betraying him, but at the same time, you deserve to know the truth. The dog tags . . . they're not real. It's just a 'bit.' "

"A 'bit'?"

"His brother didn't die in combat. I don't know how to say this but . . . They're fake. It's all fake. Some guys, not me, but yeah . . . Some guys are bad." I blew up your silly little world. I tore down your Twin Fucking Towers. You should see him for what he is and scream and throw those dog tags out the fucking window, but you nod like it's nothing, like I told you I got banana pudding because Magnolia was short on cupcakes. "Okay."

OKAY?! Okay, fine. I'll go deeper and darker. "The worst part is he doesn't even have a brother, let alone a dead one. He got the 'dog tags' at a *Top Gun*–themed bar mitzvah when he was a kid. And then his friend's little sister mistook them for *real* dog tags and . . ." No need to set a jealousy trap. You're already rubbing your forehead, bowing. "Never mind. You don't want to know how it started because, well . . . You don't want to know."

I sit on the couch and you're pacing again, slower now, still pressing your hand into your head like you're trying to stop it from exploding. He's the asshole, not you, but that's girls. That's hamsters. You blame yourselves. I'm saying all the right things—*He's not all bad . . . Every girl fell for it, not just you . . . Hell, I fell for it*—and you're nodding and maybe that's the closest girls ever come to apologizing. But love is a verb. I get off my ass and walk to you.

"You okay?"

The answer is no. You jab me in the ribs and you're a girl. I can't hit back. I won't hit back. My hands are up, I'm backing off as you batter me and I am back on the sofa. You jump me and straddle me and wrap the dog tags around my neck. It hurts, but *love hurts.* You clamp a hand over my mouth.

"You are so full of shit, Joe. Chock fucking *full* of it and you just . . . You're a *liar.*"

It's like my dad always said when my mother went to town on him: "That's how you know she still loves ya, she's still in the ring." I never thought he was right, but you yank on those dog tags and stare into my eyes like you want to slice my head open and see what's inside, find out how far I would go for you. Your breath is hot, moist. Come for me, baby. Bring it.

"The only man I ever loved and you took him away from me . . . And you . . . you just lie, lie, lie and you don't get it, do you, *Cusack*? Dick *loved* me and I loved him. He would never lie about something like a brother and I knew it. You *did* kill him and you're lying and we always came back to each other and now we can't do that and . . ." That's the grief talking. That's not you. "Do you get it now? I never loved you. Ever."

For a split second the lights go out in every corner of my body but you don't scare me and this isn't real. It's a game. I'm like a surrogate. You can't kill him—I already did that—but you have to attack *someone.* You're in a bind. Humiliated that you wasted your heart on this asshole who fooled you with *dog tags.* And that's not the worst of it. The idea of me knowing that Dick got one over on you, one of countless other girls . . . That's why you had to go to the dark. *I never loved you.* Don't worry. I know you're just afraid of losing me. It's okay, Vail. The rules of engagement couldn't be clearer: You pretend to kill me and I pretend that you could, you know, actually fucking kill me.

I think on Nerve.com they call it *edging*?

You lick your lips and I can't help it anymore. This is hot. Red Hots and Pop Rocks and I am wanted, held, seen. I rise to the occasion, and your jaw drops as you play the prudish wifey. You say it's *disgusting* that I'm turned on, but come on. Of course I'm turned on. I am yours. Bound and gagged. *Loved. Touched. Squeezed.*

You slap the side of my head. "Stop fucking smiling."

I stop fucking smiling. Game on. Here you go again.

"You are nothing to me, Joe. And if you thought killing him would change that, well . . ." You twist hard, turn the tags, turn the screw, and the game is . . . It's getting old. "It was never you and me. It was me and Dick and our road was meant to be a long one. *That's* why I loved *Serendipity,* Cusack, because in the dark with you I finally understood. Life is long. Timing is everything and that's all you are . . . a good way to pass the time. And don't do the puppy dog poor-me eyes. We didn't set out to fuck with you, but when you love someone the way I love Dick, the way he loves me . . . Everything has a way of bringing you closer. Do you know how much I loved him? Do you get it yet? You think I care about his brother or dog tags? I loved him. I forgive him without even trying to! Do you get that I know what's wrong with you because it's the same fucking thing that's wrong with *me*?"

And just like that you stop the war. You let go of the dog tags and it's the most beautiful thing in the world. Your crying is even better the fiftieth time around. At long last, you released it, the invisible weight of his cruelty, his torture. You need me now, and I am here.

"I'm not mad at you, Vail. Sometimes we need to say things out loud in order to realize. . . . Okay, sure, I'm human. None of that felt *good.* But I know you didn't mean it and it's not about me and you're right. We are the same. Cut from the same cloth. So I know how it feels, you try to go low . . ." *Even when he fucks . . . I never loved you . . .* "And you and me aren't like that . . . I mean, I know you didn't mean a word of it. We're good."

I'm not a doormat and I'm not hungry for abuse or whatever. There is no logic in love, Vail. I love you, you're it, the end. You found me, the exterminator who killed the cockroach and yep . . . I'm still here. You cross your legs and the hairs on my arms stand up a little bit.

"I got a message from him a few days before they found him. Can I . . . Can we talk about that?"

This is good, *a little more conversation, a little less you fucking strangling me.* "Of course. Do you maybe wanna order some take-out?"

You're on your feet. Mood swing. Are you a lawyer again? I hope not. Conversations are better when both people are on the sofa. "Say, Joe. Do you like Cormac McCarthy?"

I spread my legs a little. I like where this is going. "*Child of God* is my favorite."

"Cormac McCarthy was Dick's favorite author. Did you know that?"

Oh, bullshit; he jumped on that bandwagon after some girl blew him at a matinee of *All the Pretty Horses* but people die and us leftovers sit around and talk about them. No way around that. "Well, I'm not surprised. Dick had his problems, but the guy had good taste."

"Mm-hmm. On our first date, we went to his bookstore . . ." I choke up a little; I mean, seriously, Vail . . . Let it go. "And he showed me a McCarthy book and went on about how the guy never uses commas or semicolons . . ." You're not touching me but I am choking. "And he said that's why he *never* uses punctuation . . ." I might choke to death and your hands are on your lap. "And the funny thing is that I got this really weird IM from Dick before he passed. We IM a lot and I knew something was off but I couldn't put my finger on it . . . But while you were rambling on, I was thinking about IMing with you and IMing with him. You are *all* about the punctuation but Dick . . . He never used commas and semicolons. And his last message to me, well, there were a lot of commas, Joe. A lot of semicolons. Even a bracket or whatever you call it."

You are pathetic—how many times did you read that shit—and I am pathetic—how did I fuck up when I wrote that shit? I open my mouth but you punch me in the mouth. I can take it. I am Big. Strong and silent. You ram your fist into my rib cage—it really is a cage, it is broken—and this is love. Carrie hit Big, and he forgave her. I close my eyes. *No pain, no gain.* You pummel me and you *knew* that wasn't him saying all that shit and I am a sicko who went on his computer to try to make you hate yourself and no . . . No. That was him, not me. I fucked up, royally. Cyrano failure DEFCON fucking dumbass and I don't *choose* to go limp. I just do.

You smack me. "How *dare* you?"

I am not a whipping post—I'm a punching bag—but I'm still in the ring. I won't cry Uncle Angus. I won't fight back. An ass-kicking from the girl you love is good for the soul and I *like* to see you stand up for your fucking self. I *like* to feel you grow stronger by the second. Chomp on me. Smother me. *Take my breath away.* I'll just find more. I am strong enough to bear the messy, violent, zigzagging, shape-shifting, truth-spinning, self-loathing midtown Megastore hellfire that is your love. It will get warm again. Nice.

You slap my face. *Eeng.* "Stop smiling, you sicko. Say something. Own up to it."

"I'm sorry."

You're stunned. You didn't see that coming and maybe you did mess up my brain because I didn't either . . . Did I *confess*?! I did. No going back now and I take your wrists in my hands. *Gently, Joseph.*

"Vail, you're right. What I wrote was awful but that's *all* I did. I went on his computer when he passed out because I hate the way he talks about you, and that's the kinda shit he says to me. Before you even say it . . . There is no excuse. I would take it all back if I could because if you love someone, you don't want them to hurt, ever. And I hurt you, Vail . . ." I am bleeding and cracked and polymorphously pulsating with pain. "And I will spend the rest of my life making it up to you. But you need to calm down. Yes, I went on his computer. No, I did not kill him."

I loosen my grip on your wrists. You slap me. "I hate you, Joe. I hate you."

It's not the end of *When Harry Met Sally.* You're not weepy Meg Ryan speaking my language. We're not in the schoolyard where *love* means *hate* and *hate* means *love.* You hate me. You're up, lighting a yellow Fantasia. The bottom fell out. Fuck that. I dropped it. What started as a game of war became the real thing. You just *can't* let him go. That's how it is with first love. You are my first, but I am not, never will be yours. And here I am bleeding internally with a vacuum where my lungs used to be while you ash in a cold cup of coffee. I fell for you, I killed for you and it might've been a *heartbreaking work of staggering stupidity.* Your words that couldn't touch me ring true now, in the wake of my failure.

I never loved you.

I want to die. Those words are seeping into my skinsuit like cyanide. *I never loved you.* And now you never will. I popped our bubble and I hid in his computer to shit on you—was I the one on crack?!—and fuck the stupid murder. We all die eventually, but what I wrote to you, those terrible things I put in writing with fucking *commas* . . . How did I not see it until now?

My words that I passed off as his words are the cyanide in *you.*

And look at you, so calm. Back in your chair, staring out the window like you just took a really big, satisfying shit. You would trade me for him in a heartbeat. Did you ever love me, even a little? Did I ever get under your skin? Unbearable questions and I can't look at you. I may as well hand you the knife and let you stab me in the face, but that's not your weapon of choice.

I'm so lost in my head that I miss it when you bum-rush me, but here you are, back with your dog tags, wrapping them around my neck. *Hating. Touching. Squeezing.* You're in eye-for-an-eye mode, and this time you mean business. You want me gone. Dead. You're turning the screw and the chain is made of little silver beads and those beads are strong. I can't breathe and that's my windpipe. It is closing and that's okay. I want to cry Uncle Angus. You win. There is nothing left inside of me. I sealed our fate. I muddied the waters and now you'll never get over him because the closure you thought you had is gone. Mr. Mooney warned me. *A little bit of hope can do a whole lot of damage.* Is this it for me? Is the thing with feathers gonna chew at me until I bleed out and die?

The closer I get to the end, the more I pat myself on the back. It's not all my fault. I was too late. Dick ruined you, all those hours you sat in the black hole waiting for him. You didn't just turn into a hamster. He made you that way, and yes . . . My Instant Fucking Breakup was a mistake, but do I deserve to die for it? The air is playing hide-and-seek. I can't find it. Can't reach it. Every breath feels like the last one, like the first one, like I'm not so good at this, at breathing, and you're right. I am just a kid. I killed for you, and now that I'm about to die, well, no . . . I *don't* want to die and I am going, going—

The chain snaps. You spring back and scramble to your feet. You didn't see that coming and in a funny way it feels like the ghost of Dick saved us. A *real* dog tag chain wouldn't snap and stop you from doing the undoable. You're breathing. I'm breathing. The impasse is scary. *Somewhere I have never traveled.* There's a bottle of Evian by the snow globe on the table that lives by your chair. I am panting and thirsty and you reach for the bottle—there is hope for us yet—but you do not pick up the bottle of Naïve spelled backward.

You opt for the snow globe. You shake it and watch the snow settle in this way where I take it all back. I love you. I forgive you. We mesh. We dream together. I liked it in the snow globe and okay. We fucked up. We're kids. Me with my schoolyard bruises—none of it is really all *that* fucking bad—and you with your stringy sweaty hair, drowning in my sweats, in your shame, overanalyzing an IM from a man who did nothing but hurt you.

I put a message in a bottle. "That was a great day, the snow globe day."

"Yeah," you murmur. "I remember running up the stairs excited for you to see it."

This *has* to be good. You're at peace, back in the orb where the Twin Towers are still standing. The towers that feel like you and me. Weathering the white inferno, hermetically sealed and safe the way it is when you're in love, when things are so good that nothing can touch you. Yes, Vail. Lean into it. That's us in there. We can do it.

"I love you, Sitcom."

Crunk.

You hurled that snow globe at me. It wasn't a frontal lobe hit but it wasn't a missed connection. I drop to the ground. My brain is a bouncy house at a birthday party in one of your family photo albums. Is this vertigo? My eyelids flutter. Is this a concussion? Is this how I die? You are moving about the room, hunched and blurry. Giant mouse in a cartoon. A confused, meek creature unaware of its own strength, because it doesn't make sense, does it? Giant humans are so afraid of you, little you, grabbing at your boots. The dog tags clack as you wrap them around your wrist. You kiss them, not me.

"I can't be here, Joe. I can't be here."

You're out the door, but you left it open. That's you, in a nutshell. Even when you leave me, you don't leave. You didn't even have the decency to finish the job and kill me or bring me a sip of Evian and what now? What do I fucking *do*?

I'm fighting my way out of the apartment, stumbling through the stars and the fog that you brought on me. My ribs hum, and as well they fucking should. I don't want to feel better. I don't want to heal. Not without you. You ran for the same reason you always run. You're ashamed. You need me, whether you like it or not, and yours is the good kind of insanity. Temporary.

Yes, my love. Despite every Kelly Demon in your stunted, self-destructive, mousy little heart, all I want is you.

Is that love? Wanting you more than I want me. Bellying up to the bar for a Jäger bomb to ease the pain of last night's Jäger bombs? I think maybe it is. The thing with feathers is trying to beat its way back to life. I wipe the blood off my lips. *I never loved you.* I don't care. Fuck that. Fuck commas and semicolons. All couples fight, and we'll chalk this up to grief, the time you went nuts and accused me of murder, the day you lost control because you didn't know how to be loved and you were too scared to ask for directions. You lost someone you cared about and you lost your mind and yeah, okay, I shouldn't have gone in Dick's stupid computer but. . . .

Those people who say computers will be the death of us . . . They're not wrong.

You keep pausing on the stairs like you don't know where you're going, what you are. That's good, Vail. Take a beat. Give me time to get there. Sounds coming from your body. Gurgling, muttering. I don't have a concussion and I'm closer all the time, but then you're moving again. You hear me coming, calling and you drop the dog tags. *Clink.* You don't bother to retrieve them, your imaginary smoking fucking gun. Maybe that's your version of an apology. I'm sorry too. This was a bad day, but there's still time for a happy ending.

We're so close. We live in a world without Dick. You didn't lose me and I know. I know! No one in their right mind would choose this adventure. Am I in my right mind? Is any mind in love ever right? It's not easy with you, Vail. I'm still trying to catch up. Dizzy and spent. As always, you're a million steps ahead of me. Fast on your feet. I never get to you, not really. I'm slow and tired and a terrible little roach of a thought scuttles across my throbbing mind.

You might not be the only one in the world for me.

No. Fuck that. I want you to be the one and I won't judge you. I won't nitpick. I like wanting you. Letting you lift me up and put me down. That's how it goes, right?

Love chooses us. No perfect people, only perfect matches. We knew it day one. You can't read, and I can't kiss. But that's why it works. *I never loved you.* Bullshit. Craig brought us to the corner of Houston and Mercer. That was destiny. I was the Romeo in black jeans, and I still get the butterscotch-scented butterflies when I see you rounding that corner. All that potential, that feeling I only ever read about in books. *Serendipity.* Yes, the honeymoon ended and yes, my picture of us in the future is blurry, given what you did to us. But it's still inside me, driving me to put one foot in front of the other.

I know you now. You're capable of brutal acts and you love things that are bad for you. Dick and your blue fucking cape. Cigarettes and Cynthia. *Rom-coms.* You're not good at life, you almost took mine, but the skin around my heart is thickening in real time. I accept you. I belong to you. Doesn't matter if you deserve it. It's not a choice. It's an instinct.

I scoop up his dog tags. I love you. I'm your zombie. I don't quit. I picked up your scent and I want you in my life, even if it kills me, even if it means knowing you might never love me the way you loved him. One slice of bad pizza doesn't stop a guy from grabbing a slice two days later. I am a pizza guy. I want you. That's it. The end. And that has to mean something, right? That has to mean that we *are* meant to be, because if not I might be . . . Focus. If I grip the banister and close my eyes it's still there. The image of us on a sofa like Harry and Sally. We're older and wiser and calm. We made it to the place where the words flow like wine and—

Screek. Something smashes into something. City noise. Screams. The squeak of brakes. Bus brakes. High. People now, strangers. *Call 911. . . . Did you see her? Oh my God, is she dead?* There is no need for me to go back into our love nest and look out your favorite window, the one by your chair. I don't need to see it to believe it. *I know the way you know about a melon.* I know because of a hole in my gut.

That *she* was you.

Epilogue

It's been almost four years *Since U Been Gone,* and I still hear you.

I can't be here, Joe.

If you were here, you wouldn't believe the state of the world. I think that's why I take so many long walks. It's the only way to escape the noise, not the pretzel carts and the sirens—I love that shit, I do—but the noise that's more invisible, everyone so distracted, so "connected."

Your friend Cynthia has something called a *MySpace* page where she uses her pain about your untimely demise to attract suitors. Vagina is even worse. She has a *Facebook* page where she shares photos of her new life in San Diego, as if we don't know what it looks like when the sun fucking sets. In some ways, you are the John Cusack now, my dear. You are *Better Off Dead.* Did you ever see that movie? Will I ever stop asking questions that you can't answer? But I mean it. I stand in line at the Angelika, and girls are not looking at me. Girls are looking at their phones. *Everyone Poops* and now . . . everyone texts. You would not be able to handle the botanical garden of friends festering in the hands of every woman in this city.

What is so urgent? Why do people talk so much? Why not talk to me?

No, you didn't live long enough to own an iPhone and go on *Facebook,* but then again, you didn't live long enough to see them make *Closer* into a movie, to meet me at the Angelika. I buy two tickets and a box of peanut M&M's. I find our old seats, where it all began, but then again, that's not true, is it? We didn't begin on the corner of Houston and Mercer. We began with you and Dick, and that's the problem.

And four years is a long time. I'm still mourning, still missing. Will I ever love again?

Closer ends. They cut the part about temptation, and you are not here to spout off on the good and the bad, the ugly and the beautiful. I am alone, going east on Houston, torn between Mister Softee and Tasti D-Lite. I *choose my own adventure.* A vanilla cone for Mr. Tongue. It tastes like you because everything tastes like you, because four years is a blip. I still censor every semicolon; I still see you everywhere, in the bus that passes by because that is what buses do in this city.

You really did that, Vail. You got so *Carried* away that you ran into a bus like your favorite Miss Lonely in your favorite fucking play.

You did have a dark sense of humor. And maybe someday I'll be able to appreciate the irony. *Sex and the City* assistant gets run over by a *Sex and the City* tour bus. Some bystanders say it was suicide. That tracks. *I can't be here, Joe.* Others say it was an accident, and I can see that too. *I can't be here, Joe.* You just weren't that good at the world, were you?

Maybe you sensed it coming, your fixation on your quarter-life crisis . . . *Twenty-five, don't wanna stay alive.* No way to know. People *choose their own adventure,* and it's a fact of life, death. Some books leave you hanging. As the sole survivor of you, me, and Dick, it still hurts to remember. Do you know what it was like for me, Vail? Alone in our loft, listening to people on the street try to save you as they speculated and screamed. *Did she do that on purpose?*

I toss the last bit of my cone in the trash, and that feeling again that you are in the can, looking up at me. The sucker punch of a steaming hot dog stand, my old friend Jeremy.

Everything is you. Everything.

I want you, and here it comes. My new cage, meaning the aftermath of my, ahem, procedure. The pain of contemplating the pleasure.

My doctor was right. Adult fucking circumcision . . . It's no joke, Vail. I ache.

I know. You loved me *just the way I was,* in my natural state. You only disparaged me in those phony chitchats with Dick because his phantom member was crowding your extra hole, because you thought it was your role as a woman to make him feel better about his dick. But last month, your friend Cynthia got a tattoo to pay tribute to you.

See what I mean? That's the problem with MySpace. Why do I need to know about her body art?

I needed to do better. *I can't be here, Joe.* I know the feeling, Vail. I needed to kill myself, same way you did. I read a few books about circumcision. Miss Frascatore would be proud of me. I trusted Dr. Alvin McMurphy with my life. I let him drug me into a deep sleep. I allowed him to trim my foreskin, the most sensitive part of my body, my soul, my *Sex.*

I woke up in the hospital across from a woman recovering from a C-section.

"Well, I just had twins," she said, when I told her my story, and I don't really get it, but that's what women do.

You say things you don't mean. You say things just to say them. *I love you. I never loved you. I can't be here, Joe.*

The doctor warned me to give it time. When you take the one place on your body meant for pleasure and transform it into a temporary factory of pain, it's gonna take a minute to adjust. There's a reason mothers circumcise their sons before they have language, hard-ons, loneliness. It's like Dr. McMurphy said.

All pleasure will lead to pain, but then one day, it won't.

I'm still waiting, Vail. But I'm patient. A fresh start should fucking hurt, and the pain is a nice distraction from the same old pain of you. I can't help it. I bang a left and walk by the Beanery, and it's the same as ever. A new dick behind the counter. No doubt he's holding a dozen or so women hostage on his fucking laptop, luring them into his coffeehouse where most tap at their phones while a few still push their pens into spiral-bound notebooks. What the hell are they even writing in there?!

Onward, northward, and that's another thing I can't tell you. I heard that song the other day, the Bob Dylan song about loneliness, and it was like a page out of your favorite book. He wasn't bragging about going to *old Honolulu, San Francisco, or Ashtabula.* He was planning to go on those adventures, hoping to be fucking wrecked. It made me smile.

There is a thing with feathers inside of me. There is hope for me yet. A Zimmerman can become a fucking Dylan. It just takes a little time. *Seduce and Destroy.*

"Greetings, Joseph."

"Hi, Mr. Mooney."

Yeah, of course I went back to the shop. Same way I ditched SoHo and moved back to Bed-Stuy. You never liked the guy, but I'll say this. A few days after you died, he asked if I wanted to talk about it. I said no.

"Well done, Joseph."

I looked at him. I didn't get it.

"Bury the dead. They stink up the joint."

And then he winked, which is so not his kinda thing, and that's not even his line; it's from the movie *Cocktail* of all fucking things, and that's where the "old man" is not all bad. You never did give him a chance. He surprises me like that.

The idea of Mooney on the couch with Martha and meat loaf and Tom Fucking Cruise.

But it's a slow day. Deader than I want it to be. I fire up my laptop and I curse the fucking laptop. Before AOL Instant Messenger, a guy like Dick couldn't do it, Vail. He couldn't talk to seventeen women at once. He couldn't *Destroy* you without making the effort to *Seduce* you, and you couldn't sit in your messy bed putting things in writing that you don't mean, playing the beggar to let him feel like the chooser.

Oh, Vail. I wanted to save you. I tried to save you.

I know. Shit happens. Get over it. But I can't help it. *I have to wonder.* If you're out there, do you get it now? Do you get that being alone is not a worse fate than death? I am in hell, still dwelling on you, still writing to you on Hotmail knowing that it will remain here in the cold.

And I know this is weird. I know I have to stop writing to you every day, but it's kind of like the thing with my Portnoy.

I will know when it is time to pick up the knife and cut the cord. I am *unbearably sweet.* My sweetness terrified you. So much that you ran out of my apartment and smack into a bus. You didn't think you deserved it, so it doesn't matter that you did deserve it. I still love you, Vail. I still sit in this bookstore and tell you that I wish you had come back to *The Shop Around the Corner* instead of enlisting our old friend Craig. I still wish that we went to Serendipity on Day Fucking One, and there's all the small stuff too.

Angus Kaplan is dead, Vail. And no, it wasn't an overdose. His heart went on strike, and did I ever tell you about Cynthia? She came by our loft a few days after you went under the bus. She was the last girl to be in our place. It didn't feel right, having her in there, eyeing the space, eyeing me. "First Dick and now Vail. . . . I have to leave because if bad things come in threes . . . Anyway, do you want to get a drink?"

I said no. Same way I said no to Vagina when she called to check on me. Remember her? And what is it with you women? Why do you want us when you know we don't want you?

Anyway, Mooney caught Vagina with her hand in the cookie jar.

She stole a shit ton of money and offered to pay him with her extra hole. He fired her, and she left, kinda like Schlitz, who couldn't handle New York City without Dick. He moved back home to Wisconsin.

It really is like none of it ever happened, like everyone in our world went poof. That's the thing about writing to you like this.

I am keeping you alive. And I know, Vail. My Portnoy is healing. I need to live my life. I need to let you go.

I ring up books and I dust shelves. I let my mind wander like a toddler on a lawn. No dad on a mower to worry about. I remember when I diagnosed myself with cancer of the heart. It makes me laugh now. The drama of it all. I was a bit over the top, but that was me then.

I have a new lease on life. You wouldn't recognize my dick if you saw it in a Polaroid, and see how hard it is? There I go again, thinking about you. Time to go home, time to move on, but four fucking *years* and still I don't look at the girls the way I used to before you, before love. It's the upside of surgery. I *can't* look at women. There's an invisible rubber band tied around my dick. A temporary castration to protect me from all the women rendered loveless by all the cold, hard dicks. I cannot, must not be a spoon. Not yet. And it's comforting when the physical matches the emotional, when the carpets match the drapes.

At home, I pick up *The Lovely Bones* and touch the page you dog-eared. Little criminal. No attention span. Who dog-ears the third page of a fucking book?! Why do I love you?

I stomp down the stairs and set the book on the stoop. Within minutes, a woman in tight jeans bends.

"Are you giving this away?"

"Yep."

"Well, hello, universe, and thank you!"

Something shifts, Vail. My Portnoy twitches. It hurts, but it's not quite as bad. Did you see that? Did you feel it? *The Lovely Bones* was sitting on my nightstand for four fucking years and now *The Lovely*

Bones is gone. It's like it was never here and holy shit, Vail. *Lift things up and put them down.* Dick of all people to the rescue, once again, and I think that's it for us.

I think we're done.

And it's okay. It's been a while since I gave away a book, and I forgot about the high of letting go. Some books are yours for life. Some books are meant to go in one ear and out the other. Sometimes you reach the last page and toss it on the stoop for someone else and you never think about it again. I loved *The Lovely Bones.* But I don't need to own it.

A couple of days later, and I really do miss you a little less. I don't write to you anymore. You tried to love me, but you failed, same way some books fall apart in the last few chapters, and that was you, wasn't it?

Pizza for lunch. At the counter by the computer. No AOL Instant Fucking Messenger and no more writing to a dead girl who can't write back. I get it now. The computer is a strip club that never closes, always tempting, but I am a lucky guy, Vail, a broken record, I know, but I need to focus on the positive, right?

At least I am not, never will be on fucking *MySpace.*

My shift ends and I walk outside and there's a neon-pink flyer on the dirty sidewalk. A band called Martyr is playing tonight, and the lead singer is blowing a kiss to the whole city. I panic. It's not time. The pain, it still comes and goes. Truth is, I think I trusted the wrong doctor and I don't really believe I'm ever going to heal. I fear that every woman who sends Pop Rocks through my system is going to kill me, but life is a surprise, a thing with feathers and . . .

Whaddya know? It's another first. Blood flows inside of me, and at last, no more pain.

I fight a smile and walk down stairs to catch a train. Life is fast at times. A sucker punch in the dark of a warehouse. Now that I am healed, I see things as they are, as they were. And honestly . . . I feel a little guilty about the past few years. I've been haunting you, clinging.

Things are different now, and it's out of my control. I don't need you anymore and I know that I'm gonna talk to you a little less every day. It's a little sad, a little *unbearably sweet.* But it's the nature of all beasts, things with feathers, and I feel it in my bones. The truth surfaces; the subway shimmies.

The dog tags in my back pocket are pressing. It is time.

You were my first love, but it doesn't count, not really. I was your child. You and Dick weren't perfect. You lied to me and abused me at times. But like all parents, you did the best you could. First love is notoriously dangerous, and yes, you fell for the wrong man, a louse who refused to fall with you, for you. It happens, Vail. People come together and they can't make it work, so they have a child. That was you and Dick. And that was me. Your naïve first and only son. I can either spend the rest of my life turning red with shame or I can let go. Move on. Put it all behind me.

The train is slowing down and the doors are about to open. It's good timing.

I'm in no rush. I need a minute to prepare, to stop and smell the hot dogs. I don't fight the joy. If you think about it, this is a happy ending for any first love, for any family. All parents want to go first, all good ones anyway. You hoped that you'd be lucky enough to see me fly away from the nest and soar into the unknown. But that's life, that's love. The risk all expectant, misguided mothers take on when they indulge the wrong man, a roving-eyed dick who stands there smoking a cigar and sizing up a nurse while his woman is in labor, screaming. I know. I can't fixate on you and be good to any woman all at the same time. Life is too short, too crowded. You died for me, and I killed for you. It's my duty as your son to outlast you, to find someone to love and do it right. You don't have to worry. I won't repeat the mistakes of my messy, human parents. I learned a lot from you and I'm not gonna overdose or run into a bus at the young, old age of twenty-five. I know you want better for me, and I promise to do the one thing you could never pull off.

I will close the white box on you and never look back.

I made it, Vail. I'm on the edge of the East River. I reach into my pocket for the dog tags. I wait for myself to feel something, but that's how I know I've changed. Grown.

I don't cry. I don't shake. I toss the fake-ass dog tags into the fucking river. And that's it.

I made a deal and I'll honor the contract. I won't talk to you when I'm lonesome and I won't think about you when I'm lonely. It won't be easy, not at first, but every step toward Brooklyn is a move in the right direction. I'm not the man I was; I don't even have the same Portnoy. And talking about you to myself, to the next girl I meet, would be a bad thing.

After all, that *is* how you killed us. You . . . No. No more you.

The bus hit me hard, but it didn't kill me. I'm young, strong. Still open for business. And my "parents" really didn't die in vain. When I get back out there, I'll be smart. I'll make X-ray vision goggles so I can see the things I need to see, the things a young girl coming into her own doesn't *want* me to see. The important things. Her secret life . . . her little *chats*.

But then a crack in the sidewalk. What if I never love again? What if you . . . No. I don't say your name, not anymore.

They say you never forget your first. But they also say, "Never say never." I am *choosing* to erase you from the hard drive in my head. I am choosing to stop talking to myself about you, about us. Better to make room for good things.

It's like my old Aunt Misty. I only met her once when my mom took me to the nursing home where she lived. She was chomping on a Popsicle. Red juice everywhere, red tongue, white nightgown. She licked her fingers and tossed the dead stick on the floor. She never had kids. She was like a kid.

"I want a Popsicle."

"You just had one, Aunt Misty."

She didn't get mad. She just laughed. I don't think I ever saw anyone happier than Aunt Fucking Misty when my mother peeled the paper off a Popsicle and handed it over. Forgetting things comes naturally when you get old, when your time is short, as if your brain is trying to make it easier to let every Popsicle taste as sweet as the first.

We never went back to the nursing home. My mom hawked Aunt Misty's ring to pay the gas bill. "It's not like she'll miss it," she said. "Same way she won't miss us."

Aunt Misty is a good role model. The wind picks up as I buy a lighter at a newsstand. Night starts to fall. *(Touching skillfully, mysteriously) her first rose.* The smile on my face comes from within, for no reason, like an excuse you make for someone you love. I've never been in love, not yet—I'm pretty sure the other person has to be in there with you—but the thing with feathers is alive inside of me. Unflappable. A little scary, the idea of a bird in your gut that won't stop bashing the walls of your insides and maybe Mooney is right. Maybe smart, sensitive guys like me are supposed to abstain from hope altogether. I turn a little red. Who am I kidding? There are no "guys like me." I'm not a dick. And I know the way you know about a . . . I'm special. I can't lose hope, because I am hope. And it would be selfish of me to run home to my typewriters when there's a girl out there yearning for a man to love her down to the last, frostbitten drop. I can love a woman at her lowest when she feels like she's not enough, like she's disappearing. When I was a kid, I licked the Popsicle stick until it gave me a splinter on my tongue, and then I pulled out the stupid splinter and licked the stick some more. I toss my new lighter to a homeless guy. I don't need props. I have a good feeling about tonight as I line up with all the other people looking to get lost in the fog of love, in the noise of music, the pursuit of the kind of happiness you can only find in something outside yourself. A Popsicle, a girl. I'm gonna be okay. Fate is on my side, because for the first time in my life, I am too.

Acknowledgments

You First is the first book that I finished in a world without my mom. Every day we break another record. Every day it's the longest we've gone without talking. Talking leads to writing, and my mother and I talked a lot. I felt hyperaware of both my mom and my dad while bringing young Joe to life. He wasn't like that with his parents. My house was loud, and that's probably why my brother and I are . . . a little loud. It's also what made me want to give voice to characters.

But how do you do that when the first, most profoundly loving voice you ever heard is fading? I was scared of falling into the cracks of my perpetually breaking heart. I could get a THANK YOU tattoo on my forehead, but they say not to make big life decisions while you're grieving.

To Kara Cesare, author of insightful edit letters that belong in print: Your optimism inspires me. You see the big picture, the single sentence. You love. And yay for your *Sex and the City* binging! Thank you, Joe Bank . . . I mean Josh Bank. Lanie Davis, you have the superpower to hold hundreds of pages in your head. And a big heart.

Gabby Colangelo, may this one be the first of many. Thank you all for truly having my back as a writer, a daughter, and a basket case.

To my fabulous agents and managers: I feel lucky to be in this with you. Alexandra Machinist, if you had a podcast, I'd be there. Olivia Blaustein, David Stone, and Ellie Klein, thank you for believing in me and rooting for me and helping me grow.

Random House, you amaze me. Example: I gave Joseph Perez a vague, broad take on my vision for the cover and . . . Holy smokes. There it is. Gorgeous. Ayelet Durantt, Michelle Jasmine, and Peter Dyer, you make all things publishing go *up up up.* This book is a beauty because of the production team: Michelle Daniel, Sandra Sjursen, Susan Turner, and Ruby Levesque. Thank you, Andy Ward, for the constant, contagious zeal and talent that you and your team poured into these pages.

To my brother, Alex: You swept in like a hero when I needed you the most. To Beth and the best boys Jonathan and Joshua: I love you. You fed me, you are all balloons, love. You made Nana smile. Me too. To Frankie Frascatore: Morgan Fairchild would applaud your spot-on FaceTime reading of this work in progress. Thank you for helping me hear young Joe.

To my friends and family who held my hand on the phone and showed up in the haze of my turmoil and my rewrite(s) and met me on the dance floor, in the kitchen, on the Cape, in the parking lot, in the yard, in the hospital, in Birds, and at Sam's, always with your distinctive zest and glory, your love: A good friend is a run-on sentence that never ends, even when it does. And you know how I feel about run-on sentences. ☺ Thank you for feeding my soul. I love you.

To my mom: As I said in the *Providence* dedication . . . Thank you for life. You too, Daddos.

Our time on this planet is kinda like a relationship with Joe Goldberg. We don't get out alive. So thank you, dear reader, for choosing to spend your precious hours with my words and feelings. It is an honor, always.

About the Author

Caroline Kepnes is the author of *You, Hidden Bodies, You Love Me, For You and Only You,* and *Providence.* Her work has been translated into a multitude of languages and inspired a television series adaptation of *You,* currently on Netflix. Kepnes graduated from Brown University and worked as a pop culture journalist for *Entertainment Weekly* and a TV writer for *7th Heaven* and *The Secret Life of the American Teenager.* She grew up on Cape Cod, Massachusetts, and now lives in Los Angeles.

carolinekepnes.com
Facebook.com/CarolineKepnes
X: @CarolineKepnes
Instagram: @carolinekepnes

About the Type

This book was set in Baskerville, a typeface designed by John Baskerville (1706–75), an amateur printer and typefounder, and cut for him by John Handy in 1750. The type became popular again when the Lanston Monotype Corporation of London revived the classic roman face in 1923. The Mergenthaler Linotype Company in England and the United States cut a version of Baskerville in 1931, making it one of the most widely used typefaces today.